中文详注剑桥莎士比亚精选

麦克白

原版创始主编：[英] 瑞克斯·吉布森（Rex Gibson）
原版主编：[英] 瑞查德·安褚斯（Richard Andrews）
　　　　　[英] 维姬·维南德（Vicki Wienand）
原版编注：[英] 琳孜·布雷迪（Linzy Brady）
　　　　　[英] 戴维·詹慕斯（David James）
总主编：陈国华
分册主编：胡玫　李亮

社图号 21044

Cambridge School Shakespeare: Macbeth [Third edition] [978-1-107-61549-6] was first published by Cambridge University Press in 2014. All rights reserved.
This Simplified Chinese edition for the People's Republic of China is published by arrangement with the Press Syndicate of the University of Cambridge, Cambridge, United Kingdom.
© Cambridge University Press & Beijing Language and Culture University Press 2021.
This book is in copyright. No reproduction of any part may take place without the written permission of Cambridge University Press or Beijing Language and Culture University Press.
本书版权由剑桥大学出版社和北京语言大学出版社共同所有。本书任何部分之文字及图片，如未获得出版者书面同意，不得用任何方式抄袭、节录或翻印。
This edition is for sale in the People's Republic of China (excluding Hong Kong SAR, Macao SAR and Taiwan Province) only.
此版本仅限在中华人民共和国境内销售。

北京市版权局著作权合同登记图字：01-2020-4097 号

图书在版编目（CIP）数据

中文详注剑桥莎士比亚精选．麦克白／陈国华总主编；胡玫，李亮分册主编．-- 北京：北京语言大学出版社，2021.7
书名原文：Cambridge School Shakespeare：Macbeth
ISBN 978-7-5619-5871-1

Ⅰ. ①中⋯ Ⅱ. ①陈⋯ ②胡⋯ ③李⋯ Ⅲ. ①多幕剧－剧本－英国－中世纪 Ⅳ. ① I561.33

中国版本图书馆 CIP 数据核字（2021）第 104089 号

中文详注剑桥莎士比亚精选：麦克白
ZHONGWEN XIANG ZHU JIANQIAO SHASHIBIYA JINGXUAN: MAIKEBAI

项目策划：李 亮	**责任编辑**：孙冠群 李 亮
封面设计：乔 剑	**排版制作**：北京创艺涵文化发展有限公司
责任印制：周 燚	

出版发行：北京语言大学出版社

社　　址：	北京市海淀区学院路 15 号，100083
网　　址：	www.blcup.com
电子信箱：	service@blcup.com
电　　话：	编辑部　8610-82301019/0178
	发行部　8610-82303650/3591/3648
	北语书店　8610-82303653
	网购咨询　8610-82303908
印　　刷：	北京博海升彩色印刷有限公司

版　次：2021 年 7 月第 1 版	**印　次**：2021 年 7 月第 1 次印刷
开　本：787 毫米 × 1092 毫米 1/16	**印　张**：12.75
字　数：374 千字	
定　价：79.00 元	

PRINTED IN CHINA

序

由于观察角度不同，评判标准不同，关于哪个国家哪位诗人或小说家的成就最大，世人可能难以达成一致；可是说到剧作家，大家的共识是，莎士比亚不仅是英语国家有史以来最伟大的剧作家，也是全世界最伟大的剧作家，在知名度、影响力和传世作品的数量上，没有任何一位剧作家可以与之比肩。正是由于其公认的文学成就和人文精神，在过去400多年里，莎士比亚戏剧的演出在英语国家和许多非英语国家经久不衰，莎剧的阅读和鉴赏已成为这些国家英文教学的必选内容。

莎剧进入中国，已经有100多年历史，莎士比亚全集已经有了四个中文译本。不懂英文的人可以通过译本来欣赏莎士比亚剧作。然而文学作品的语言，尤其是诗歌的语言，具有相当程度的不可译性，而几乎所有莎剧的大部分台词都是素体诗（blank verse）。例如《哈慕雷》（*Hamlet*）里主人公的名言"To be, or not to be, that is the question"，不论怎样译，都难以完全再现原文的深刻内涵和形式特点。要想真正欣赏莎士比亚的语言和戏剧艺术，还得阅读其英文原作。最早由剑桥大学出版社出版的这套莎剧精选，收录了最受读者和观众喜爱的14部剧目，涵盖莎剧的各个类别，以其独具匠心的设计和编排，成为所有英文原版莎剧中最适合英语学习者阅读、最适合戏剧爱好者排演的莎剧选集。

本选集的创始主编瑞克斯·吉布森（Rex Gibson）在本书引言（Introduction）里指出："不论做什么，都要记住，莎士比亚写下他的剧本是为了演出、观看和享受的。"秉承这一宗旨，这一新版莎剧选集有四个鲜明的区别性特点：

一、书的开本和页面的宽高比例特别适合学校的老师和学生以及剧团的导演和演员在排练莎剧时把书打开，拿在手里，随时参阅，而且左边页面上有许多有关排演活动的建议。

二、书中配有大量世界各国莎剧演出的彩色剧照，为莎剧爱好者和剧团排演莎剧提供了灵感。

三、书的正文部分打开后，右页是未经删减、原汁原味的剧本原文，左页是多种不同栏目，包括导演技巧（Stagecraft）、剧中语言（Language in the play）、人物分析（Characters）、主题分析（Themes）、写作练习（Write about it）及词语注释等。每幕之间（本幕回顾）和最后一幕后（本剧回顾）有与剧情相关的各种思考题。

四、在剧本之后有各种针对全剧的专题论述，以《哈慕雷》为例，包括视角与主题（Perspectives and themes）、人物分析（Characters）、《哈慕雷》的语言（The language of *Hamlet*）、《哈慕雷》的演出（*Hamlet* in performance）、笔论莎士比亚（Writing about Shakespeare）、笔论《哈慕雷》（Writing about *Hamlet*），还有一份莎翁年表（William Shakespeare 1564–1616）。

左页上的栏目对于解读和排演莎剧特别有帮助，剧本后面的专题论述对于撰写有关莎士比亚的文章特别有帮助，而参加莎剧排演，背诵台词，撰写论文，又是提高英语水平的极好途径。

为了方便更多的中国读者阅读、欣赏、排演莎士比亚原作，北京语言大学出版社携手剑桥大学出版社，将这套莎剧精选引入中国。我有幸应邀担任这套书的中文版总主编，组织起一个团队，对原版进行一定程度的改编和汉化，以适应中国读者的需求。我们不仅将原版提供的关键注释基本译成了中文，而且针对中国英语学习者和莎剧爱好者阅读理解上的难点，主要做了以下四件事：

一、参考 *The Oxford Dictionary of Original Shakespearean Pronunciation* (David Crystal 2016)、*Oxford Dictionary of Pronunciation for Current English* (Clive Upton 2003) 和 *Shakespeare's Names: A Pronouncing Dictionary* (Helge Kökeritz 1950)，给每个剧本前面人物表里的人名加上了国际音标。为了便于读者识别，我们将第一本发音词典里一般中国读者不认识的个别音标替换成了大家熟悉的近似音标。

二、为左页顶端的剧情简介添加中文译文。

三、左页中以及剧本后面论文部分里有一些具有挑战性的词和术语（如tableau），我们为其中的大部分添加了相应的中文释义。

四、适当增加了原版里没有的词语注释。

给剧中人物的名字加了国际音标之后，我们发现，现有莎剧中文译本里一些人名的中文译名与原文的读音差别较大且互不相同。根据定名不咎、译音循本、音义兼顾、音系对应的原则，我们给出了新译名。根据前两个原则，我们将剧本 *Julius Caesar* /ˈdʒuːlɪəs ˈsiːzə(r)/ 译成《儒略·恺撒》，而没有采用《尤利/力乌斯·恺撒》《裘利/力斯·凯撒》《居里厄斯·恺撒》等现成译名中的任何一个，因为从公元前1世纪到公元16世纪西方使用的儒略历（Julian calendar）就是以这位 Julius Caesar（拉丁文读音是 /ˈjuːlɪʊs ˈkae̯sar/）命名的。根据音义兼顾的原则，我们将剧本 *Hamlet* /ˈ(h)amlət/ 译成《哈慕雷》而不是《哈姆莱特》或《哈姆雷特》，因为"慕雷"比"姆莱"或"姆雷"更适合用来给男子起名，结尾的辅音 /t/ 在实际说话中往往不发音。根据音系对应的原则，我们借鉴了曹禺的译法，将剧本 *Romeo and Juliet* 译成《柔密欧与茱丽叶》，没有将 Romeo 译成更常见的"罗密欧"，因为"柔 /rou/"比"罗 /luo/"更接近原名 Romeo /ˈroːmɪoː/ 的读音；同时我们将 Juliet /ˈdʒuːlɪət/ 译成"茱丽叶"而不是"朱丽叶"，因为这样做不容易让人误以为这个女孩姓"朱"。

这套经过改编并且带中文注释的《中文详注剑桥莎士比亚精选》不仅可以用作中国高中和大学的英文教材，而且适合中国所有具有较高英语能力的莎剧爱好者阅读和欣赏，将戏剧从书中提升到自己心中，将剧本从课堂搬演到戏台。

相信《中文详注剑桥莎士比亚精选》会带给中国广大英语爱好者一个惊喜。

2020年5月于英国剑桥家中

Contents 目录

Introduction 引言 iv
Photo gallery 剧照精选 v

Macbeth 《麦克白》
List of characters 人物表 1
Act 1 第 1 幕 3
Act 2 第 2 幕 39
Act 3 第 3 幕 65
Act 4 第 4 幕 99
Act 5 第 5 幕 133

Perspectives and themes 视角与主题 160
The contexts of *Macbeth* 《麦克白》的创作背景 162
Characters 人物分析 166
The language of *Macbeth* 《麦克白》的语言 170
Macbeth in performance 《麦克白》的演出 174
Writing about Shakespcare 笔论莎士比亚 182
Writing about *Macbeth* 笔论《麦克白》 184
William Shakespeare 1564–1616 莎翁年表 186
Acknowledgements 鸣谢 187

Introduction 引言

This *Macbeth* is part of the **Cambridge School Shakespeare** series. Like every other play in the series, it has been specially prepared to help all students in schools and colleges.

The **Cambridge School Shakespeare** *Macbeth* aims to be different. It invites you to lift the words from the page and to bring the play to life in your classroom, hall or drama studio. Through enjoyable and focused activities, you will increase your understanding of the play. Actors have created their different interpretations of the play over the centuries. Similarly, you are invited to make up your own mind about *Macbeth*, rather than having someone else's interpretation handed down to you.

Cambridge School Shakespeare does not offer you a cut-down or simplified version of the play. This is Shakespeare's language, filled with imaginative possibilities. You will find on every left-hand page: a summary of the action, an explanation of unfamiliar words, and a choice of activities on Shakespeare's stagecraft, characters, themes and language.

Between each act and in the pages at the end of the play, you will find notes, illustrations and activities. These will help to encourage reflection after every act, and give you insights into the background and context of the play as a whole.

This edition will be of value to you whether you are studying for an examination, reading for pleasure or thinking of putting on the play to entertain others. You can work on the activities on your own or in groups. Many of the activities suggest a particular group size, but don't be afraid to make up larger or smaller groups to suit your own purposes. Please don't think you have to do every activity: choose those that will help you most.

Although you are invited to treat *Macbeth* as a play, you don't need special dramatic or theatrical skills to do the activities. By choosing your activities, and by exploring and experimenting, you can make your own interpretations of Shakespeare's language, characters and stories.

Whatever you do, remember that Shakespeare wrote his plays to be acted, watched and enjoyed.

Rex Gibson
Founding editor

This new edition contains more photographs, more diversity and more supporting material than previous editions, whilst remaining true to Rex's original vision. Specifically, it contains more activities and commentary on stagecraft and writing about Shakespeare, to reflect contemporary interest. The glossary has been enlarged too. Finally, this edition aims to reflect the best teaching and learning possible, and to represent not only Shakespeare through the ages, but also the relevance and excitement of Shakespeare today.

Richard Andrews and Vicki Wienand
Series editors

This edition of *Macbeth* uses the text of the play established by A. R. Braunmuller in **The New Cambridge Shakespeare**.

Macbeth dramatises the story of a brave soldier who is tempted by witches and urged by his wife to murder his way to the throne of Scotland. It is a play about ambition, murder, intrigue (阴谋), manipulation (操纵), seduction and betrayal.

Three Witches make prophecies about Macbeth's future and tempt him to murder. The Witches have been portrayed in very different ways on stage: as supernatural harbingers (先兆) of chaos; as instruments of evil to tempt Macbeth to destruction; as figures of destiny or fate; and as figments (臆造之事) of Macbeth's overwrought (过度紧张) imagination. You can find other pictures of the Witches on pages 8, 10, 37 and 131.

Shakespeare gives the Witches a style of speaking all their own, a rhythmic language of charms (咒语) and curses, to emphasise the theme of magic and the supernatural in the play.

What is the relationship between Macbeth and his wife? Although she dominates him in the first two acts, many productions show a loving relationship between them.

The complex relationship between Macbeth and Lady Macbeth develops rapidly over the course of the play. Their interdependence is complicated by manipulation, murder and an increasing alienation (陌生，疏远) from each other. You can find other portrayals of the Macbeths on pages 44, 74, 86, 97, 166, 171, 177 and 178.

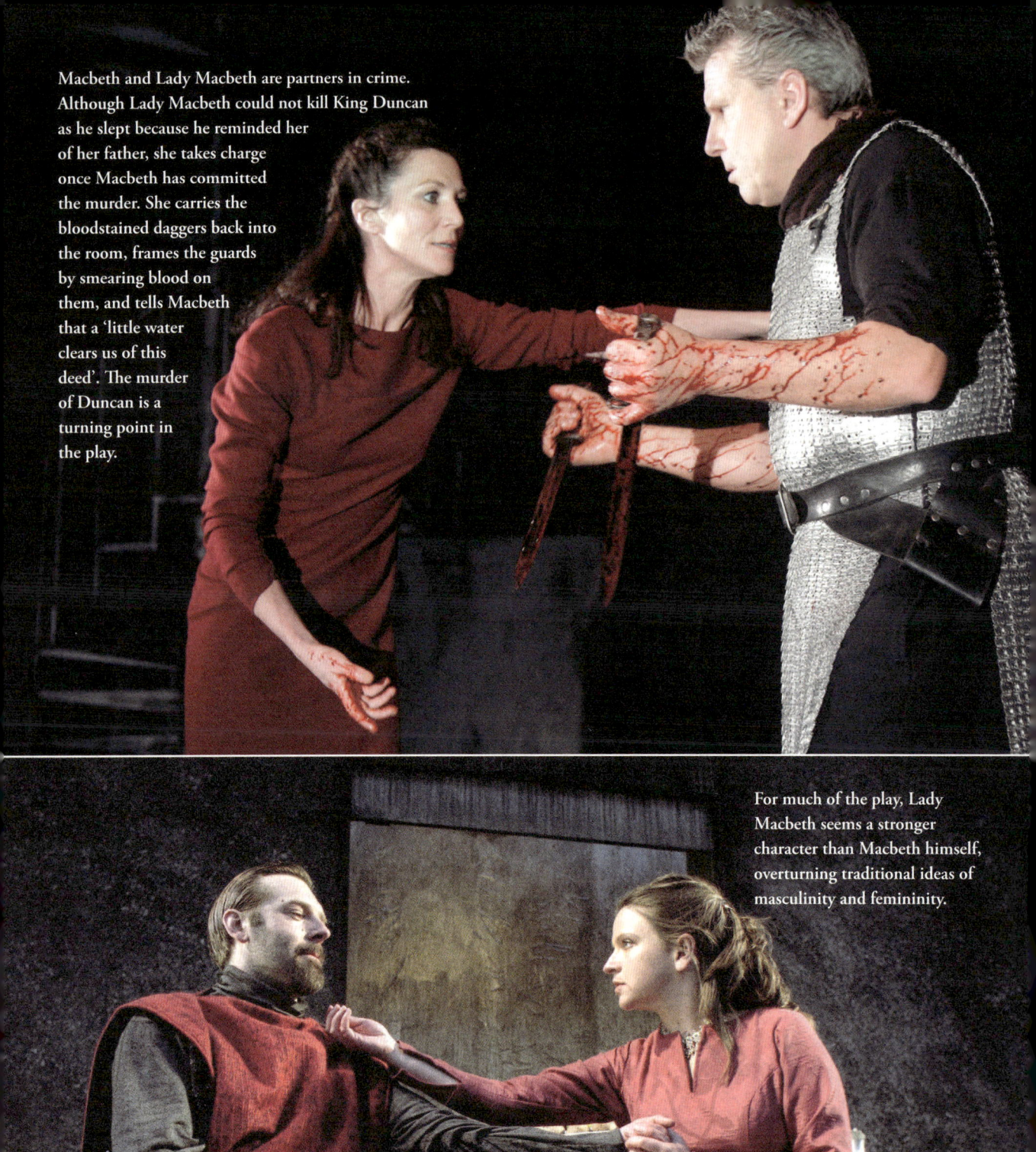

Macbeth and Lady Macbeth are partners in crime. Although Lady Macbeth could not kill King Duncan as he slept because he reminded her of her father, she takes charge once Macbeth has committed the murder. She carries the bloodstained daggers back into the room, frames the guards by smearing blood on them, and tells Macbeth that a 'little water clears us of this deed'. The murder of Duncan is a turning point in the play.

For much of the play, Lady Macbeth seems a stronger character than Macbeth himself, overturning traditional ideas of masculinity and femininity.

They maintain an innocent appearance of grief and modesty to hide their evil deeds and ambitious desires. This 'false face' is only threatened in the famous banquet scene, as Macbeth reacts violently to the sight of Banquo's ghost while Lady Macbeth tries to keep up appearances (撑场面) (shown here in a Chinese adaptation of the play).

As something of a contrast to the dark atmosphere of the play, the Porter provides some comic relief in Act 2 Scene 3. The Porter's joke about 'an equivocator' (someone who does not tell the truth) echoes the theme of deception and the conflict between appearance and reality that runs through the play.

Lady Macbeth is increasingly consumed by guilt and alienated from Macbeth as he tries to shield her from more murder. Lady Macbeth's repression of this guilt leads to self-destructive behaviour and mental instability. At the end of the play, we see her walking in her sleep, in terror of darkness, obsessively washing her hands and ultimately suicidal.

As king, Macbeth becomes increasingly tyrannical (专横) and paranoid (多疑，疑惧). He murders all who threaten him, embarks on wars to defend his position, and continues to seek out the Witches to hear what they have to say about his future. He is so caught up with defending the throne and analysing the Witches' predictions that he has no time to mourn the death of Lady Macbeth.

▶ In Act 5 Scene 8, Macduff confronts Macbeth, the man responsible for the murder of his family. Macbeth realises that the Witches have misled him and falsely promised safety in battle. Despite this, he fights on – choosing death over the humiliation of being paraded like a 'baited bear in front of the rabble (乌合之众)'.

▼ In the final speech of the play, Malcolm, son of Duncan, becomes king and grants earldoms (伯爵爵位) to Macduff and the other thanes (子爵). Although order has been restored after Macbeth's death, the audience is left to wonder if peace has really returned to Scotland.

List of characters 人物表

The Royal House of Scotland 苏格兰王室

DUNCAN /ˈdʌŋkən/ (邓肯) King of Scotland
MALCOLM /ˈmalkəm/ (马尔肯) his elder son
DONALDBAIN /ˈdɒnəlˌbeɪn/ (道讷尔本) his younger son

Thanes (noblemen of Scotland), their households and supporters 众子爵及其家人和支持者

MACBETH /məkˈbeθ/ (麦克白) Thane of Glamis /glɑːmz/ (格拉姆斯)
  later Thane of Cawdor /ˈkɔːdə(r)/ (考德)
  later King of Scotland
LADY MACBETH
BANQUO /ˈbaŋkwoː/ (班阔)
FLEANCE /ˈfliːəns/ (弗利恩) Banquo's son
MACDUFF /məkˈdʌf/ (麦克达) Thane of Fife /faɪf/ (法夫)
LADY MACDUFF
SON OF MACDUFF
GENTLEWOMAN Lady Macbeth's attendant (服侍麦克白夫人的贵妇)
SEYTON /ˈseɪtən/ (撒顿) Macbeth's armour bearer
PORTER (门房) at Macbeth's castle
CAPTAIN wounded in battle
AN OLD MAN
DOCTOR of physic (医师)
FIRST MURDERER
SECOND MURDERER
THIRD MURDERER
ROSS /rɒs/ (若斯)
LENNOX /ˈlenəks/ (伦诺克斯)
MENTEITH /menˈtiːθ/ (门蒂斯)
ANGUS /ˈaŋgəs/ (安格斯)
CAITHNESS /ˈkaθnes/ (凯斯内斯)
} other thanes

The supernatural world 灵魔世界

THREE WITCHES the wïrd sisters
THREE APPARITIONS (幽灵)
HECATE /ˈ(h)ekətiː/ (赫柯媂，又译作"赫卡忒") Queen of Witchcraft
THREE OTHER WITCHES

The English 英格兰人

SIWARD /ˈsjuːə(r)d/ (修沃) Earl of Northumberland /nɔː(r)ˈθʌmbə(r)lənd/ (诺森伯兰伯爵)
YOUNG SIWARD his son
ENGLISH DOCTOR at the court of King Edward the Confessor

Lords, Soldiers, Attendants, Servants, Messengers

The play is set in Scotland and England.

Three Witches vow to meet Macbeth after the battle. They respond to the calls of their familiar spirits. They leave, chanting ominous words. In Scene 2, Duncan hopes for a battle report from a wounded Captain.

剧情简介：三个女巫发誓战斗结束后去见麦克白。她们回应熟悉的妖精发出的呼唤，动身离去，口中叨念着一些凶兆。第二场，邓肯希望从一名负伤的排长那里听到战报。

Stagecraft 导演技巧

Dramatic entrance (in small groups, then by yourself)

Shakespeare makes *Macbeth* literally start with a bang. The Witches enter the scene with a clap of thunder, which in Shakespeare's day may have been created backstage by rolling a cannonball across wooden boards.

a Look at the photographs of modern productions in the 'Looking back' section on page 37, then talk about how you would stage this opening scene in your own modern production. How do the Witches look and sound? How do they move, enter and exit? What sound effects might add to the menacing mood (危险气氛)? How would you heighten the dramatic effect of this scene?

b In role as the director of a new modern production of *Macbeth*, write a letter to a close friend describing your ideas for staging this scene.

Write about it 写作练习

Confusion and ambiguity (in threes)

Read Scene 1 aloud with two other people. Try to explain to one another what each line means. If the meaning of any lines is obscure, consider why Shakespeare may have written those lines so they were deliberately confusing. After the discussion, write a paragraph that explains how Shakespeare uses ambiguity and contradiction to heighten the dramatic interest of the scene.

1 hurly-burly 混战
2 ere = before
3 heath 荒野
4 I come （这是女巫在回应灰猫精的呼唤）
5 Graymalkin 灰猫精（这是这个词第一次出现在英文里；Gray = Grey）
6 Paddock 蟾蜍精（paddock 是一种蛙或蟾蜍的名称）
7 Anon 马上，立刻
8 Fair 美
9 foul 丑
10 Hover 翱翔，盘旋
11 Exeunt （两个以上演员）退场，下场
12 Alarum 号角声（警示战斗或危险）
13 within 在后台
14 plight 境况
15 newest state 最新战况
16 sergeant 士官（可任班排长）
17 hardy 勇敢
18 fought / 'Gainst my captivity 解救我
19 Hail 你好

1 Diabolic (魔鬼般) language (whole class, then by yourself)

a Identify the Witches' use of rhythm and rhyme. Saying the words out loud should help you hear a beat that creates a chant-like rhythm (DUM da DUM da DUM da DUM). This rhythm is called trochaic tetrameter (扬抑四音步). While reading the lines out loud, shift your weight (or walk slowly round the classroom) in time to the beat. If you find this difficult, clap your hands at each stressed syllable to find the beat.

b In lines 1–7, the Witches speak in short, rhythmic lines, and this scene finishes with a couplet (two lines that end in the same rhyme). Make up your own rhyming couplet (押韵二行连句；对偶句) for Hecate, a fourth witch who joins these three later in the play.

Macbeth

Act 1 Scene 1
A desolate place

Thunder and lightning. Enter three WITCHES

FIRST WITCH	When shall we three meet again?	
	In thunder, lightning, or in rain?	
SECOND WITCH	When the hurly-burly's[1] done,	
	When the battle's lost, and won.	
THIRD WITCH	That will be ere[2] the set of sun.	5
FIRST WITCH	Where the place?	
SECOND WITCH	Upon the heath[3].	
THIRD WITCH	There to meet with Macbeth.	
FIRST WITCH	I come[4], Graymalkin[5].	
SECOND WITCH	Paddock[6] calls.	10
THIRD WITCH	Anon[7].	
ALL	Fair[8] is foul[9], and foul is fair,	
	Hover[10] through the fog and filthy air.	

Exeunt[11]

Act 1 Scene 2
King Duncan's camp near Forres

Alarum[12] *within*[13]. *Enter King* [DUNCAN,] MALCOLM, DONALD-BAIN, LENNOX, *with Attendants, meeting a bleeding* CAPTAIN

DUNCAN	What bloody man is that? He can report,	
	As seemeth by his plight[14], of the revolt	
	The newest state[15].	
MALCOLM	This is the sergeant[16]	
	Who like a good and hardy[17] soldier fought	
	'Gainst my captivity[18]. Hail[19], brave friend;	5

The wounded Captain reports that although the rebel Macdonald had strong forces, Macbeth personally killed him. Facing an assault by fresh Norwegian troops, Macbeth and Banquo fought on undaunted.

剧情简介：受伤的排长禀报说，尽管反贼麦克道讷尔兵强马壮，麦克白还是亲手杀了他。面对挪威新增援部队的进攻，麦克白和班阔继续战斗，百折不挠。

Language in the play 剧中语言
The Captain's report (by yourself)

The Captain's words are carefully chosen to capture the battle and paint a picture for his onstage audience (Duncan and the noblemen), as well as for the audience in the theatre.

Read lines 16–23 aloud. Identify four visual images that help the audience picture key moments in the battle. For example, you might want to look for images that depict Macbeth in the fray ('his brandished steel, / Which smoked with bloody execution') or when he meets his enemy ('And fixed his head upon our battlements'). When you have selected your four visual images, draw them or write a short paragraph for each one describing the impact it has.

Write about it 写作练习
First impressions (by yourself, then in pairs)

a Imagine you fought in the battle that the Captain describes. Using details from the script opposite, write a diary entry at the end of the day describing your impression of Macbeth. How would you turn some of the visual images into a straightforward eye-witness account?

b Swap your piece of writing with a classmate. Read each other's entries and then talk together about the difference Shakespeare's language makes in evoking (挑起) the battle. How do the visual images created by the Captain's words have a different impact from the narrative details in your own account of the battle? (For example, look at descriptions such as 'two spent swimmers that do cling together' or 'cannons over-charged with double cracks'.)

1 The wounded Captain writes home

Imagine you are the wounded Captain. You have had your wounds dressed and now you write home to tell your family what has happened. Base your letter on lines 7–42.

1 broil 厮杀，混战
2 spent 精疲力竭
3 choke their art 掣肘（例如二人在水中相互拉扯，彼此妨碍，结果双双溺水）
4 for to that 为了那个目的
5 multiplying 成倍增加
6 kerns 爱尔兰步兵（配备刀剑或弓箭）
7 galloglasses 爱尔兰骑兵（配备战斧）
8 Fortune 命运女神（常被比作反复无常的妓女）
9 damnèd quarrel 输定的事业
10 brandished 挥舞
11 steel 钢刀，钢剑
12 smoked 冒热气
13 Valour's minion 勇气的宠臣
14 carved out his passage 杀出一条血路
15 unseamed him 开了他的膛
16 from … th'chaps 从肚脐至下巴
17 battlements 城垛
18 cousin （泛指）亲戚（党肯和麦克白确实是表兄弟，他们都是苏格兰国王马尔肯二世的外孙）
19 'gins his reflection 开始其回归
20 direful 可怕
21 spring 春天
22 Mark 注意
23 skipping 溜得快
24 trust their heels 脚底板抹油，溜之大吉
25 surveying vantage 瞅准机会
26 furbished 补充
27 Dismayed 胆寒
28 say sooth 说实话
29 cracks 弹药
30 doubly redoubled 翻番再翻番
31 reeking 热血汩汩
32 memorise 让人想起
33 Golgotha 各各他（= Calvary [骷髅地]，泛指杀人地；耶稣是在耶路撒冷郊外一座名叫各各他的小山上被钉死在十字架上的）
34 gashes 很深的伤口

MACBETH ACT 1 SCENE 2
麦克白

	Say to the king the knowledge of the broil[1]
	As thou didst leave it.
CAPTAIN	Doubtful it stood,
	As two spent[2] swimmers that do cling together
	And choke their art[3]. The merciless Macdonald –
	Worthy to be a rebel, for to that[4]
	The multiplying[5] villainies of nature
	Do swarm upon him – from the Western Isles
	Of kerns[6] and galloglasses[7] is supplied,
	And Fortune[8] on his damnèd quarrel[9] smiling,
	Showed like a rebel's whore. But all's too weak,
	For brave Macbeth – well he deserves that name –
	Disdaining Fortune, with his brandished[10] steel[11],
	Which smoked[12] with bloody execution,
	Like Valour's minion[13] carved out his passage[14]
	Till he faced the slave,
	Which ne'er shook hands, nor bade farewell to him,
	Till he unseamed him[15] from the nave to th'chaps[16]
	And fixed his head upon our battlements[17].
DUNCAN	O valiant cousin[18], worthy gentleman.
CAPTAIN	As whence the sun 'gins his reflection[19],
	Shipwrecking storms and direful[20] thunders,
	So from that spring[21] whence comfort seemed to come,
	Discomfort swells. Mark[22], King of Scotland, mark,
	No sooner justice had, with valour armed,
	Compelled these skipping[23] kerns to trust their heels[24],
	But the Norwegian lord, surveying vantage[25],
	With furbished[26] arms and new supplies of men
	Began a fresh assault.
DUNCAN	Dismayed[27] not this our captains, Macbeth and Banquo?
CAPTAIN	Yes, as sparrows, eagles, or the hare, the lion.
	If I say sooth[28], I must report they were
	As cannons over-charged with double cracks[29];
	So they doubly redoubled[30] strokes upon the foe.
	Except they meant to bathe in reeking[31] wounds
	Or memorise[32] another Golgotha[33],
	I cannot tell.
	But I am faint, my gashes[34] cry for help.

Line numbers: 10, 15, 20, 25, 30, 35, 40

Ross tells that Macbeth has triumphed, capturing Cawdor and obtaining ransom and a favourable peace treaty from the King of Norway. Duncan sentences Cawdor to death and confers his title on Macbeth.

 剧情简介：若斯说麦克白已经获胜，活捉了考德，正从挪威王那里获得赎金和条件优越的和平条约。邓肯判处考德死刑，将考德的爵位封给了麦克白。

1 What is Macbeth like? (in small groups)

In your groups, talk about and then draw up a list of the qualities you think Macbeth possesses. Include some quotations from the play so far. Present a tableau (活人画；定格) (a 'human sculpture', like a still photograph) that shows Macbeth as he has been described up to this point in the play. Your tableau might represent a moment in the battle or it could be a more symbolic depiction of Macbeth's qualities.

Language in the play 剧中语言
What is Duncan like? (in pairs)

Duncan's language is formal and his vocabulary ('honour', 'worthy', 'noble') associates him with qualities that are both admirable and kingly. With a partner, discuss how you would advise an actor playing Duncan to speak his lines in this scene. How would they contrast with the speeches made by the other characters? After the discussion, read those lines out loud in the style you have decided on.

▼ Macbeth's world is brutal and violent. How do scenes like the one pictured here create a specific ideal of masculinity?

1	become	相配，相称
2	smack	有……味道
3	worthy Thane of Ross	尊贵的若斯子爵
4	looks	流露出
5	Fife	法夫（苏格兰中部东海岸的一个半岛，曾是一个郡，现在是一个地区）
6	flout	嘲弄，藐视
7	Norway	挪威王
8	numbers	大军
9	Cawdor	考德（苏格兰高地地区奈恩郡 [Nairn] 的一个村子，位于奈恩镇和印威内斯市 [Inverness] 之间）
10	dismal	凶险
11	Bellona	碧娄娜（罗马神话中的女战神）
12	bridegroom	新郎（麦克白酷爱战争，所以被比作碧娄娜的新郎）
13	lapped in proof	身着盔甲
14	self-comparisons	势均力敌
15	Point against point	刀尖对刀尖
16	Curbing	遏制
17	lavish	嚣张
18	Norways'	挪威人的
19	craves	恳求
20	composition	和平条约
21	deign	允许
22	disbursèd	从钱袋里掏出
23	Saint Colm's Inch	（今天爱丁堡附近的 Isle of Inchcolm [因奇科姆岛]；参见第60页图）
24	dollars = talers / thalers	（泰勒，古时德国的一种大银币）
25	bosom interest	内心的关切
26	present	即刻
27	former title	之前的称号（即"考德子爵"）

MACBETH ACT 1 SCENE 2
麦克白

DUNCAN So well thy words become[1] thee as thy wounds;
They smack[2] of honour both. Go get him surgeons.
　　　　　　　　　　[*Exit Captain, attended*]

　　　　　　　　Enter ROSS *and* ANGUS

Who comes here?
MALCOLM 　　　　　　The worthy Thane of Ross[3].　　　　　　　45
LENNOX What a haste looks[4] through his eyes! So should he look
That seems to speak things strange.
ROSS 　　　　　　　　　　　　God save the king.
DUNCAN Whence cam'st thou, worthy thane?
ROSS 　　　　　　　　　　　　From Fife[5], great king,
Where the Norwegian banners flout[6] the sky
And fan our people cold.　　　　　　　　　　　　50
Norway[7] himself, with terrible numbers[8],
Assisted by that most disloyal traitor,
The Thane of Cawdor[9], began a dismal[10] conflict,
Till that Bellona's[11] bridegroom[12], lapped in proof[13],
Confronted him with self-comparisons[14],　　　　55
Point against point[15], rebellious arm 'gainst arm,
Curbing[16] his lavish[17] spirit. And to conclude,
The victory fell on us –
DUNCAN 　　　Great happiness! –
ROSS 　　　　　　　　　　That now Sweno,
The Norways'[18] king, craves[19] composition[20].
Nor would we deign[21] him burial of his men　　　60
Till he disbursèd[22] at Saint Colm's Inch[23]
Ten thousand dollars[24] to our general use.
DUNCAN No more that Thane of Cawdor shall deceive
Our bosom interest[25]. Go pronounce his present[26] death
And with his former title[27] greet Macbeth.　　　65
ROSS I'll see it done.
DUNCAN What he hath lost, noble Macbeth hath won.
　　　　　　　　　　　　　　　　　　Exeunt

The Witches await Macbeth. They plot to torment a sea captain whose wife has insulted them. A drum signals the approach of Macbeth.

剧情简介：女巫们等待麦克白。她们设局折磨一名船长，因为这名船长的妻子冒犯过她们。鼓声响起，示意麦克白的到来。

1 Historical witches (in pairs)

a The First Witch is angry with a sailor's wife who would not give her some chestnuts. The wife's response gives us some insights into the way witches were viewed in Shakespeare's day. With a partner, discuss what this passage tells us about the Witches and their supposed powers over both people and nature.

b Look at the images below of witches as they have been represented historically, and identify the witch-like qualities depicted there. Then read the script opposite and add to your list.

c How do the qualities on your list differ from depictions of witches and other supernatural characters in popular movies and books today? Describe these differences in a letter to a younger student interested in contemporary representations of the supernatural.

1 quoth 说
2 Aroint thee 你滚开
3 rump-fed 猪屁股喂大的
4 runnion 癞婆娘
5 Aleppo 阿勒坡（叙利亚北部的一个商贸城，曾属土耳其帝国）
6 Tiger "老虎号"（1606年这艘英格兰的商船经历了567天灾难性航海后最终回到英国）
7 sieve 筛子（乘坐筛子航海被认为是女巫的惯常做法）
8 thither = to / towards that place
9 wind （女巫能呼风唤雨）
10 very ports they blow 风吹的所有港口
11 quarters 方向
12 card 地图
13 penthouse lid = eyelid （眼睑）
14 forbid 受诅咒
15 sennights = seven nights （周，星期）
16 nine times nine 九乘九
17 dwindle 消瘦
18 peak, and pine 消瘦，萎靡
19 bark 小船
20 tempest-tossed 在暴风雨中颠簸
21 pilot 领航员

Language in the play 剧中语言

Metaphor (隐喻) for life (in pairs)

The image of a ship tossed by the winds and the waves, struggling to make it to a safe harbour, has often been used as a **metaphor** for life. Life is seen as a voyage during which we face difficulties, experience adventures and make discoveries. Discuss the impact the Witches have on the 'voyage' of the sailor in the script opposite. What does this metaphor reveal about the Witches' plans to meet with Macbeth?

Act 1 Scene 3
A heath

Thunder. Enter the three WITCHES

FIRST WITCH	Where hast thou been, sister?	
SECOND WITCH	Killing swine.	
THIRD WITCH	Sister, where thou?	
FIRST WITCH	A sailor's wife had chestnuts in her lap	
	And munched, and munched, and munched. 'Give me', quoth[1] I.	
	'Aroint thee[2], witch', the rump-fed[3] runnion[4] cries.	5
	Her husband's to Aleppo[5] gone, master o'th'Tiger[6]:	
	But in a sieve[7] I'll thither[8] sail,	
	And like a rat without a tail,	
	I'll do, I'll do, and I'll do.	
SECOND WITCH	I'll give thee a wind[9].	10
FIRST WITCH	Thou'rt kind.	
THIRD WITCH	And I another.	
FIRST WITCH	I myself have all the other,	
	And the very ports they blow[10],	
	All the quarters[11] that they know	15
	I'th'shipman's card[12].	
	I'll drain him dry as hay:	
	Sleep shall neither night nor day	
	Hang upon his penthouse lid[13];	
	He shall live a man forbid[14].	20
	Weary sennights[15] nine times nine[16],	
	Shall he dwindle[17], peak, and pine[18].	
	Though his bark[19] cannot be lost,	
	Yet it shall be tempest-tossed[20].	
	Look what I have.	
SECOND WITCH	Show me, show me.	25
FIRST WITCH	Here I have a pilot's[21] thumb,	
	Wrecked as homeward he did come.	

Drum within

THIRD WITCH	A drum, a drum;
	Macbeth doth come.

The Witches chant a spell to prepare for their meeting with Macbeth. They amaze him with predictions that he will be Thane of Cawdor and King of Scotland. Banquo demands to know his own future.

 剧情简介：女巫叨念咒语，准备与麦克白会面。她们预见麦克白会当上考德子爵和苏格兰王，这使他大吃一惊。班阔也要求知道自己的未来。

Stagecraft 导演技巧

A charmed space (in small groups)

The Witches wind up a charm immediately before Macbeth and Banquo enter the scene. Read lines 30–5 with your group.

a The rhythmic, chant-like language of the Witches gives clues about their movements on stage, such as what they are doing when creating the charm, when they speed up and when they stop. In your groups, talk about how you would stage this part of the scene so that you can show Macbeth and Banquo walking into this 'charmed' space.

b Prepare a dramatised reading of the whole passage opposite. Look at Banquo's speech in lines 37–45 for more clues about what is happening on stage.

1 weïrd sisters 命运姐妹（盎格鲁-撒克逊神话里Wyrd是命运女神；weïrd = Wyrd）
2 Posters 神行侠
3 about 转
4 Thrice … mine 三次朝向你，三次朝向我（女巫们似乎在跳圆圈舞）
5 Peace 别出声，安静
6 charm 魔咒
7 wound up 上好弦了；马上就灵
8 foul and fair 又糟又好（天气糟但战况好）
9 How … Forres? 离福里斯还有多远？（is't called = is it; Forres是苏格兰一个镇的名字，距麦克白的城堡不远；见第60页地图）
10 withered 枯瘦
11 wild 怪异
12 attire 装束
13 on't = of it
14 Live you 你们是活人吗
15 aught = anything
16 choppy 皲裂
17 All hail 万福
18 Glamis 格拉姆斯（麦克白的家族封地，位于苏格兰邓迪市[Dundee]北部）
19 start 吃惊
20 ye = you
21 fantastical 虚幻
22 present grace 眼下的殊荣
23 noble having 加官晋爵
24 royal hope 称王的希望
25 rapt 着迷
26 seeds of time 时间的种子（指将来）

▼ 'Speak if you can', Macbeth demands. Speak the Witches' predictions in lines 46–8 as you think they would deliver them.

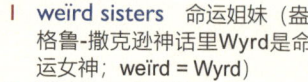

ALL	The weïrd sisters[1], hand in hand,	30
	Posters[2] of the sea and land,	
	Thus do go, about[3], about,	
	Thrice to thine, and thrice to mine[4],	
	And thrice again, to make up nine.	
	Peace[5], the charm's[6] wound up[7].	35

Enter MACBETH *and* BANQUO

MACBETH	So foul and fair[8] a day I have not seen.	
BANQUO	How far is't called to Forres?[9] What are these,	
	So withered[10] and so wild[11] in their attire[12],	
	That look not like th'inhabitants o'th'earth,	
	And yet are on't[13]? – Live you[14], or are you aught[15]	40
	That man may question? You seem to understand me,	
	By each at once her choppy[16] finger laying	
	Upon her skinny lips; you should be women,	
	And yet your beards forbid me to interpret	
	That you are so.	
MACBETH	Speak if you can: what are you?	45
FIRST WITCH	All hail[17] Macbeth, hail to thee, Thane of Glamis[18].	
SECOND WITCH	All hail Macbeth, hail to thee, Thane of Cawdor.	
THIRD WITCH	All hail Macbeth, that shalt be king hereafter.	
BANQUO	Good sir, why do you start[19] and seem to fear	
	Things that do sound so fair? – I'th'name of truth	50
	Are ye[20] fantastical[21], or that indeed	
	Which outwardly ye show? My noble partner	
	You greet with present grace[22] and great prediction	
	Of noble having[23] and of royal hope[24]	
	That he seems rapt[25] withal. To me you speak not.	55
	If you can look into the seeds of time[26]	
	And say which grain will grow and which will not,	
	Speak then to me, who neither beg nor fear	
	Your favours nor your hate.	
FIRST WITCH	Hail.	60
SECOND WITCH	Hail.	
THIRD WITCH	Hail.	

The Witches prophesy that Banquo's descendants will be kings, but he himself will not. Refusing to answer Macbeth's questions, the Witches vanish. Ross brings news of Duncan's delight at Macbeth's victory.

剧情简介：女巫预言班阔的后代会当国王，但他自己不会。女巫拒绝回答麦克白的问题，随后消失。若斯带来消息说，麦克白的胜利令党肯大为欣喜。

Stagecraft 导演技巧
How do the Witches vanish?

Every director of the play has to solve the practical problem of the stage direction '*Witches vanish*'. At the beginning of Roman Polanski's movie version, the Witches vanished by walking away from the camera along a dismal beach, fading into specks that dissolved (消散) into the opening credits (片头字幕). On Shakespeare's stage there were obvious limitations to the way the Witches could vanish. They may have left on foot or via a trapdoor (地板门), or have somehow 'flown' off stage.

Write out your own suggestions for making the Witches vanish convincingly in a letter to a director working on a production in a modern theatre, which will later be turned into a film.

Characters 人物分析
To be 'rapt withal' (in pairs)

Macbeth and Banquo are 'rapt withal' by the Witches' prophecies. Read the scene again, from their entrance after line 35, then write out five questions for these two characters. Step into role as either Macbeth or Banquo and answer your partner's questions.

1 Actors' experiments (in pairs)

Imagine you are an actor in rehearsal, taking advice from a director who wants to experiment with different ways of representing the scene opposite. Read the director's instructions below:

- In lines 68–76, Macbeth just can't believe what he has heard. He wants answers urgently. So speak the lines quickly and angrily *or* in a way that shows he is confused and frustrated.
- In lines 77–86, the two men are deeply puzzled and amazed by what they have seen and heard. So speak the lines slowly and wonderingly *or* fearfully and suspiciously.
- In lines 87–98, Ross wants to give Macbeth and Banquo important news from the king. So speak the lines pompously (自负，傲慢) and grandly *or* with friendliness and excitement.

Choose how you want to interpret these lines, then take turns to perform your version of this scene to the rest of the class.

1 Lesser than Macbeth, and greater 地位低于麦克白，但更伟大
2 get = beget（做……之父/父母）
3 Stay 等一等
4 imperfect 话不说完/明白
5 Finel 法依讷尔（麦克白的父亲）
6 Stands … belief 不在可信前景的范围内
7 intelligence 消息
8 blasted 荒凉
9 charge 命令
10 bubbles 气泡（意思是这些女巫突然消失就像气泡突然破灭一样）
11 Whither = To what place
12 corporal 有形体，有肉身
13 the insane root 毒堇（hemlock）、天仙子（henbane）或颠茄（nightshade）等植物的根（人食后会精神失常）
14 takes the reason prisoner 将理智困为囚犯
15 selfsame tune 意思完全相同
16 reads 考虑到
17 stout 勇猛
18 Nothing afeard 毫无畏惧
19 As thick as tale （比喻密集得就像算筹一根接一根掷下；tale = tally, tally sticks [理货棒，算筹]）
20 post with post 驿马/邸报接踵而至

FIRST WITCH	Lesser than Macbeth, and greater[1].
SECOND WITCH	Not so happy, yet much happier.
THIRD WITCH	Thou shalt get[2] kings, though thou be none.
	So all hail Macbeth and Banquo.
FIRST WITCH	Banquo and Macbeth, all hail.
MACBETH	Stay[3], you imperfect[4] speakers. Tell me more.
	By Finel's[5] death, I know I am Thane of Glamis,
	But how of Cawdor? The Thane of Cawdor lives
	A prosperous gentleman, and to be king
	Stands not within the prospect of belief[6],
	No more than to be Cawdor. Say from whence
	You owe this strange intelligence[7], or why
	Upon this blasted[8] heath you stop our way
	With such prophetic greeting? Speak, I charge[9] you.

Witches vanish

BANQUO	The earth hath bubbles[10], as the water has,
	And these are of them. Whither[11] are they vanished?
MACBETH	Into the air, and what seemed corporal[12],
	Melted, as breath into the wind. Would they had stayed.
BANQUO	Were such things here as we do speak about?
	Or have we eaten on the insane root[13],
	That takes the reason prisoner[14]?
MACBETH	Your children shall be kings.
BANQUO	You shall be king.
MACBETH	And Thane of Cawdor too: went it not so?
BANQUO	To th'selfsame tune[15] and words – who's here?

Enter ROSS and ANGUS

ROSS	The king hath happily received, Macbeth,
	The news of thy success, and when he reads[16]
	Thy personal venture in the rebels' sight,
	His wonders and his praises do contend
	Which should be thine or his. Silenced with that,
	In viewing o'er the rest o'th'selfsame day,
	He finds thee in the stout[17] Norwegian ranks,
	Nothing afeard[18] of what thyself didst make,
	Strange images of death. As thick as tale[19]
	Came post with post[20], and every one did bear
	Thy praises in his kingdom's great defence,
	And poured them down before him.

Macbeth is amazed to hear that he is now Thane of Cawdor. Angus explains that the treacherous thane has been sentenced to death. Banquo warns that the Witches' predictions might lead to evil.

 剧情简介：麦克白惊奇地听到他现在被封为考德子爵了。安格斯解释说那个叛徒子爵已经被判死刑。班阔警告说女巫的预言可能会导致罪恶。

Themes 主题分析
Honour and kingship

Angus tells that the present Thane of Cawdor is alive, but has committed treason and sided with the enemy. Use lines 107–15 to help you write the official notice that gives reasons for Cawdor's conviction for treason and announces his imminent execution. You may find it helpful to start by considering the themes and ideas of kingship, honour and masculinity that are raised here, perhaps in the form of a mind map or as bullet points.

1. earnest 承诺
2. addition 新爵位
3. Who = He who
4. heavy judgement 重判（即死刑）
5. line 支持
6. vantage 有利条件（如额外的兵员、武器、金钱等）
7. laboured 努力做
8. wrack 毁灭，颠覆
9. capital = punishable by death (可判死刑)
10. overthrown 打翻在地；使遭殃
11. The greatest 压轴大戏，重头戏
12. pains 辛苦，费心
13. home = completely (完全)
14. enkindle 使燃起欲望
15. win = bring
16. instruments of darkness 恶魔的工具/走卒（指女巫）
17. Win ... consequence 小事情上说真话，却在有严重后果的事情上撒谎

1 Secret desires (in pairs)

Macbeth and Banquo are comrades in arms, who have fought together and won a great victory. But how might the Witches' prophecies affect them and their relationship?

a With a partner, read out Macbeth's and Banquo's lines opposite. Talk together about the meaning of Banquo's words in lines 121–5 in relation to the theme of appearance versus reality. (See p. 161 for more information on this theme.) What do you think counts as 'reality' here?

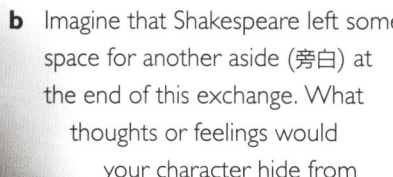

b Imagine that Shakespeare left some space for another aside (旁白) at the end of this exchange. What thoughts or feelings would your character hide from his comrade in arms? In role as either Macbeth or Banquo, speak out your secret thoughts about the Witches and each other. Write out these thoughts in **blank verse** (无韵诗；素体诗) (see p. 172), modelled on the speeches Shakespeare has given the characters in this scene.

ANGUS	We are sent
	To give thee from our royal master thanks;
	Only to herald thee into his sight, 100
	Not pay thee.
ROSS	And for an earnest[1] of a greater honour,
	He bade me, from him, call thee Thane of Cawdor:
	In which addition[2], hail most worthy thane,
	For it is thine.
BANQUO	What, can the devil speak true? 105
MACBETH	The Thane of Cawdor lives. Why do you dress me
	In borrowed robes?
ANGUS	Who[3] was the thane, lives yet,
	But under heavy judgement[4] bears that life
	Which he deserves to lose.
	Whether he was combined with those of Norway, 110
	Or did line[5] the rebel with hidden help
	And vantage[6], or that with both he laboured[7]
	In his country's wrack[8], I know not,
	But treasons capital[9], confessed and proved,
	Have overthrown[10] him.
MACBETH	[Aside] Glamis, and Thane of Cawdor: 115
	The greatest[11] is behind. – Thanks for your pains[12]. –
	[To Banquo] Do you not hope your children shall be kings,
	When those that gave the Thane of Cawdor to me
	Promised no less to them?
BANQUO	That trusted home[13],
	Might yet enkindle[14] you unto the crown, 120
	Besides the Thane of Cawdor. But 'tis strange,
	And oftentimes, to win[15] us to our harm,
	The instruments of darkness[16] tell us truths;
	Win us with honest trifles, to betray's
	In deepest consequence[17]. – 125
	Cousins, a word, I pray you.

Macbeth weighs the moral implications of the Witches' prediction. He is horrified at the thought of killing Duncan, but resolves to accept whatever has to be. He proposes that he and Banquo talk together later.

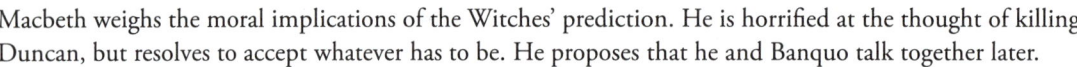

剧情简介：麦克白掂量了女巫预言的道德含义。一想到要杀死邓肯，他感到恐惧，但下定决心无论何去何从他都接受。他提出晚些时候同班阔谈谈。

1 Macbeth's private thoughts (in pairs)

An aside is a dramatic device that gives important insights into a character's thoughts and feelings. In lines 126–43, Macbeth processes the news that he is now the Thane of Cawdor and that one of the Witches' prophecies has come true.

In pairs, one person reads these lines aloud, pausing at every punctuation mark. The other person says 'Hail Macbeth, King of Scotland' in these pauses, either in a tempting voice or echoing the way the Witches might have said it. Work out how many times Macbeth refers to the murder of Duncan. Afterwards, talk together about whether you think this prediction is uppermost in Macbeth's mind each time he speaks.

2 Punctuation clues

Macbeth's confusion is evident in this section, as he wavers between murderous thoughts and an awareness of good and evil. Think about how the language makes you feel as you read the lines opposite while walking round the classroom. As you walk, you should change direction on each punctuation mark, using the following rules:

- At each full stop make a full about-turn (180 degrees).
- At each comma make a half turn (90 degrees to your right or left).

Which words or lines stood out for you during this activity? How did this activity improve your understanding of Macbeth's thoughts and feelings?

Language in the play 剧中语言

Borrowed robes (in pairs)

Earlier in this scene, in lines 106–7, the first of many images of clothing is used. There is also a subtle reference to clothes in line 111, where 'line' also means the lining or reinforcement of a cloak (Cawdor had reinforced the rebel forces).

a Look for imagery relating to clothing in the script opposite. Discuss how this adds depth to the language and links different ideas. Remember that 'rapt' (line 141) means spellbound (着魔，入迷), but also sounds like 'wrapped', as in 'wrapped up in a new cloak'.

b Start compiling a list of imagery that relates to clothing, and add to this as you read through the rest of the play.

1 swelling act　大戏拉开帷幕
2 Of the imperial theme　有关登基称王的话题
3 soliciting　诱惑
4 ill　恶意
5 unfix my hair　让我毛发竖立
6 seated　安安稳稳
7 use　常态
8 Present … imaginings　现实中的可怕事物远不如想象中的可怕
9 single state　健全状态
10 function　行动能力
11 surmise　想象
12 stir　动手
13 strange　新；没有穿惯
14 cleave not to their mould　穿在身上不服帖
15 Come what come may　听天由命吧
16 Time … day　日子再不平静也会一天天过去
17 Give me your favour　敬请海涵，请多包涵
18 wrought　搅乱
19 registered … leaf　记在我每天翻的本子上了（leaf指一张纸，喻指记事本）
20 chanced = happened
21 at more time　过一段时间
22 The interim having weighed it　这期间把这事再掂量一下
23 free hearts　畅所欲言
24 Till then, enough　到时再谈

MACBETH	[*Aside*] Two truths are told,	
	As happy prologues to the swelling act[1]	
	Of the imperial theme[2]. – I thank you, gentlemen. –	
	This supernatural soliciting[3]	
	Cannot be ill[4], cannot be good. If ill,	130
	Why hath it given me earnest of success,	
	Commencing in a truth? I am Thane of Cawdor.	
	If good, why do I yield to that suggestion,	
	Whose horrid image doth unfix my hair[5]	
	And make my seated[6] heart knock at my ribs	135
	Against the use[7] of nature? Present fears	
	Are less than horrible imaginings[8].	
	My thought, whose murder yet is but fantastical,	
	Shakes so my single state[9] of man that function[10]	
	Is smothered in surmise[11], and nothing is,	140
	But what is not.	
BANQUO	Look how our partner's rapt.	
MACBETH	If chance will have me king, why chance may crown me	
	Without my stir[12].	
BANQUO	New honours come upon him	
	Like our strange[13] garments, cleave not to their mould[14],	
	But with the aid of use.	
MACBETH	Come what come may[15],	145
	Time and the hour runs through the roughest day[16].	
BANQUO	Worthy Macbeth, we stay upon your leisure.	
MACBETH	Give me your favour[17]. My dull brain was wrought[18]	
	With things forgotten. Kind gentlemen, your pains	
	Are registered where every day I turn	150
	The leaf[19] to read them. Let us toward the king.	
	[*To Banquo*] Think upon what hath chanced[20] and at more time[21],	
	The interim having weighed it[22], let us speak	
	Our free hearts[23] each to other.	
BANQUO	Very gladly.	
MACBETH	Till then, enough[24]. – Come, friends.	155
	Exeunt	

Malcolm reports that the Thane of Cawdor died a repentant and dignified death. Duncan reflects that it is impossible to judge anyone by their outward appearance. He warmly welcomes Macbeth.

剧情简介：马尔肯报告说考德子爵死了，死前表示悔意，死得有尊严。邓肯反思，认为不可能从外表看清一个人。他热情欢迎麦克白到来。

Stagecraft 导演技巧

Offstage events (whole class)

Because of the limitations of the Jacobean (詹姆斯一世时代) theatre, important events often took place off stage – such as the battle involving Macbeth and the Norwegian forces, or Cawdor's execution. Today, directors often take the same approach in television programmes and movies.

Do you think offstage battles, executions or other important and dramatic events in a story add to or limit an audience's enjoyment and understanding? Write down your ideas, then report back to the rest of the class. Afterwards, hold a class discussion on the benefits and drawbacks of having some events take place off stage.

Themes 主题分析

Appearance and reality

Duncan claims that you cannot tell what people are like from their appearance ('There's no art / To find the mind's construction in the face'). Discuss with others in your class how far you think this observation is true. Consider your own experiences. Have you ever been judged by what you look like rather than who you really are? Do you think society today judges people more by their appearance than anything else? If you feel comfortable doing so, share these experiences with your class.

1. *Flourish* 号角齐鸣（表示身份高贵的人物上场）
2. *in commission* 负责此事
3. *My liege* 陛下
4. *Implored* 恳求
5. *repentance* 悔恨
6. *Became* 适合
7. *the leaving it* 离生命而去
8. *studied in* 在如何……上排练过
9. *owed* = owned
10. *As 'twere a careless trifle* = As if it were a careless trifle（仿佛那是什么不值钱的小玩意儿）
11. *far before* 远远超出（我奖赏你的能力）
12. *wing of recompense* 奖赏的速度
13. *That … mine* = So that … mine（那样我就能公平地奖赏你了）
14. *More … pay* 你应得到的奖赏多于任何人能给你的全部奖赏

1 Dramatic irony (戏剧反讽)

Dramatic irony occurs when the audience knows something that the characters in the play do not. There is a good example of dramatic irony in the script opposite. Just at the moment when Duncan is saying that he wrongly trusted Cawdor ('He was a gentleman on whom I built / An absolute trust'), the man who is thinking of killing him enters.

Imagine you are a director and write notes to the cast about how you would like this crucial entrance to be played. To what extent do you want the actors to emphasise the use of dramatic irony?

Act 1 Scene 4
Duncan's palace at Forres

Flourish[1]. *Enter King* DUNCAN, LENNOX, MALCOLM,
DONALDBAIN, *and Attendants*

DUNCAN   Is execution done on Cawdor, or not
Those in commission[2] yet returned?

MALCOLM   My liege[3],
They are not yet come back. But I have spoke
With one that saw him die, who did report
That very frankly he confessed his treasons,   5
Implored[4] your highness' pardon, and set forth
A deep repentance[5]. Nothing in his life
Became[6] him like the leaving it[7]. He died
As one that had been studied in[8] his death,
To throw away the dearest thing he owed[9]   10
As 'twere a careless trifle[10].

DUNCAN   There's no art
To find the mind's construction in the face.
He was a gentleman on whom I built
An absolute trust.

Enter MACBETH, BANQUO, ROSS, *and* ANGUS

                        O worthiest cousin,
The sin of my ingratitude even now   15
Was heavy on me. Thou art so far before[11],
That swiftest wing of recompense[12] is slow
To overtake thee. Would thou hadst less deserved,
That the proportion both of thanks and payment
Might have been mine[13]. Only I have left to say,   20
More is thy due than more than all can pay[14].

MACBETH   The service and the loyalty I owe,
In doing it, pays itself. Your highness' part

Macbeth declares his loyalty to Duncan, who (after promising honours to Macbeth and Banquo) announces that his son, Malcolm, shall succeed to the throne. Macbeth is appalled and broods ominously.

剧情简介：麦克白宣称忠于邓肯。邓肯保证给麦克白和班阔名誉地位，随后宣布他的儿子马尔肯将继承王位。麦克白大为震惊，预感不妙。

Characters 人物分析

King and future king (in small groups)

This is an important scene, because we see both Duncan and Macbeth develop as characters.

- Duncan is often portrayed on stage as a gentle, kindly king. The language Shakespeare uses here – of reward and growth – reinforces this idea of a generous ruler. But in his decision to name Malcolm as his successor, Duncan also shows himself to be a clever and ruthless (无情，冷酷) politician.
- In lines 22–7, Macbeth is publicly loyal to his king. In lines 48–53, however, he admits to himself that he must find a way to prevent Malcolm being appointed Duncan's heir. It is important to note that in Scotland at the time, kingship was not automatically inherited. This explains Macbeth's disappointment, especially given the Witches' prophecy.

Experiment with different ways of staging the script opposite to show how the characters of Duncan and Macbeth have changed. Think about how each character reacts as the other is talking. Is Duncan being devious (阴险) or kind? Is Macbeth justified in his response? Remember to consider characters such as Malcolm and Donaldbain, who do not speak in this section but whose lives will be affected by this exchange. How would you play them?

1 Power relationships (in small groups)

Talk about how the characters in this scene would be depicted in a formal portrait. Then take roles and prepare for a group portrait. A 'portrait painter' should arrange the characters in the most diplomatic way. Remember that to accurately show the status of each group of sitters, they should be positioned so that the most important is nearest the king. How do the figures in the Tudor painting below relate to your arrangement?

1 **Safe toward** = For the safeguard of
2 **hither** = to this place
3 **plant** 培养，扶持
4 **enfold** 拥抱
5 **Wanton** 放纵，止不住
6 **We … upon** 朕要将朕的千秋大业置于……的肩上
7 **Prince of Cumberland** 坎伯兰亲王（坎伯兰是英格兰西北部靠近苏格兰的一个历史地区，曾属于苏格兰；坎伯兰亲王是王储的封号，相当于英格兰的威尔士亲王）
8 **invest** 封为
9 **Inverness** 印威内斯（麦克白的封地）
10 **bind us further to you** 让朕（因您的款待）对您心存更多感激
11 **harbinger** 先行官（任务是打前站）
12 **make … approach** = make my wife joyful with the hearing of your approach（麦克白此时说话有些语无伦次）
13 **The … hand** 让眼暂时闭上，不要看手
14 **let that be** = let that be done
15 **full so valiant** 完全（像你说的）那样英勇
16 **commendations** 表扬
17 **peerless** 举世无双

	Is to receive our duties, and our duties	
	Are to your throne and state, children and servants,	25
	Which do but what they should by doing everything	
	Safe toward[1] your love and honour.	
DUNCAN	Welcome hither[2].	
	I have begun to plant[3] thee and will labour	
	To make thee full of growing. Noble Banquo,	
	That hast no less deserved, nor must be known	30
	No less to have done so, let me enfold[4] thee	
	And hold thee to my heart.	
BANQUO	There if I grow,	
	The harvest is your own.	
DUNCAN	My plenteous joys,	
	Wanton[5] in fullness, seek to hide themselves	
	In drops of sorrow. Sons, kinsmen, thanes,	35
	And you whose places are the nearest, know:	
	We will establish our estate upon[6]	
	Our eldest, Malcolm, whom we name hereafter	
	The Prince of Cumberland[7], which honour must	
	Not unaccompanied invest[8] him only,	40
	But signs of nobleness like stars shall shine	
	On all deservers. [*To Macbeth*] From hence to Inverness[9]	
	And bind us further to you[10].	
MACBETH	The rest is labour which is not used for you;	
	I'll be myself the harbinger[11] and make joyful	45
	The hearing of my wife with your approach[12].	
	So humbly take my leave.	
DUNCAN	My worthy Cawdor.	
MACBETH	[*Aside*] The Prince of Cumberland: that is a step	
	On which I must fall down, or else o'erleap,	
	For in my way it lies. Stars, hide your fires,	50
	Let not light see my black and deep desires,	
	The eye wink at the hand[13]. Yet let that be[14],	
	Which the eye fears when it is done to see. *Exit*	
DUNCAN	True, worthy Banquo, he is full so valiant[15],	
	And in his commendations[16] I am fed;	55
	It is a banquet to me. Let's after him,	
	Whose care is gone before to bid us welcome:	
	It is a peerless[17] kinsman.	
	Flourish	
	Exeunt	

Lady Macbeth reads her husband's letter telling of the Witches' prophecy of kingship. She analyses his nature, fearing that he is too decent and squeamish to murder Duncan for the crown.

剧情简介：麦克白夫人读了丈夫的来信，里面讲了女巫有关王位的预言。她分析了丈夫的本性，担心他为人太正派，神经太脆弱，不会为了王位而谋杀邓肯。

Characters 人物分析

Lady Macbeth: first impressions (in pairs)

This is Lady Macbeth's first appearance. Some directors are keen to suggest that she is psychologically unstable right from the start, while others stress how close she is to her absent husband and how ambitious she is for both of them.

a Read lines 1–28, then write down your immediate thoughts on how Shakespeare presents this important character.

b With your partner, act out this speech. One person should perform the part of Lady Macbeth and the other should take the role of director.

c Write down your impressions of being both a director and an actor: what have you learned about Lady Macbeth?

Language in the play 剧中语言

Prose (散文；散体) and verse (韵文；韵体) (in pairs)

Macbeth's letter is in prose, but Lady Macbeth speaks in a much richer, poetic language. Look closely at the imagery she uses as she scrutinises (审视) her husband, almost as if he is present. With a partner, talk about Lady Macbeth's evaluation of his character. What does she see as his strengths? Perhaps more importantly, what does she consider his major failings? Draw up a list of Macbeth's strengths and weaknesses, then compare your list with your partner's.

◀ Lines 1–12 may be just part of Macbeth's letter, concerning only the Witches. What other news might he have reported to his wife?

1 They 她们（这里指代女巫）
2 in the day of success 战斗胜利那天
3 perfectest 最可靠
4 mortal knowledge 凡人的见识
5 missives 信使
6 the coming on of time 未来的时间
7 deliver 告诉
8 the dues of rejoicing 应得的快乐
9 Lay it to thy heart 将它铭记在心吧
10 What thou art promised 别人向你许诺的（即当上国王）
11 milk of human kindness 仁爱之奶
12 catch the nearest way 明白最近的道（指谋杀）
13 illness 邪恶
14 attend = accompany
15 holily 正大光明，符合道义
16 play false 耍手腕，搞阴谋
17 wrongly win 用不正当的方式得到
18 cries = cries out
19 Hie 快来
20 chastise 清洗
21 impedes 阻止
22 golden round 金圈圈（指金王冠）
23 metaphysical 超自然
24 withal = as well
25 tidings 消息

Act 1 Scene 5
Macbeth's castle at Inverness

Enter LADY MACBETH *alone, with a letter*

LADY MACBETH [*Reads*] 'They[1] met me in the day of success[2], and I have learned by the perfectest[3] report they have more in them than mortal knowledge[4]. When I burned in desire to question them further, they made themselves air, into which they vanished. Whiles I stood rapt in the wonder of it, came missives[5] from the king who all-hailed me Thane of Cawdor, by which title before these weïrd sisters saluted me and referred me to the coming on of time[6] , with "Hail, king that shalt be." This have I thought good to deliver[7] thee, my dearest partner of greatness, that thou mightst not lose the dues of rejoicing[8] by being ignorant of what greatness is promised thee. Lay it to thy heart[9] and farewell.'

    Glamis thou art, and Cawdor, and shalt be
    What thou art promised[10]; yet do I fear thy nature,
    It is too full o'th'milk of human kindness[11]
    To catch the nearest way[12]. Thou wouldst be great,
    Art not without ambition, but without
    The illness[13] should attend[14] it. What thou wouldst highly,
    That wouldst thou holily[15]; wouldst not play false[16],
    And yet wouldst wrongly win[17]. Thou'dst have, great Glamis,
    That which cries[18], 'Thus thou must do' if thou have it;
    And that which rather thou dost fear to do,
    Than wishest should be undone. Hie[19] thee hither,
    That I may pour my spirits in thine ear
    And chastise[20] with the valour of my tongue
    All that impedes[21] thee from the golden round[22],
    Which fate and metaphysical[23] aid doth seem
    To have thee crowned withal[24].

Enter [ATTENDANT]

    What is your tidings[25]?

ATTENDANT The king comes here tonight.

The Attendant gives news that Macbeth is approaching. Lady Macbeth calls on evil spirits to assist her plans for Duncan's murder. She greets Macbeth with thoughts of future greatness.

 剧情简介：侍从通报说麦克白快到了。麦克白夫人呼唤恶鬼助她完成谋杀邓肯的计划。她迎接麦克白时心里想着未来的荣耀。

Stagecraft 导演技巧
Addressing the audience

Lady Macbeth's speech can be divided into three sections (lines 38–45, 45–8 and 48–52), each beginning with the word 'Come'. Some people think that Shakespeare did this deliberately, so that the actor playing Lady Macbeth could say essentially the same thing to the three different sections of the audience (the right, the centre and the left).

Write down a summary of each part of the speech. As you write, ask yourself if Lady Macbeth says anything new in each of these sections, or if she simply expresses the same desire each time.

Language in the play 剧中语言
Lady Macbeth's soliloquy (独白) (in threes)

Lines 36–52 form a **soliloquy** until Macbeth arrives. The language is excited and its rhythm is varied. The pace changes throughout, which adds to the sense of compressed time and of hurrying fate. This is a powerful speech, full of verbs and metaphors ('fill me from the crown to the toe', 'make thick my blood', 'Shake', 'take my milk for gall'), and it reaches a climax with 'Hold, hold'.

In groups of three, experiment with the pacing of this speech, taking it in turns to speak the various sections and thinking about which words you would stress. Discuss your choices with the rest of the group.

1 Ambitious or evil? (in pairs)

a With a partner, discuss what you think Lady Macbeth most wants, and consider how this challenges conventional views of feminine behaviour. Remember that when the play was written and first performed, all the parts were played by male actors. Does this affect your interpretation of the character of Lady Macbeth?

b Many people find this speech shocking. Pick out the images that you feel contribute most to this impression and sketch the ones you think are the most powerful. Share these with a partner and put together a wall display of the strongest and most shocking images.

---

1 were't so = if it were so
2 So please you = If you please（启禀夫人；这是当时下级对上级表示谦卑的一种用语）
3 had the speed of 赶在了……的前面
4 make up 说完
5 tending 照料
6 tend on mortal thoughts 照管凡人意念
7 unsex me 去除我的性别
8 topfull = completely full
9 Stop up 堵上
10 compunctious 内疚，惭愧
11 visitings of nature 本能的感受
12 fell purpose 无情的计划
13 keep … it 让计划与其实现彼此相安（即不去执行计划）
14 for gall 当作胆汁（此处喻指苦药/毒药）
15 murd'ring ministers 谋杀的执行者
16 sightless substances 看不见的形体
17 pall 裹上
18 dunnest 最黑
19 keen 锋利；热切
20 by the all-hail 按照"all-hail"的说法
21 in the instant 就在眼前
22 purposes = intends

LADY MACBETH	Thou'rt mad to say it.

    Is not thy master with him? Who, were't so[1],
    Would have informed for preparation.

ATTENDANT So please you[2], it is true: our thane is coming.
    One of my fellows had the speed of[3] him;
    Who almost dead for breath, had scarcely more
    Than would make up[4] his message.

LADY MACBETH   Give him tending[5],
    He brings great news.

Exit [Attendant]

                    The raven himself is hoarse
    That croaks the fatal entrance of Duncan
    Under my battlements. Come, you spirits
    That tend on mortal thoughts[6], unsex me[7] here
    And fill me from the crown to the toe topfull[8]
    Of direst cruelty; make thick my blood,
    Stop up[9] th'access and passage to remorse
    That no compunctious[10] visitings of nature[11]
    Shake my fell purpose[12] nor keep peace between
    Th'effect and it[13]. Come to my woman's breasts
    And take my milk for gall[14], you murd'ring ministers[15],
    Wherever in your sightless substances[16]
    You wait on nature's mischief. Come, thick night,
    And pall[17] thee in the dunnest[18] smoke of hell,
    That my keen[19] knife see not the wound it makes,
    Nor heaven peep through the blanket of the dark,
    To cry, 'Hold, hold.'

Enter MACBETH

                Great Glamis, worthy Cawdor,
    Greater than both by the all-hail[20] hereafter,
    Thy letters have transported me beyond
    This ignorant present, and I feel now
    The future in the instant[21].

MACBETH   My dearest love,
    Duncan comes here tonight.

LADY MACBETH   And when goes hence?

MACBETH Tomorrow, as he purposes[22].

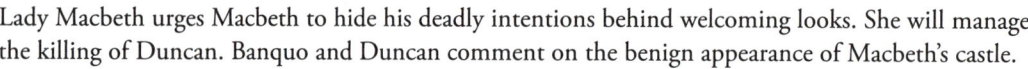

Lady Macbeth urges Macbeth to hide his deadly intentions behind welcoming looks. She will manage the killing of Duncan. Banquo and Duncan comment on the benign appearance of Macbeth's castle.

剧情简介：麦克白夫人敦促麦克白将杀人的意图隐藏起来，脸上要显得热情。她会操办刺杀邓肯这件事。班阔和邓肯评价麦克白城堡的外观如何惹人喜爱。

Language in the play 剧中语言
Double meanings (in pairs)

Lady Macbeth's lines 64–8 are filled with double meaning: 'provided for' = fed (or killed); 'business' = feasting (or murder); 'dispatch' = being welcoming (or killing). Discuss why Shakespeare uses such phrases. Do you think it is because:

- Lady Macbeth is subtly testing Macbeth to see how he will respond to the suggestion that they kill Duncan?
- Lady Macbeth is still unsure of doing such a deed and so has to disguise her words, even to herself?
- Shakespeare is adding to the tension of the play – in showing that they have not decided what to do, there is still some uncertainty about how the action will unfold?

Experiment with different ways of staging these lines. Think about what might be motivating Lady Macbeth to speak in this way and how Macbeth would respond.

Themes 主题分析
Appearance and reality (in threes)

Act 1 Scene 6 continues to develop the theme of appearance and reality that emerged at the end of the previous scene. Both Duncan and Banquo speak favourably of Macbeth's castle. Look closely at the glossary and discuss the use of:

- dramatic irony (the pleasant and healthy positioning of the castle)
- extended metaphor (the ideas of flight, freedom and protection suggested by the 'temple-haunting martlet' that nests and breeds under its shelter).

1 Don't trust appearances!

Work out how to stage lines 1–10 of Scene 6 to bring out the dramatic irony of Duncan's and Banquo's praise of the benign appearance of Macbeth's castle. Remember – the audience has just heard Lady Macbeth planning Duncan's murder with the words 'look like th'innocent flower, / But be the serpent under't' (look friendly, but act treacherously).

1. O ... see = O the sun shall never see that morrow（哼，太阳永远也休想见到那个明天；morrow = tomorrow）
2. as = like
3. beguile the time 蒙蔽世人
4. under't = under it
5. Give solely sovereign sway 让我们得到君王的权势
6. look up clear 表现泰然自若
7. To ... fear 神色有异就是恐惧（favour：脸色）
8. Hautboys 高音大喇叭
9. torches 火炬（表明此场景为夜晚）
10. seat 位置
11. temple-haunting martlet 在庙堂飞出飞进的雨燕（雨燕是一种候鸟，在莎士比亚时代也指代容易上当受骗的人）
12. approve 说明
13. By his loved mansionry 通过它喜欢的住处（his = its）
14. wooingly 吸引人
15. jutty frieze 外凸的中楣（西方古典建筑中横架在柱头 [capital] 之上、支撑上层建筑的构件称为柱顶 [entablature]，其上部称为壁带 [cornice]，向外凸出；中部称为中楣 [frieze]；下部称为过梁 [lintel]。古代希腊和罗马建筑的中楣上多刻有浮雕，最著名的是希腊卫城帕得嫩 [Parthenon，又译作"帕特农"] 神庙的大理石中楣。）
16. Buttress 扶壁（支撑墙壁预防其倒塌的建筑构件）
17. coign of vantage 观景台（现在称为vantage point）
18. pendent bed 悬空床
19. procreant cradle 幼鸟摇篮

LADY MACBETH   O never
             Shall sun that morrow see[1].
             Your face, my thane, is as[2] a book where men
             May read strange matters. To beguile the time[3],
             Look like the time, bear welcome in your eye,
             Your hand, your tongue; look like th'innocent flower,
             But be the serpent under't[4]. He that's coming
             Must be provided for, and you shall put
             This night's great business into my dispatch,
             Which shall to all our nights and days to come
             Give solely sovereign sway[5] and masterdom.
MACBETH   We will speak further –
LADY MACBETH   Only look up clear[6];
             To alter favour ever is to fear[7].
             Leave all the rest to me.

                                                    Exeunt

Act 1 Scene 6
Outside Macbeth's castle

Hautboys[8], and torches[9]. Enter King DUNCAN, MALCOLM, DONALDBAIN, BANQUO, LENNOX, MACDUFF, ROSS, ANGUS, *and attendants*

DUNCAN   This castle hath a pleasant seat[10]; the air
             Nimbly and sweetly recommends itself
             Unto our gentle senses.
BANQUO   This guest of summer,
             The temple-haunting martlet[11], does approve[12]
             By his loved mansionry[13] that the heaven's breath
             Smells wooingly[14] here. No jutty frieze[15],
             Buttress[16], nor coign of vantage[17] but this bird
             Hath made his pendent bed[18] and procreant cradle[19];
             Where they most breed and haunt, I have observed
             The air is delicate.

Lady Macbeth welcomes Duncan with elaborately courteous language. She speaks of loyalty, obedience and gratefulness for past honours.

剧情简介：麦克白夫人用十分恭敬的语言迎接邓肯，表达了忠诚、恭顺和对以往所获荣誉的感激。

1 Duncan beware! (in fours)

The script opposite has many instances of dramatic irony relating to the way that pleasing appearances can hide a darker reality. In your groups, two students read aloud the duologue (对白) between Duncan and Lady Macbeth, while the other two listen carefully and call out 'Duncan beware!' whenever they believe he has misjudged his hostess, or when she is being insincere. Write short notes to the actors playing the parts of Lady Macbeth and Duncan to explain how they should behave with each other.

Themes 主题分析

Duncan and Lady Macbeth (in pairs)

This is the first and last time that Lady Macbeth and Duncan are seen to talk to each other. The language is formal, as you would expect between a king and his subject and a hostess and her guest. Even so, Shakespeare uses words that continue to develop key themes already explored in the play. Look carefully at the exchange between Duncan and Lady Macbeth, then discuss the following:

- the imagery of pursuit and hunting
- the theme of duty
- the use of the word 'love'.

2 Duncan's last night (by yourself)

Imagine you are Duncan staying with the Macbeths. Write his journal entry or a letter to his wife the night he arrives at Glamis Castle. What does he think of Macbeth? Lady Macbeth? The castle? While doing this, keep in mind the dramatic irony of what you write: Duncan does not know what his hosts have planned for him, but you do. Alternatively, write a 'deleted scene' in which Duncan talks about events so far and his plans for the future. Write this as a soliloquy in modern prose, modern poetry, or imitating Shakespeare's language in the rest of this scene.

1 The love … love 随朕而来的效忠有时是朕带来的麻烦，不过朕仍将之视作效忠而心存感激
2 Herein 就此
3 bid God yield us 祈求上帝回报朕
4 Were poor and single = Would be poor and small （不足挂齿）
5 contend / Against 与……衡量，相比
6 loads 装满
7 those of old 过去的（荣华）
8 late dignities 最近的富贵
9 We rest your hermits 我们永远是您的祈祷者
10 coursed 追赶
11 purveyor 鞍前马后之人
12 sharp as his spur 如他的马刺般锐利
13 holp = helped
14 Your servants ever 您的奴仆们（指麦克白夫妇）已经
15 Have … count 将他们的奴仆、他们本人和他们的一切都列入账目（count = account）
16 make … pleasure 在陛下您高兴之时审计核算
17 Still to return your own 甘愿把原本您的还给您（Still = Contented）
18 By your leave 承蒙您许可

MACBETH ACT 1 SCENE 6
麦克白

Enter LADY [MACBETH]

DUNCAN
See, see, our honoured hostess. – The love
That follows us sometime is our trouble,
Which still we thank as love[1]. Herein[2] I teach you
How you shall bid God yield us[3] for your pains
And thank us for your trouble.

LADY MACBETH
　　　　　　　　　All our service, 15
In every point twice done and then done double,
Were poor and single[4] business to contend
Against[5] those honours deep and broad wherewith
Your majesty loads[6] our house. For those of old[7],
And the late dignities[8] heaped up to them, 20
We rest your hermits[9].

DUNCAN
　　　　　　　　Where's the Thane of Cawdor?
We coursed[10] him at the heels and had a purpose
To be his purveyor[11], but he rides well,
And his great love, sharp as his spur[12], hath holp[13] him
To his home before us. Fair and noble hostess, 25
We are your guest tonight.

LADY MACBETH
　　　　　　　　　Your servants ever[14]
Have theirs, themselves, and what is theirs in count[15]
To make their audit at your highness' pleasure[16],
Still to return your own[17].

DUNCAN
　　　　　　　　Give me your hand;
Conduct me to mine host: we love him highly 30
And shall continue our graces towards him.
By your leave[18], hostess.
　　　　　　　　　　　　　Exeunt

Macbeth struggles with his conscience: killing Duncan will result in vengeance; there are compelling reasons against the murder. Heaven itself will abhor the deed. Only ambition spurs him on.

 剧情简介：麦克白的良心在挣扎：杀了邓肯会招致报复；有一些不可抗拒的理由反对谋杀。上天本身会憎恨这种行为。只有野心在鼓动他。

1 To kill or not to kill? (in small groups)

Macbeth agonises over killing Duncan. Experiment with ways of speaking his soliloquy to bring out his uneasy feelings. In groups of three or four, read aloud one sentence each, making sure you either use emphasis or pause where appropriate. Afterwards, write down as many reasons as you can think of for why Duncan should not be killed.

2 'A deed without a name' (in pairs)

In Act 4 Scene 1, line 48, the Witches talk of 'A deed without a name'. In the script opposite, Macbeth, like Lady Macbeth (Act 1 Scene 5, lines 61–8), seems unable to speak directly of killing Duncan. Instead, he uses less brutal language (including euphemism [委婉语]): 'it', 'assassination', 'his surcease', 'this blow', 'these cases', 'ingredience', 'the deed', 'bear the knife', 'his taking-off', 'horrid deed', 'my intent'.

Read the soliloquy but replace these euphemisms with the words 'killing Duncan'. Talk together about the effect this has on the soliloquy. Think of some modern euphemisms that say the same thing (they can be formal or informal phrases).

1 *service* 食物
2 *over* = across
3 *If … quickly* = If it would be done when it were done, then it would be good if it were done quickly（it 指谋杀邓肯）
4 *trammel up the consequence* 收拾/摆平后果
5 *his surcease* 他（邓肯）的死亡
6 *that but* = if only
7 *the be-all and the end-all* 一锤子就搞定一切的买卖
8 *shoal* 浅滩
9 *jump the life to come* 拿后半生来下赌注/冒险（jump = stake, risk）
10 *here that*（here: 心里；that = in that）
11 *but teach / Bloody instructions* 只要教授杀人之法
12 *plague th'inventor* 让其发明者不得安宁
13 *even-handed* 公正
14 *ingredience* 杯中之物
15 *chalice* 杯盏
16 *Strong both against the deed* 都有强大的理由不让我做这件事
17 *faculties* 权威
18 *clear* 清白
19 *deep damnation* 罪大恶极
20 *his taking-off* 把他（邓肯）解决掉
21 *Striding the blast* 乘风而行（如同骑着一匹天马）
22 *cherubin* 小天使
23 *sightless couriers* 盲人信使
24 *have … intent* 没有马刺来扎我意图的双肋（这里麦克白将其杀人意图比喻成一匹马，将杀人动机喻为策马前行的马刺）
25 *Vaulting* 极度膨胀
26 *th'other –* = the other side（此处话未说完即被他夫人的到来打断）
27 *How now?* = How is it going?

30

Act 1 Scene 7
Macbeth's castle Near the Great Hall

Hautboys. Torches. Enter a butler and many servants with dishes and service[1] over[2] the stage. Then enter MACBETH

MACBETH If it were done when 'tis done, then 'twere well
It were done quickly[3]. If th'assassination
Could trammel up the consequence[4] and catch
With his surcease[5], success, that but[6] this blow
Might be the be-all and the end-all[7] – here,   5
But here, upon this bank and shoal[8] of time,
We'd jump the life to come[9]. But in these cases,
We still have judgement here that[10] we but teach
Bloody instructions[11], which being taught, return
To plague th'inventor[12]. This even-handed[13] justice   10
Commends th'ingredience[14] of our poisoned chalice[15]
To our own lips. He's here in double trust:
First, as I am his kinsman and his subject,
Strong both against the deed[16]; then, as his host,
Who should against his murderer shut the door,   15
Not bear the knife myself. Besides, this Duncan
Hath borne his faculties[17] so meek, hath been
So clear[18] in his great office, that his virtues
Will plead like angels, trumpet-tongued against
The deep damnation[19] of his taking-off[20].   20
And pity, like a naked newborn babe
Striding the blast[21], or heaven's cherubin[22] horsed
Upon the sightless couriers[23] of the air,
Shall blow the horrid deed in every eye,
That tears shall drown the wind. I have no spur   25
To prick the sides of my intent[24], but only
Vaulting[25] ambition which o'erleaps itself
And falls on th'other –[26]

Enter LADY [MACBETH]

How now?[27] What news?

Macbeth says he has decided not to kill Duncan. Lady Macbeth accuses him of cowardice and lack of manliness. She would kill her own child rather than break such a promise.

 剧情简介：麦克白说他已决定不杀邓肯。麦克白夫人怪他胆小懦弱，没有大丈夫气概。她宁愿杀死自己的孩子也不会违背这样的承诺。

1 A wife taunts (奚落) her husband (in small groups)

One person reads the part of Macbeth; all the others play Lady Macbeth. Macbeth sits or stands in the centre; the Lady Macbeths walk or stand around him. Work through lines 28–82, with each Lady Macbeth reading only up to a punctuation mark before handing on to another person. Deliver your words to Macbeth in any way you think appropriate. Afterwards, discuss which sentence or phrase of Lady Macbeth's you think has the greatest effect on Macbeth in making him decide to carry out the murder.

Language in the play 剧中语言
Shocking imagery

In this scene, Shakespeare uses imagery that links newborn babies, pity and violence. Look closely at lines 18–25 and lines 54–9 in this scene. Using a clean copy of these lines, underline the words that relate to this imagery and make notes in the margins. When you have done so, carry out the following activities.

a This is highly visceral (发自肺腑) language, but what is actually being said in these lines? Paraphrase the section so that you have a clear understanding of its meaning.

b What visual images do the lines evoke for you and why are these images shocking or strange? Discuss this in pairs.

c Write a paragraph exploring how Shakespeare's language creates vivid images that evoke complex responses in an audience and influence how we view the characters.

2 Did the Macbeths have children?

Imagery associated with children occurs throughout the play. Some critics have argued that the Macbeths are motivated by the loss of a child, but Shakespeare makes very little of this.

Do you think it helps us understand their behaviour if we believe they have lost a child, or is it unimportant? Write an imagined secret history of the Macbeths – their untold story – in a few paragraphs.

1 supped 吃完晚饭
2 bought / Golden opinions = won glowing praise
3 Which ... gloss 我想趁其现在金光闪闪把它穿在身上
4 wakes it = it wakes
5 green and pale 脸色苍白
6 At ... freely 回顾此前的大胆畅想（it指hope）
7 Such I account thy love = I regard thy love as a drunken hope / boast
8 afeard = afraid
9 valour 勇气
10 the ornament of life 人生的最高荣耀（王冠）
11 Letting ... would = Letting "I dare not" wait upon "I would"（wait upon：伴随）
12 Like ... i'th'adage 像格言里的那只可怜的猫（格言是That cat wanted to fish but dared not get her feet wet；adage = proverb）
13 Prithee 恳求你
14 become = befit（适合）
15 Who ... none = Anyone who dares do more is not a man
16 break this enterprise 透露（杀死邓肯）这个计划
17 Did then adhere 当时合适
18 made themselves = made themselves adhere
19 fitness 合适（指时机的成熟）
20 unmake 摧毁
21 given suck 喂奶
22 boneless 无牙（牙齿也是一种骨头）
23 had ... this = if I had sworn to this, as you have done（假如我已经承诺做这件事，就像你那样）

MACBETH ACT 1 SCENE 7
麦克白

LADY MACBETH   He has almost supped[1]. Why have you left the chamber?
MACBETH   Hath he asked for me?
LADY MACBETH   Know you not, he has?
MACBETH   We will proceed no further in this business.
He hath honoured me of late, and I have bought
Golden opinions[2] from all sorts of people,
Which would be worn now in their newest gloss[3],
Not cast aside so soon.
LADY MACBETH   Was the hope drunk
Wherein you dressed yourself? Hath it slept since?
And wakes it[4] now to look so green and pale[5]
At what it did so freely[6]? From this time,
Such I account thy love[7]. Art thou afeard[8]
To be the same in thine own act and valour[9],
As thou art in desire? Wouldst thou have that
Which thou esteem'st the ornament of life[10],
And live a coward in thine own esteem,
Letting I dare not wait upon I would[11],
Like the poor cat i'th'adage[12]?
MACBETH   Prithee[13], peace.
I dare do all that may become[14] a man;
Who dares do more is none[15].
LADY MACBETH   What beast was't then
That made you break this enterprise[16] to me?
When you durst do it, then you were a man.
And to be more than what you were, you would
Be so much more the man. Nor time, nor place
Did then adhere[17], and yet you would make both.
They have made themselves[18] and that their fitness[19] now
Does unmake[20] you. I have given suck[21] and know
How tender 'tis to love the babe that milks me:
I would, while it was smiling in my face,
Have plucked my nipple from his boneless[22] gums
And dashed the brains out, had I so sworn
As you have done to this[23].

Lady Macbeth will make the king's bodyguards so drunk that murdering Duncan (and blaming the bodyguards) will be easy. Macbeth applauds her. He says that they should veil their evil designs with pleasant looks.

 剧情简介：麦克白夫人要把国王的卫士灌得烂醉，这样谋杀邓肯（并且栽赃卫士）会容易些。麦克白赞同她的计划，说他们应该面目和善以掩盖这一罪恶图谋。

1 'We fail?' (in small groups)

There are many ways of speaking these two words. Explore them using your own approaches. You might want to say them as a simple statement of resignation, as a question or with scorn.

2 The art of questioning (in pairs)

Macbeth and Lady Macbeth use questions for different purposes in this scene. As you read through the script opposite, consider different ways of delivering each of these questions. Experiment with Macbeth having trouble maintaining eye contact, or with Lady Macbeth moving around freely while Macbeth stands still, or with both characters staring intently at each other throughout the duologue. What do you think is the state of mind of each character in this section? What is their motivation?

> ### Write about it 写作练习
> **'Bring forth men-children only' (in pairs)**
>
> Lady Macbeth convinces her husband to murder Duncan. Macbeth, in turn, praises her strength of character. Write one paragraph each answering the following questions:
>
> - What do Macbeth's words in lines 72–4 tell us about the position of women in Scotland at the time the play is set? Refer to Lady Macbeth's speech in Act 1 Scene 5, lines 36–52 to support your points.
> - What does this section tell us about the relationship between Lady Macbeth and her husband?

3 Imagery

Lady Macbeth uses two metaphors familiar to Jacobean audiences:

- 'But screw your courage to the sticking-place' (line 60) suggests an archer turning the screw of his crossbow to adjust the cord to receive an arrow, or a musician tightening the strings of a violin.
- Lines 65–7 use an elaborate image from alchemy (魔力). Drunkenness will make the king's attendants forget their duties because noxious vapours will befuddle (使糊涂) their reason ('memory, the warder of the brain, / Shall be a fume'). 'Receipt' and 'limbeck' were items of apparatus used by alchemists (炼金术士).

As you read through the rest of the play, look out for other examples of imagery that you think might have struck a particular chord with audiences in Shakespeare's day.

1 But = Just
2 screw ... sticking-place 鼓足您的勇气（这里将勇气比作琴弦或弩弦；screw的意思是"拧/绷紧"，sticking-place 指固定弦之处，如琴头拧紧琴弦的弦轴 [peg] 或弩机钩住弓弦的牙 [sear]；今天相同意思的英文表达是 pluck up your courage）
3 the rather = no sooner than
4 chamberlains 侍从
5 wassail 祝酒，痛饮
6 convince 制服
7 warder 警卫
8 fume = vapour （水汽；旧时人们认为让人醉的是从酒里挥发出来的气体）
9 receipt 容器
10 limbeck = alembic （蒸馏罐）
11 swinish 猪一样（打鼾）
12 drenchèd natures 酩酊的本性
13 put upon 强加
14 spongy 浸满酒（像海绵一样）
15 quell 谋杀
16 Bring forth 要生就生
17 undaunted mettle 大无畏的气质
18 received 接受；相信
19 clamour 号啕
20 settled 打定主意
21 bend up 绷紧了；做好准备了
22 Each corporal agent 身体的每个器官
23 mock the time 欺骗世界

MACBETH   If we should fail?
LADY MACBETH   We fail?
　　　　　　But[1] screw your courage to the sticking-place[2],   60
　　　　　　And we'll not fail. When Duncan is asleep,
　　　　　　Whereto the rather[3] shall his day's hard journey
　　　　　　Soundly invite him, his two chamberlains[4]
　　　　　　Will I with wine and wassail[5] so convince[6]
　　　　　　That memory, the warder[7] of the brain,   65
　　　　　　Shall be a fume[8], and the receipt[9] of reason
　　　　　　A limbeck[10] only. When in swinish[11] sleep
　　　　　　Their drenchèd natures[12] lies as in a death,
　　　　　　What cannot you and I perform upon
　　　　　　Th'unguarded Duncan? What not put upon[13]   70
　　　　　　His spongy[14] officers, who shall bear the guilt
　　　　　　Of our great quell[15]?
MACBETH   Bring forth[16] men-children only,
　　　　　　For thy undaunted mettle[17] should compose
　　　　　　Nothing but males. Will it not be received[18],
　　　　　　When we have marked with blood those sleepy two   75
　　　　　　Of his own chamber, and used their very daggers,
　　　　　　That they have done't?
LADY MACBETH   Who dares receive it other,
　　　　　　As we shall make our griefs and clamour[19] roar
　　　　　　Upon his death?
MACBETH   I am settled[20] and bend up[21]
　　　　　　Each corporal agent[22] to this terrible feat.   80
　　　　　　Away, and mock the time[23] with fairest show,
　　　　　　False face must hide what the false heart doth know.
　　　　　　　　　　　　　　　　　　　　　　　　　　　　　　Exeunt

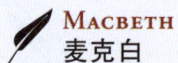

MACBETH
麦克白

Looking back at Act 1 第1幕回顾
Activities for groups or individuals

1 Contrasting scenes

Shakespeare uses the dramatic technique of juxtaposing (并置) scenes: each scene contrasts with, or comments on, the preceding scene. For example, the ghostly supernatural world of Scene 1 is followed by the harsh military world of Scene 2 (the former is entirely made up of female characters, the latter of male characters). Write a tabloid newspaper (小报) headline for each scene in Act 1. For example, Scene 2 could be: *'Victory! Captain tells of amazing win for Duncan's men.'*

2 Witches: stereotypes and conventions

Although the Witches have many stereotypical features of historical witches (see p. 8), they are only called 'witch' once in the play (Scene 3, line 5). Later on they call themselves the 'weïrd sisters' (Scene 3, line 30) and are called 'weïrd women' by Banquo (Act 3 Scene 1, line 2), which in Anglo-Saxon mythology referred to the goddess Fate, or 'Wyrd'.

Look at the images of the Witches in different productions on the page opposite and in the photo gallery at the beginning of this book. Write a paragraph explaining how you would portray them. Select descriptions of the Witches from the play to support your decisions.

3 Imagery

In Act 1, imagery that links pity, milk, blood and babies provokes strong responses from us. Find examples of this imagery, then carry out the activities below.

a Create a tableau based on one example. Try to capture the symbolism rather than an exact representation. Be as imaginative as you can.

b Pick out phrases or sentences that strike you and explain why they have this effect. Is it the visual image they conjure up, the way the words sound, the repetition or the vocabulary?

4 Men and women

In Macbeth's world, what qualities does a 'man' have? What qualities does a 'woman' have? Copy the table below and add examples. Some have been provided for you.

	What qualities?	Who has them?	Where are they?
Man	Bravery	Macbeth	1.2.16
	Ruthlessness	Lady Macbeth	2.2.55–60
Woman	Manipulative	Lady Macbeth	1.5.60–8
	Deceitful	Lady Macbeth	1.6.15–21

Discuss how Macbeth and Lady Macbeth conform to these ideas at the beginning and end of Act 1. Have they changed over the course of this act? Has Shakespeare challenged traditional ideas of 'masculinity' and 'femininity'?

5 Act 1 on screen

a Watch the openings of two different movie adaptations of *Macbeth*, then discuss which is the most effective and why. You may want to consider:

- the craft of filmmaking: the setting, soundtrack, camera angles and lighting
- any changes made to Shakespeare's script.

b Imagine you are a director working on a new film of *Macbeth*. Which actors would you choose to play Macbeth and Lady Macbeth? Who would you cast as Duncan and Banquo? Why? You may also want to think about *when* and *where* you would set it: for example, would you set your version in medieval Scotland or modern-day America? Now discuss these choices in groups.

Banquo tells of Duncan's gratitude for the Macbeths' hospitality. When Banquo says he has dreamt of the Witches, Macbeth replies with a lie. Banquo won't be tempted by Macbeth into betraying Duncan.

剧情简介： 班阔告诉麦克白夫妇，邓肯感激他们的殷勤款待。班阔说到他梦到女巫时，麦克白说谎敷衍他。班阔不肯受麦克白劝诱而背叛邓肯。

Language in the play 剧中语言
'husbandry in heaven' (in pairs)

The opening duologue between Banquo and his son, Fleance, describes the threatening atmosphere. Darkness has been associated with evil before (in Act 1 Scene 4, lines 50–1 and Scene 5, line 48), but here it seems even more ominous. In pairs, analyse the language that Banquo and Fleance use to describe the intensity of the night. What themes are explored through this imagery? How effectively does it create the mood of this scene?

Characters 人物分析
Banquo and Macbeth (in threes)

Here, Shakespeare dramatises the difference between Banquo, the honourable man and protective father, and Macbeth, the deceiver (who is alone). Banquo uses kind and open words in his report of Duncan ('He hath been in unusual pleasure'); he wishes to stay free of guilt ('keep / My bosom franchised') and remain loyal ('allegiance clear') to Duncan. Tellingly, he asks for his sword when Macbeth appears. In sharp contrast, Macbeth speaks untruths: 'A friend'; 'Being unprepared'; 'I think not of them'. He tries to tempt Banquo to his side ('cleave to my consent') in return for honour (lines 25–6).

Write advice for the actors on how to show the men's increasingly uneasy relationship, and how to alert the audience to the contrast between them. How would you position the actors? Would they speak face to face throughout these lines? How would you convey their real intentions? In groups of three (with Banquo, Macbeth and the director) create tableaux, taking it in turns to swap roles to try out different interpretations.

1 Fleance's point of view (in pairs)

Discuss how much you think Fleance knows: what does he make of the conversation between his father and Macbeth? Then write a diary entry of at least 100 words, in which Fleance describes what he sees, hears and feels about lines 10–30.

1 **How goes the night** 这夜晚走到几点了
2 **she**（指月亮，也可能指时钟）
3 **I take't** 我想
4 **husbandry** 节俭（把星光都吹灭了）
5 **candles** 蜡烛（指星光、月光）
6 **A … sleep** 睡意袭来，上眼皮像铅一样重，但我却不敢睡觉
7 **merciful powers** 仁慈的神力
8 **cursèd thoughts** 该诅咒的念头（指女巫在他内心深处激发出的念头）
9 **in repose** = in sleep
10 **largess to your offices** 给您家仆人丰厚的犒赏
11 **shut up** 结束（这里指上床睡觉）
12 **Our … defect** 我们一心效劳却招待不周（这句话的字面意思是"我们东道主的意愿成了瑕疵的奴仆"）
13 **Which … wrought** 不然这意愿本应该大显身手（free = freely）
14 **entreat an hour to serve** 挤出一个钟头来为我们所用
15 **cleave to my consent** 与我一条心（cleave = stick / adhere）
16 **when 'tis** 到时候
17 **So** = As long as
18 **augment** 增加
19 **franchised** 无必须承诺的义务（即保持心胸坦荡）
20 **allegiance** 忠心
21 **I shall be counselled** 我就听您的高见

Act 2 Scene 1
Macbeth's castle The courtyard

Enter BANQUO, *and* FLEANCE *with a torch-bearer before him*

BANQUO How goes the night[1], boy?
FLEANCE The moon is down; I have not heard the clock.
BANQUO And she[2] goes down at twelve.
FLEANCE   I take't[3], 'tis later, sir.
BANQUO Hold, take my sword. – There's husbandry[4] in heaven,
Their candles[5] are all out. – Take thee that too.   5
A heavy summons lies like lead upon me,
And yet I would not sleep[6]; merciful powers[7],
Restrain in me the cursèd thoughts[8] that nature
Gives way to in repose[9].

Enter MACBETH, *and a Servant with a torch*

              Give me my sword –
Who's there?   10
MACBETH A friend.
BANQUO What, sir, not yet at rest? The king's abed.
He hath been in unusual pleasure
And sent forth great largess to your offices[10].
This diamond he greets your wife withal,   15
[*Gives Macbeth a diamond*]
By the name of most kind hostess, and shut up[11]
In measureless content.
MACBETH   Being unprepared,
Our will became the servant to defect[12],
Which else should free have wrought[13].
BANQUO   All's well.
I dreamed last night of the three weïrd sisters;   20
To you they have showed some truth.
MACBETH   I think not of them;
Yet when we can entreat an hour to serve[14],
We would spend it in some words upon that business,
If you would grant the time.
BANQUO   At your kind'st leisure.
MACBETH If you shall cleave to my consent[15], when 'tis[16],   25
It shall make honour for you.
BANQUO   So[17] I lose none
In seeking to augment[18] it, but still keep
My bosom franchised[19] and allegiance[20] clear,
I shall be counselled[21].

Alone, Macbeth hallucinates, thinking he sees a blood-stained dagger. As he moves to murder Duncan, his thoughts are filled with evil images.

 剧情简介：麦克白独处时出现幻视，以为自己看到一把沾了鲜血的匕首。他起身去谋杀邓肯，脑子里充满了邪恶的形象。

1 Macbeth sees the dagger (in pairs)

Macbeth's hallucination of the dagger is both a warning and an invitation. At first he dismisses the 'fatal vision' as something created by his unreliable senses, but soon he becomes convinced that he has to murder Duncan.

With a partner, discuss the various turning points in this soliloquy. Consider the issues Macbeth raises and how he answers them, then write these down in a list with two columns (issues and answers). Compare the points you have listed with those identified by others in your class.

2 Acting the horror (in small groups, then by yourself)

Work out your own presentation of Macbeth's soliloquy. Use the following ideas to help you:

- As one person reads the soliloquy a short section at a time, others silently act out what Macbeth does at each moment.
- Allocate short sections of the soliloquy to different members of the group. Each person should deliver their lines in a different style (for example, lines 33–4 could be spoken in horror, or in fear, or with faltering control). Experiment with the volume, pitch and pace of this speech in your performance.

After the presentations, write a detailed account of the one you found most interesting or dramatic. Why were some presentations more successful than others?

Stagecraft 导演技巧

Is there a dagger on the stage? (by yourself)

Think about how you would stage lines 33–47 to greatest dramatic effect. Should a dagger actually be shown on stage (for example, as a holograph [全息图])? What sound effects might you add at particular lines? Write a letter to a director describing your views about the use of props (道具), sound effects, lighting and Macbeth's movement on the stage in the script opposite.

---

1 **Good repose the while** = Have a good sleep in the mean time
2 **the like** = the same
3 **toward** 朝……招手
4 **have** = hold
5 **fatal vision** 不祥的幻影
6 **sensible / To feeling** 摸得到
7 **Proceeding from** 来自，始于
8 **heat-oppressèd** 发烧的
9 **yet** = still
10 **palpable** 有形，感知得到
11 **marshall'st** 引导
12 **blade and dudgeon** 剑锋和剑柄
13 **gouts** 一滴滴
14 **informs** 成形
15 **one half-world** 半个世界（指夜间）
16 **Hecate's off'rings** 给赫柯婑的献祭（在希腊神话中赫柯婑[又译作"赫卡忒"]是一尊三身女神，掌管天、地、海和冥界，后世认为她也是巫术和魔法之神）
17 **Alarumed** 召唤；唤醒
18 **sentinel** 卫士，哨兵
19 **stealthy pace** 鬼鬼祟祟的脚步
20 **Tarquin** 塔昆（古罗马王政时代最后一位君王之子，强奸了鲁克丽丝 [Lucrece]，导致王国覆灭；莎士比亚的长诗《鲁克丽丝遭强暴记》[*The Rape of Lucrece*] 即叙述此事）
21 **ravishing strides** 恶狼般的大步
22 **prate of** 说出
23 **threat** = threaten
24 **Words … gives** 火热行动中说的话只不过是呼出的一口冷气
25 **knell** 丧钟

MACBETH	Good repose the while[1].	
BANQUO	Thanks, sir; the like[2] to you.	30

[Exeunt] Banquo[, Fleance, and Torch-bearer]

MACBETH [*To Servant*] Go bid thy mistress, when my drink is ready,
She strike upon the bell. Get thee to bed.

Exit [Servant]

Is this a dagger which I see before me,
The handle toward[3] my hand? Come, let me clutch thee:
I have[4] thee not, and yet I see thee still.   35
Art thou not, fatal vision[5], sensible
To feeling[6] as to sight? Or art thou but
A dagger of the mind, a false creation,
Proceeding from[7] the heat-oppressèd[8] brain?
I see thee yet[9], in form as palpable[10]   40
As this which now I draw.
Thou marshall'st[11] me the way that I was going,
And such an instrument I was to use.
Mine eyes are made the fools o'th'other senses,
Or else worth all the rest. I see thee still,   45
And on thy blade and dudgeon[12] gouts[13] of blood,
Which was not so before. There's no such thing:
It is the bloody business which informs[14]
Thus to mine eyes. Now o'er the one half-world[15]
Nature seems dead, and wicked dreams abuse   50
The curtained sleep. Witchcraft celebrates
Pale Hecate's off'rings[16], and withered murder,
Alarumed[17] by his sentinel[18], the wolf,
Whose howl's his watch, thus with his stealthy pace[19],
With Tarquin's[20] ravishing strides[21], towards his design   55
Moves like a ghost. Thou sure and firm-set earth,
Hear not my steps, which way they walk, for fear
Thy very stones prate of[22] my whereabout,
And take the present horror from the time,
Which now suits with it. Whiles I threat[23], he lives;   60
Words to the heat of deeds too cold breath gives[24].

A bell rings

I go, and it is done. The bell invites me.
Hear it not, Duncan, for it is a knell[25]
That summons thee to heaven or to hell.   *Exit*

Lady Macbeth, exhilarated by drink, awaits Macbeth's return from Duncan's room. She has drugged Duncan's bodyguards, but fears that the murder has not been done. Macbeth returns and says he has killed the king.

剧情简介：麦克白夫人饮酒后兴奋不已，等着麦克白从邓肯卧室回来。她已经给邓肯的卫士下了药，但担心谋杀没有成功。麦克白回来说他已将国王杀死。

1 Offstage murder (in pairs)

Once again a major event – Duncan's murder – takes place off stage. Why do you think Shakespeare does this? Is it to preserve the dignity of Duncan (and of monarchy)? Is it to shield us from the true horror of Macbeth's crime? Talk about this with a partner, and then compile a list of the elements of stagecraft that make this scene so dramatically effective.

Write about it 写作练习
Language and meaning

Analyse the language used by Macbeth and Lady Macbeth. Write two paragraphs on each character, detailing what you have learned about them by line 24. Below are some points you might want to consider.

- Even though she has been drinking, Lady Macbeth's opening two lines appear carefully composed. Look not only at their meaning but also at their structure. Contrast them with Macbeth's lines.
- Why does Lady Macbeth decide not to kill Duncan herself? What does this tell us about her? Compare her words here with her speeches in Act 1 Scene 7.

Stagecraft 导演技巧
After the murder (in pairs)

Take parts as Lady Macbeth and Macbeth. Read straight through the whole of Scene 2. (Don't pause to worry over words you are not sure of.) What should be the pace of playing different sections of the scene? Write notes advising the actors where and why they might speak quickly, and where they could adopt a different style of speech.

2 Stichomythia (针锋对话) (in pairs)

Lines 13–24 alternate rapidly between Macbeth and Lady Macbeth to increase pace and tension. They are an example of **stichomythia** and are usually spoken quickly on stage. As you read these lines aloud, make a list of words that describe how you feel and how an audience might feel on hearing these lines. Then draft your own dialogue between two frightened or two guilty people who find themselves in a dark and dangerous situation.

1 **quenched** 浇灭（对于酒瘾大发者，酒可以浇灭酒瘾，就像水可以浇灭口渴者的喉咙之火）
2 **owl** 猫头鹰（不祥之鸟）
3 **Hark** 听
4 **fatal bellman** 敲丧钟的人（在处决犯人的前一天晚上敲钟的看守）
5 **stern'st good-night** 最凄厉的晚安（即死亡）
6 **surfeited** 酒足饭饱
7 **grooms** 侍从
8 **mock their charge** 玩忽职守
9 **possets** 甜奶酒（旧时用热牛奶加啤酒或葡萄酒和香料调制而成）
10 **contend about** 为……相争
11 **Alack** 啊呀（表示担心的叹词）
12 **Confounds us** 毁掉我们
13 **Had he not resembled** 要不是他长得像
14 **Ay = Aye** （是的，对）
15 **sorry** 凄惨

Act 2 Scene 2
Macbeth's castle Near Duncan's room

Enter LADY MACBETH

LADY MACBETH   That which hath made them drunk, hath made me bold;
What hath quenched[1] them, hath given me fire.
[*An owl[2] shrieks*]
                                                                    Hark[3], peace!
It was the owl that shrieked, the fatal bellman[4]
Which gives the stern'st good-night[5]. He is about it.
The doors are open, and the surfeited[6] grooms[7]   5
Do mock their charge[8] with snores. I have drugged their possets[9],
That death and nature do contend about[10] them,
Whether they live, or die.

Enter MACBETH [*with two bloody daggers*]

MACBETH   Who's there? What ho?
LADY MACBETH   Alack[11], I am afraid they have awaked,
And 'tis not done; th'attempt and not the deed   10
Confounds us[12]. Hark! I laid their daggers ready,
He could not miss 'em. Had he not resembled[13]
My father as he slept, I had done't. My husband?
MACBETH   I have done the deed. Didst thou not hear a noise?
LADY MACBETH   I heard the owl scream and the crickets cry.   15
Did not you speak?
MACBETH   When?
LADY MACBETH   Now.
MACBETH   As I descended?
LADY MACBETH   Ay[14].   20
MACBETH   Hark, who lies i'th'second chamber?
LADY MACBETH   Donaldbain.
MACBETH   This is a sorry[15] sight.
LADY MACBETH   A foolish thought, to say a sorry sight.

Macbeth is obsessed by his inability to say 'Amen', and by a voice crying that he has murdered sleep and will never sleep again. Lady Macbeth dismisses his hallucinations and orders him to return the daggers. He refuses.

剧情简介：麦克白感到困扰，因为自己说不出"阿门"，还因为听到一个声音叫喊着他谋杀了睡眠，因而他再也无法安眠。麦克白夫人对他的幻觉不予理睬，命他把匕首放回去，遭到他的拒绝。

Characters 人物分析

Does Macbeth have a conscience? (in pairs)

Macbeth seems suddenly conscience-stricken (良心不安): he is unable to say 'Amen', and cannot pray. Not being able to say 'Amen' suggests that God has already judged him and condemned him to eternal damnation (永坠地狱). Many actors portray Macbeth talking to himself, ignoring his wife. Others show him almost obsessively telling her his story.

a Discuss how you would act lines 25–46 to show how each character is developing and how their relationship has suddenly changed due to their murderous act.

b Read through Macbeth's lines, with one person in role as Macbeth and the other person speaking the words of his conscience at the end of each line, asking questions to reveal what he is really feeling.

1 Images of sleep (in groups of four or more)

In lines 38–43, Shakespeare uses vivid images to portray sleep.

a Sleep deprivation (剥夺睡眠) is used as a form of torture. Discuss with others in your group what you think are the psychological effects of loss of sleep; you could research this outside the classroom.

b How do you visualise these images? Try drawing them very quickly and showing them to the rest of the group. How do they compare with Shakespeare's words? What is lost and what is gained by turning them into pictures?

c Work out a mime (哑剧) for each image. Extend your mime by adding the results of lack of sleep promised by the First Witch in Act 1 Scene 3, lines 18–22.

1 addressed them 自己准备好
2 Amen 阿门（用于基督徒祈祷或圣歌结束时，表示诚心所愿）
3 hangman's hands 刽子手的双手（刽子手常将死犯开膛，因此双手会沾满鲜血）
4 Methought = I thought
5 ravelled sleeve of care 心事那开了线的袖子
6 death of each day's life 每日生活的终结（指睡眠）
7 sore labour's bath 辛苦劳作后的泡澡
8 Balm 药膏
9 second course 第二道菜（主菜）
10 unbend 松懈
11 brain-sickly 胡思乱想
12 filthy witness 污秽的证据

◀ 'Why did you bring these daggers?' What postures do you think the Macbeths should have at this point in the play?

MACBETH	There's one did laugh in's sleep, and one cried, 'Murder!',	25
	That they did wake each other; I stood, and heard them,	
	But they did say their prayers and addressed them[1]	
	Again to sleep.	
LADY MACBETH	There are two lodged together.	
MACBETH	One cried 'God bless us!' and 'Amen'[2] the other,	
	As they had seen me with these hangman's hands[3].	30
	List'ning their fear, I could not say 'Amen'	
	When they did say 'God bless us.'	
LADY MACBETH	Consider it not so deeply.	
MACBETH	But wherefore could not I pronounce 'Amen'?	
	I had most need of blessing and 'Amen'	35
	Stuck in my throat.	
LADY MACBETH	These deeds must not be thought	
	After these ways; so, it will make us mad.	
MACBETH	Methought[4] I heard a voice cry, 'Sleep no more:	
	Macbeth does murder sleep', the innocent sleep,	
	Sleep that knits up the ravelled sleeve of care[5],	40
	The death of each day's life[6], sore labour's bath[7],	
	Balm[8] of hurt minds, great nature's second course[9],	
	Chief nourisher in life's feast.	
LADY MACBETH	What do you mean?	
MACBETH	Still it cried, 'Sleep no more' to all the house;	
	'Glamis hath murdered sleep', and therefore Cawdor	45
	Shall sleep no more: Macbeth shall sleep no more.	
LADY MACBETH	Who was it, that thus cried? Why, worthy thane,	
	You do unbend[10] your noble strength to think	
	So brain-sickly[11] of things. Go get some water	
	And wash this filthy witness[12] from your hand.	50
	Why did you bring these daggers from the place?	
	They must lie there. Go carry them and smear	
	The sleepy grooms with blood.	
MACBETH	I'll go no more.	
	I am afraid to think what I have done;	
	Look on't again, I dare not.	

Lady Macbeth takes the daggers to smear Duncan's blood on his servants' faces. A knocking sound frightens Macbeth, but his wife tells him to pull himself together. She plans an alibi.

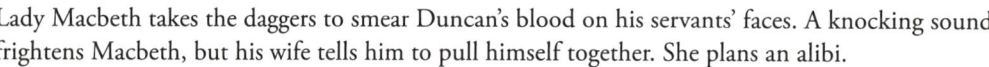**剧情简介**：麦克白夫人拿过匕首，准备把邓肯的血抹在他仆人们的脸上。敲门声吓坏了麦克白，但他妻子让他振作起来。她计划制造不在犯罪现场的证据。

Themes 主题分析

Masculinity and femininity (in groups of five or six)

This is an important scene for many reasons, but in particular for how we view the two central characters. We might expect Lady Macbeth to be more shaken than her husband, the warrior, by Duncan's murder, but the opposite seems to be true. Look at lines 47–53, 55–60 and 67–75, then discuss how and why Shakespeare seems to challenge traditional views of masculine and feminine behaviour.

- Does Lady Macbeth understand the full implications of Macbeth's actions?
- Has Lady Macbeth's wish to be 'unsexed' in Act 1 Scene 5, line 39 come true?
- Is she behaving in this way to protect her husband as well as herself?
- Are her actions those of a rational individual (理性的个体)?

Now create your own list of questions to ask the Macbeths at this point in the play. You should aim to explore the characters' motivations, inner logic and unexpressed feelings. Take turns to step into role as either Lady Macbeth or Macbeth and sit in the hot-seat*, ready to answer questions from the rest of your group.

1 Guilty – and guiltier? (whole class)

Divide into two groups to stage a debate. One group argues that Lady Macbeth is morally less defensible than her husband by the end of this scene. The other half of the class takes the opposite view: that Macbeth is the guiltier of the two. If you use quotations from the script to support your argument, make them no more than five words long. Write notes about which arguments you find the most convincing. At the end of the debate take a vote to find out which character the class feels is most guilty.

Language in the play 剧中语言

Images of death

Look closely at the language used by both Lady Macbeth and Macbeth, focusing in particular on lines 56–8 and 63–6. Write two paragraphs analysing the imagery used by both characters. Which character do you think best understands the reality of the situation? Or are they both delusional? Explain your reasons with evidence from the script.

1 **Infirm of purpose!** 意志薄弱！
2 **'tis … devil** 只有小孩子才会害怕画中的魔鬼
3 **gild** 涂红（gild 的本义是"镀金"，掺了红铜的金子时间久了会泛红）
4 **withal** = with it （用血）
5 **appals** 吓坏
6 **Neptune** 尼普顿（又译作"涅普顿"，罗马神话里的海神，相当于希腊神话中的 **Poseidon** [波塞冬]）
7 **multitudinous seas** 浩瀚无际的海洋
8 **incarnadine** 变成血色
9 **Making the green one red** 把绿海变成红海
10 **shame** 感到羞耻
11 **wear** 怀有
12 **white** 懦弱（旧时认为血液与胆量有关，血液少的心脏颜色发白，导致缺乏勇气）
13 **Your … unattended** 您那不渝的忠心已经让您不知所措
14 **lest occasion call us** 以备有人发现情况后喊我们去
15 **show us to be watchers** 暴露出我们是醒着的
16 **Be … thoughts** 别这样神情恍惚
17 **To … self** 与其认清我干了什么，还不如不认识我自己

* **hot seat** 热座位，一种课堂游戏，玩法是请一位同学坐到讲台上的一把椅子上，其他同学轮番给他/她出难题，哪个问题他/她回答不出就算输。

MACBETH ACT 2 SCENE 2
麦克白

LADY MACBETH   Infirm of purpose![1]   55
Give me the daggers. The sleeping and the dead
Are but as pictures; 'tis the eye of childhood
That fears a painted devil[2]. If he do bleed,
I'll gild[3] the faces of the grooms withal[4],
For it must seem their guilt.   *Exit*

Knock within

MACBETH   Whence is that knocking?   60
How is't with me, when every noise appals[5] me?
What hands are here? Ha: they pluck out mine eyes.
Will all great Neptune's[6] ocean wash this blood
Clean from my hand? No: this my hand will rather
The multitudinous seas[7] incarnadine[8],   65
Making the green one red[9].

Enter LADY [MACBETH]

LADY MACBETH   My hands are of your colour, but I shame[10]
To wear[11] a heart so white[12].

Knock [within]

                    I hear a knocking
At the south entry. Retire we to our chamber;
A little water clears us of this deed.   70
How easy is it then! Your constancy
Hath left you unattended[13].

Knock [within]

                    Hark, more knocking.
Get on your night-gown, lest occasion call us[14]
And show us to be watchers[15]. Be not lost
So poorly in your thoughts[16].   75

MACBETH   To know my deed, 'twere best not know my self[17].

Knock [within]

Wake Duncan with thy knocking: I would thou couldst.
                    Exeunt

Macbeth's Porter imagines himself keeper of Hell's gate. He talks about admitting to Hell a greedy farmer, a liar and a cheating tailor. He jokes with Macduff about the effects of too much drink.

剧情简介：麦克白的门卫想象自己是地狱之门的守卫。他谈到地狱接收了一个贪婪的农夫、一个撒谎者和一个偷工减料的裁缝，又拿饮酒过量产生的醉意同麦克达开玩笑。

Stagecraft 导演技巧

The Porter: comic relief? (in small groups)

Some directors cut the 'Porter scene' because they consider it irrelevant to the action. Read the scene, then discuss why you think Shakespeare wrote it. Here are some ideas to help you:

- **Light relief** (轻松的情节) Given the intensity of the play, this comes as a welcome moment of humour. Also, Shakespeare's theatre company – the King's Men – always had one actor who specialised in comic parts. Here, the Porter acts as the funny man to Macduff's straight man.
- **Dramatic function** The Porter's scene further develops key themes in the play, including damnation ('th'everlasting bonfire'), the supernatural ('Beelzebub'), ambition (the greedy farmer), deceit (the equivocator), theft (the tailor), desire and achievement (lust and the effects that drink has on it). The Porter's use of bathos* (the sudden descent from the sublime to the absurd) slows the action and, in doing so, heightens the tension as we wait to see what happens next.
- **A link with older plays** In medieval mystery plays, a porter admitted sinners to hell. Here, Shakespeare links Macbeth's castle with hell. (See 'The Contexts of *Macbeth*', pp. 164–5.)

1 Acting it out (in pairs or small groups)

Break down the language in the Porter's speech to make it as vivid as possible. You could have two or more people miming the actions described, or have just one person responding as someone else reads the words aloud. Use your imagination, and make it as funny as you can!

Language in the play 剧中语言

Verse and prose

The Porter's colloquial vocabulary and imagery are a sharp contrast to the dense, poetic imagery of the previous scene. His rambling prose is further contrasted with the sharp, repetitive beat of the banging at the gate. Rewrite one or two extracts from Macbeth's soliloquy in Scene 1, lines 33–61 to show how it may have sounded in prose (in the way the Porter speaks). What have you discovered about the distinction between Shakespeare's poetry and prose?

1 **have old** 老是
2 **i'th'name of Beelzebub** 以巴力西卜的名义（"巴力西卜"意思是"蝇王"，又译作"别西卜"，圣经中提到的魔王；in the name of... 仅是一种发泄表达式）
3 **on th'expectation of plenty** 因预计会有大丰收（这里的农夫指囤积居奇的农夫）
4 **napkins** 手巾（擦汗用）
5 **th'other devil** 另外那个恶魔（即圣经里的路西法 [Lucifer]，又名"撒旦"，门卫一时没有想起来他的名字）
6 **Faith** 实在话（语气温和的诅咒词，同 hell [该死] 有明显差异）
7 **equivocator** 巧舌如簧者，说谎者（这里指耶稣会神父 Henry Garnet，他谎称自己没有参与1605年11月5日试图炸掉英国议会大厦、炸死国王詹姆斯一世的火药阴谋 [Gunpowder Plot]，不过仍被绞死）
8 **scales** （正义女神的）天平
9 **French hose** 法式紧腿裤（这种裤子紧绷双腿，因此裁缝无法在裁剪时做手脚偷顾客的布料；英格兰裁缝当时被视为惯于偷工减料）
10 **goose** 鹅型熨斗（裁缝用的熨斗，握柄似鹅颈）
11 **primrose way** 通向毁灭的繁花之路（primrose指报春花）
12 **everlasting bonfire** 永久的篝火（即地狱之火）
13 **remember the porter** 记得给门房赏钱
14 **carousing** 开怀畅饮
15 **second cock** 鸡叫二遍（指凌晨三点）
16 **Marry** 马利亚（Mary的变体写法，相当于"不瞒您说"）
17 **nose-painting** 红鼻头（饮酒过量所致）
18 **urine** 撒尿
19 **Lechery** 淫欲
20 **makes ... him** 成也是它，败也是它
21 **sets ... off** 让人雄起，又让人瘫软
22 **stand to** 直立
23 **giving him the lie** 忽悠他一把

* **bathos** 突降法，一种修辞手法，指美好、庄重的内容突然变得平庸可笑。这种效果常常不是言者有意所为。

Act 2 Scene 3
The entrance to Macbeth's castle

Enter a PORTER. *Knocking within*

PORTER   Here's a knocking indeed: if a man were porter of hell-gate, he should have old[1] turning the key. (*Knock*) Knock, knock, knock. Who's there i'th'name of Beelzebub[2]? Here's a farmer that hanged himself on th'expectation of plenty[3]. Come in time – have napkins[4] enough about you, here you'll sweat for't. (*Knock*) Knock, knock. Who's there in th'other devil's[5] name? Faith[6], here's an equivocator[7] that could swear in both the scales[8] against either scale, who committed treason enough for God's sake, yet could not equivocate to heaven. O, come in, equivocator. (*Knock*) Knock, knock, knock. Who's there? Faith, here's an English tailor come hither for stealing out of a French hose[9]. Come in, tailor, here you may roast your goose[10]. (*Knock*) Knock, knock. Never at quiet: what are you? But this place is too cold for hell. I'll devil-porter it no further: I had thought to have let in some of all professions that go the primrose way[11] to th'everlasting bonfire[12]. (*Knock*) Anon, anon. I pray you, remember the porter[13]. [*Opens door*]

Enter MACDUFF *and* LENNOX

MACDUFF   Was it so late, friend, ere you went to bed,
That you do lie so late?

PORTER   Faith, sir, we were carousing[14] till the second cock[15], and drink, sir, is a great provoker of three things.

MACDUFF   What three things does drink especially provoke?

PORTER   Marry[16], sir, nose-painting[17], sleep, and urine[18]. Lechery[19], sir, it provokes, and unprovokes: it provokes the desire, but it takes away the performance. Therefore much drink may be said to be an equivocator with lechery: it makes him, and it mars him[20]; it sets him on, and it takes him off[21]; it persuades him and disheartens him, makes him stand to[22] and not stand to. In conclusion, equivocates him in a sleep, and giving him the lie[23], leaves him.

Macduff has come to meet Duncan. Macbeth shows him to Duncan's room. Lennox tells of the terrible events of the night. Horrified, Macduff returns from Duncan's room.

剧情简介：麦克达是来见邓肯的。麦克白带他来到邓肯的房间。伦诺克斯讲述了夜里发生的恐怖事件。麦克达心惊胆寒，从邓肯的房间返回。

1 'the earth / Was feverous and did shake'
(in small groups)

Lines 46–53 describe the terrible night that Lennox has experienced. In small groups, carry out *one* of the following activities.

a As one person speaks Lennox's lines, the others provide appropriate sound effects.

b Create a picture that conveys the horror of the night. Select images from the script that develop the dark mood. Either draw the images or create a collage (拼贴画) with pictures from the Internet or magazines.

2 Another transition (in threes)

This part of the scene acts as an important transition: the Porter's humorous interlude breaks the tension between the murder scene and the scene in which the murder is discovered. In groups of three, act out lines 35–55. Think carefully about how Macbeth would behave in light of what he has just done. There is strong emphasis on dramatic irony here, but to what extent do you think Macbeth should behave differently?

◀ The Porter is usually portrayed as a comic figure, but some productions choose to depict him in a more sober way. How would the Porter in your own production behave?

1. i'the ... me 忽悠到了我的嗓子眼儿（on = of）
2. requited him for his lie 回报了他的忽悠
3. took up my legs 让我腿软
4. made ... him 略施小计，让他摔了一跤
5. stirring 起身
6. Good morrow = Good morning
7. timely 及早
8. slipped 错过
9. The ... pain 快意之事不觉辛苦
10. limited service 所负之责
11. Lamentings 哀号
12. dire combustion 可怕的熊熊大火（暗指Gunpowder Plot）
13. obscure bird 黑暗之鸟（指猫头鹰，常与死亡联系在一起）
14. livelong 漫漫
15. feverous 发烧
16. 'Twas a rough night 这一夜晚不平静
17. parallel / A fellow to it 找出一个与之类似的
18. Tongue ... thee 有心想不到，有口也说不出你来

Write about it 写作练习

The divine right of kings (君权神授) (by yourself)

Find out more about the divine right of kings in Shakespeare's time, focusing on the possible consequences to a nation if that right is challenged (as Macbeth has done). Now think about why Shakespeare may have wanted to link the murderous events that have just taken place with the wider world. What would be the effect on Shakespeare's audience (including the king and courtiers [侍臣])? Write two short paragraphs exploring possible links between the killing of Duncan and the 'dire combustion and confused events' that Lennox describes.

MACDUFF	I believe drink gave thee the lie last night.	
PORTER	That it did, sir, i'the very throat on me[1], but I requited him for his lie[2], and, I think, being too strong for him, though he took up my legs[3] sometime, yet I made a shift to cast him[4].	

Enter MACBETH

MACDUFF	Is thy master stirring[5]?	35
	Our knocking has awaked him: here he comes.	

[*Exit Porter*]

LENNOX	Good morrow[6], noble sir.	
MACBETH	Good morrow, both.	
MACDUFF	Is the king stirring, worthy thane?	
MACBETH	Not yet.	
MACDUFF	He did command me to call timely[7] on him; I have almost slipped[8] the hour.	
MACBETH	I'll bring you to him.	40
MACDUFF	I know this is a joyful trouble to you, but yet 'tis one.	
MACBETH	The labour we delight in physics pain[9]. This is the door.	
MACDUFF	I'll make so bold to call, for 'tis my limited service[10]. *Exit*	
LENNOX	Goes the king hence today?	
MACBETH	He does – he did appoint so.	45
LENNOX	The night has been unruly: where we lay, Our chimneys were blown down, and, as they say, Lamentings[11] heard i'th'air, strange screams of death And prophesying with accents terrible Of dire combustion[12] and confused events, New hatched to th'woeful time. The obscure bird[13] Clamoured the livelong[14] night. Some say, the earth Was feverous[15] and did shake.	50
MACBETH	'Twas a rough night[16].	
LENNOX	My young remembrance cannot parallel A fellow to it[17].	55

Enter MACDUFF

MACDUFF	O horror, horror, horror, Tongue nor heart cannot conceive, nor name thee[18].
MACBETH *and* LENNOX	What's the matter?

Macduff, horror-struck, reveals the murder of Duncan. He tells Macbeth and Lennox to see for themselves. He shouts to awake Banquo and the king's sons. Lady Macbeth pretends concern and amazement.

剧情简介：麦克达惊恐万分，透露了邓肯被谋杀一事。他让麦克白和伦诺克斯自己去看看。他高声唤醒班阔和国王的两个儿子。麦克白夫人佯装关切和惊愕。

1 'Confusion now hath made his masterpiece'

Macduff imagines 'Confusion' as a perverse (性情乖张) artist who has created a 'masterpiece'. To gain a sense of the great confusion that results from Duncan's murder, try the following activity. You will need a large space such as a hall or drama studio (a cleared classroom will also be fine).

Everybody reads the whole page opposite, but each person begins at a different line. Start anywhere you wish in lines 59–83. As you walk around the room, greet others with a single line or sentence from the script. They will reply with a different line or sentence. Then move on to greet others. Greet as many people as you can, using a different line from the script each time. Keep the activity going for several minutes, then meet in small groups of four or five. Read through again, taking turns to read a sentence at a time. After your activity:

- Identify as many images as you can, and suggest what each describes.
- Write notes on how to stage the lines for greatest dramatic effect.

Language in the play 剧中语言
'Murder and treason!' (in pairs)

Macduff's language in lines 67–74 is dramatic and urgent. As well as waking the sleepers of the house, he compares the horror of 'death itself' with popular images of death and Judgement Day.

a Identify the language features in this section that suggest chaos, urgency and clamour.

b Look at the 'great doom's image' as depicted on the wall of the Guild Chapel in Stratford-upon-Avon, next door to Shakespeare's school (p. 164). Identify the details that are referenced in the script opposite.

Characters 人物分析
'gentle lady'? (by yourself)

Macduff calls Lady Macbeth 'gentle' and says the news is too cruel for a woman's hearing (lines 76–9). From your knowledge of her so far, write some notes to the actor playing Lady Macbeth. How would you advise her to behave in this part of the scene? Write down between five and ten adjectives other than 'gentle' that you think appropriately describe her at this point in the play.

1 Confusion　以下犯上
2 sacrilegious　亵渎神明（旧时认为君权神授，刺杀国王被认为是冒犯神明的重罪）
3 ope = open
4 The Lord's anointed temple　君主涂过圣油的庙堂（指邓肯的身体；君王加冕时由大主教为其敷圣油，君主被看作是上帝在俗世的代表）
5 thence = from there
6 Gorgon　戈耳贡（又译作"戈尔工"，希腊神话中三个蛇发女怪之一，人见之即化为石头）
7 Shake … itself　摆脱这鸭绒般的睡眠、这死亡的替身，看看死亡本身
8 The great doom's image　末日大审判的景象
9 As … sprites　从坟墓中升起，像鬼魂一样行走（末日审判时，死去的基督徒的魂灵被认为会从坟墓里钻出）
10 countenance　支持，强化
11 hideous trumpet　凄厉的号角
12 parley　会谈
13 murder as it fell　一说出口就会杀了她
14 Duff　（对麦克达的昵称）
15 contradict　否认

MACDUFF	Confusion[1] now hath made his masterpiece:
	Most sacrilegious[2] murder hath broke ope[3] 60
	The Lord's anointed temple[4] and stole thence[5]
	The life o'th'building.
MACBETH	What is't you say, the life?
LENNOX	Mean you his majesty?
MACDUFF	Approach the chamber and destroy your sight 65
	With a new Gorgon[6]. Do not bid me speak:
	See and then speak yourselves.

Exeunt Macbeth and Lennox

                Awake, awake!
Ring the alarum bell! Murder and treason!
Banquo and Donaldbain! Malcolm, awake,
Shake off this downy sleep, death's counterfeit, 70
And look on death itself[7]. Up, up, and see
The great doom's image[8]. Malcolm, Banquo,
As from your graves rise up and walk like sprites[9]
To countenance[10] this horror.

Bell rings. Enter LADY [MACBETH]

LADY MACBETH	What's the business
	That such a hideous trumpet[11] calls to parley[12] 75
	The sleepers of the house? Speak, speak.
MACDUFF	O gentle lady,
	'Tis not for you to hear what I can speak.
	The repetition in a woman's ear
	Would murder as it fell[13]. –

Enter BANQUO

                  O Banquo, Banquo,
Our royal master's murdered.

LADY MACBETH	Woe, alas. 80
	What, in our house?
BANQUO	Too cruel, anywhere.
	Dear Duff[14], I prithee contradict[15] thyself
	And say it is not so.

Macbeth says that Duncan's death empties the world of meaning. Duncan's sons are told the news of their father's murder. Macbeth defends his killing of the bodyguards. Lady Macbeth faints and is carried out.

剧情简介：麦克白说邓肯的死让一切都失去意义。邓肯的两个儿子被告知父亲被谋杀了。麦克白为自己杀死邓肯的卫士辩解。麦克白夫人昏了过去，被抬下。

Language in the play 剧中语言

Is Macbeth sincere? (in pairs)

Look closely at Macbeth's first speech (lines 84–9). Some believe that, in contrast with Macduff's hurried and passionate reaction to finding Duncan's body, Macbeth's words are so carefully constructed and so rich in elaborate imagery that they reveal his insincerity. With a partner, talk about how you would deliver this speech and what you would try to convey to the audience about Macbeth's state of mind.

1 'O, by whom?' (in sevens)

Of the seven characters on stage, only two know who killed Duncan. Take parts and prepare a tableau of line 93 to show just how everyone looks at the moment when Malcolm asks his question. Who is suspicious of whom? Who is making eye contact, and who is avoiding it? Compare the tableaux of each group and discuss why you have made your choices.

Characters 人物分析

'Look to the lady' (whole class)

Spend some time analysing Macbeth's second, longer, speech. Look at the imagery he uses, as well as the use of devices such as repetition and rhetorical questions. As with lines 84–9, Macbeth seems to have prepared this speech in advance, but behind his words he is justifying another significant murder: that of the only other witnesses to Duncan's killing (he has also taken a long time to announce this shocking news).

a Why do you think Lady Macbeth faints at this point? Is she sincere? What dramatic purpose does it serve?

b Discuss how to stage this part of the scene, and experiment by directing a group of volunteers who enact your suggestions. Try the lines without Lady Macbeth fainting. What difference does it make to the effect of the scene?

1 chance 事件
2 There's nothing serious in mortality 人生已毫无意义可言
3 All is but toys 万事皆空
4 renown 名誉
5 The ... drawn 生命的美酒已经抽干
6 lees 残渣
7 vault 酒窖
8 brag 吹嘘
9 amiss 出差错
10 The spring, the head 源泉，源头
11 your blood 你们家的血脉
12 stopped 阻断
13 badged 标记
14 distracted 糊涂不清
15 repent 后悔
16 Wherefore = Why
17 temp'rate 冷静，克制
18 Loyal and neutral 忠诚而中立（忠于国王又中立地对待杀手）
19 expedition 迅速
20 pauser 犹豫者
21 silver 银白色
22 golden 红色 (参见第46页注解3)
23 breach 缺口
24 ruin's wasteful entrance 废墟毁掉的入口
25 Steeped 浸泡
26 Unmannerly breeched 不堪入目地沾满
27 gore 凝血
28 refrain 克制
29 Look to 留心

Enter MACBETH *and* LENNOX

MACBETH Had I but died an hour before this chance[1],
I had lived a blessèd time, for from this instant,
There's nothing serious in mortality[2].
All is but toys[3]; renown[4] and grace is dead,
The wine of life is drawn[5], and the mere lees[6]
Is left this vault[7] to brag[8] of.

Enter MALCOLM *and* DONALDBAIN

DONALDBAIN What is amiss[9]?
MACBETH You are, and do not know't.
The spring, the head[10], the fountain of your blood[11]
Is stopped, the very source of it is stopped[12].
MACDUFF Your royal father's murdered.
MALCOLM O, by whom?
LENNOX Those of his chamber, as it seemed, had done't.
Their hands and faces were all badged[13] with blood,
So were their daggers which, unwiped, we found
Upon their pillows. They stared and were distracted[14];
No man's life was to be trusted with them.
MACBETH O, yet I do repent[15] me of my fury
That I did kill them.
MACDUFF Wherefore[16] did you so?
MACBETH Who can be wise, amazed, temp'rate[17], and furious,
Loyal and neutral[18], in a moment? No man.
Th'expedition[19] of my violent love
Outran the pauser[20], reason. Here lay Duncan,
His silver[21] skin laced with his golden[22] blood
And his gashed stabs looked like a breach[23] in nature,
For ruin's wasteful entrance[24]. There the murderers,
Steeped[25] in the colours of their trade; their daggers
Unmannerly breeched[26] with gore[27]. Who could refrain[28],
That had a heart to love and in that heart
Courage to make's love known?
LADY MACBETH Help me hence, ho.
MACDUFF Look to[29] the lady.

[*Exit Lady Macbeth, helped*]

Donaldbain and Malcolm fear for their future. Banquo and the others swear to investigate the murder. Duncan's sons, suspecting danger, resolve to flee: Malcolm to England, Donaldbain to Ireland.

剧情简介：道讷尔本和马尔肯担心自己的未来。班阔和其他众人发誓要调查这起谋杀事件。邓肯的两个儿子疑心会有危险，决定逃命：马尔肯逃往英格兰，道讷尔本去了爱尔兰。

1 Donaldbain and Malcolm: should they stay or should they go? (in pairs)

Should Malcolm and Donaldbain stay in Scotland and find the murderer? Or should they flee? Improvise (即兴创作) the arguments for and against each of these actions. Which do you think is the stronger argument? Which is the braver course of action? Do you think they even trust each other now? When considering these arguments, remember that Duncan has already appointed Malcolm as his heir (Act 1 Scene 4, lines 37–8), so he stands to gain most from his father's death. But the younger brother, Donaldbain, has also moved one step closer to the throne with Duncan's death.

2 The qualities of a king

With Malcolm and Donaldbain having fled to England and Ireland respectively, Scotland urgently needs a king. Create a hastily gathered royal court to draw up a job description and outline the qualities the ideal candidate should have. Discuss this as a group and, if you feel strongly about a particular character, argue for them to be crowned king.

Themes 主题分析

Fate and free will (by yourself)

Imagine you are a psychiatrist. You are faced with characters who seem unable to determine whether it is fate or their own free will that informs their actions. Provide a written report of five key points about one character in Scene 3, telling them what you think is shaping their fate and how they should best respond to this.

Language in the play 剧中语言

Deception and suspicion (in pairs)

The theme of deceptive appearance emerges again in this part of the play, as we see Malcolm and Donaldbain's fearful suspicion of those around them. Present line 133 in the most imaginative way you can, as a tableau, a collection of images or a sketch.

1 that ... ours 最有权为我们的论点发声
2 auger hole 钻头洞（指微小的窟窿眼）
3 tears are not yet brewed 眼泪尚未酿好（即还不到哭的时候）
4 upon the foot of motion 落到行动的脚上（即到表达悲伤的时候）
5 naked frailties 赤裸脆弱之体
6 question 深究
7 scruples 疑虑
8 the great hand of God 上帝的巨手（法力）
9 undivulged pretence 不可告人的目的
10 treasonous malice 叛逆的恶行
11 briefly 立即
12 put on manly readiness 显出男子汉的样子
13 Well contented 好主意
14 consort 与……在一起
15 To show ... easy 表演假悲伤对惯作假的人来说很容易
16 Our ... safer 咱们各奔前程会让咱俩更安全
17 the nea'er ... bloody （与邓肯）血缘越近，距离血腥越近
18 shaft 箭支
19 lighted 着地
20 dainty of 讲究
21 leave-taking 告辞
22 shift away 离开
23 steals itself 偷偷溜走

MALCOLM [*To Donaldbain*] Why do we hold our tongues, that most may claim
This argument for ours¹?
DONALDBAIN [*To Malcolm*] What should be spoken here,
Where our fate hid in an auger hole² may rush   115
And seize us? Let's away. Our tears are not yet brewed³.
MALCOLM [*To Donaldbain*] Nor our strong sorrow upon the foot of motion⁴.
BANQUO Look to the lady,
And when we have our naked frailties⁵ hid
That suffer in exposure, let us meet   120
And question⁶ this most bloody piece of work
To know it further. Fears and scruples⁷ shake us:
In the great hand of God⁸ I stand and thence
Against the undivulged pretence⁹ I fight
Of treasonous malice¹⁰.
MACDUFF And so do I.
ALL So all.   125
MACBETH Let's briefly¹¹ put on manly readiness¹²
And meet i'th'hall together.
ALL Well contented¹³.

Exeunt [*all but Malcolm and Donaldbain*]

MALCOLM What will you do? Let's not consort¹⁴ with them.
To show an unfelt sorrow is an office
Which the false man does easy¹⁵. I'll to England.   130
DONALDBAIN To Ireland, I. Our separated fortune
Shall keep us both the safer¹⁶. Where we are,
There's daggers in men's smiles; the nea'er in blood,
The nearer bloody¹⁷.
MALCOLM This murderous shaft¹⁸ that's shot
Hath not yet lighted¹⁹, and our safest way   135
Is to avoid the aim. Therefore to horse,
And let us not be dainty of²⁰ leave-taking²¹,
But shift away²². There's warrant in that theft
Which steals itself²³ when there's no mercy left.

Exeunt

Ross and an Old Man talk about the darkness and unnaturalness of events that mirror Duncan's murder. The sun is obscured, owls kill falcons, and Duncan's horses eat each other. Macduff arrives.

 剧情简介：若斯和一位老丈谈到邓肯被谋杀一事反映出的黑暗和反常。太阳被遮住，猫头鹰杀死猎鹰，邓肯的马相互撕咬。麦克达来了。

Stagecraft 导演技巧
The pathetic fallacy (借物喻情)

The shocking events taking place inside the castle seem to be mirrored by events in the wider world ('Tis unnatural / Even like the deed that's done'). This use of the **pathetic fallacy** (a literary device used to make the external world seem to be an extension of the moods and actions of the characters) and apocalyptic (末日般) imagery is intended to create a great impression on the audience. Why do you think Shakespeare uses it here? How successful is it? As you read the rest of the play, add to your notes when you see similar techniques being used.

Characters 人物分析
Who is the Old Man? (in pairs)

This is the Old Man's only appearance in the play. His dramatic function is rather like the chorus in a Greek tragedy. The role of the chorus was threefold:

- to comment on the action
- to show the universality of the action (how the action is reflected in nature and society)
- to represent the views of ordinary people.

Discuss whether the Old Man fulfils these three roles, then draft a conversation between two people who have different views about the importance of this part of the play. Would you include lines 1–20 in a production at your school?

1 An unimportant scene? (in pairs)

On the surface, the purpose of this scene seems to be simply to inform the audience of recent events. But look closer. Ross is a thane, a high-ranking nobleman, who seems to be mocking an old man. Also, he claims that he saw Duncan's horses eat each other, but do you think this is true? What reason might Ross have for lying about such an event?

Discuss how you would stage this scene to give the two characters more depth and to highlight key themes in the play, such as appearance and reality, the supernatural, hidden evil, and any others that you think are relevant. Write out your ideas as a set of notes to inspire and prompt two actors to bring the script opposite to life as you would want.

1. Threescore and ten　70年（即一生）
2. sore　残暴
3. Hath trifled former knowings　使以前知道的事都变得无足轻重
4. father　老爹
5. heavens / act / stage　天棚/幕/戏台（都是与剧院有关的词语）
6. strangles　扼杀；扑灭
7. travelling lamp　行走的灯（指太阳）
8. predominance　主宰
9. the day's shame　白昼的受辱（指邓肯被害）
10. entomb　埋葬
11. falcon　猎鹰
12. tow'ring　翱翔
13. pride of place　崇高位置
14. mousing owl　逮老鼠的猫头鹰（一般不会飞上天空捉猛禽）
15. hawked at　在空中被捉住
16. minions　典范
17. flung out　冲出来
18. Contending 'gainst　反抗
19. as = as if
20. good　（与麦克白对比，麦克达第一次这样被描述）
21. How goes the world　这个世道怎么了

Act 2 Scene 4
Outside Macbeth's castle

Enter ROSS, *with an* OLD MAN

OLD MAN Threescore and ten[1] I can remember well;
Within the volume of which time, I have seen
Hours dreadful and things strange, but this sore[2] night
Hath trifled former knowings[3].

ROSS   Ha, good father[4],
Thou seest the heavens[5], as troubled with man's act[5],   5
Threatens his bloody stage[5]. By th'clock 'tis day
And yet dark night strangles[6] the travelling lamp[7].
Is't night's predominance[8], or the day's shame[9],
That darkness does the face of earth entomb[10]
When living light should kiss it?

OLD MAN   'Tis unnatural,   10
Even like the deed that's done. On Tuesday last,
A falcon[11] tow'ring[12] in her pride of place[13]
Was by a mousing owl[14] hawked at[15] and killed.

ROSS And Duncan's horses, a thing most strange and certain,
Beauteous and swift, the minions[16] of their race,   15
Turned wild in nature, broke their stalls, flung out[17],
Contending 'gainst[18] obedience as[19] they would
Make war with mankind.

OLD MAN   'Tis said, they eat each other.

ROSS They did so, to th'amazement of mine eyes
That looked upon't.

Enter MACDUFF

                    Here comes the good[20] Macduff.   20
How goes the world[21], sir, now?

MACDUFF   Why, see you not?

Macduff tells that Duncan's sons bribed the killers and have now fled. Macbeth has been elected king, and has gone to Scone to be crowned. Macduff will not attend the ceremony. The Old Man blesses peacemakers.

剧情简介：麦克达告诉他们，邓肯的两个儿子贿赂了杀手，现已潜逃。麦克白已被推选为王，已经前往斯贡接受加冕。麦克达不会出席加冕仪式。老丈祝福创造和平的人。

Characters 人物分析

Macduff: diplomatic or naïve? (in pairs)

This part of the scene is an exposition: it allows the audience to catch up with events that have taken place since the murder of Duncan. Macduff tells us that Duncan's sons bribed the killers and have now fled. He also seems unwilling to comment on the crowning of Macbeth as King of Scotland, although he admits that he is not going to the coronation ceremony.

How does the character of Macduff develop over these twenty lines? With a partner, read through the script opposite. Show by your choice of tone, pace, pause and gesture whether you think Macduff is being diplomatic or naïve, and whether Ross is being deceptive or sincere. Write out your view of each character in a short paragraph.

▼ 'Where the place?' The map below shows the locations of the play. It also shows the rough locations of the territories of the thanes.

1. Those ... slain 麦克白杀掉的人
2. pretend 打算，企图
3. suborned 被收买（杀邓肯）
4. 'Gainst nature still 根本违反天性
5. Thriftless ... means 野心无节制，必将吞噬自家性命
6. Then ... Macbeth 王权最有可能落入麦克白之手
7. named 提名，推选
8. Scone 斯贡（位于珀斯 [Perth] 附近，苏格兰君王的传统加冕地）
9. invested 加冕
10. Colmkill （即爱奥那 [Iona]，苏格兰的一个岛，古时苏格兰君王的埋葬地）
11. I will thither 我会去那里
12. Adieu 再见，再会
13. Lest ... new 以免新的袍子还没旧的穿着舒服（比喻侍奉旧主习惯了，不知新的君主会怎样）
14. benison 祝福
15. make good of bad 化恶为善

MACBETH ACT 2 SCENE 4
麦克白

ROSS	Is't known who did this more than bloody deed?	
MACDUFF	Those that Macbeth hath slain[1].	
ROSS	Alas the day,	
	What good could they pretend[2]?	
MACDUFF	They were suborned[3].	
	Malcolm and Donaldbain, the king's two sons,	25
	Are stol'n away and fled, which puts upon them	
	Suspicion of the deed.	
ROSS	'Gainst nature still[4].	
	Thriftless ambition that will ravin up	
	Thine own life's means[5]. Then 'tis most like	
	The sovereignty will fall upon Macbeth[6].	30
MACDUFF	He is already named[7] and gone to Scone[8]	
	To be invested[9].	
ROSS	Where is Duncan's body?	
MACDUFF	Carried to Colmkill[10],	
	The sacred storehouse of his predecessors	
	And guardian of their bones.	
ROSS	Will you to Scone?	35
MACDUFF	No, cousin, I'll to Fife.	
ROSS	Well, I will thither[11].	
MACDUFF	Well may you see things well done there. Adieu[12],	
	Lest our old robes sit easier than our new[13].	
ROSS	Farewell, father.	
OLD MAN	God's benison[14] go with you, and with those	40
	That would make good of bad[15], and friends of foes.	
	Exeunt	

MACBETH
麦克白

Looking back at Act 2 第2幕回顾
Activities for groups or individuals

1 'the bloody business'

Blood is a recurring symbol throughout *Macbeth*, but in Act 2, with the murder of Duncan, it is used particularly vividly. Find all the images of blood in Act 2 and consider the different ways it is represented. You could act out each section, or create tableaux of the most powerful lines in groups.

2 Storyboarding the main action

Act 2 moves at real pace. Storyboard the main points of action: which scenes will you choose, and what lines will you select to illustrate each image? What will you decide to leave out, and why? Put each image together into a continuous sequence, either using pen and paper, or a computer with a film-editing program.

3 A favourite speech

This act has many powerful speeches. Choose your favourite (between ten and twenty lines) and set yourself the challenge of learning those lines. Think about the rhythm, the stresses, the tone and the meaning you wish to convey. Try filming your interpretation of these lines and then show your work to the rest of your class. Discuss the decisions you made in building your performance.

4 Thinking about the big themes

Working by yourself, make a list of what you consider to be the main themes in Act 2. When you have your list, get together with the rest of your class. Each person should explain their choices. Together, agree on the five most important themes in this act.

Next, take five large pieces of paper and write one key theme in the middle of each piece. Split into five groups and take one piece of paper each. Discuss the theme on your piece of paper for five minutes, writing down your thoughts. At the end of five minutes, pass on your piece of paper and move on to the next theme, writing down your thoughts and responding to those that the previous groups have written down. Keep going until each group has considered all five themes. Afterwards, keep these pieces of paper and add to them as you continue to work through the rest of the play.

If you wanted to continue this activity, you could explore an additional area: the link between themes. For example, you could investigate the connections between the themes of loyalty and ambition, conscience and action.

5 Macbeth: hero or villain?

At the end of Act 2, it is possible to see the character of Macbeth in a number of different ways:

- He is a heartless killer who has murdered a kind king purely for his own benefit.
- He is politically clever and acts ruthlessly simply because he lives in ruthless times.
- He is easily manipulated by a wife he loves, and acts to prove to her that he is a man.
- He has no choice: the Witches told him what was going to happen and it was fated to be so.
- He is a hero who has been selected by the thanes to rescue Scotland in its hour of need.

Which of these interpretations do you think is the most valid? Write down your reasons, using quotations where appropriate. Now list them in order of priority and debate your choices with each other. Can you think of any other ways to see Macbeth at this point in the play?

Banquo fears that Macbeth has become king by evil means, but he takes heart from the Witches' predictions for his own descendants. Macbeth requests Banquo to attend tonight's banquet.

剧情简介：班阔害怕麦克白是通过邪恶手段当上国王的，但他因为女巫有关他自己后代的预言而受到鼓舞。麦克白请求班阔出席当晚的宴会。

1 Noble Banquo?

Initially, Banquo – like Macbeth – dwells on the words of the Witches. His thoughts are interrupted by the entrance of Macbeth and Lady Macbeth.

a Was he saying 'hush, no more' to rebuke the thoughts that might have led him to evil, or so that the Macbeths would not hear him? What might he have said if he had carried on? Compose an extension to this aside to reveal Banquo's thoughts and feelings further.

b How would you enact lines 15–18? Would Banquo be noble and sincere or hypocritical and deceptive? Experiment with ways of saying these lines aloud, varying the emphasis and intonation to reveal different meanings.

1 **stand in thy posterity** 延续到你的子孙后代
2 **father / Of many kings** （詹姆斯一世［即苏格兰詹姆斯六世］认为自己是班阔的后裔）
3 **shine** 灵验
4 **verities** 实现
5 **made good** 被证实
6 **my oracles** 关于我的预言
7 **set me up in hope** 燃起我的希望
8 *Sennet sounded* 号角/喇叭响起（伊丽莎白时代的戏台指令）
9 **all thing unbecoming** 完全不合礼节（all thing = completely）
10 **solemn** 隆重
11 **Command upon me** 吩咐我，给我下旨
12 **indissoluble tie** 牢不可破的纽带

▼ Macbeth now wears the crown of Scotland, but what does his face reveal about his 'mind's construction'?

Act 3 Scene 1
The royal palace at Forres

Enter BANQUO *dressed for riding*

BANQUO Thou hast it now, King, Cawdor, Glamis, all,
As the weïrd women promised, and I fear
Thou played'st most foully for't; yet it was said
It should not stand in thy posterity[1],
But that myself should be the root and father 5
Of many kings[2]. If there come truth from them —
As upon thee, Macbeth, their speeches shine[3] —
Why by the verities[4] on thee made good[5],
May they not be my oracles[6] as well
And set me up in hope[7]? But hush, no more. 10

Sennet sounded[8]. *Enter* MACBETH *as King,* LADY [MACBETH *as Queen*], LENNOX, ROSS, *Lords, and Attendants*

MACBETH Here's our chief guest.
LADY MACBETH   If he had been forgotten,
It had been as a gap in our great feast
And all thing unbecoming[9].
MACBETH Tonight we hold a solemn[10] supper, sir,
And I'll request your presence.
BANQUO   Let your highness 15
Command upon me[11], to the which my duties
Are with a most indissoluble tie[12]
Forever knit.

Macbeth claims that Duncan's sons are spreading malicious rumours. He checks that Fleance will ride this afternoon with Banquo, then dismisses the court. A servant confirms two men (the Murderers) are waiting.

剧情简介：麦克白声称邓肯的两个儿子在散布恶毒的谣言。他查明了弗利恩会在当天下午与班阔一起骑马外出后，然后退了朝。一个仆人证实有两个人（即杀手）在恭候。

Themes 主题分析

Hidden evil (in pairs)

Macbeth flatters Banquo as a valued adviser. He pretends to be interested in Banquo's ride that afternoon, but in his heart Macbeth has evil intentions for his friend. His order 'Fail not our feast' is deeply ironic, because Macbeth intends that Banquo will never return from his ride.

With a partner, read slowly all Macbeth's words in lines 19–41. As one person reads, the other says 'false face' or 'hypocrite' (虚伪) every time he says something insincere. At each point, give a reason why Macbeth is false, or describe what is really on his mind.

1 'strange invention' (by yourself)

Malcolm has escaped to England and Donaldbain to Ireland. Macbeth accuses them of influencing the king and people there with tales of 'strange invention'. Step into role as either Malcolm or Donaldbain. Write your side of the story in the form of a speech to be delivered to the people of England or Ireland (or any other country) who might support your cause. Why have you not confessed to 'cruel parricide' and what do you intend to do to clear your name?

Characters 人物分析

Why is Lady Macbeth dismissed? (in pairs)

In many productions, Lady Macbeth approaches Macbeth at line 45, obviously wanting to talk to him, but is dismissed with everyone else when he says 'While then, God be with you'. Does Macbeth send his wife away because the evil they have committed is beginning to drive them apart? Or is Macbeth just distracted by his plans for getting rid of Banquo?

With a partner, improvise the conversation that might have taken place between Macbeth and Lady Macbeth if they were left on stage together at this point.

1 still = always
2 grave　重要
3 prosperous　卓有成果
4 take tomorrow　明天再议
5 'Twixt this and supper = Between now and supper
6 Go … better　如果我的马跑得不快
7 borrower of the night　夜行者
8 twain = two
9 bloody　沾有鲜血（杀过人的）
10 cousins　（指马尔肯和道讷尔本）
11 bestowed　安身于
12 parricide　弑父
13 strange invention　离奇的谎言
14 therewithal = with it also
15 Craving us jointly　要求你我共同关注此事
16 Hie you　您快些吧
17 be master of his time　支配自己的时间
18 While = Until
19 Sirrah　小子（称呼社会地位低的人）
20 attend those men / Our pleasure　那些人在等本王的吩咐吗
21 without = outside

MACBETH ACT 3 SCENE 1
麦克白

MACBETH	Ride you this afternoon?	
BANQUO	Ay, my good lord.	20
MACBETH	We should have else desired your good advice	
	Which still[1] hath been both grave[2] and prosperous[3]	
	In this day's council: but we'll take tomorrow[4].	
	Is't far you ride?	
BANQUO	As far, my lord, as will fill up the time	25
	'Twixt this and supper[5]. Go not my horse the better[6],	
	I must become a borrower of the night[7]	
	For a dark hour, or twain[8].	
MACBETH	Fail not our feast.	
BANQUO	My lord, I will not.	30
MACBETH	We hear our bloody[9] cousins[10] are bestowed[11]	
	In England and in Ireland, not confessing	
	Their cruel parricide[12], filling their hearers	
	With strange invention[13]. But of that tomorrow,	
	When therewithal[14] we shall have cause of state	35
	Craving us jointly[15]. Hie you[16] to horse; adieu,	
	Till you return at night. Goes Fleance with you?	
BANQUO	Ay, my good lord; our time does call upon's.	
MACBETH	I wish your horses swift and sure of foot,	
	And so I do commend you to their backs.	40
	Farewell.	

Exit Banquo

	Let every man be master of his time[17]	
	Till seven at night; to make society	
	The sweeter welcome, we will keep ourself	
	Till supper-time alone. While[18] then, God be with you.	45

Exeunt [all but Macbeth and a Servant]

	Sirrah[19], a word with you: attend those men
	Our pleasure[20]?
SERVANT	They are, my lord, without[21] the palace gate.

67

Macbeth broods on his fears that Banquo's descendants will become kings. The two Murderers enter, and Macbeth reminds them of an earlier conversation when he told them that Banquo is their enemy.

 剧情简介：麦克白因害怕班阔的后代会成为国王而闷闷不乐。两个杀手上场，麦克白提醒他们之前的谈话，当时他告诉他们班阔是他们的敌人。

1 Thoughts of Banquo (in pairs)

As he waits for the Murderers, Macbeth reveals how much he fears Banquo. Interestingly, while he earlier acted to ensure that the Witches' prophecy would come true (so he could be king), he now takes steps to ensure their prophecy for Banquo's descendants will *not* come true.

To experience how much Macbeth now fears Banquo, read through the soliloquy while your partner echoes any word referring to Banquo (his name, 'he', 'his', 'him') in an angry voice, and any word referring to Macbeth ('I', 'my', 'me') in a complaining voice.

Language in the play 剧中语言
Fruitless and barren (in pairs)

Macbeth speaks bitterly of the 'fruitless crown' and 'barren sceptre' that the Witches have given him. He is jealous of Banquo because of the prophecy that Banquo will be 'father to a line of kings'.

a With a partner, draw up a list of images or phrases that signify fruitfulness or honour for Banquo, and those that suggest barrenness and dishonour for Macbeth. Talk together about which image is the most striking. Why is this so?

b Write two short paragraphs: one on Macbeth's use of language and the other on the insight it gives into his mental state. Swap your paragraphs with your partner and compare your perspectives. Are they the same?

2 'our last conference' (in threes)

Macbeth had an earlier meeting with the Murderers. He told them ('passed in probation with you') that Banquo had deceived them ('borne in hand'), and it was all Banquo's doing that they were so poor and out of luck ('held you so under fortune').

Improvise that earlier conversation as Macbeth lays all the blame on Banquo. Take lines 77–83 and 85–9 as your starting point and use either modern English or blank verse in the style of Shakespeare.

1 thus 如此（指做国王）
2 royalty of nature 称王的潜质
3 Reigns 最为显著
4 dauntless 无畏
5 being 存在
6 genius 守护神
7 rebuked 斥责
8 chid 训斥
9 fruitless 后继无人
10 barren sceptre 光杆权杖（暗指麦克白没有后代）
11 gripe 紧握
12 wrenched 夺走
13 with an unlineal hand 借外姓人之手
14 issue 子嗣，后代
15 filed 玷污
16 rancours 毒药；折磨
17 vessel 杯子
18 eternal jewel 不朽的灵魂
19 common enemy 人类的公敌（指魔鬼撒旦）
20 seeds 后代
21 list 比武场，决斗场
22 champion me to th'utterance 一决生死（champion：发起挑战；utterance：极限，极端）
23 he （指班阔）
24 conference 商谈，会面
25 passed in probation 证明
26 borne in hand 哄骗
27 crossed 被出卖
28 half a soul 傻瓜
29 notion crazed 头脑糊涂的人

MACBETH Bring them before us.

Exit Servant

To be thus[1] is nothing,
But to be safely thus. Our fears in Banquo   50
Stick deep, and in his royalty of nature[2]
Reigns[3] that which would be feared. 'Tis much he dares,
And to that dauntless[4] temper of his mind,
He hath a wisdom that doth guide his valour
To act in safety. There is none but he,   55
Whose being[5] I do fear; and under him
My genius[6] is rebuked[7], as it is said
Mark Antony's was by Caesar. He chid[8] the sisters
When first they put the name of king upon me
And bade them speak to him. Then prophet-like,   60
They hailed him father to a line of kings.
Upon my head they placed a fruitless[9] crown
And put a barren sceptre[10] in my gripe[11],
Thence to be wrenched[12] with an unlineal hand[13],
No son of mine succeeding. If't be so,   65
For Banquo's issue[14] have I filed[15] my mind;
For them, the gracious Duncan have I murdered,
Put rancours[16] in the vessel[17] of my peace
Only for them, and mine eternal jewel[18]
Given to the common enemy[19] of man,   70
To make them kings, the seeds[20] of Banquo kings.
Rather than so, come Fate into the list[21],
And champion me to th'utterance[22]. Who's there?

Enter Servant and two MURDERERS

[*To Servant*] Now go to the door and stay there till we call.

Exit Servant

Was it not yesterday we spoke together?   75

MURDERERS It was, so please your highness.

MACBETH Well then, now have you considered of my speeches? Know, that it was he[23] in the times past which held you so under fortune, which you thought had been our innocent self. This I made good to you in our last conference[24]; passed in probation[25]   80
with you how you were borne in hand[26], how crossed[27]; the instruments, who wrought with them, and all things else that might to half a soul[28] and to a notion crazed[29] say, 'Thus did Banquo.'

Macbeth taunts the Murderers, urging them to show they are men, not dogs. If they can prove their manhood, he will help them to kill Banquo. The Murderers claim that they are so desperate they'll do anything.

 剧情简介：麦克白嘲笑杀手，鼓动他们表现得像男子汉而不是狗。如果他们能证明自己的男子汉气概，他会帮助他们杀死班阔。杀手宣称他们无所顾忌，愿意做任何事情。

Write about it 写作练习
Men and dogs

Earlier in the play, Lady Macbeth questioned Macbeth's manhood in an attempt to manipulate him into murdering Duncan. Now Macbeth does the same thing with the Murderers. He describes a variety of dogs ('Shoughs', 'water-rugs', 'demi-wolves') and lists their different qualities ('swift', 'slow', 'subtle'). He suggests that men can similarly be ranked by their qualities. As he does this, Macbeth shifts from prose to verse at line 91. Convert the prose to verse, and the verse to prose. What difference does it make?

1 Murder and manipulation (in small groups)

Prepare a dramatic reading of the script opposite. Use the following questions to help you:

- Would Macbeth be seated while the Murderers stand, or would all stand?
- Would Macbeth remain hidden in the shadows or would he tower above the Murderers?
- Would he have freedom of movement and a wide vocal range to show his power over the Murderers, who fearfully stay in one place on the stage?
- Would the Murderers be restless, wild and violent men who gradually become subject to Macbeth's manipulation (操纵)?

1 so gospelled 如此相信福音
2 beggared yours 让你们的家人沦为乞丐
3 catalogue 注册簿
4 hounds 猎犬
5 greyhounds 格力犬，灵猩（一种身细腿长且善跑的狗，俗称"灰狗"）
6 mongrels 混种狗
7 spaniels 西班牙猎犬，獚
8 curs 杂种狗
9 Shoughs 莎夫狗（一种原产于冰岛的卷毛小宠物狗）
10 water-rugs 水猎犬（一种原产于英格兰的水禽猎犬，现已灭绝）
11 demi-wolves 狼犬
12 clept 称为
13 valued file 犬种价目表
14 housekeeper 看门狗
15 closed 附上
16 Particular addition 特质，特性
17 bill 单子
18 station in the file 表里的位置
19 rank 等级
20 put … bosoms 向你们托付一件心头事
21 execution 实施，执行
22 Grapples 紧密连在一起
23 in his life 只要他还活着
24 perfect 健康无恙
25 spite 重创
26 tugged with 被……摧残
27 set my life 冒生命危险

MACBETH ACT 3 SCENE 1
麦克白

FIRST MURDERER   You made it known to us.

MACBETH   I did so, and went further, which is now our point of 85
second meeting. Do you find your patience so predominant in
your nature, that you can let this go? Are you so gospelled[1], to
pray for this good man and for his issue, whose heavy hand
hath bowed you to the grave and beggared yours[2] forever?

FIRST MURDERER   We are men, my liege. 90

MACBETH   Ay, in the catalogue[3] ye go for men,
As hounds[4], and greyhounds[5], mongrels[6], spaniels[7], curs[8],
Shoughs[9], water-rugs[10], and demi-wolves[11] are clept[12]
All by the name of dogs. The valued file[13]
Distinguishes the swift, the slow, the subtle, 95
The housekeeper[14], the hunter, every one
According to the gift which bounteous nature
Hath in him closed[15], whereby he does receive
Particular addition[16] from the bill[17]
That writes them all alike. And so of men. 100
Now, if you have a station in the file[18]
Not i'th'worst rank[19] of manhood, say't,
And I will put that business in your bosoms[20],
Whose execution[21] takes your enemy off,
Grapples[22] you to the heart and love of us 105
Who wear our health but sickly in his life[23],
Which in his death were perfect[24].

SECOND MURDERER   I am one, my liege,
Whom the vile blows and buffets of the world
Hath so incensed that I am reckless what I do
To spite[25] the world.

FIRST MURDERER   And I another, 110
So weary with disasters, tugged with[26] fortune,
That I would set my life[27] on any chance
To mend it or be rid on't.

MACBETH   Both of you know
Banquo was your enemy.

MURDERERS   True, my lord.

Macbeth says that Banquo is his enemy, but he cannot kill him openly. He will arrange a time and place for the Murderers to assassinate Banquo and Fleance, so that no suspicion falls upon himself.

剧情简介：麦克白说班阔是他的敌人，但他不能公然杀死他。他将安排一个时间和地点让杀手去刺杀班阔和弗利恩，这样人们不会怀疑到他身上。

Stagecraft 导演技巧

A tyrant and his thugs (暴徒)

Like all tyrants, Macbeth hires thugs and villains to do his dirty work for him. Note that Macbeth does not simply order the Murderers to kill Banquo, but gives them reasons for his orders and takes them into his confidence.

a Read the script again and identify where Macbeth seems to relate to the Murderers in ways that are:
  - friendly and confidential
  - anxious
  - threatening
  - contemptuous or dismissive (轻蔑).

b Explore ways of staging this part of the script for a modern production, taking into account the factors below and trying out some of the movements or gestures you would want the actors to use:
  - Stage space – how would the actors exploit this?
  - Lighting – how would the stage be lit to emphasise the intensity of this manipulation scene?
  - Sound effects – what music or other sounds would you use here?
  - Movement, expressions and gestures – experiment with these to characterise Macbeth and the Murderers.

Language in the play 剧中语言

Killing the killers (in pairs)

Macbeth's last two lines before he has Banquo murdered (140–1) are in the form of a rhyming couplet. His last two lines before murdering Duncan are in the same form (Act 2 Scene 1, lines 63–4).

a Write out these two sets of rhyming couplets. Why do you think Shakespeare used this device to craft Macbeth's language before the death of two significant characters?

b Imagine that Macbeth intends to kill the two Murderers after they have murdered Banquo. Write a rhyming couplet of your own, revealing Macbeth's intention to kill the killers.

---

1 distance   冲突（两个剑客之间的纷争）
2 his being   他活着
3 near'st of life   最接近生命处（即心脏）
4 barefaced   公开
5 bid my will avouch it   宣布我要做的就是对的
6 wail   悲泣
7 make love   表示热爱
8 common eye   公众视线
9 sundry weighty reasons   各种有分量的理由
10 Though our lives   哪怕我们的性命
11 plant   埋伏
12 perfect spy o'th'time   最佳窥视点
13 something from the palace   离王宫稍远的地方
14 always … clearness   千万记住，必须撇清我的嫌疑
15 rubs nor botches   失手或有纰漏
16 absence   不在了（死亡）
17 material   重要
18 Resolve yourselves apart   你们自己下去定个主意
19 straight   立即
20 abide within   待在里面
21 thy soul's flight   你灵魂的飞翔（死亡被想象成离开身体、飞入天堂或地狱的鸟）

MACBETH ACT 3 SCENE 1
麦克白

MACBETH	So is he mine, and in such bloody distance[1]	115
	That every minute of his being[2] thrusts	
	Against my near'st of life[3]; and though I could	
	With barefaced[4] power sweep him from my sight	
	And bid my will avouch it[5], yet I must not,	
	For certain friends that are both his and mine,	120
	Whose loves I may not drop, but wail[6] his fall	
	Who I myself struck down. And thence it is	
	That I to your assistance do make love[7],	
	Masking the business from the common eye[8]	
	For sundry weighty reasons[9].	
SECOND MURDERER	We shall, my lord,	125
	Perform what you command us.	
FIRST MURDERER	Though our lives[10] –	
MACBETH	Your spirits shine through you. Within this hour at most,	
	I will advise you where to plant[11] yourselves,	
	Acquaint you with the perfect spy o'th'time[12],	
	The moment on't, for't must be done tonight,	130
	And something from the palace[13]: always thought,	
	That I require a clearness[14]. And with him,	
	To leave no rubs nor botches[15] in the work,	
	Fleance, his son that keeps him company,	
	Whose absence[16] is no less material[17] to me	135
	Than is his father's, must embrace the fate	
	Of that dark hour. Resolve yourselves apart[18],	
	I'll come to you anon.	
MURDERERS	We are resolved, my lord.	
MACBETH	I'll call upon you straight[19]; abide within[20].	
	[*Exeunt Murderers*]	
	It is concluded. Banquo, thy soul's flight[21],	140
	If it find heaven, must find it out tonight. *Exit*	

Lady Macbeth is troubled. She advises Macbeth not to brood on what's done, but he is still racked by fears and insecurity. He even envies the peace of death that Duncan enjoys.

剧情简介：麦克白夫人心烦意乱。她劝麦克白不要再忧虑已经做过的事了，但麦克白仍受恐惧和不安的折磨，甚至羡慕邓肯享受死亡带来的安宁。

1 Apocalyptic dreams (in pairs)

This scene marks a change in the relationship between Macbeth and Lady Macbeth. Both are uneasy about their present position: Lady Macbeth says 'Nought's had, all's spent' and Macbeth is full of 'sorriest fancies'. However, Lady Macbeth's advice to her husband is simply to forget the events of the past because they cannot be changed – 'what's done, is done'.

a Identify some of the reasons Macbeth gives about why it is impossible for him to forget the past. Improvise a scenario in which Macbeth unburdens his mind more fully. Imagine him on a psychoanalyst's couch, telling of the terrible dreams that torment him and giving a truthful account of everything that is troubling him (lines 13–26).

b Study the photograph below. Pick out lines from this scene that could make a suitable caption.

1 Nought's ... spent   啥也没得到，费了好大劲
2 doubtful joy   疑惑不定的欢乐（矛盾修辞法）
3 sorriest fancies   悲惨的妄想（指下谋杀令）
4 without all remedy   根本无法改变
5 be without regard   不考虑
6 what's done, is done   什么事做了就做了（谚语：What is done cannot be undone.）
7 scorched   砍伤
8 close, and be herself   愈合并恢复元气
9 poor malice   斩草未除根（指谋杀邓肯）
10 let ... disjoint   让宇宙大厦垮塌
11 both the worlds suffer   两个世界（今生和来世）被摧毁
12 affliction   折磨，痛苦
13 lie / In restless ecstasy   好像躺在刑具上惴惴不安
14 fitful   一阵阵
15 sleeps well   睡得安稳（永眠）
16 Malice domestic   内战
17 foreign levy   外国军队
18 touch   伤害

Act 3 Scene 2
A room in Macbeth's palace

Enter LADY MACBETH, *and a* SERVANT

LADY MACBETH   Is Banquo gone from court?
SERVANT   Ay, madam, but returns again tonight.
LADY MACBETH   Say to the king, I would attend his leisure
For a few words.
SERVANT   Madam, I will.   *Exit*
LADY MACBETH   Nought's had, all's spent[1]
Where our desire is got without content.
'Tis safer to be that which we destroy
Than by destruction dwell in doubtful joy[2].

Enter MACBETH

How now, my lord, why do you keep alone,
Of sorriest fancies[3] your companions making,
Using those thoughts which should indeed have died
With them they think on? Things without all remedy[4]
Should be without regard[5]; what's done, is done[6].

MACBETH   We have scorched[7] the snake, not killed it;
She'll close, and be herself[8], whilst our poor malice[9]
Remains in danger of her former tooth.
But let the frame of things disjoint[10], both the worlds suffer[11],
Ere we will eat our meal in fear, and sleep
In the affliction[12] of these terrible dreams
That shake us nightly. Better be with the dead
Whom we, to gain our peace, have sent to peace,
Than on the torture of the mind to lie
In restless ecstasy[13]. Duncan is in his grave.
After life's fitful[14] fever, he sleeps well[15];
Treason has done his worst; nor steel nor poison,
Malice domestic[16], foreign levy[17], nothing
Can touch[18] him further.

Macbeth tells his wife to pay special regard to Banquo at the banquet. He speaks contemptuously of having to flatter deceitfully. He hints darkly that terrible deeds will be performed that night.

 剧情简介：麦克白让妻子在宴会上要对班阔特殊对待。他语气轻蔑地说要虚情假意奉承班阔。他模糊地暗示当晚会发生可怕的事情。

1 Statement and replies (whole class)

Stand in a circle around one student, who is going to address different people in the circle with a 'statement' from the script opposite. He or she (in role as Lady Macbeth or Macbeth) should walk up to various people in the circle to say the line and hear their response. If you are standing in the circle, you should memorise the 'reply' so that you can say it in response with your choice of intonation, emotion, volume and accompanying gestures. Try both statements below, then find other lines from the play to experiment with in this way.

- Statement: You must leave this.
  Reply: O, full of scorpions is my mind, dear wife!
- Statement: What's to be done?
  Reply: Be innocent of the knowledge, dearest chuck

Language in the play 剧中语言

Scorpions, bats, beetles and crows (in pairs)

Shakespeare uses animal imagery for sinister (阴险，不祥) and dramatic effect in lines 36–53. For example, a bat is a creature that fulfils Hecate's orders. The words 'seeling' and 'scarf' relate to falconry, where the falconer would temporarily blind the hawk so that it would remain dependent on him until it was fully trained. List the animals mentioned and describe the roles they have in the creation of a chillingly dark atmosphere in this part of the scene.

Write about it 写作练习

Close reading (by yourself)

Macbeth's language in lines 46–50 is rich and visceral in its personification (拟人) of night and day. It evokes vivid images of blood and blindness, evil and darkness, adding to the drama of the scene.

a What effect does Macbeth's strikingly poetic language have when contrasted with the sinister atmosphere created by his invocation (祈求) to evil? Write a paragraph describing the impact of Macbeth's language, using embedded quotations as you refer to the script opposite.

b In role as either Macbeth or Lady Macbeth, write about your thoughts and feelings in a secret diary at the end of this scene.

1 Sleek　使光滑
2 rugged　粗犷；满脸皱纹
3 jovial　快乐
4 remembrance　关注
5 present him eminence　抬举他，向他致敬
6 unsafe the while　此时还不安稳
7 lave　冲洗
8 vizards　面具
9 Nature's copy's not eterne　繁衍不会永恒
10 assailable　易受攻击
11 jocund　高兴
12 cloistered flight　在寺院回廊里飞旋
13 shard-born beetle　生在粪里的屎壳郎
14 yawning peal　打着哈欠（即张着大嘴）的钟
15 note　名声（也指乐曲，延续上文的比喻）
16 chuck　宝贝
17 Be … deed　事前不必知道，事后鼓掌就好
18 seeling night　封人双眼的夜晚（驯鹰时封上鹰眼使之看不见）
19 Scarf up　蒙上
20 bond　契约
21 Light thickens　天色变暗
22 makes wing　展翅飞翔
23 rooky wood　白嘴乌鸦的树林
24 hold thee still　保持镇定

LADY MACBETH	Come on. Gentle my lord,
	Sleek[1] o'er your rugged[2] looks, be bright and jovial[3]
	Among your guests tonight.
MACBETH	So shall I, love,
	And so I pray be you. Let your remembrance[4] 30
	Apply to Banquo, present him eminence[5]
	Both with eye and tongue; unsafe the while[6], that we
	Must lave[7] our honours in these flattering streams
	And make our faces vizards[8] to our hearts,
	Disguising what they are.
LADY MACBETH	You must leave this. 35
MACBETH	O, full of scorpions is my mind, dear wife!
	Thou know'st that Banquo and his Fleance lives.
LADY MACBETH	But in them Nature's copy's not eterne[9].
MACBETH	There's comfort yet, they are assailable[10];
	Then be thou jocund[11]: ere the bat hath flown 40
	His cloistered flight[12], ere to black Hecate's summons
	The shard-born beetle[13] with his drowsy hums
	Hath rung night's yawning peal[14], there shall be done
	A deed of dreadful note[15].
LADY MACBETH	What's to be done?
MACBETH	Be innocent of the knowledge, dearest chuck[16], 45
	Till thou applaud the deed[17]. Come, seeling night[18],
	Scarf up[19] the tender eye of pitiful day
	And with thy bloody and invisible hand
	Cancel and tear to pieces that great bond[20]
	Which keeps me pale. Light thickens[21], 50
	And the crow makes wing[22] to th'rooky wood[23];
	Good things of day begin to droop and drowse,
	Whiles night's black agents to their preys do rouse.
	Thou marvell'st at my words, but hold thee still[24];
	Things bad begun, make strong themselves by ill. 55
	So prithee, go with me.
	Exeunt

A third Murderer has joined the other two to await their victims. They kill Banquo, but Fleance escapes.
剧情简介：第三个杀手加入另外两个杀手，一起等待受害者。他们杀死了班阔，但弗利恩逃脱了。

Stagecraft 导演技巧

Hidden clues (in small groups)

Shakespeare's stage was quite bare and the actors didn't have time to rehearse the play in detail (see 'Macbeth in performance', pp. 174).

a Read the script opposite and look for clues that Shakespeare gives the actors for internal stage directions (information about what to do on stage). Look out also for lines that help the audience imagine what is happening on the stage. Copy the table below and fill it in, adding further examples.

Quotation	Action for actor	Imagination for audience
'But who did bid thee join with us?' (line 1)	A third actor walks on stage	
'The west yet glimmers with some streaks of day' (line 5)		It is twilight and nearly dark
'Hark, I hear horses.' (line 8)		
'A light, a light!' (line 15)		
'Stand to't.' (line 17)		

b How would you direct this murder scene for a new movie production set in your school? Think about the people you would cast, music for the score (配乐), set and props, use of camera angles and special effects.

c Write out your ideas for filming this scene, or create a storyboard. In groups, have a go at filming the section, then hold a screening session in class to review everyone's version of the scene.

1 He needs not our mistrust 我们不用怀疑他（第三个杀手）
2 offices 任务
3 To the direction just 严格遵照指令
4 spurs the lated traveller apace 迟到的旅客策马飞奔
5 timely 及时
6 The subject of our watch 我们等候的客人
7 within the note of expectation 在嘉宾的名单上
8 go about 绕路而走（马由马夫牵回）
9 Make it their walk 他们步行（马夫牵马使之凉快下来，班阔和弗利恩步行大概一英里到城堡）
10 Stand to't 准备好
11 treachery 叛逆
12 slave 卑鄙小人
13 best half of our affair 我们的一大半任务

Act 3 Scene 3
A lonely place near Forres

Enter three MURDERERS

FIRST MURDERER But who did bid thee join with us?
THIRD MURDERER Macbeth.
SECOND MURDERER He needs not our mistrust[1], since he delivers
Our offices[2] and what we have to do
To the direction just[3].
FIRST MURDERER [*To Third Murderer*] Then stand with us.
The west yet glimmers with some streaks of day; 5
Now spurs the lated traveller apace[4]
To gain the timely[5] inn, and near approaches
The subject of our watch[6].
THIRD MURDERER Hark, I hear horses.
BANQUO (*Within*) Give us a light there, ho!
SECOND MURDERER Then 'tis he; the rest
That are within the note of expectation[7] 10
Already are i'th'court.
FIRST MURDERER His horses go about[8].
THIRD MURDERER Almost a mile; but he does usually,
So all men do, from hence to th'palace gate
Make it their walk[9].

Enter BANQUO *and* FLEANCE, *with a torch*

SECOND MURDERER A light, a light! 15
THIRD MURDERER 'Tis he.
FIRST MURDERER Stand to't[10].
BANQUO It will be rain tonight.
FIRST MURDERER Let it come down.
[*The Murderers attack. First Murderer strikes out the light*]
BANQUO O, treachery[11]!
Fly, good Fleance, fly, fly, fly! 20
Thou mayst revenge – O slave[12]! [*Dies. Fleance escapes*]
THIRD MURDERER Who did strike out the light?
FIRST MURDERER Was't not the way?
THIRD MURDERER There's but one down; the son is fled.
SECOND MURDERER We have lost best half of our affair[13].
FIRST MURDERER Well, let's away, and say how much is done. 25
Exeunt[, *with Banquo's body*]

Macbeth welcomes his guests to the banquet and mixes with them. The First Murderer reports Banquo's death. The news of Fleance's escape disturbs Macbeth and renews his fears.

 剧情简介：麦克白欢迎来参加宴会的宾客，与他们觥筹交错。杀手甲报告班阔死了，弗利恩逃跑的消息让麦克白心烦意乱，他又开始害怕起来。

Themes 主题分析
The humble host? (in pairs)

False and deceptive behaviour recurs throughout the play, contributing to the theme of appearance and reality.

a How does Macbeth create the appearance of peace and harmony at the beginning of this scene? How is this undercut by the presence of the Murderers, who have secret instructions from the king?

b Macbeth avoids naming the deed (murder). Listen to the difference it makes when you read his lines to the Murderer and substitute 'kill' or 'murder' for Macbeth's evasive language.

c List four euphemisms for murder that Macbeth uses in his conversation with the Murderer (lines 15–28). Describe how they relate to the theme of appearance and reality.

1 Stark contrasts (鲜明对比) (in pairs or small groups)

Macbeth uses stark contrasts to express his disappointment that Fleance has escaped (lines 21–5). Read these lines and work with a partner or a group to create a tableau of each of the two images Macbeth describes. Switch from one to the other to show the difference between appearance and reality – and to demonstrate Macbeth's fears for the future – as you present your tableaux to the class.

Stagecraft 导演技巧
'Is he dispatched?'

Macbeth's place at the banqueting table is in the middle among his guests. He plans to 'drink a measure / The table round', but first leaves to talk to the Murderers.

Imagine you are an audience member at a performance that has just played this scene well, allowing the audience to hear the conversation between Macbeth and the Murderer, but not the guests at the banquet. How was this conversation staged? What effect might this scene have on an audience if staged the way you imagine it?

1 your own degrees 你们各自的级别（知道该坐哪儿）
2 society 众爱卿
3 keeps her state 坐在她的宝座（常带华盖）上
4 encounter thee 向你致意（可能是在敬酒）
5 Be large in mirth 尽情欢乐，开怀畅饮
6 drink … round 环席敬一轮酒 (measure: 祝酒，敬酒)
7 better … within （血）在你体外比在班阔体内好
8 nonpareil 无与伦比
9 scaped = escaped
10 fit 犯病
11 founded 坚固
12 broad and general 自由自在
13 casing 周围
14 cabined, cribbed, confined 被幽禁，被拘束，被限制
15 saucy 放肆，无礼
16 safe 安稳（委婉语）
17 ditch 沟
18 trenchèd 裂开
19 The least 最小的一个

Act 3 Scene 4
The banqueting hall at Forres

Banquet prepared. Two thrones are placed on stage. Enter MACBETH *as King,* LADY MACBETH *as Queen,* ROSS, LENNOX, LORDS, *and attendants. Lady Macbeth sits*

MACBETH You know your own degrees[1], sit down; at first and last, the hearty welcome.

[*The Lords sit*]

LORDS Thanks to your majesty.

MACBETH Our self will mingle with society[2] and play the humble host; our hostess keeps her state[3], but in best time we will require her welcome.

LADY MACBETH Pronounce it for me, sir, to all our friends, for my heart speaks, they are welcome.

Enter FIRST MURDERER

MACBETH See, they encounter thee[4] with their hearts' thanks.
Both sides are even; here I'll sit i'th'midst.
Be large in mirth[5], anon we'll drink a measure
The table round[6]. [*To First Murderer*] There's blood upon thy face.

FIRST MURDERER 'Tis Banquo's then.

MACBETH 'Tis better thee without, than he within[7].
Is he dispatched?

FIRST MURDERER My lord, his throat is cut; that I did for him.

MACBETH Thou art the best o'th'cut-throats,
Yet he's good that did the like for Fleance;
If thou didst it, thou art the nonpareil[8].

FIRST MURDERER Most royal sir, Fleance is scaped[9].

MACBETH Then comes my fit[10] again: I had else been perfect;
Whole as the marble, founded[11] as the rock,
As broad and general[12] as the casing[13] air:
But now I am cabined, cribbed, confined[14], bound in
To saucy[15] doubts and fears. But Banquo's safe[16]?

FIRST MURDERER Ay, my good lord: safe in a ditch[17] he bides,
With twenty trenchèd[18] gashes on his head,
The least[19] a death to nature.

Macbeth consoles himself that Fleance is too young to do harm yet. Lady Macbeth bids him welcome his guests. The sight of Banquo's Ghost unnerves Macbeth. Lady Macbeth attempts to calm the Lords.

剧情简介：麦克白安慰自己说弗利恩还太年轻，不会对他造成伤害。麦克白夫人让他招呼宾客。班阔的鬼魂出现在麦克白眼前，让他心慌意乱。麦克白夫人试图让众臣镇静。

Stagecraft 导演技巧

Ghost or no ghost? (in pairs)

Every time *Macbeth* is performed, the director must decide whether or not to bring on a Ghost that the audience can see, or whether to leave it to the audience's imagination. On Shakespeare's stage, an actor was made up with animal blood and possibly with flour to give him a deathly white complexion. With a partner, decide how you would stage the scene in a theatre production. Would your Ghost be visible or invisible? Why? Explain your decision to the class, then take a vote.

Write about it 写作练习

Dramatic irony

The appearance of Banquo's Ghost on stage gives much opportunity for dramatic irony, and there are several points where the audience is more aware of what is happening than the characters are.

a Look at the following quotations from the script and give at least two versions of what the statement might mean:
  - Macbeth: 'Sweet remembrancer!' (line 37)
  - Macbeth: 'Here had we now our country's honour roofed, / Were the graced person of our Banquo present' (lines 40–1)
  - Ross: 'His absence, sir, / Lays blame upon his promise' (lines 43–4)
  - Macbeth: 'Which of you have done this?' (line 49). Remember, Macbeth is not aware that no one else can see the Ghost. His question assumes that this is a practical joke.

b Write three or four paragraphs describing how the Ghost adds to the horror and intrigue in this scene, as well as contributing to its dramatic irony.

1 grown serpent 长成的大蛇（指班阔）
2 worm 幼虫（指弗利恩，把他比作一条迟早会长成毒蛇的小虫子）
3 venom 毒液
4 breed 产生
5 hear ourselves 一起商量
6 give the cheer 祝酒
7 the feast … a-making 东道主在宴会上若不时时招呼客人（vouched），那宴会就成了饭铺了
8 To … home 单纯吃饭还是在家吃最好
9 From thence 离开家
10 sauce to meat is ceremony 待客礼仪是饭食的调味品
11 remembrancer 提醒者
12 wait on 伺候
13 honour 显贵，贵族
14 roofed 相聚一堂
15 Here … present = Here we would now have all our country's nobility under this roof if the favoured person of our Banquo were present
16 Who … mischance 我希望他的缺席是因为不近人情而不是因为遭遇不测
17 His absence … promise 他没有出席，应该怪他言而无信
18 grace 赏光，赏脸
19 The table's full 餐桌坐满了（麦克白找不到空座位）
20 moves 使不安（麦克白对鬼的反应）
21 gory locks 沾血的头发
22 keep seat 请继续坐着
23 upon a thought 一小会儿（谚语：as swift as thought）
24 note him 盯着他看
25 passion 犯病；情绪爆发

MACBETH ACT 3 SCENE 4
麦克白

MACBETH   Thanks for that.
There the grown serpent[1] lies; the worm[2] that's fled
Hath nature that in time will venom[3] breed[4],   30
No teeth for th'present. Get thee gone; tomorrow
We'll hear ourselves[5] again.
                                Exit [First] Murderer
LADY MACBETH   My royal lord,
You do not give the cheer[6]; the feast is sold
That is not often vouched while 'tis a-making[7],
'Tis given with welcome. To feed were best at home[8]:   35
From thence[9], the sauce to meat is ceremony[10],
Meeting were bare without it.

            Enter the Ghost of Banquo and sits in Macbeth's place

MACBETH   Sweet remembrancer[11]!
Now good digestion wait on[12] appetite,
And health on both.
LENNOX   May't please your highness, sit.
MACBETH   Here had we now our country's honour[13] roofed[14],   40
Were the graced person of our Banquo present[15],
Who may I rather challenge for unkindness
Than pity for mischance[16].
ROSS   His absence, sir,
Lays blame upon his promise[17]. Please't your highness
To grace[18] us with your royal company?   45
MACBETH   The table's full[19].
LENNOX   Here is a place reserved, sir.
MACBETH   Where?
LENNOX   Here, my good lord. What is't that moves[20] your highness?
MACBETH   Which of you have done this?
LORDS   What, my good lord?
MACBETH   Thou canst not say I did it; never shake   50
Thy gory locks[21] at me!
ROSS   Gentlemen, rise, his highness is not well.
                        [Lady Macbeth joins the Lords]
LADY MACBETH   Sit, worthy friends. My lord is often thus,
And hath been from his youth. Pray you, keep seat[22].
The fit is momentary; upon a thought[23]   55
He will again be well. If much you note him[24]
You shall offend him and extend his passion[25].
Feed, and regard him not. [*To Macbeth*] Are you a man?

83

Lady Macbeth rebukes Macbeth for his display of fear. The Ghost leaves. Macbeth broods on how the dead return. He recovers his composure, reassures the thanes and proposes a toast. The Ghost re-enters.

剧情简介：麦克白夫人责怪麦克白面露恐惧。鬼魂离开。麦克白焦虑不安，纳闷死人怎么会回来。他恢复镇定，打消众子爵的顾虑，向大家敬酒。鬼魂再次上场。

Characters 人物分析
'O proper stuff!'

Lady Macbeth ridicules and insults Macbeth in an attempt to get him to come to his senses. Practise reading lines 60–8 with as much disgust as possible. Take note of her short sentences, rhetorical question and references to horror stories told by old women. What do you think is the most devastating aspect of her outburst? What effect do you think it has on Macbeth?

Stagecraft 导演技巧
Staging the banquet (in pairs)

How would you advise the actors in this scene? Imagine you are a director and you want to explore ways of using stage space, gesture, pitch and pace. Create a stage plan on A3 paper and include a page of written instructions to the actors. Remember to look at the clues Shakespeare has given in the internal stage directions (especially lines 67, 70 and 88). Give particular attention to the following:

- the secret conversation between Lady Macbeth and Macbeth (lines 59–73)
- the Ghost's exit (line 73)
- Macbeth's horror (expressed either to himself or to Lady Macbeth in lines 75–83)
- Macbeth's awareness of his guests and their reactions (remember that no one else can see the Ghost)
- the re-entry of the Ghost just as Macbeth proposes the toast he promised at the beginning of the scene (line 88)

Swap and compare your stage plan and instructions with another pair, then evaluate the most effective way of staging this scene.

1 proper stuff　好一派胡言
2 very painting　真实图像
3 air-drawn dagger　凭空想象的匕首
4 Led you to Duncan　指引您到了邓肯跟前（麦克白夫人嘲笑丈夫杀害邓肯之前的幻象）
5 flaws　冲动，情绪爆发
6 Impostors to　与……相比的冒牌货
7 woman's … fire　主妇在冬天炉火边讲的故事
8 Authorised by her grandam　由她祖母证实（即从她祖母那儿听来的）
9 Shame itself!　真丢人！
10 Behold　看哪
11 lo = look
12 charnel-houses　地下墓室
13 monuments　坟墓
14 maws of kites　鸢的嗉子
15 unmanned　受了阉割；没有胆量
16 folly　愚蠢
17 If I stand here　千真万确（谚语：as true as I stand here）
18 Fie, for shame　呸，真丢人
19 Ere … weal　在人道的法律将邪恶涤荡出文明国家之前
20 mortal　致命
21 crowns　头顶（也指班阔的后世子孙将戴在头上的王冠）
22 lack　需要
23 muse　感到惊奇
24 infirmity　弱点
25 love and health to all　祝大家互爱、健康（麦克白如在本场开头保证的那样向大家祝酒）

MACBETH	Ay, and a bold one, that dare look on that	
	Which might appal the devil.	
LADY MACBETH	O proper stuff[1]!	60
	This is the very painting[2] of your fear;	
	This is the air-drawn dagger[3] which you said	
	Led you to Duncan[4]. O, these flaws[5] and starts,	
	Impostors to[6] true fear, would well become	
	A woman's story at a winter's fire[7]	65
	Authorised by her grandam[8]. Shame itself![9]	
	Why do you make such faces? When all's done	
	You look but on a stool.	
MACBETH	Prithee, see there! Behold[10], look, lo[11]! How say you?	
	[*To Ghost*] Why, what care I? If thou canst nod, speak too.	70
	If charnel-houses[12] and our graves must send	
	Those that we bury back, our monuments[13]	
	Shall be the maws of kites[14].	

[*Exit Ghost of Banquo*]

LADY MACBETH	What, quite unmanned[15] in folly[16]?	
MACBETH	If I stand here[17], I saw him.	
LADY MACBETH	Fie, for shame[18].	
MACBETH	Blood hath been shed ere now, i'th'olden time,	75
	Ere humane statute purged the gentle weal[19];	
	Ay, and since too, murders have been performed	
	Too terrible for the ear. The time has been	
	That when the brains were out, the man would die,	
	And there an end. But now they rise again	80
	With twenty mortal[20] murders on their crowns[21]	
	And push us from our stools. This is more strange	
	Than such a murder is.	
LADY MACBETH	My worthy lord,	
	Your noble friends do lack[22] you.	
MACBETH	I do forget –	
	Do not muse[23] at me, my most worthy friends.	85
	I have a strange infirmity[24] which is nothing	
	To those that know me. Come, love and health to all[25],	
	Then I'll sit down. Give me some wine; fill full!	

Enter Ghost [*of Banquo*]

I drink to th'general joy o'th'whole table,

Macbeth, his composure recovered, proposes a toast to Banquo and the guests. On seeing the Ghost again, he bursts into violent language, commanding him away. Lady Macbeth orders the Lords to leave.

剧情简介：麦克白恢复了镇定，向班阔和众宾客祝酒。他再次看见了鬼魂的时候，突然大骂起来，命令鬼魂走开。麦克白夫人命众臣退席。

Characters 人物分析
A state dinner to remember

The guests are bewildered and the banquet descends into chaos as Macbeth reacts in horror to the presence of the Ghost.

a Describe how the Ghost enters and behaves during Macbeth's violent outbursts (lines 89–107).

b What does Lady Macbeth make of these events? In some productions she starts to drink heavily during the banquet, and becomes increasingly drunk and exhausted by the end of the scene. Other productions show her directing operations and holding everything together throughout a disastrous dinner. How would you convey the stress she might feel as a result of Duncan's murder and Macbeth's strange behaviour?

c Step into role as Lady Macbeth and imagine what she would write in her secret diary at the end of this scene. Describe what she saw and did at the banquet. How does this make her feel and what is she thinking now?

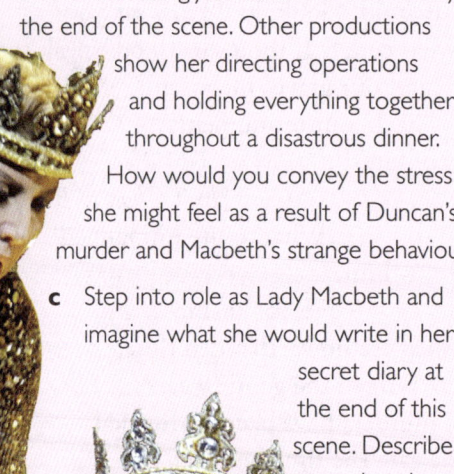

1 him we thirst 我们渴望他（班阔）
2 Our duties and the pledge 向我们的职责和誓言致敬（前面省略了to）
3 Avaunt 滚开
4 marrowless 缺少骨髓（没有生命力）
5 no speculation 没有视力
6 peers 众爱卿
7 a thing of custom 司空见惯的事
8 rugged 粗野
9 arm'd rhinoceros （以厚皮和尖角）武装起来的犀牛
10 Hyrcan tiger 赫卡虎（又称里海虎 [Caspian tiger]，栖息于里海东南的赫卡尼亚 [Hyrcania] 地区，现已灭绝）
11 Take any shape but that 随你以什么样子出现，只是别那样（以班阔的鬼魂出现）
12 dare me to the desert 在沙漠里向我挑战
13 If … girl 假如我发抖，就把我当成小姑娘的玩偶
14 Hence 走开
15 admired 令人诧异
16 overcome 让人吃惊
17 make … owe 使我不像平常的自己
18 ruby 红润
19 blanched 变得苍白
20 Question 提问
21 enrages 激怒
22 Stand not upon 不必考虑
23 order 等级次序

	And to our dear friend Banquo, whom we miss.		90
	Would he were here! To all, and him we thirst[1],		
	And all to all.		
LORDS	Our duties and the pledge[2].		
MACBETH	Avaunt[3] and quit my sight! Let the earth hide thee!		
	Thy bones are marrowless[4], thy blood is cold;		
	Thou hast no speculation[5] in those eyes		95
	Which thou dost glare with.		
LADY MACBETH	Think of this, good peers[6],		
	But as a thing of custom[7]. 'Tis no other,		
	Only it spoils the pleasure of the time.		
MACBETH	What man dare, I dare;		
	Approach thou like the rugged[8] Russian bear,		100
	The armed rhinoceros[9], or th'Hyrcan tiger[10],		
	Take any shape but that[11], and my firm nerves		
	Shall never tremble. Or be alive again,		
	And dare me to the desert[12] with thy sword;		
	If trembling I inhabit then, protest me		105
	The baby of a girl[13]. Hence[14] horrible shadow,		
	Unreal mock'ry hence.		

[*Exit Ghost of Banquo*]

	Why so, being gone,		
	I am a man again. – Pray you, sit still.		
LADY MACBETH	You have displaced the mirth, broke the good meeting		
	With most admired[15] disorder.		
MACBETH	Can such things be,		110
	And overcome[16] us like a summer's cloud,		
	Without our special wonder? You make me strange		
	Even to the disposition that I owe[17],		
	When now I think you can behold such sights		
	And keep the natural ruby[18] of your cheeks,		115
	When mine is blanched[19] with fear.		
ROSS	What sights, my lord?		
LADY MACBETH	I pray you speak not; he grows worse and worse.		
	Question[20] enrages[21] him. At once, good night.		
	Stand not upon[22] the order[23] of your going,		
	But go at once.		

The Lords leave. Macbeth broods on murder and unnaturalness. He vows to visit the Witches to know his future, swearing that from now on there is no turning back. He will kill anyone standing in his way.

 剧情简介：众臣退席。麦克白因谋杀和反常现象忧虑不安，立誓要去拜访女巫，以了解自己的未来，发誓从现在起做事绝不回头。他会杀掉任何挡住他去路的人。

Themes 主题分析

Evil and blood (by yourself)

After the disturbed action of the banquet, the final episode of the scene is usually played slowly in a still and eerie (神秘兮兮) atmosphere. Macbeth and his wife are left alone together and Macbeth seems to enter a mysterious, personal world of evil and renewed energy.

In role as a psychologist, write an analysis of either Macbeth or Lady Macbeth. Remember to use quotations from the script opposite (especially those that refer to blood as a symbol of guilt or addiction to evil). Refer also to the impact of sleep deprivation and guilt, and the allure of evil for the characters at this point in the play (lines 122–38).

1 'O, full of scorpions' (in tens)

From the first act, Lady Macbeth has influenced her husband by challenging him and manipulating him to murder Duncan and take the throne. During Act 3, we see the impact of the shame that takes hold of Macbeth after he has committed the murder. He tells his wife of his guilt and the strange dreams that haunt him.

Allocate everyone one of the lines below, taken from the play up to this point. Use the following activity to explore Macbeth's mental state at the end of Act 3.

- 'Are you a man?' (Act 3 Scene 4, line 58)
- 'Infirm of purpose!' (Act 2 Scene 2, line 55)
- 'Was the hope drunk / Wherein you dressed yourself?' (Act 1 Scene 7, lines 35–6)
- 'Art thou afeard / To be the same in thine own act and valour, / As thou art in desire?' (Act 1 Scene 7, lines 39–41)
- 'From this time, / Such I account thy love.' (Act 1 Scene 7, lines 38–9)
- 'My hands are of your colour, but I shame / To wear a heart so white.' (Act 2 Scene 2, lines 67–8)
- 'Be not lost / So poorly in your thoughts.' (Act 2 Scene 2, lines 74–5)
- 'This is the very painting of your fear' (Act 3 Scene 4, line 61)
- 'What, quite unmanned in folly?' (Act 3 Scene 4, line 73)
- 'Shame itself! / Why do you make such faces?' (Act 3 Scene 4, lines 66–7)

Take turns being Macbeth and stand in the middle of the circle as everyone says their lines aggressively, scornfully, insultingly and with force. Feed back to the class your experience of being Macbeth – how did it feel to face such insults and abuse? Afterwards, discuss whether Lady Macbeth's advice to get more sleep is either perfectly acceptable or totally inadequate.

1 Augures, and understood relations　预言和因果关系
2 maggot-pies, and choughs　喜鹊和乌鸦
3 secret'st man of blood　隐藏最深的杀手
4 What is the night?　夜里什么时辰了？
5 at odds with　与……争执
6 How sayst thou that　你怎么看……
7 denies his person　拒绝出席
8 great bidding　正式邀请
9 send　派人
10 by the way　碰巧，偶然
11 them　（指苏格兰贵族）
12 keep a servant feed　安插了一个我收买的用人（feed是fee的过去分词形式）
13 will = will go
14 betimes　及早
15 bent　一心想
16 worst means　最恶毒的方法
17 in … hand　想到的就要做到
18 acted … scanned　不用反复斟酌，立即动手
19 initiate　生手
20 wants hard use　缺少历练
21 young in deed　行动上青涩

LENNOX	Good night, and better health	120
	Attend his majesty.	
LADY MACBETH	A kind good night to all.	

[Exeunt] Lords [and Attendants]

MACBETH   It will have blood they say: blood will have blood.
Stones have been known to move and trees to speak.
Augures, and understood relations[1], have
By maggot-pies, and choughs[2], and rooks brought forth   125
The secret'st man of blood[3]. What is the night?[4]

LADY MACBETH   Almost at odds with[5] morning, which is which.

MACBETH   How sayst thou that[6] Macduff denies his person[7]
At our great bidding[8]?

LADY MACBETH   Did you send[9] to him, sir?

MACBETH   I hear it by the way[10], but I will send.   130
There's not a one of them[11] but in his house
I keep a servant feed[12]. I will[13] tomorrow –
And betimes[14] I will – to the weïrd sisters.
More shall they speak. For now I am bent[15] to know
By the worst means[16], the worst; for mine own good,   135
All causes shall give way. I am in blood
Stepped in so far that should I wade no more,
Returning were as tedious as go o'er.
Strange things I have in head that will to hand[17],
Which must be acted ere they may be scanned[18].   140

LADY MACBETH   You lack the season of all natures, sleep.

MACBETH   Come, we'll to sleep. My strange and self-abuse
Is the initiate[19] fear that wants hard use[20];
We are yet but young in deed[21].

Exeunt

Hecate rebukes the Witches for speaking to Macbeth without involving her. She instructs them to meet her at the pit of Acheron to tell Macbeth of his destiny. She promises to use magic to ruin the over-confident Macbeth.

剧情简介：女魔赫柯媂斥责三女巫没有让她参与就同麦克白交谈。她吩咐她们在地狱里愁苦河的洼地见她，好告诉麦克白他的命运如何。她保证用魔法毁掉过于自信的麦克白。

1 Is it by Shakespeare? (in pairs)

Scene 5 links the previous scene, in which Macbeth decides to visit the Witches, with the opening of Act 4, when he meets them. But there have been many arguments about whether Shakespeare himself wrote the scene. It is generally accepted that another playwright, Thomas Middleton, wrote this scene, as well as some of the Witches' songs in Act 4. The scene opposite has a different rhythmic quality from the rest of the play. It also includes an extra witch, who vanishes dramatically. (The 'foggy cloud' in line 35 may have allowed Hecate a spectacular flying exit.)

In role as director, discuss with a partner (your producer) the reasons for including this scene in a production at your school. Think about how you would cut it down a little, then type out the edited speech with instructions for your actors.

2 Find the lines

Identify the sections in lines 2–35 that match the following parts of Hecate's meaning:

- reasons for anger
- self-centred Macbeth
- meet tomorrow with spells
- I'm off to collect moon-vapour for magic to ruin Macbeth
- Macbeth's future
- my spirit calls.

Language in the play 剧中语言

Trochaic (扬抑，即前音节重，后音节轻) and **iambic** (抑扬，即前音节轻，后音节重) **rhythm (in pairs)**

Earlier in the play, the Witches' lines had a distinct **trochaic** rhythm:

Fair is foul and foul is fair,
Hover through the fog and filthy air.

In this scene, Hecate's lines have an **iambic** rhythm:

And I the mistress of your charms,
The close contriver of all harms,

Can you hear the difference between the rhythms in these lines? Describe in your own words the difference between trochaic and iambic rhythm (see 'Verse and prose', p. 172). How is this scene as a whole different to the previous scenes that the Witches appear in? Research these rhythms further by finding extracts from other famous texts and describing the impact of the rhythm in each example.

---

1 angerly 生气，愤怒
2 beldams 老妖婆
3 Saucy 放肆
4 traffic 交往
5 close contriver 秘密发明者
6 bear my part 让我参加
7 wayward 刚愎，任性
8 Spiteful 满怀恶意
9 Loves for his own ends 为了他个人目的（关心魔法和预言）
10 pit 低洼处
11 Acheron 阿刻戎河（希腊神话里的地狱之河，又称愁苦河 [river of woe]）
12 vessels 器皿
13 spells 符咒
14 spend 花（时间）
15 dismal 邪恶，阴险
16 business 工作
17 vap'rous drop 露珠
18 profound 魔力高深
19 sleights 手法，技巧
20 artificial sprites 虚幻的精灵
21 illusion 错觉，幻觉
22 spurn 摒弃，唾弃
23 bear … fear 把自己的希望凌驾于智慧、美德和恐惧之上
24 security 盲目自信

Act 3 Scene 5
A desolate place

Thunder. Enter the three WITCHES, *meeting* HECATE

FIRST WITCH   Why how now, Hecate, you look angerly[1]?
HECATE   Have I not reason, beldams[2], as you are,
Saucy[3] and over-bold? How did you dare
To trade and traffic[4] with Macbeth
In riddles and affairs of death?   5
And I the mistress of your charms,
The close contriver[5] of all harms,
Was never called to bear my part[6]
Or show the glory of our art?
And which is worse, all you have done   10
Hath been but for a wayward[7] son,
Spiteful[8] and wrathful, who, as others do,
Loves for his own ends[9], not for you.
But make amends now. Get you gone,
And at the pit[10] of Acheron[11]   15
Meet me i'th'morning. Thither he
Will come to know his destiny.
Your vessels[12] and your spells[13] provide,
Your charms and every thing beside.
I am for th'air. This night I'll spend[14]   20
Unto a dismal[15] and a fatal end.
Great business[16] must be wrought ere noon.
Upon the corner of the moon
There hangs a vap'rous drop[17] profound[18];
I'll catch it ere it come to ground;   25
And that distilled by magic sleights[19],
Shall raise such artificial sprites[20]
As by the strength of their illusion[21]
Shall draw him on to his confusion.
He shall spurn[22] fate, scorn death, and bear   30
His hopes 'bove wisdom, grace, and fear[23].
And you all know, security[24]
Is mortals' chiefest enemy.

Lennox comments guardedly and ironically on Macbeth's guilt as he recounts the killing of Duncan, Banquo and the grooms. He hints at Macbeth's murderous intentions towards Malcolm, Donaldbain and Fleance.

剧情简介：伦诺克斯在讲述邓肯、班阔和马夫被杀时，谨慎而嘲讽地表示这些都应归罪于麦克白。他暗示麦克白有意暗杀马尔肯、道讷尔本和弗利恩。

1 Tyranny and dictatorship (in pairs)

Under a dictatorship, everyone must watch their language. It is dangerous to voice your thoughts openly. Even though the script opposite is more like a monologue (独白) than a dialogue, it marks a turning point as the formerly frightened Scots begin to speak out.

Turn Lennox's lines 1–24 into a conversation by speaking small sections in turn and experimenting with using:

- hushed voices
- fearful gestures
- a guarded and suspicious manner
- long, pregnant pauses (意味深长的停顿)
- monosyllables (单音节) for emphasis or double meaning (see line 7)
- marked statement of 'official' perspectives (see line 6)
- insinuating (暗示的) or suggestive gestures.

How would you advise an actor to speak Lennox's lines to show he is on his guard and afraid to speak the truth plainly? What actions might Lennox and his listener use to express this?

2 Dramatic grammar (by yourself)

Read Lennox's lines opposite by yourself as you walk around the room. Pay particular attention to the grammar by changing direction as you walk:

- At each full stop make a full 'about-turn' (180 degrees).
- At each comma make a half turn (90 degrees to your right or left).
- Think of a gesture to make at every question mark (such as stamping your foot or clicking your fingers).

Think about your feelings as you enhance the words with these actions. How might the grammatical structure of the script reflect the character's feelings and experiences?

1	but hit your thoughts　与您的想法不谋而合
2	only I say　我只是说
3	strangely borne　处理得蹊跷
4	pitied of　受到……哀悼
5	right-valiant　非常英勇
6	too late　太晚（在夜里）
7	want the thought　不觉得，不认为
8	fact　罪恶行径
9	grieve　使难过
10	pious　尽职尽责
11	delinquents　罪犯
12	thralls　奴才
13	under his key　被他关押起来
14	an't = if it
15	broad words　坦诚地讲
16	Where he bestows himself?　他现在身居何处？

Write about it 写作练习

Living under the rule of a murderer

Write a journalist's report describing what life is like for the people of Scotland under the rule of a murderous king. Why does Shakespeare want to provide this perspective on Macbeth's rule?

Music, and a song[, 'Come away, come away', within]

Hark, I am called: my little spirit, see,
Sits in a foggy cloud, and stays for me. [*Exit*] 35

FIRST WITCH Come, let's make haste; she'll soon be back again.

Exeunt

Act 3 Scene 6
The castle of Lennox

Enter LENNOX *and another* LORD

LENNOX My former speeches have but hit your thoughts[1]
Which can interpret further; only I say[2]
Things have been strangely borne[3]. The gracious Duncan
Was pitied of[4] Macbeth; marry, he was dead.
And the right-valiant[5] Banquo walked too late[6], 5
Whom you may say, if't please you, Fleance killed,
For Fleance fled. Men must not walk too late.
Who cannot want the thought[7] how monstrous
It was for Malcolm and for Donaldbain
To kill their gracious father? Damnèd fact[8], 10
How it did grieve[9] Macbeth! Did he not straight
In pious[10] rage the two delinquents[11] tear,
That were the slaves of drink and thralls[12] of sleep?
Was not that nobly done? Ay, and wisely too,
For 'twould have angered any heart alive 15
To hear the men deny't. So that I say,
He has borne all things well, and I do think
That had he Duncan's sons under his key[13] –
As, an't[14] please heaven, he shall not – they should find
What 'twere to kill a father. So should Fleance. 20
But peace, for from broad words[15], and 'cause he failed
His presence at the tyrant's feast, I hear
Macduff lives in disgrace. Sir, can you tell
Where he bestows himself[16]?

The unnamed Lord tells of Malcolm's warm welcome in England, and of Macduff's plea to King Edward for an army to overthrow Macbeth's tyranny. He reports Macduff's refusal to visit Macbeth.

剧情简介：一位无名大臣透露马尔肯在英格兰受到热情欢迎，还说麦克达恩求爱德华王派兵推翻麦克白的暴政。他告知大家麦克达拒绝觐见麦克白。

1 Who is the unnamed Lord? (in small groups)

The unnamed Lord has a similar dramatic function to the Old Man of Act 2 Scene 4, who represented the ordinary people of Scotland. In this scene, the Lord has words of hope for the eventual peace and prosperity of Scotland.

Identify some of these positive words in lines 24–39. Prepare a tableau contrasting the characters of the Old Man and the unnamed Lord, thinking in terms of 'present Scotland' and 'future Scotland' (for example, starving in the present versus feasting in the future, sleeplessness versus tranquil [安静] sleep).

2 'The cloudy messenger' (in pairs)

In several of Shakespeare's plays, the messenger that brings bad news gets into trouble merely for reporting it. Macbeth's 'cloudy messenger' of lines 41–4 is obviously resentful of Macduff's refusal to return to Scotland. It will hinder ('clog') the messenger's career prospects.

Imagine what the messenger travelling back to Macbeth with the bad news of Macduff's answer might say. With a partner, compose the script for the scene in which he tells Macbeth the truth, while hoping to avoid punishment. Experiment with ways of performing your script.

Themes 主题分析

Internal violence (by yourself)

In Act 1 Scene 2, there are vivid images of violence from the battles fought by the rulers of Scotland to defend the country from Norwegian enemies. In this scene, however, there is evidence of violence and tyranny unleashed (发动) against the citizens of Scotland as a result of the evil that has invaded the country through Macbeth's behaviour. Create a table or a Venn diagram (文氏图) that compares the imagery, language and distress of Scotland in these scenes. For example, in Act 1 Scene 2, the battle is described with reference to 'two spent swimmers that do cling together / And choke their art', while in Act 3 Scene 6, Scotland is described as a 'suffering country / Under a hand accursed'.

1 son of Duncan （指马尔肯）
2 holds the due of birth　窃取了他生来的权利（指继承王位的权利）
3 Edward　（指忏悔者爱德华 [Edward the Confessor]，英格兰国王，1042年—1066年在位）
4 with … respect　仍以礼相待，不因他时运不济而薄待半分（malevolence：恶意，怨恨）
5 pray　请求
6 warlike　骁勇
7 him above　（指上帝）
8 ratify　恩准
9 Do faithful homage　忠诚拥戴
10 pine　渴望
11 this report　（对马尔肯在英国的状况的描述）
12 exasperate their king　激怒了他们的国王（麦克白）
13 attempt of war　进攻，开战
14 absolute　坚决
15 'Sir, not I'　（这是麦克达说的话）
16 cloudy　面带愠怒
17 hums　嘟囔
18 rue the time　后悔这件事
19 clogs　添堵
20 to a caution　小心提防
21 accursed　受诅咒

LORD	The son of Duncan[1],	
	From whom this tyrant holds the due of birth[2],	25
	Lives in the English court and is received	
	Of the most pious Edward[3] with such grace,	
	That the malevolence of fortune nothing	
	Takes from his high respect[4]. Thither Macduff	
	Is gone to pray[5] the holy king upon his aid	30
	To wake Northumberland and warlike[6] Siward,	
	That by the help of these, with him above[7]	
	To ratify[8] the work, we may again	
	Give to our tables meat, sleep to our nights,	
	Free from our feasts and banquets bloody knives,	35
	Do faithful homage[9] and receive free honours,	
	All which we pine[10] for now. And this report[11]	
	Hath so exasperate their king[12] that he	
	Prepares for some attempt of war[13].	
LENNOX	Sent he to Macduff?	40
LORD	He did. And with an absolute[14], 'Sir, not I'[15],	
	The cloudy[16] messenger turns me his back	
	And hums[17], as who should say, 'You'll rue the time[18]	
	That clogs[19] me with this answer.'	
LENNOX	And that well might	
	Advise him to a caution[20] t'hold what distance	45
	His wisdom can provide. Some holy angel	
	Fly to the court of England and unfold	
	His message ere he come, that a swift blessing	
	May soon return to this our suffering country	
	Under a hand accursed[21].	
LORD	I'll send my prayers with him.	50
	Exeunt	

MACBETH
麦克白

Looking back at Act 3 第3幕回顾
Activities for groups or individuals

1 Silent witnesses

Act 3 opens shortly after Macbeth has been crowned at Scone as High King (高王，苏格兰诸王之一) of Scotland, and it includes the dramatic invasion of a stately banquet by the Ghost of Banquo. Step into role as a thane at either event. Invent your thane's title and write *either* an account of the unstaged coronation as seen by a participant *or* an account of the banquet as the thanes are abruptly dismissed in Scene 4. You might like to write this account in your journal or in a letter to a trusted friend.

2 Thematic focus

Look back at the Themes boxes on the left-hand pages, then create a mind map of the themes that have been developed in Act 3. Draw a chart to show how they relate to each other, and support your chart with quotations from the play. Remember that the following themes are interrelated in the play: the relationship between appearance and reality; the manifestation of evil, and honour and loyalty; how selfishness and ambition sit with kingship and honour.

Now present a case to the rest of the class: which are the most important combinations of themes? Why? How have the events of this act contributed to your understanding of them?

3 'Good things of day begin to droop and drowse'

One critic thought that line 52 in Scene 2 was 'the motto of the entire tragedy'. Look through this act in pairs to find other lines that might similarly capture the essence of *Macbeth*, or lines that might work as a subtitle to the play. Write out the lines and explain to other pairs why you think they are significant.

4 Changing relationships

Act 3 is the last time the Macbeths appear together, and we see how their relationship has changed since the beginning of the play. The following activity will help you compare their relationship at the end of Act 1 with their relationship at the end of Act 3.

Create a line diagram to show the changing relationship between this couple. Along the horizontal axis, mark out Act 1, Act 2 and Act 3. Along the vertical axis, mark out the level of power and control the character has, both personally and within the relationship. The highest level shows them to be controlling and manipulative, while the lowest level shows them to be out of control and unsure of what is happening in the relationship. Your line graph should reveal at a glance how the Macbeths' relationship has changed throughout the play so far.

5 The Macbeths psychoanalysed

In role as a psychoanalyst, use your line graph to report on the differences in the Macbeths' states of mind and relationship. You may also want to consider:

- how they speak to each other
- how they talk about the future
- the language and imagery they use
- their ideas of 'manhood' and 'womanhood'
- their mental suffering and anxiety.

Write at least two paragraphs, and remember to identify quotations from the play that would give your report more detail. Finish with an additional paragraph predicting what will happen to the Macbeths in the final two acts of the play.

97

The Witches' familiars have declared the time has come to meet Macbeth. Engrossed in their ugly ritual, they chant as they circle the cauldron, throwing in repulsive ingredients to make a sickening brew.

剧情简介： 女巫的密友们宣布会见麦克白的时机已到。她们全神贯注地举行邪恶的仪式，一边围着大锅转，一边念念有词，把令人厌恶的食材丢进锅里，熬成浓粥。

Stagecraft 导演技巧
What is happening on stage? (in pairs)

The script opposite has a pattern to it: each Witch is given a long speech, and in between they chant a rhyming couplet together. What might each Witch be doing on stage while delivering these lines? With a partner, write detailed stage directions for ten lines from this section. Consider the context and setting for your production to help you work out the characters' movements.

Language in the play 剧中语言
The Witches' words (by yourself)

Shakespeare uses lists that accumulate words or phrases to increase dramatic effect and add to the sinister atmosphere. In a few paragraphs written for a younger student, describe some of the patterns in the language used by the Witches in the script opposite. Identify features of rhyme, rhythm and language such as **assonance*** and **alliteration****. (See 'The language of *Macbeth*', pp. 170–3.)

1 Hyphenated adjectives (in pairs)

Find some examples of Shakespeare's hyphenated adjectives in the script opposite. Here are other examples from later in Act 4: 'gold-bound brow'; 'two-fold balls'; 'blood-boltered Banquo'.

a How does this use of language convey striking images or add depth of description to what the Witches are saying? What rhythms or repetitions of sound do they create?

b Write your own hyphenated adjectives as you invent a recipe for either a divine stew, with pleasant ingredients, or another 'hell-broth' with disgusting ingredients.

1 *cauldron* 大锅；缶
2 *brindled* 有斑纹
3 *hedge-pig* = hedgehog （刺猬）
4 *whined* 嗷嗷叫
5 *Harpier* （女巫密友之一，为鸟身女妖 [harpy]）
6 *entrails* 内脏
7 *Sweltered venom sleeping got* 睡眠中获得的体内渗出的毒液
8 *Fillet* 肉片
9 *fenny* 沼泽里的
10 *newt* 蝾螈
11 *Adder's fork* 蝰蛇的叉型舌
12 *blind-worm* 蛇蜥
13 *howlet* 猫头鹰雏
14 *charm* 魔咒，咒语
15 *hell-broth* （术士配制的）地狱羹
16 *mummy* 木乃伊，干尸
17 *maw and gulf* 胃和咽喉
18 *ravined* 血盆大口的
19 *hemlock* 毒堇
20 *blaspheming* 亵渎神灵
21 *Jew / Turk / Tartar* 犹太人/土耳其人/鞑靼人（这些人都不是基督徒）
22 *slips of yew* 紫杉（一种毒树）的枝
23 *Slivered* 砍下
24 *moon's eclipse* 月食（旧时认为月食时是采魔药的最佳时刻）
25 *Ditch-delivered* 沟渠里娩出
26 *drab* 妓女
27 *gruel* 粥
28 *slab* 黏稠
29 *chawdron* 肠肚

* **assonance** 半谐音，半韵，例如sonnet和porridge押第一个音节元音/ɒ/的韵；cold和killed押/-ld/的韵。

** **alliteration** 头韵，指诗句里两个或多个词的第一个辅音相同，如 sing a song of sixpence，类似中文的双声。

Act 4 Scene 1
A desolate place near Forres

Thunder. Enter the three WITCHES [*with a cauldron*[1]]

FIRST WITCH	Thrice the brindled[2] cat hath mewed.	
SECOND WITCH	Thrice and once the hedge-pig[3] whined[4].	
THIRD WITCH	Harpier[5] cries, ''Tis time, 'tis time.'	
FIRST WITCH	Round about the cauldron go;	
	In the poisoned entrails[6] throw.	5
	Toad, that under cold stone	
	Days and nights has thirty-one	
	Sweltered venom sleeping got[7],	
	Boil thou first i'th'charmèd pot.	
ALL	Double, double toil and trouble;	10
	Fire burn, and cauldron bubble.	
SECOND WITCH	Fillet[8] of a fenny[9] snake,	
	In the cauldron boil and bake:	
	Eye of newt[10], and toe of frog,	
	Wool of bat, and tongue of dog,	15
	Adder's fork[11], and blind-worm's[12] sting,	
	Lizard's leg, and howlet's[13] wing,	
	For a charm[14] of powerful trouble,	
	Like a hell-broth[15], boil and bubble.	
ALL	Double, double toil and trouble,	20
	Fire burn, and cauldron bubble.	
THIRD WITCH	Scale of dragon, tooth of wolf,	
	Witches' mummy[16], maw and gulf[17]	
	Of the ravined[18] salt-sea shark,	
	Root of hemlock[19], digged i'th'dark;	25
	Liver of blaspheming[20] Jew[21],	
	Gall of goat, and slips of yew[22],	
	Slivered[23] in the moon's eclipse[24];	
	Nose of Turk[21], and Tartar's[21] lips,	
	Finger of birth-strangled babe,	30
	Ditch-delivered[25] by a drab[26],	
	Make the gruel[27] thick and slab[28].	
	Add thereto a tiger's chawdron[29]	
	For th'ingredience of our cauldron.	

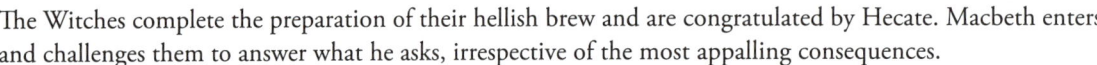

The Witches complete the preparation of their hellish brew and are congratulated by Hecate. Macbeth enters and challenges them to answer what he asks, irrespective of the most appalling consequences.

剧情简介：女巫们完成了地狱之羹的熬制，赫柯婍向她们表示祝贺。麦克白上场，逼着她们回答自己的问题，全然不顾这样会带来什么恶果。

1 Tell me – though destruction follows
(in small groups)

Macbeth is obsessed with one thought: the desire to know the future. He appeals to the Witches to answer him, even if the result is the destruction of the world. His language is like that of the Witches: 'I conjure you' is the beginning of a spell or incantation (咒语). Using lines 49–60, try one or more of the following activities:

a One person whispers the lines; the others echo every 'though' for emphasis.

b Experiment with changing the order of words in the list. How would you order it? Do you think that the order Shakespeare chose was the most powerful and dramatic?

c One person reads the lines and the others request clarification from the speaker at the end of each line or phrase (use questions that start with 'what,' 'why,' 'when,' 'where'). The speaker then repeats the line or phrase, emphasising the important parts of the speech.

Themes 主题分析
Images of chaos (in pairs)

a List some of the verbal images of chaos that appear in this section of the script, then talk with a partner about how this disorder relates to Macbeth's evil and selfish ambition.

b Collect photographs or pictures from magazines that might represent the chaos evident in the script opposite. Annotate each picture with relevant quotations.

c What can you decipher (辨认) (or discover through research) about beliefs in Shakespeare's day about personal disorder and cosmic chaos?

Language in the play 剧中语言
Shared lines (in fours)

Macbeth has 545 part-lines that are shared between characters. Find examples of shared lines in the script opposite. In your groups, read these out without breaking the rhythm of the line. What effect do the shared lines have in this part of the scene, and in the play as a whole?

---

1 I commend your pains 你们大家辛苦了
2 pricking 刺痛
3 black 恶毒
4 hags 巫婆
5 conjure 恳请
6 yeasty 有泡沫
7 Confound 掀翻
8 navigation 航船
9 Though bladed corn be lodged 哪怕刚结穗的麦子被压倒（迷信观念认为女巫能将庄稼从一个地方移到另一个地方，或压平庄稼形成形状复杂的麦田圈）
10 topple 坍塌
11 warders 看守
12 slope 倾斜
13 nature's germen 万物的种子
14 sicken 厌恶
15 masters 主人（即幽灵）

ALL	Double, double toil and trouble,	35
	Fire burn, and cauldron bubble.	
SECOND WITCH	Cool it with a baboon's blood,	
	Then the charm is firm and good.	

Enter HECATE, *and the other three Witches*

HECATE	O well done! I commend your pains[1],	
	And every one shall share i'th'gains;	40
	And now about the cauldron sing	
	Like elves and fairies in a ring,	
	Enchanting all that you put in.	

Music, and a song, 'Black spirits, etc.'
[*Exeunt Hecate and the other three Witches*]

SECOND WITCH	By the pricking[2] of my thumbs,	
	Something wicked this way comes;	45
	Open locks, whoever knocks.	

Enter MACBETH

MACBETH	How now, you secret, black[3], and midnight hags[4]!	
	What is't you do?	
ALL THE WITCHES	A deed without a name.	
MACBETH	I conjure[5] you by that which you profess,	
	Howe'er you come to know it, answer me.	50
	Though you untie the winds and let them fight	
	Against the churches, though the yeasty[6] waves	
	Confound[7] and swallow navigation[8] up,	
	Though bladed corn be lodged[9] and trees blown down,	
	Though castles topple[10] on their warders'[11] heads,	55
	Though palaces and pyramids do slope[12]	
	Their heads to their foundations, though the treasure	
	Of nature's germen[13] tumble altogether	
	Even till destruction sicken[14]: answer me	
	To what I ask you.	
FIRST WITCH	Speak.	
SECOND WITCH	Demand.	
THIRD WITCH	We'll answer.	60
FIRST WITCH	Say, if thou'dst rather hear it from our mouths,	
	Or from our masters'[15]?	
MACBETH	Call 'em, let me see 'em.	

The Witches show their Apparitions. An armed Head warns Macbeth: 'beware Macduff'. A bloody Child tells him that no naturally born man can harm him. Macbeth, though reassured, swears to kill Macduff.

剧情简介：三女巫展示她们的幽灵。一颗戴着头盔的头颅警告麦克白："要提防麦克达。" 一个浑身是血的小孩儿告诉他自然出生的人伤害不了他。麦克白虽然心里踏实了，但仍发誓要杀麦克达。

1 Prophetic apparitions (by yourself)

In a table like the one below, briefly describe the three Apparitions, their warnings and what each might symbolise.

Apparition	Warning	Symbolism

Themes 主题分析
Disorder and evil (in small groups)

a Design *either* a puppet for use on stage to represent one of the Apparitions, *or* an object that one of the Apparitions would hold. You might find inspiration for this from the striking visual and dramatic language in this part of the play. Look for images of dismembered limbs, armour, blood and children. You may also like to refer to objects and images that have a modern (and scary) resonance.

b In your groups, *either* stage the scene as an animation or puppet show, *or* work out a note from a director to his set designer describing how you would like to see the scene staged in the scariest way possible.

Language in the play 剧中语言
Hendiadys (一语二体；重言法) (in pairs)

Upon seeing the Third Apparition, Macbeth describes the crown on the child's head as 'the round / And top of sovereignty' (lines 87–8). Shakespeare uses two nouns, instead of an adjective and a noun (round top or rounded top), to describe what Macbeth sees. This is known as a **hendiadys** and it carries more layers of meaning than just saying 'crown'. What different meanings do the words 'round' and 'top' carry in this hendiadys?

Try out your own creative ideas to imitate Shakespeare's device and make up your own hendiadys from these adjective and noun pairs: furious sound; angelic ministers of grace; thankful payment; widely universal theatre; bodily beauty; heavenly grace.

---

1 sow 母猪
2 farrow 猪崽
3 sweaten 渗出
4 the murderer's gibbet 处死杀人犯的绞架
5 high or low 不管级别高低
6 office 职责；行使职责
7 deftly 灵巧，熟练
8 Thane of Fife 法夫子爵（指麦克达）
9 Dismiss 让……走
10 caution 警告
11 harped 道出
12 potent 厉害
13 resolute 坚决，果断
14 assurance double sure 双倍可靠的担保
15 take a bond of fate 拿到一纸命运的契约
16 round / And top of sovereignty 王冠

FIRST WITCH	Pour in sow's[1] blood, that hath eaten	
	Her nine farrow[2]; grease that's sweaten[3]	
	From the murderer's gibbet[4] throw	65
	Into the flame.	
ALL THE WITCHES	Come high or low[5]:	
	Thyself and office[6] deftly[7] show.	

Thunder. [Enter] FIRST APPARITION, *an armed Head*

MACBETH	Tell me, thou unknown power –	
FIRST WITCH	He knows thy thought;	
	Hear his speech, but say thou nought.	
FIRST APPARITION	Macbeth, Macbeth, Macbeth: beware Macduff,	70
	Beware the Thane of Fife[8]. Dismiss[9] me. Enough. *Descends*	
MACBETH	Whate'er thou art, for thy good caution[10], thanks;	
	Thou hast harped[11] my fear aright. But one word more –	
FIRST WITCH	He will not be commanded. Here's another,	
	More potent[12] than the first.	75

Thunder. [Enter] SECOND APPARITION, *a bloody Child*

SECOND APPARITION	Macbeth, Macbeth, Macbeth.	
MACBETH	Had I three ears, I'd hear thee.	
SECOND APPARITION	Be bloody, bold, and resolute[13]; laugh to scorn	
	The power of man, for none of woman born	
	Shall harm Macbeth. *Descends*	80
MACBETH	Then live, Macduff, what need I fear of thee?	
	But yet I'll make assurance double sure[14]	
	And take a bond of fate[15]: thou shalt not live,	
	That I may tell pale-hearted fear it lies,	
	And sleep in spite of thunder.	

Thunder. [Enter] THIRD APPARITION, *a Child crowned, with a tree in his hand*

	What is this,	85
	That rises like the issue of a king	
	And wears upon his baby-brow the round	
	And top of sovereignty[16]?	
ALL THE WITCHES	Listen, but speak not to't.	

The Third Apparition promises that Macbeth will not be defeated until Birnam Wood comes to Dunsinane. Macbeth demands to know more about the future. The Witches present a procession of eight kings and Banquo.

剧情简介：第三个鬼魂保证麦克白在伯南林来到丹悉嫩之前不会被打败。麦克白要求知道更多未来之事。女巫一连展现了八个王和班阔。

Stagecraft 导演技巧

A show of eight kings (in small groups)

Many people believe that Shakespeare had King James I very much in mind as he wrote *Macbeth* (see 'The contexts of *Macbeth*', pp. 162–3). The eight kings are supposed to represent the ancestors of James (represented in the photograph below as eight babies delivered by the Witches). King James saw the play shortly after it was written. One story is that the eighth king carried a mirror ('glass') and, at lines 118–19, focused it on the watching King James, who therefore saw his own reflection and heard the promise that his descendants ('many more') would rule England. Read lines 99–123, then in groups:

a Talk about how you would stage the appearances of the eight kings and Banquo's ghost.

b Create a suitable action or gesture for the actors at key points in the script.

c Describe the props you would like the actors to have. For example, perhaps you would like a blindfold for Macbeth to wear, to make it seem like he was hallucinating.

d Consider the soundtrack or sound effects that would increase dramatic tension.

1 lion-mettled　狮子般勇敢
2 Who … conspirers　谁担心，谁愤怒，或密谋者在何处
3 vanquished　被征服，被击败
4 Great Birnam Wood　大伯南林（离丹悉嫩山12英里远的一片山林；丹悉嫩是珀斯东北方的一座山峰）
5 impress　征兵
6 Sweet bodements　称心如意的预言
7 high-placed　地位崇高
8 the lease of nature　天年之期
9 mortal custom　正常寿命
10 Throbs　悸动
11 I will be satisfied　我一定要听到满意答案
12 sinks　（可能通过舞台上的一个地板门来实现，双簧管的乐声会掩盖其打开的声音）
13 glass　镜子或神秘的水晶
14 sear　灼烧
15 gold-bound brow　头戴王冠
16 Start　（从眼窝里）鼓出来
17 th'crack of doom　最后审判日的霹雳
18 two-fold balls　两个宝球（象征詹姆斯一世在苏格兰和英格兰两次加冕时手持的两个王权宝球）
19 treble sceptres　三根权杖（代表詹姆斯一世统治的三片王土：苏格兰、英格兰和爱尔兰）
20 blood-boltered　身上溅满血
21 points at them for his　表明他们是他的子嗣

MACBETH ACT 4 SCENE 1
麦克白

THIRD APPARITION	Be lion-mettled[1], proud, and take no care	
	Who chafes, who frets, or where conspirers[2] are.	90
	Macbeth shall never vanquished[3] be until	
	Great Birnam Wood[4] to high Dunsinane hill	
	Shall come against him. *Descends*	
MACBETH	That will never be:	
	Who can impress[5] the forest, bid the tree	
	Unfix his earthbound root? Sweet bodements[6], good.	95
	Rebellious dead, rise never till the wood	
	Of Birnam rise, and our high-placed[7] Macbeth	
	Shall live the lease of nature[8], pay his breath	
	To time and mortal custom[9]. Yet my heart	
	Throbs[10] to know one thing. Tell me, if your art	100
	Can tell so much, shall Banquo's issue ever	
	Reign in this kingdom?	
ALL THE WITCHES	Seek to know no more.	
MACBETH	I will be satisfied[11]. Deny me this,	
	And an eternal curse fall on you. Let me know.	
	[*Cauldron descends.*] *Hautboys*	
	Why sinks[12] that cauldron? And what noise is this?	105
FIRST WITCH	Show!	
SECOND WITCH	Show!	
THIRD WITCH	Show!	
ALL THE WITCHES	Show his eyes and grieve his heart,	
	Come like shadows, so depart.	110

[*Enter*] *a show of eight kings, and* [*the*] *last with a glass*[13] *in his hand*[; *Banquo's Ghost following*]

MACBETH   Thou art too like the spirit of Banquo. Down!
Thy crown does sear[14] mine eyeballs. And thy hair,
Thou other gold-bound brow[15], is like the first;
A third, is like the former. – Filthy hags,
Why do you show me this? – A fourth? Start[16], eyes!   115
What, will the line stretch out to th'crack of doom[17]?
Another yet? A seventh? I'll see no more.
And yet the eighth appears, who bears a glass
Which shows me many more. And some I see,
That two-fold balls[18] and treble sceptres[19] carry.   120
Horrible sight! Now I see 'tis true,
For the blood-boltered[20] Banquo smiles upon me,
And points at them for his[21].
        [*Exeunt show of kings and Banquo's Ghost*]
            What, is this so?

Having presented Banquo's descendants as kings, the Witches dance, then vanish, to Macbeth's anger. Hearing of Macduff's flight, Macbeth resolves to kill every member of Macduff's family he can catch.

 剧情简介：女巫展现班阔的后代成为国王后，跳起舞来，随后消失，这让麦克白愤怒不已。听说麦克达逃跑了，麦克白决心杀死他能抓到的麦克达的每一个家人。

1 Getting the Witches off the stage (in small groups)

Lines 124–31 are thought to have been written by Thomas Middleton, and are often cut in production. But many critics argue that the final two lines (130–1) represent another example of Shakespeare flattering King James, and were probably spoken directly to him at a performance in 1606. Whether or not that is true, every new production faces the practical problem of how the Witches leave the stage.

Rewrite the stage direction after line 131 to give more information for actors in a modern production. In your stage direction, include a suitable dance sequence ('antic round', line 129) for the Witches that enables them to 'vanish' as dramatically as possible. Experiment with ways of performing the lines as you think about this.

2 'dread exploits' (in pairs)

The depth of brutality to which Macbeth has now sunk is revealed in his determination to massacre innocent women and children in Macduff's castle. In pairs, take turns to try out different ways of speaking lines 143–54 as:

- private, whispered thoughts
- the words of a very fearful man
- the words of an angry tyrant.

Afterwards, take turns to position your partner into a statue representing the different ways Macbeth could deliver the speech.

Themes 主题分析

Battling with Time (by yourself)

In his soliloquy, Macbeth expresses a great sense of urgency, as if he is in a battle with Time. He decides that intentions without action are useless, and resolves simply to follow his first instincts without time for second thoughts or the objections of his conscience.

Write a paragraph, using embedded quotations, to consider other references to time in the play so far, and to describe how this theme is developed in the script opposite.

1 amazedly 惊慌失措（如同身处迷宫）
2 sprites 情绪，精神
3 antic round 古雅圆圈舞
4 did his welcome pay 向他表示国王应受有的尊敬
5 pernicious 不祥，险恶
6 Stand aye accursèd 永远遭受诅咒之苦
7 without there 从外面
8 anticipat'st 抢先一步
9 dread 可怕
10 flighty purpose 一闪而过的念头
11 never is o'ertook 不会被赶超
12 The very … hand 我心里最先想到什么，双手就要去干什么
13 thought and done 想到就行动（如同谚语no sooner said than done表达的意思）
14 surprise 奇袭
15 give … o'th'sword 交付刀刃（即杀死）
16 trace him in his line 与他同一血脉

FIRST WITCH Ay, sir, all this is so. But why
Stands Macbeth thus amazedly[1]? 125
Come, sisters, cheer we up his sprites[2],
And show the best of our delights.
I'll charm the air to give a sound,
While you perform your antic round[3]
That this great king may kindly say, 130
Our duties did his welcome pay[4].

Music. The Witches dance, and vanish

MACBETH Where are they? Gone? Let this pernicious[5] hour,
Stand aye accursèd[6] in the calendar.
Come in, without there[7]!

Enter LENNOX

LENNOX What's your grace's will?
MACBETH Saw you the weïrd sisters?
LENNOX No, my lord. 135
MACBETH Came they not by you?
LENNOX No indeed, my lord.
MACBETH Infected be the air whereon they ride,
And damned all those that trust them. I did hear
The galloping of horse. Who was't came by?
LENNOX 'Tis two or three, my lord, that bring you word 140
Macduff is fled to England.
MACBETH Fled to England?
LENNOX Ay, my good lord.
MACBETH [*Aside*] Time, thou anticipat'st[8] my dread[9] exploits;
The flighty purpose[10] never is o'ertook[11]
Unless the deed go with it. From this moment, 145
The very firstlings of my heart shall be
The firstlings of my hand[12]. And even now
To crown my thoughts with acts, be it thought and done[13].
The castle of Macduff I will surprise[14];
Seize upon Fife; give to th'edge o'th'sword[15] 150
His wife, his babes, and all unfortunate souls
That trace him in his line[16]. No boasting like a fool;
This deed I'll do before this purpose cool,
But no more sights. – Where are these gentlemen?
Come, bring me where they are. 155

Exeunt

Macduff's wife interprets his flight to England as madness, fear, or lack of love for his family. Ross comforts her: Macduff knows best, and even though the times are dangerous, they will improve.

剧情简介：麦克达的妻子认为丈夫逃到英格兰是疯狂、恐惧或对家庭缺少爱的表现。若斯安慰她说，麦克达知道怎样做最好，还说尽管眼下世道危险，但情况会好转。

Write about it 写作练习

'He loves us not' (by yourself)

Write Lady Macduff's perspective at this point in the play, in the form of a diary entry or a letter to her husband. Does she take comfort from Ross's words and his opinion that evil always gives way to good?

1 Crocodile tears?

In this part of the scene, Ross leaves near to tears. However, in Roman Polanski's 1971 movie, Ross is an obvious hypocrite. As he leaves Macduff's castle, he waves the Murderers in to kill everyone inside, adding to the sense of Scotland's corruption. In other versions, Ross is good-hearted and his words of comfort to Lady Macduff are sincere, but he is naïve in that he underestimates the power of evil against them. Write notes for an actor to explain how you think they should play Ross. Give the actor specific instructions about how to speak and act when playing this scene.

Stagecraft 导演技巧

Scene change (in pairs)

The setting for the action changes from a desolate heath with Witches, bloody Apparitions, rituals and Macbeth's violent thoughts in Scene 1, to Macduff's castle and the innocence of Macduff's wife and child in Scene 2. How would you perform the scene change and set the scene to heighten this contrast? Make two sketches of the designs you would use for the contrasting scenes.

1	titles	特权
2	wants the natural touch	缺少家庭的天生亲情
3	wren	鹪鹩
4	diminutive	微小
5	All … love	他心里全是恐惧，没有丝毫的爱
6	coz	表姐（指麦克达夫人）
7	school	控制
8	judicious	明智
9	The fits o'th'season	时事的混乱
10	hold … fear	因内心害怕而听信谣言
11	Each way and none	四处漂泊，居无定所
12	cousin	表侄（指麦克达夫人的儿子）
13	Fathered … fatherless	他虽有生父，但生父不在身边
14	my disgrace and your discomfort	（若斯害怕自己会哭起来，让对方感到不舒服）

▲ What style of sets would you choose for a production of *Macbeth*? Traditional or modern? Sparse or elaborate?

Act 4 Scene 2
Fife The castle of Macduff

Enter LADY MACDUFF, *her* SON, *and* ROSS

LADY MACDUFF What had he done, to make him fly the land?
ROSS You must have patience, madam.
LADY MACDUFF He had none;
His flight was madness. When our actions do not,
Our fears do make us traitors.
ROSS You know not
Whether it was his wisdom or his fear.   5
LADY MACDUFF Wisdom? To leave his wife, to leave his babes,
His mansion, and his titles[1] in a place
From whence himself does fly? He loves us not.
He wants the natural touch[2], for the poor wren[3],
The most diminutive[4] of birds, will fight,   10
Her young ones in her nest, against the owl.
All is the fear, and nothing is the love[5];
As little is the wisdom, where the flight
So runs against all reason.
ROSS My dearest coz[6],
I pray you school[7] yourself. But for your husband,   15
He is noble, wise, judicious[8], and best knows
The fits o'th'season[9]. I dare not speak much further,
But cruel are the times when we are traitors
And do not know ourselves, when we hold rumour
From what we fear[10], yet know not what we fear,   20
But float upon a wild and violent sea,
Each way and none[11]. I take my leave of you;
Shall not be long but I'll be here again.
Things at the worst will cease, or else climb upward
To what they were before. My pretty cousin[12],   25
Blessing upon you.
LADY MACDUFF Fathered he is, and yet he's fatherless[13].
ROSS I am so much a fool, should I stay longer
It would be my disgrace and your discomfort[14].
I take my leave at once.   *Exit*

Macduff's son teases his mother affectionately. Behind his playful words are glimpses of the dangerous times: traps for the innocent and widespread treachery. A messenger arrives to warn of danger.

剧情简介：麦克达的儿子亲热地逗母亲开心。他俏皮的话中隐藏着对危险时事的觉察：对无辜者的陷害和无处不在的背叛。一位信使上场，警告他们有危险。

Themes 主题分析

A man's duty (whole class)

Macduff has fled to England to raise enough forces to overthrow the increasingly murderous Macbeth. However, in doing so he has left his wife and family behind, and they are now at risk themselves. Lady Macduff tells her son that his father is 'dead' and a 'traitor'. She seems to want to remove him from their lives, perhaps to protect her son. But the boy continues to intelligently question the truth of what she says.

As a class, debate Macduff's actions. Should he have stayed and protected his family (which would mean that perhaps many more would be killed by Macbeth)? Or was he right to act as he did? Ask yourselves: should our first sense of duty be to ourselves, our loved ones or our country?

Characters 人物分析

The 'mind's construction' (in pairs)

The photograph of Lady Macduff below prompts comparisons with depictions of Lady Macbeth.

a What are the main differences between these women, specifically in terms of their ideas about children, husband and family?

b In conversation with your partner, suggest several ways in which this image conveys the innocence and vulnerability that Macbeth is determined to destroy.

1 **Sirrah** 小伙子（此处为sir的亲昵用法）
2 **your father's dead** 您父亲要是死了
3 **lime / pitfall / gin** （捉鸟的方法：涂在树上的粘鸟胶/罗网/鸟夹子）
4 **Poor ... for** 这些圈套对不值钱的鸟没有危险
5 **How ... father** 你没了父亲可怎么办呢？
6 **i'faith** = in faith （说真的）
7 **swears and lies** 立下誓言又毁掉誓言
8 **monkey** 小猴子（亲昵的称呼）
9 **prattler** 话匣子
10 **I ... known** 您不认识我
11 **in ... perfect** 我深知您的尊贵和贤淑
12 **doubt** 担心

LADY MACDUFF	Sirrah¹, your father's dead²,	30
	And what will you do now? How will you live?	
SON	As birds do, mother.	
LADY MACDUFF	What, with worms and flies?	
SON	With what I get I mean, and so do they.	
LADY MACDUFF	Poor bird, thou'dst never fear the net, nor lime³,	
	the pitfall³, nor the gin³.	35
SON	Why should I, mother? Poor birds they are not set for⁴.	
	My father is not dead for all your saying.	
LADY MACDUFF	Yes, he is dead. How wilt thou do for a father⁵?	
SON	Nay, how will you do for a husband?	
LADY MACDUFF	Why, I can buy me twenty at any market.	40
SON	Then you'll buy 'em to sell again.	
LADY MACDUFF	Thou speak'st with all thy wit, and yet i'faith⁶	
	with wit enough for thee.	
SON	Was my father a traitor, mother?	
LADY MACDUFF	Ay, that he was.	45
SON	What is a traitor?	
LADY MACDUFF	Why, one that swears and lies⁷.	
SON	And be all traitors, that do so?	
LADY MACDUFF	Every one that does so is a traitor and must be	
	hanged.	50
SON	And must they all be hanged that swear and lie?	
LADY MACDUFF	Every one.	
SON	Who must hang them?	
LADY MACDUFF	Why, the honest men.	
SON	Then the liars and swearers are fools, for there are liars and	55
	swearers enough to beat the honest men and hang up them.	
LADY MACDUFF	Now God help thee, poor monkey⁸, but how wilt	
	thou do for a father?	
SON	If he were dead, you'd weep for him; if you would not, it were	
	a good sign that I should quickly have a new father.	60
LADY MACDUFF	Poor prattler⁹, how thou talk'st!	

Enter a MESSENGER

MESSENGER	Bless you, fair dame. I am not to you known¹⁰,	
	Though in your state of honour I am perfect¹¹;	
	I doubt¹² some danger does approach you nearly.	

The messenger warns Lady Macduff to flee with her children because terrible danger is near. The Murderers enter, seeking Macduff. They kill his son and pursue Macduff's wife to murder her off stage.

剧情简介：信使提醒麦克达夫人赶快带着孩子逃跑，因为可怕的危险近在咫尺。杀人凶手上场，搜寻麦克达。他们杀死麦克达的儿子，然后追赶他的妻子退场，到幕后将她杀死。

Themes 主题分析

Slaughter of the Innocents (in pairs)

One critic compared this scene to the biblical Slaughter of the Innocents. Macbeth's murder of future life and youthful hopefulness, as well as his cruelty and depravity, take on epic proportions through this biblical allusion (圣经典故).

Find pictures of the Slaughter of the Innocents and then look at Lady Macduff's lines 70–4. Why are Macbeth's murderous intentions so disturbing in this part of the play? Use the style and tone of the front page of a tabloid newspaper (小报) to report these events.

Stagecraft 导演技巧

On stage or off stage?

In Greek tragedy, all killings took place off stage. The audience did not see the act of violence, but heard it reported later. Shakespeare devotes very few lines to the murders, but productions vary greatly in their presentation, often showing Lady Macduff killed on stage.

How would you stage the final few lines? Should she be killed on or off stage? How would you advise the actor playing Lady Macduff to show her bravery and defiance as she insults the Murderers? How would you portray the son's loyalty to his father and his bravery in the face of death? Write a paragraph giving reasons for your decisions.

1 Murderers most foul (in small groups)

Think about status, gestures and interaction between the characters in this murder scene. Split your group into people of high and low status. Experiment with ways of interacting with each other, following these rules:

- Give high-status characters strong gestures, upright postures, with lifted eyes and movements forward with purpose.
- Give low-status characters insecure gestures, slouching (无精打采) postures, lowered eyes and shuffling (拖鞋走路) movements that have no purpose.

How does this activity give you more insight into the scene and the tragedy that develops?

1 homely man　普通人
2 methinks　在我看来
3 savage　无礼，粗野
4 fell cruelty　致命的凶残
5 Which … person　与您近在咫尺（nigh：接近）
6 laudable　值得称赞
7 unsanctified　不圣洁
8 shag-haired　头发蓬乱
9 egg　小坏蛋
10 Young fry of treachery　叛贼的小孽种（fry：鱼苗；注意生育繁殖的形象egg和fry被用作骂人的词汇）

MACBETH ACT 4 SCENE 2

              If you will take a homely man's[1] advice,   65
              Be not found here. Hence with your little ones.
              To fright you thus, methinks[2] I am too savage[3];
              To do worse to you were fell cruelty[4],
              Which is too nigh your person[5]. Heaven preserve you,
              I dare abide no longer.   *Exit*

LADY MACDUFF   Whither should I fly?   70
              I have done no harm. But I remember now
              I am in this earthly world where to do harm
              Is often laudable[6], to do good sometime
              Accounted dangerous folly. Why then, alas,
              Do I put up that womanly defence,   75
              To say I have done no harm?

                        Enter MURDERERS

                                What are these faces?

A MURDERER   Where is your husband?
LADY MACDUFF   I hope in no place so unsanctified[7],
              Where such as thou mayst find him.
A MURDERER   He's a traitor.
SON   Thou liest, thou shag-haired[8] villain.
A MURDERER   What, you egg[9]!   80
              Young fry of treachery[10]!
                      [*Kills him*]
SON   He has killed me, mother,
              Run away, I pray you!
                      Exit [*Lady Macduff*] *crying 'Murder'*[, *pursued by*
                                      Murderers with her Son]

Macduff urges Malcolm to go to the defence of Scotland, which is suffering under Macbeth's tyranny. Malcolm voices his suspicions that Macduff is Macbeth's agent and has good reasons to betray him to Macbeth.

剧情简介：麦克达敦促马尔肯保卫苏格兰免遭麦克白暴政蹂躏。马尔肯表示他怀疑麦克达是麦克白派来的奸细，说麦克达完全有理由将他出卖给麦克白。

Stagecraft 导演技巧

England: design the scene (in pairs)

Work out a simple but effective way of showing the audience that this scene takes place in England at the palace of King Edward.

1 Malcolm's suspicions about Macduff
(in small groups)

Malcolm builds a strong case for his mistrust of Macduff:

- He is not sure that Macduff is telling the truth (line 11).
- Macbeth was once thought to be honest (lines 12–13).
- Macduff was a friend of Macbeth (line 13).
- Macbeth has left Macduff unharmed (line 14).
- Macduff may betray Malcolm to Macbeth (lines 14–15).
- Macduff may kill Malcolm for Macbeth (lines 16–17).
- Macbeth is a traitor (line 18).
- Even a good man may obey a wicked king (lines 19–20).
- Evil often tries to look like good (lines 21–3).
- Macduff has abruptly left his family behind in danger (lines 26–8).
- Malcolm is suspicious for his own safety (lines 29–30).

Imagine you are Malcolm and draw up a list of questions that you would like to ask Macduff. Afterwards, take turns playing Macduff and answering the questions from the rest of the group.

Language in the play 剧中语言

Religious imagery

There is much religious imagery in the speeches opposite, including references to sorrow that strikes heaven on the face (line 6), an innocent lamb (line 16) and to angels and fallen angels (line 22).

Write an extended paragraph describing this imagery to a younger student. How do these images relate to themes of good and evil, deceptive appearances and disorder in the natural world? How can each of them apply to Macbeth himself? To extend your ideas, look through the act to find other examples of religious imagery.

1 desolate shade 僻静之处
2 fast 紧紧
3 Bestride our downfall birthdom 保卫我们沦丧的出生地
4 resounds 回响
5 Like syllable of dolour 类似悲恸的声音
6 redress 矫正，匡正
7 time to friend 有利时机
8 perchance 可能
9 You … me 您可以从我身上隐约看到他（麦克白）的影子
10 and wisdom = it is wisdom
11 appease 安抚
12 recoil / In an imperial charge 在王权威严命令下畏缩
13 crave 恳求
14 transpose 转变
15 the brightest 最亮眼的（即路西法 [Lucifer]，又名"撒旦"，原本是天使中最得上帝恩宠的天使长，因不服上帝管束而叛变为魔鬼）
16 the brows of grace 美德的面容，慈眉善目
17 rawness 仓皇（指对妻儿不管不顾）

Act 4 Scene 3
England The palace of King Edward

Enter MALCOLM *and* MACDUFF

MALCOLM Let us seek out some desolate shade[1] and there
Weep our sad bosoms empty.

MACDUFF   Let us rather
Hold fast[2] the mortal sword and like good men
Bestride our downfall birthdom[3]; each new morn,
New widows howl, new orphans cry, new sorrows   5
Strike heaven on the face, that it resounds[4]
As if it felt with Scotland and yelled out
Like syllable of dolour[5].

MALCOLM   What I believe, I'll wail;
What know, believe; and what I can redress[6],
As I shall find the time to friend[7], I will.   10
What you have spoke, it may be so perchance[8].
This tyrant, whose sole name blisters our tongues,
Was once thought honest; you have loved him well –
He hath not touched you yet. I am young, but something
You may discern of him through me[9], and wisdom[10]   15
To offer up a weak, poor, innocent lamb
T'appease[11] an angry god.

MACDUFF I am not treacherous.

MALCOLM   But Macbeth is.
A good and virtuous nature may recoil
In an imperial charge[12]. But I shall crave[13] your pardon: 20
That which you are, my thoughts cannot transpose[14];
Angels are bright still, though the brightest[15] fell.
Though all things foul would wear the brows of grace[16],
Yet grace must still look so.

MACDUFF   I have lost my hopes.

MALCOLM Perchance even there where I did find my doubts.   25
Why in that rawness[17] left you wife and child,
Those precious motives, those strong knots of love,
Without leave-taking? I pray you,

Malcolm's suspicions dismay Macduff. Malcolm tells him that he has English troops to support his cause, but that his own vices are far worse than Macbeth's.

剧情简介：马尔肯的疑心让麦克达心灰意冷。马尔肯告诉他英格兰军会支持他的义举，但他自己的罪恶比麦克白的严重得多。

Characters 人物分析

Inner thoughts (in fours)

Malcolm is testing Macduff's sincerity. The terror of Macbeth's regime has made him suspect all visitors – after all, they may be Macbeth's secret agents. He now embarks on a strange way of testing Macduff's honesty, claiming that his own vices far exceed Macbeth's. To explore the complexity of motive and expression in this scene, try the following activity.

Split your group into two pairs. One pair reads the script in role as Malcolm and Macduff. As you read, pause after each speech so that the second pair can voice Malcolm's and Macduff's inner thoughts. If you are in the second pair, try speaking over the shoulder of – or while seated behind – the character whose inner thoughts you are revealing. Talk together about why Malcolm embarks on (着手实施) this bizarre strategy, how effective you think it is going to be and the impact it has on Macduff.

1 jealousies　猜疑
2 lay thou thy basis sure　把你的基业奠定安稳吧（对麦克白说的话）
3 check　限制，抑制
4 wear thou thy wrongs　头顶着你的罪恶（即窃取的王冠）
5 affeered　确认（也就是说麦克白的王位坐稳了）
6 Fare thee well　再会，再见
7 to boot　也，此外
8 the yoke　受奴役，受压迫
9 withal　此外，也
10 hands uplifted in my right　众人拥戴我夺我应得的王位
11 England = the King of England（即Edward the Confessor）
12 grafted　扎根；嫁接
13 be opened　萌发
14 confineless harms　无限的邪恶
15 legions　众多，一大群

Language in the play 剧中语言

Language and themes

In the script opposite, Shakespeare uses:

- personification (of Scotland)
- symbolic language (black, white)
- religious imagery (hell, devil).

Identify examples of each of these uses of language. How do they relate to the themes of evil, ambition, deception and power that have been developed in the play so far?

MACBETH ACT 4 SCENE 3
麦克白

                Let not my jealousies[1] be your dishonours,
                But mine own safeties; you may be rightly just,
                Whatever I shall think.
MACDUFF   Bleed, bleed, poor country.
                Great tyranny, lay thou thy basis sure[2],
                For goodness dare not check[3] thee; wear thou thy wrongs[4],
                The title is affeered[5]. Fare thee well[6], lord,
                I would not be the villain that thou think'st
                For the whole space that's in the tyrant's grasp,
                And the rich East to boot[7].
MALCOLM   Be not offended.
                I speak not as in absolute fear of you:
                I think our country sinks beneath the yoke[8];
                It weeps, it bleeds, and each new day a gash
                Is added to her wounds. I think withal[9]
                There would be hands uplifted in my right[10],
                And here from gracious England[11] have I offer
                Of goodly thousands. But for all this,
                When I shall tread upon the tyrant's head,
                Or wear it on my sword, yet my poor country
                Shall have more vices than it had before,
                More suffer, and more sundry ways than ever,
                By him that shall succeed.
MACDUFF   What should he be?
MALCOLM It is myself I mean – in whom I know
                All the particulars of vice so grafted[12]
                That when they shall be opened[13], black Macbeth
                Will seem as pure as snow, and the poor state
                Esteem him as a lamb, being compared
                With my confineless harms[14].
MACDUFF   Not in the legions[15]
                Of horrid hell can come a devil more damned
                In evils to top Macbeth.

Malcolm lists Macbeth's vices, but claims that his own sexual desire is limitless, and he is infinitely greedy. Macduff finds reasons to excuse Malcolm's ungovernable lust and avarice.

 剧情简介：马尔肯列举麦克白的罪恶，但声称他自己纵欲无度，而且极其贪婪。麦克达找理由原谅马尔肯难以抑制的性欲和贪欲。

Characters 人物分析

Show Macbeth's evil (in large groups)

Malcolm begins by naming eight of Macbeth's evils. He is 'bloody' (murderous), 'luxurious' (lecherous), 'avaricious' (greedy), 'false', 'deceitful', 'sudden' (violent), 'malicious', and possesses 'every sin / That has a name' (the seven deadly sins). The activity below provides an interesting way to explore the language in lists such as the one in lines 57–60.

Work out a sequence of tableaux or short mimes to show Macbeth's nature. Each scene in your tableaux should show one of the evils listed. Add a commentary to your presentation.

1. Luxurious 淫荡，放纵
2. avaricious 贪婪
3. Sudden 冲动
4. smacking 有……的风味
5. voluptuousness 淫欲
6. matrons 保姆
7. cistern 水箱（大容器）
8. continent impediments 自我约束的障碍
9. o'erbear 压倒
10. Boundless intemperance 无限制的纵欲
11. hoodwink 蒙骗
12. there … inclined 那么多佳人巴望着为君献身，您胃口再大，也受用不尽的（vulture：兀鹫，比喻贪婪之徒）
13. ill-composed affection 扭曲的品性
14. stanchless avarice 无法遏制的贪婪
15. forge 制造，创造
16. summer-seeming 如盛夏般（火热而短暂）
17. foisons 丰富的资源
18. your mere own 单是您自己的
19. portable 可以忍受

1 Lust and greed: 'portable' sins? (in pairs)

Malcolm claims that he is infinitely lustful and excessively greedy. He says that when he is king, he will satisfy his desire for sex and money. Macduff dismisses these sins as personal flaws that are unimportant as long as a man shows 'other graces', such as the duties owed by a king to his country.

a Do you agree that lust and greed are unimportant in a leader? Does it matter if a ruler is promiscuous (淫乱) or embezzles (盗用，侵吞) public money?
Talk together about Macduff's reasoning and what it suggests about his character.

b Research and then make a list of real leaders who fit Malcolm's sins. Use examples of the much-publicised sexual and financial activities of modern politicians, as well as leaders of the past.

MALCOLM   I grant him bloody,
Luxurious¹, avaricious², false, deceitful,
Sudden³, malicious, smacking⁴ of every sin
That has a name. But there's no bottom, none,
In my voluptuousness⁵: your wives, your daughters,
Your matrons⁶, and your maids could not fill up
The cistern⁷ of my lust, and my desire
All continent impediments⁸ would o'erbear⁹
That did oppose my will. Better Macbeth,
Than such an one to reign.

MACDUFF   Boundless intemperance¹⁰
In nature is a tyranny; it hath been
Th'untimely emptying of the happy throne
And fall of many kings. But fear not yet
To take upon you what is yours: you may
Convey your pleasures in a spacious plenty
And yet seem cold. The time you may so hoodwink¹¹.
We have willing dames enough; there cannot be
That vulture in you to devour so many
As will to greatness dedicate themselves,
Finding it so inclined¹².

MALCOLM   With this, there grows
In my most ill-composed affection¹³ such
A stanchless avarice¹⁴ that, were I king,
I should cut off the nobles for their lands,
Desire his jewels, and this other's house,
And my more-having would be as a sauce
To make me hunger more, that I should forge¹⁵
Quarrels unjust against the good and loyal,
Destroying them for wealth.

MACDUFF   This avarice
Sticks deeper, grows with more pernicious root
Than summer-seeming¹⁶ lust, and it hath been
The sword of our slain kings; yet do not fear,
Scotland hath foisons¹⁷ to fill up your will
Of your mere own¹⁸. All these are portable¹⁹,
With other graces weighed.

Malcolm claims that he has no good qualities whatsoever, and seeks only to create chaos. Macduff condemns Malcolm as unfit to rule. Malcolm says that Macduff's reaction has removed his suspicions. He denies all vices.

剧情简介：马尔肯声称他没有任何优良品质，只想制造混乱。麦克达谴责马尔肯不适合统治国家。马尔肯说麦克达的反应消除了他的怀疑。他否认以上所有罪恶。

1 The good king (in small groups)

In lines 92–4, Malcolm lists twelve qualities that a good king should possess: 'justice' (fairness), 'verity' (truthfulness), 'temp'rance' (self-control), 'stableness' (even-temperedness), 'bounty' (generosity), 'perseverance' (endurance), 'mercy' (forgiveness), 'lowliness' (humility), 'devotion' (piety), 'patience', 'courage' and 'fortitude' (strength). Do you agree? List these qualities in the order you think is the most important for a good king. Share your list with other groups in the class to see if there is general agreement or not. Remember to justify your top three qualities.

2 Who's who? (in pairs)

Macduff's impassioned outburst in lines 102–14 includes references to Malcolm, Macbeth, Duncan, Duncan's wife, Scotland and Macduff himself. As one person reads a line at a time, the other identifies aloud to whom (or what) Macduff is referring (for example, in line 102 it is 'Malcolm', in line 103, 'Malcolm' and 'Scotland').

Language in the play 剧中语言
Visual images of chaos and uproar

Macduff can tolerate no more of Malcolm's self-condemnation, and rejects him as unfit to live. Look at lines 97–100 and draw an image prompted by the language. How do the images here relate to other visual images in the play based on milk, hell and uproar?

▼ How can costumes reveal what qualities a character possesses?

1 verity 诚实
2 fortitude 刚毅
3 relish 嗜好
4 division 各种变化
5 several 各自，个别
6 concord 和谐
7 Uproar 搅乱
8 untitled 名分不正
9 wholesome 健康，健全
10 truest issue 最合法的后人（指马尔肯）
11 interdiction 禁令
12 blaspheme his breed 诋毁他的血统
13 upon her knees 下跪（祈祷）
14 Died every day she lived 每日刻苦修行
15 repeat'st 讲述，提及
16 breast 心
17 black scruples 邪恶的猜忌
18 trains 诡计
19 modest wisdom 常识
20 over-credulous haste 过于轻信而草率为之
21 Unspeak 收回前言
22 detraction 毁谤
23 abjure 声明放弃，否认
24 For = As
25 forsworn 不守誓言，做伪证

MALCOLM   But I have none. The king-becoming graces –
           As justice, verity[1], temp'rance, stableness,
           Bounty, perseverance, mercy, lowliness,
           Devotion, patience, courage, fortitude[2] –
           I have no relish[3] of them, but abound   95
           In the division[4] of each several[5] crime,
           Acting it many ways. Nay, had I power, I should
           Pour the sweet milk of concord[6] into hell,
           Uproar[7] the universal peace, confound
           All unity on earth.
MACDUFF   O Scotland, Scotland!   100
MALCOLM   If such a one be fit to govern, speak.
           I am as I have spoken.
MACDUFF   Fit to govern?
           No, not to live. O nation miserable!
           With an untitled[8] tyrant, bloody-sceptred,
           When shalt thou see thy wholesome[9] days again,   105
           Since that the truest issue[10] of thy throne
           By his own interdiction[11] stands accursed
           And does blaspheme his breed[12]? Thy royal father
           Was a most sainted king; the queen that bore thee,
           Oft'ner upon her knees[13] than on her feet,   110
           Died every day she lived[14]. Fare thee well,
           These evils thou repeat'st[15] upon thyself
           Hath banished me from Scotland. O my breast[16],
           Thy hope ends here.
MALCOLM   Macduff, this noble passion,
           Child of integrity, hath from my soul   115
           Wiped the black scruples[17], reconciled my thoughts
           To thy good truth and honour. Devilish Macbeth
           By many of these trains[18] hath sought to win me
           Into his power, and modest wisdom[19] plucks me
           From over-credulous haste[20]; but God above   120
           Deal between thee and me, for even now
           I put myself to thy direction and
           Unspeak[21] mine own detraction[22], here abjure[23]
           The taints and blames I laid upon myself,
           For[24] strangers to my nature. I am yet   125
           Unknown to woman, never was forsworn[25],

Malcolm asserts his virtue and declares he is now ready to invade Scotland. The Doctor tells how King Edward cures sick people by his touch. Malcolm says the gift of healing is passed down to future kings.

剧情简介：马尔肯明确肯定自己的德行，宣布他现在已准备好进攻苏格兰。医生告诉他爱德华王如何以触摸治愈病人。马尔肯说这种能治愈疾病的天赋会传给后世君王。

1 'Why are you silent?' (in small groups)

Macduff's outburst finally convinces Malcolm that Macduff is sincere. In response, Malcolm reveals his true nature (lines 125–31) and confesses that he has been testing him. How does Macduff react (see line 137)? Some productions make Macduff's disorientation (迷惑) a comic moment; others imply that Macduff might now feel unsure about his alliance with Malcolm.

Take turns as Macduff and answer questions from the rest of the group about his thoughts, feelings, hopes and fears at this point in the play. Then write an aside to insert into the scene, so that an audience will have a greater understanding of Macduff's character and motivations.

Characters 人物分析

Dramatic contrast (by yourself)

The Doctor's description highlights a contrast between the two kings: Macbeth is dedicated to destruction, King Edward to healing. Where Macbeth unleashes violence and death in his kingdom, King Edward is concerned for his nation's moral and spiritual health.

Identify the images of saintliness found in the description of the ceremony of healing, then compare these with images that have been used to describe Macbeth so far (revisit lines 55–7, 104, 117). Write an obituary (讣告) for both kings, using these images and your own ideas.

▼ 'This good king'. Imagine that King Edward makes an appearance on stage. How would you have him look, move and speak to set him apart as the 'good king' to Macbeth's 'evil king'?

1	coveted	觊觎，垂涎
2	here-approach	到来
3	at a point	准备好（上战场）
4	Now we'll together = Now let's go together	
5	chance of goodness	好运降临
6	warranted quarrel	正义之战
7	more anon	等会儿再说
8	a crew	一群
9	stay his cure	等待他的回春妙手
10	their … art	他们的疾病击败了医术最大的努力（最精湛的医术）
11	sanctity	神圣
12	amend	康复
13	the Evil	邪病（即淋巴结核；当时人们迷信国王能治愈这种病，因此也被称为the King's Evil [国王邪病]）
14	here-remain	逗留，暂住
15	solicits	恳求
16	strangely visited	异乎寻常染上这种病
17	ulcerous	溃疡
18	mere	完全
19	golden stamp	金币
20	succeeding royalty	后世君主
21	healing benediction	能治病的恩赐
22	With this strange virtue	除了这种不寻常的神功
23	speak	表明，显示

	Scarcely have coveted¹ what was mine own,
	At no time broke my faith, would not betray
	The devil to his fellow, and delight
	No less in truth than life. My first false speaking
	Was this upon myself. What I am truly
	Is thine, and my poor country's, to command:
	Whither indeed, before thy here-approach²,
	Old Siward with ten thousand warlike men
	Already at a point³ was setting forth.
	Now we'll together⁴, and the chance of goodness⁵
	Be like our warranted quarrel⁶. Why are you silent?
MACDUFF	Such welcome and unwelcome things at once,
	'Tis hard to reconcile.

Enter a DOCTOR

MALCOLM Well, more anon⁷. —
Comes the king forth, I pray you?

DOCTOR Ay, sir: there are a crew⁸ of wretched souls
That stay his cure⁹; their malady convinces
The great assay of art¹⁰, but at his touch,
Such sanctity¹¹ hath heaven given his hand,
They presently amend¹². *Exit*

MALCOLM I thank you, doctor.
MACDUFF What's the disease he means?
MALCOLM 'Tis called the Evil¹³.
A most miraculous work in this good king,
Which often since my here-remain¹⁴ in England
I have seen him do. How he solicits¹⁵ heaven
Himself best knows, but strangely visited¹⁶ people
All swoll'n and ulcerous¹⁷, pitiful to the eye,
The mere¹⁸ despair of surgery, he cures,
Hanging a golden stamp¹⁹ about their necks
Put on with holy prayers, and 'tis spoken
To the succeeding royalty²⁰ he leaves
The healing benediction²¹. With this strange virtue²²,
He hath a heavenly gift of prophecy,
And sundry blessings hang about his throne
That speak²³ him full of grace.

Enter ROSS

MACDUFF See who comes here.

Ross reports that in Scotland suffering goes unremarked and good men's lives are short. He says that Macduff's family is well. Rebellion against Macbeth is rumoured. Malcolm reveals his plan to invade Scotland.

剧情简介：若斯报告说，在苏格兰，疾苦无人问津，好人活不长久；麦克达家人安好；有传闻说发生了反对麦克白的叛乱。马尔肯透露了他进攻苏格兰的计划。

Themes 主题分析

'Alas, poor country' (in pairs)

Under Macbeth's rule, Scotland is a country that is 'Almost afraid to know itself' and uncertain of its own identity. Life there has become so full of suffering that 'violent sorrow' is commonplace. Death is so much a fact of everyday experience that good men are more vulnerable than plucked flowers: they do not live as long.

Do you think it is possible for a country to have an identity? Write down words that you would associate with your own country's identity. Use these words to write ten lines of blank verse describing your country and the experiences of specific people living there today.

Language in the play 剧中语言

Key words and images (in pairs)

Read through lines 166–75 slowly. Try to work out an action or gesture for a key word or image in each line. Afterwards, identify some of the language features Shakespeare uses in the script (look for personification, lists, metaphors, visual images, symbols). Record your findings in a table that shows:

- quotations
- language features
- the effect of these language features on an audience or reader.

1 Bringing bad news (in fours)

Ross knows what has happened to Macduff's family. But he does not immediately tell his terrible news, saying rather that they are 'well' and 'at peace'. What different meanings do these key phrases have? Why does Ross delay telling Macduff what has happened? How does this add to the dramatic tension and pathos (感染力) of the scene?

Read through lines 178–82 in role as Ross, Macduff and Malcolm, with the fourth member of your group acting as an observer. Discuss with the observer your reasons for the pace and tone of each speech, the words to which you gave special emphasis and how you used pauses or gesture for dramatic effect. Using this information, each group's observer reports back to the rest of the class.

1 betimes 迅速
2 means 情况
3 once 曾经
4 rend 撕破
5 not marked 没人注意
6 modern ecstasy 司空见惯的忘形
7 relation 叙述
8 nice 准确
9 doth hiss the speaker 对说话人发出嘘声
10 teems 产生
11 battered 破坏，殴打
12 niggard 吝啬鬼；囤积者
13 heavily 心情沉痛
14 out 揭竿而起
15 power 军队
16 afoot 行进
17 eye 露面（以"眼睛"代指人，为"提喻法"修辞）
18 doff 脱去（喻指摆脱）

MALCOLM	My countryman, but yet I know him not.	
MACDUFF	My ever gentle cousin, welcome hither.	
MALCOLM	I know him now. Good God betimes[1] remove	
	The means[2] that makes us strangers.	
ROSS	Sir, amen.	165
MACDUFF	Stands Scotland where it did?	
ROSS	Alas, poor country,	
	Almost afraid to know itself. It cannot	
	Be called our mother, but our grave, where nothing,	
	But who knows nothing, is once[3] seen to smile;	
	Where sighs, and groans, and shrieks that rend[4] the air	170
	Are made, not marked[5]; where violent sorrow seems	
	A modern ecstasy[6]. The deadman's knell	
	Is there scarce asked for who, and good men's lives	
	Expire before the flowers in their caps,	
	Dying or ere they sicken.	
MACDUFF	O relation[7]	175
	Too nice[8], and yet too true.	
MALCOLM	What's the newest grief?	
ROSS	That of an hour's age doth hiss the speaker[9];	
	Each minute teems[10] a new one.	
MACDUFF	How does my wife?	
ROSS	Why, well.	
MACDUFF	And all my children?	
ROSS	Well, too.	
MACDUFF	The tyrant has not battered[11] at their peace?	180
ROSS	No, they were well at peace when I did leave 'em.	
MACDUFF	Be not a niggard[12] of your speech: how goes't?	
ROSS	When I came hither to transport the tidings	
	Which I have heavily[13] borne, there ran a rumour	
	Of many worthy fellows that were out[14],	185
	Which was to my belief witnessed the rather	
	For that I saw the tyrant's power[15] afoot[16].	
	Now is the time of help. [*To Malcolm*] Your eye[17] in Scotland	
	Would create soldiers, make our women fight	
	To doff[18] their dire distresses.	
MALCOLM	Be't their comfort	190
	We are coming thither. Gracious England hath	
	Lent us good Siward and ten thousand men –	

Ross tells of the murder of Macduff's family. Malcolm tries to comfort Macduff, who struggles with his grief over the slaughter of his wife and children.

 剧情简介：若斯讲述麦克达的家人已被谋杀。看到麦克达在妻儿被屠杀的痛苦中挣扎，马尔肯试图安慰他。

1 Approach, retreat or manoeuvre (in threes)

Take parts as Ross, Macduff and Malcolm and speak everything from line 195 ('But I have words') to the end of the scene. After you have read it through once, perform it again on your feet, using the following three actions: approach, retreat or manoeuvre (巧妙移动). Use these gestures at appropriate times as you read your character's lines. Ask yourselves the following questions as you think about which gestures work best:

- Why might you approach someone or something in everyday life?
- Why might you retreat from something or someone?
- Why might you manoeuvre or reposition yourself in the same space?

1	latch	抓住
2	The general cause	所有人的事
3	fee-grief	一个人的悲伤
4	single breast	单独一颗心脏
5	Pertains to	属于
6	possess	抓住；占据
7	heaviest	最悲伤
8	quarry	一堆被杀的鹿
9	pull … brows	拉低帽子遮住眉眼（悲伤的姿势）
10	o'erfraught	过于沉重，不堪重负
11	from thence	离开家
12	hell-kite	地狱之鸢（比喻杀人魔）
13	dam	母鸟
14	fell swoop	从天而降（麦克达把自己的妻儿比作母鸡和小鸡，把麦克白比作突袭他们的老鹰）

Stagecraft 导演技巧

Telling the terrible news

Notice that Ross still delays, then reports bluntly in lines 206–7. What might be happening on stage to make him suddenly break the news like this? Also notice how Macduff presses for detail, then incredulously repeats 'all' four times in lines 218–21, as though he is unable to believe the enormity of what has happened.

How would you advise an actor to use this repetition to greatest dramatic effect? How would you advise him to use pauses and gesture in this scene? Write out your advice and look carefully at any clues for actions (such as in line 210) as you do so.

	An older and a better soldier none
	That Christendom gives out.
ROSS	Would I could answer
	This comfort with the like. But I have words
	That would be howled out in the desert air,
	Where hearing should not latch[1] them.
MACDUFF	What concern they?
	The general cause[2], or is it a fee-grief[3]
	Due to some single breast[4]?
ROSS	No mind that's honest
	But in it shares some woe, though the main part
	Pertains to[5] you alone.
MACDUFF	If it be mine,
	Keep it not from me; quickly let me have it.
ROSS	Let not your ears despise my tongue forever
	Which shall possess[6] them with the heaviest[7] sound
	That ever yet they heard.
MACDUFF	H'm – I guess at it.
ROSS	Your castle is surprised; your wife and babes
	Savagely slaughtered. To relate the manner
	Were on the quarry[8] of these murdered deer
	To add the death of you.
MALCOLM	Merciful heaven –
	What, man, ne'er pull your hat upon your brows[9]:
	Give sorrow words; the grief that does not speak,
	Whispers the o'erfraught[10] heart and bids it break.
MACDUFF	My children too?
ROSS	Wife, children, servants, all
	That could be found.
MACDUFF	And I must be from thence[11]?
	My wife killed too?
ROSS	I have said.
MALCOLM	Be comforted.
	Let's make us med'cines of our great revenge
	To cure this deadly grief.
MACDUFF	He has no children. All my pretty ones?
	Did you say all? O hell-kite[12]! All?
	What, all my pretty chickens and their dam[13]
	At one fell swoop[14]?

Macduff cannot hide his grief. He feels that he is to blame for his family's death. He vows vengeance on Macbeth. Malcolm declares that the time is ripe to overthrow Macbeth, as heaven itself is against him.

剧情简介：麦克达难掩悲痛，觉得自己应该为家人的死负责。他发誓要向麦克白复仇。马尔肯宣布推翻麦克白的时机已经成熟，因为连上天也反对他。

Write about it 写作练习

What is a man? (in pairs)

Planning the murder of Duncan, Lady Macbeth taunted Macbeth for not behaving like 'a man', and at the banquet she accused him of being 'unmanned'. Now Malcolm (lines 222 and 238) and Macduff (line 224) express different interpretations of what it is to be a man.

With a partner, talk about whether you agree with their representations of masculinity. Afterwards, write two paragraphs comparing two or more different representations of masculinity in the play so far. Remember to use embedded quotations and to consider how context (the battlefield, domestic sphere, in exile, on the throne) impacts on masculinity.

Characters 人物分析

Malcolm's motivation (by yourself)

Earlier in the scene, Malcolm had engaged in a deception to test Macduff's integrity. His words now pose a moral question. Is Malcolm genuinely trying to help Macduff cope with his grief, or is he seizing an opportunity to urge him into the common cause against Macbeth? Step into role as Malcolm and write a letter to Donaldbain, currently in self-imposed exile in Ireland, telling him why you behaved as you did throughout this scene.

1 Dispute 抗争
2 take their part 站在他们一边
3 Naught 恶人，罪人
4 demerits 过错
5 whetstone 磨刀石
6 play … eyes 像女人一样哭泣
7 braggart 自夸，吹嘘
8 intermission 暂停，中断
9 Front to front 面对面
10 scape = escape
11 tune 气魄
12 Our … leave 我们就只缺一声告别了
13 powers above 上天的神力
14 instruments 武器

1 The longest scene (whole class)

Some directors do not include the whole of this scene in their stage productions because it is so long.

a Imagine you are about to put on the play. Split the class in half. One half argues for cutting the scene, the other half for keeping it as it is. Listen carefully to your opponents' reasons to cut or not to cut, and try to answer them.

b Assume you have decided to compromise. You will keep the scene but try to reduce its length. Explore ways of presenting it in the briefest time while still keeping all its major elements.

MACBETH ACT 4 SCENE 3
麦克白

MALCOLM	Dispute[1] it like a man.
MACDUFF	I shall do so;

But I must also feel it as a man;
I cannot but remember such things were   225
That were most precious to me. Did heaven look on,
And would not take their part[2]? Sinful Macduff,
They were all struck for thee. Naught[3] that I am,
Not for their own demerits[4] but for mine,
Fell slaughter on their souls. Heaven rest them now.   230

MALCOLM Be this the whetstone[5] of your sword, let grief
Convert to anger. Blunt not the heart, enrage it.

MACDUFF O, I could play the woman with mine eyes[6]
And braggart[7] with my tongue. But gentle heavens,
Cut short all intermission[8]. Front to front[9]   235
Bring thou this fiend of Scotland and myself;
Within my sword's length set him. If he scape[10],
Heaven forgive him too.

MALCOLM   This tune[11] goes manly.
Come, go we to the king; our power is ready;
Our lack is nothing but our leave[12]. Macbeth   240
Is ripe for shaking, and the powers above[13]
Put on their instruments[14]. Receive what cheer you may:
The night is long that never finds the day.

                                            Exeunt

MACBETH
麦克白

Looking back at Act 4 第4幕回顾
Activities for groups or individuals

1 Dramatic range and scale

The three scenes of Act 4 contain great dramatic range:

- Ritual: the Witches around the cauldron
- Spectacle: the Apparitions and the show of eight kings
- Domestic family life: Lady Macduff and her son
- Horrific violation: the murders in Macduff's castle
- Deception and moral complexity: Malcolm's testing of Macduff
- Deep personal grief: Macduff hears of his family's slaughter.

a Try to reduce the dramatic range and scale of this act to a short text. As you do so, consider how each scene is juxtaposed (并列) to position the audience to understand the themes of the play.

b Write the script for a newsflash based on events in each scene. Try to limit your newsflash to 100 words.

c Create a haiku (俳句，日本古典短诗，由 "五—七—五" 共十七个音节组成) based on each scene. For example:

> Sheltered innocence,
> Object of ambitious greed:
> Gone, in one fell swoop.

2 A tempting letter from Macbeth

In Scene 3, Malcolm says that Macbeth has tried to lure him with offers of women, money and other incentives (lines 117–20). Write a letter from Macbeth, tempting Malcolm to return to Scotland.

3 'How many children had Lady Macbeth?'

'He has no children', cries Macduff in Scene 3 as he is advised to seek revenge on Macbeth. But in Act 1 Scene 7, Lady Macbeth says that she has suckled (哺育) a child at her breast. The critic L. C. Knights wrote a famous essay titled 'How many children had Lady Macbeth?' His answer was that the question is unimportant, because *Macbeth* should be read as a dramatic poem rather than as a study of characters. Some productions of *Macbeth* have made 'children' a central concept. Does it matter, in the play, whether Lady Macbeth has children or not? How would you explain the significance of children, childlessness and violence against children as recurring ideas in this play?

4 Dramatic reading

a In groups, prepare a dramatic reading of an important passage relating to notions of kingship from Act 4 (at least ten lines). There are many ways in which each extract can be spoken and presented: consider tone, pauses, emphasis, speech, repetitions, movement, gesture and accompanying sound effects.

b List the various representations of kingship that are covered in this act. Include the positive and the negative and try to match each item with a relevant quotation.

5 Tableaux quotations

In groups, choose a key quotation from this act and present a physical representation of it for the rest of your class to guess the quotation. Give the class five clues as they try to guess your quotation.

6 Witchcraft and superstition

a In small groups, stage a mock trial of the Witches to determine the role they have played in Macbeth's destiny. Together, assemble a list of questions to ask them, then take turns to answer these questions in role as one of the Witches.

b Look at the photographs showing the Witches from different stage productions on the page opposite and at the end of Act 1. Write your opinions about the extent to which the Witches are to blame for what happens in the play. Include a description of how you would portray them on stage to convey your interpretation to the audience.

The Gentlewoman reports to the Doctor that she has seen Lady Macbeth sleepwalking. She refuses to tell what her mistress has said in her sleep. Lady Macbeth, asleep, enters with a candle.

剧情简介： 女官告诉医生她看见麦克白夫人梦游，但拒绝透露女主人睡觉时说了什么。梦游的麦克白夫人手持一根蜡烛上场。

1 The sleepwalking scene: act it out (in threes)

This is one of the most famous scenes in world drama.

a In groups of three, work out how you would stage it to maximum dramatic effect by preparing notes for the actors. Advise them on how they should speak and move, as well as what props you think they should use.

b Staying in your groups, experiment with ways of performing this scene, taking turns as Lady Macbeth. Remember to listen to the advice of the others in your group.

Write about it 写作练习
What does Lady Macbeth write? (by yourself)

The Gentlewoman tells how she has seen Lady Macbeth carefully take paper, fold it, write on it, read it and seal it – all in her sleep. What do you think Lady Macbeth is writing? Is it a confession? A letter to Macbeth? A warning to Lady Macduff? Or something else? How honest might she be, bearing in mind that she is writing when she is unconscious? Write Lady Macbeth's letter, using modern English or imitating the prose used in this scene.

Themes 主题分析
Obsessive Compulsive Disorder (强迫症)?

This scene is filled with unnatural and disturbed behaviour ('A great perturbation in nature'), so it is appropriate that Shakespeare wrote it in prose rather than verse. The language is uneven and lacking in the rich fluency of poetry. Lady Macbeth's obsessive washing of her hands, coupled with her sleepwalking, are telling signs of mental illness.

Find out some more about somnambulism (梦游症) and the illness known as Obsessive Compulsive Disorder (OCD). What causes these conditions? How might they be treated today? Report back to your class after you have learned more, focusing on the accuracy of Shakespeare's description.

1 DOCTOR OF PHYSIC 医生
2 WAITING-GENTLEWOMAN 女官（莎士比亚时代女王或王后的女官为贵族女性）
3 his majesty 陛下（指麦克白）
4 went into the field 上战场
5 closet （放贵重物品的）柜子
6 seal 封缄（在信的封口滴上热封蜡，趁热加盖私人印章以确保隐私性和真实性）
7 perturbation 不安，扰乱
8 effects 表现
9 watching 清醒
10 slumbery agitation 睡眠中的焦躁不安
11 actual 活动的
12 report after her 背着她告诉旁人
13 meet 合适
14 no ... speech 没有证人证明我说了什么（女官担心因此犯叛国罪）
15 taper 蜡烛
16 guise 方式，样子
17 close 隐藏
18 seem 似乎
19 set down 写下
20 satisfy ... strongly 让我记得更牢一些

Act 5 Scene 1
A room in Dunsinane Castle

Enter a DOCTOR OF PHYSIC[1], *and a* WAITING-GENTLEWOMAN[2]

DOCTOR I have two nights watched with you, but can perceive no truth in your report. When was it she last walked?

GENTLEWOMAN Since his majesty[3] went into the field[4], I have seen her rise from her bed, throw her night-gown upon her, unlock her closet[5], take forth paper, fold it, write upon't, read it, afterwards seal[6] it, and again return to bed, yet all this while in a most fast sleep.

DOCTOR A great perturbation[7] in nature, to receive at once the benefit of sleep and do the effects[8] of watching[9]. In this slumbery agitation[10], besides her walking and other actual[11] performances, what at any time have you heard her say?

GENTLEWOMAN That, sir, which I will not report after her[12].

DOCTOR You may to me, and 'tis most meet[13] you should.

GENTLEWOMAN Neither to you, nor anyone, having no witness to confirm my speech[14].

Enter LADY [MACBETH], *with a taper*[15]

Lo you, here she comes. This is her very guise[16] and, upon my life, fast asleep. Observe her, stand close[17].

DOCTOR How came she by that light?

GENTLEWOMAN Why, it stood by her. She has light by her continually, 'tis her command.

DOCTOR You see her eyes are open.

GENTLEWOMAN Ay, but their sense are shut.

DOCTOR What is it she does now? Look how she rubs her hands.

GENTLEWOMAN It is an accustomed action with her, to seem[18] thus washing her hands; I have known her continue in this a quarter of an hour.

LADY MACBETH Yet here's a spot.

DOCTOR Hark, she speaks; I will set down[19] what comes from her to satisfy my remembrance the more strongly[20].

Lady Macbeth, fast asleep, tries to wash imagined blood from her hands. Her fragmented language echoes her own and Macbeth's words about past murders: Duncan, Lady Macduff, Banquo.

剧情简介：梦游的麦克白夫人试图洗掉手上她想象的血污。她的话支离破碎，重现了她本人和麦克白说过的关于谋杀党肯、麦克达夫人和班阔的话。

Stagecraft 导演技巧
'will these hands ne'er be clean?'

Some modern productions (such as Polanski's movie) have highlighted the use of hands in *Macbeth* as a powerful motif (主题) that runs throughout the play. At times, the characters' hands seem almost removed from their bodies, acting separately to their wishes. Lighting can be employed very effectively to pick out actors' hands at key points in the play, as can film and projections.

How would you stage this scene so that the various actors' hands convey different emotions? Try storyboarding or filming to explore this aspect of the scene. Alternatively, create a tableau that emphasises the importance of hands.

1 Act out Lady Macbeth's dreams (in fives or sixes)

Lady Macbeth's sleepwalking language is dreamlike: short and disjointed recollections of Macbeth's deeds. There are twenty-six sentences in all. In groups, work on the script so that one of you speaks the lines and the other members of the group become other characters from the play. These might include King Duncan, Lady Macduff and her children, Banquo, the Witches, Malcolm, Donaldbain and Macbeth. As Lady Macbeth speaks, each character reacts using facial expressions, hand gestures and other forms of silent communication. Afterwards, talk together about the emotions you have explored as actors.

1 **One, two** （麦克白夫人可能在想象敲响的钟声）
2 **murky** 黑暗
3 **call our power to account** 冒大不韪要我们自证清白
4 **You … starting** 您的退缩毁了一切
5 **Go to** 算了（作为批评语或表示无可奈何）
6 **perfumes of Arabia** 阿拉伯香料
7 **sorely charged** 负担太多痛苦
8 **for … body** 为了全身尊荣（女官的意思是：即使给我王后之位我也不愿心中有愧）
9 **Pray God it be** 请上帝治好她吧
10 **practice** 医术
11 **holily** 安详
12 **on's** = of his
13 **Directly** 立即
14 **Foul whisp'rings are abroad** 污言秽语在悄悄传播
15 **divine** 神父
16 **annoyance** 伤害
17 **mated** 搞糊涂，使困惑

LADY MACBETH Out, damned spot! Out, I say! One, two[1]. Why then 'tis time to do't. Hell is murky[2]. Fie, my lord, fie, a soldier, and afeard? What need we fear? Who knows it, when none can call our power to account[3]? Yet who would have thought the old man to have had so much blood in him?

DOCTOR Do you mark that?

LADY MACBETH The Thane of Fife had a wife. Where is she now? What, will these hands ne'er be clean? No more o'that, my lord, no more o'that. You mar all with this starting[4].

DOCTOR Go to[5], go to; you have known what you should not.

GENTLEWOMAN She has spoke what she should not, I am sure of that. Heaven knows what she has known.

LADY MACBETH Here's the smell of the blood still; all the perfumes of Arabia[6] will not sweeten this little hand. O, O, O.

DOCTOR What a sigh is there! The heart is sorely charged[7].

GENTLEWOMAN I would not have such a heart in my bosom for the dignity of the whole body[8].

DOCTOR Well, well, well –

GENTLEWOMAN Pray God it be[9], sir.

DOCTOR This disease is beyond my practice[10]; yet I have known those which have walked in their sleep who have died holily[11] in their beds.

LADY MACBETH Wash your hands, put on your night-gown, look not so pale. I tell you yet again, Banquo's buried; he cannot come out on's[12] grave.

DOCTOR Even so?

LADY MACBETH To bed, to bed; there's knocking at the gate. Come, come, come, come, give me your hand; what's done cannot be undone. To bed, to bed, to bed.   *Exit*

DOCTOR Will she go now to bed?

GENTLEWOMAN Directly[13].

DOCTOR Foul whisp'rings are abroad[14]; unnatural deeds
Do breed unnatural troubles; infected minds
To their deaf pillows will discharge their secrets.
More needs she the divine[15] than the physician.
God, God forgive us all. Look after her;
Remove from her the means of all annoyance[16],
And still keep eyes upon her. So, good night,
My mind she has mated[17], and amazed my sight.
I think, but dare not speak.

GENTLEWOMAN   Good night, good doctor.
                                Exeunt

News! Malcolm, Macduff, Siward and the English army approach; young men flock to join them; Macbeth is troubled by internal revolt – his soldiers obey him only out of fear, and his conscience oppresses him.

 剧情简介：重大消息！马尔肯、麦克达、修沃和英格兰军逼近；年轻人成群结队加入他们的队伍；麦克白正被内部叛乱困扰——他的士兵只是因为害怕才听从他的命令，而且他备受良心压迫。

Characters 人物分析
'Those he commands, move only in command'
(by yourself, then whole class)

Macbeth's men are serving him not out of love and duty, but only because they have to. Many will desert him as the battle nears its end.

Imagine that you are one of Macbeth's soldiers. Write down three questions you would like to ask Macbeth as you consider your sense of duty to him as king. As a class, decide which question is the most important.

1 Hope! (in fours)

The four thanes are full of hope because of Macbeth's difficulties and the approach of Malcolm's army. They can see, not far ahead, freedom from tyranny. Speak lines 1–31 in two ways:

- Take parts as the four thanes and read through the scene.
- Do not take parts, but take turns to read up to a punctuation mark, then hand on. Speak in whispers, as conspirators.

Which reading most powerfully conveys a sense of mounting optimism?

Language in the play 剧中语言
Propaganda (in pairs)

The language Caithness and Angus use in lines 12–22 portrays Macbeth in a very negative way. Identify and write out three images from these lines that strongly capture their opinion of Macbeth. With a partner, talk about which image you think is the most powerful. Why did Shakespeare choose to describe Macbeth so negatively at this point in the play?

▶ Views of Macbeth: in pairs, one person reads the negative descriptions while the other mimes (以哑剧形式表现) them.

1 *Drum and colours* 鼓手和旗手
2 *uncle Siward* 修沃姥爷（修沃应为马尔肯的外祖父）
3 *their … man* 他们的崇高事业甚至能激励死人，回应流血牺牲的号角
4 *file* 名单
5 *gentry* 贵族
6 *unrough* 没长胡子（指没有经过考验）
7 *Protest their first of manhood* 发誓要证明自己是男子汉
8 *buckle … rule* 将其病态的统治维持在法律的范围内
9 *Now … faith-breach* 每分钟都有叛乱声讨他的犯上作乱
10 *pestered* 错乱，纠缠
11 *When … there* 他内心的一切都憋在那里而与自己交战
12 *med'cine of the sickly weal* 治愈患病国家的良医（指马尔肯）
13 *purge* 清洗；泻药

Act 5 Scene 2
Scotland Open country

Drum and colours[1]. *Enter* MENTEITH, CAITHNESS, ANGUS, LENNOX, *Soldiers*

MENTEITH The English power is near, led on by Malcolm,
His uncle Siward[2], and the good Macduff.
Revenges burn in them, for their dear causes
Would to the bleeding and the grim alarm
Excite the mortified man[3].

ANGUS   Near Birnam Wood
Shall we well meet them; that way are they coming.

CAITHNESS Who knows if Donaldbain be with his brother?

LENNOX For certain, sir, he is not. I have a file[4]
Of all the gentry[5]; there is Siward's son
And many unrough[6] youths that even now
Protest their first of manhood[7].

MENTEITH   What does the tyrant?

CAITHNESS Great Dunsinane he strongly fortifies.
Some say he's mad; others that lesser hate him
Do call it valiant fury, but for certain
He cannot buckle his distempered cause
Within the belt of rule[8].

ANGUS   Now does he feel
His secret murders sticking on his hands.
Now minutely revolts upbraid his faith-breach[9];
Those he commands, move only in command,
Nothing in love. Now does he feel his title
Hang loose about him, like a giant's robe
Upon a dwarfish thief.

MENTEITH   Who then shall blame
His pestered[10] senses to recoil and start,
When all that is within him does condemn
Itself for being there[11]?

CAITHNESS   Well, march we on
To give obedience where 'tis truly owed;
Meet we the med'cine of the sickly weal[12],
And with him pour we in our country's purge[13],
Each drop of us.

Macbeth, receiving news of desertions from his army, recalls the Apparitions' predictions. He rages at a soldier who tells of Malcolm's approach. He knows the coming battle will make or break him.

 剧情简介：麦克白得到消息说他军队里很多人开了小差，他回想起幽灵的预言。有士兵向他报告马尔肯正逼近，他大发雷霆。他知道即将开始的战斗要么成就他，要么摧毁他。

Stagecraft 导演技巧
The return of Macbeth (in threes)

This is our first sight of Macbeth since Act 4 Scene 1. In the previous scene, the thanes talk of how desperate he has become. In groups of three, plot Macbeth's rise and fall on a graph. When is he at his most successful and when is he at his lowest point? Share your work with the rest of the class. Do your graphs look similar to one another?

Characters 人物分析
Macbeth's mood swings (in pairs)

Faced with bad news, Macbeth tries to cheer himself by recalling the words of the Apparitions ('Birnam Wood' and 'no man that's born of woman'). His mood was described in the previous scene as 'mad' or 'valiant fury', and his mood swings are evident in this scene.

a   To help you understand Macbeth's varying moods, speak all he says in lines 1–61. Share his lines between you, speaking sentences alternately. Identify the points where Macbeth's mood and tone of voice change in the scene.

b   Prepare notes for an actor playing Macbeth in this scene, advising him how he might speak.

1 'let them fly all' (in threes)

Macbeth hears of thanes who have deserted him to join the English forces, and he sees the fear in the face of the servant who brings him news of ten thousand English soldiers. It is clear that there are many who will not fight with Macbeth: they are either fighting against him or have fled in terror of the invading army.

Improvise Macbeth's servants discussing life at the castle. What have you witnessed since the king and queen were last seen in the play? What rumours have you heard about the English army?

1 dew the sovereign flower 滋润王位的鲜花（让合法的君王复位）
2 them （指那些不忠的领主）
3 taint 感染
4 mortal consequences 人生命运的结局
5 epicures 饕餮之徒
6 sway by 统治
7 sag 消沉
8 cream-faced 面色苍白
9 loon 混蛋，蠢货
10 goose-look 呆鹅样儿
11 over-red 涂一层血
12 lily-livered 胆小（传统上认为肝脏司人的热情和胆量，如果一个人肝脏为百合色，则胆小）
13 patch 笨蛋，蠢货
14 linen 惨白（表示胆小）
15 counsellors 顾问
16 whey-face 苍白脸
17 Seyton 撒顿（可能与Satan[撒旦魔王]同音）
18 push 进攻
19 cheer … now 要么让我从此王位稳坐，要么立刻废黜我

LENNOX	Or so much as it needs To dew the sovereign flower[1] and drown the weeds. Make we our march towards Birnam.	30

Exeunt, marching

Act 5 Scene 3
Dunsinane Castle

Enter MACBETH, DOCTOR, *and Attendants*

MACBETH	Bring me no more reports, let them[2] fly all; Till Birnam Wood remove to Dunsinane, I cannot taint[3] with fear. What's the boy Malcolm? Was he not born of woman? The spirits that know All mortal consequences[4] have pronounced me thus: 'Fear not, Macbeth, no man that's born of woman Shall e'er have power upon thee.' Then fly false thanes And mingle with the English epicures[5]; The mind I sway by[6] and the heart I bear Shall never sag[7] with doubt nor shake with fear.	5 10

Enter SERVANT

	The devil damn thee black, thou cream-faced[8] loon[9]. Where got'st thou that goose-look[10]?	
SERVANT	There is ten thousand –	
MACBETH	Geese, villain?	
SERVANT	Soldiers, sir.	
MACBETH	Go prick thy face and over-red[11] thy fear, Thou lily-livered[12] boy. What soldiers, patch[13]? Death of thy soul, those linen[14] cheeks of thine Are counsellors[15] to fear. What soldiers, whey-face[16]?	15
SERVANT	The English force, so please you.	
MACBETH	Take thy face hence!	

[Exit Servant]

	Seyton[17]! – I am sick at heart, When I behold – Seyton, I say! – this push[18] Will cheer me ever or disseat me now[19].	20

Macbeth reflects on a bleak future. He determines to fight to the death, and orders rumour-mongers to be killed. When the Doctor tells him he cannot cure mental disorders, Macbeth dismisses medicine.

剧情简介：麦克白认真考虑了黯淡的前景。他决心战斗到死，并下令处死散布谣言的人。当医生告诉麦克白他治不好精神错乱时，麦克白放弃了药物治疗。

Characters 人物分析
Not 'honour' but 'mouth-honour' (in pairs)

Macbeth wearily broods on the unhappy future that awaits him. In line 25 he lists four things that old people hope for, and in lines 27–8 two things he is likely to receive. Actors try to speak such 'lists' using a different tone of voice for each 'item'.

In pairs, explore Macbeth's innermost thoughts. One person speaks the lines and the other improvises deeper reflections that are unspoken in the play. Take it in turns to do this and then compare your approaches.

1 'a mind diseased'

The language Macbeth uses in lines 41–6 is rich in metaphor and is both lyrical and tender. Try to sketch out the metaphors in these lines, visualising the rich imagery. Discuss your work with the rest of the class, explaining what you hoped to capture in your sketches. You could add your work to the wall displays you are developing on *Macbeth*.

Write about it 写作练习
Lady Macbeth: her psychoanalyst's report

Three hundred years before Sigmund Freud, Shakespeare seems to have invented psychoanalysis. Macbeth's description of 'a mind diseased' (line 41) exactly captures the anxiety, depression and sorrow that Freud sought to cure by psychoanalysis. Freud's method (sometimes known as 'the talking cure') resembles what the Doctor says in line 46–7: 'Therein the patient / Must minister to himself.' This expresses the heart of psychoanalytic practice: the patient, by talking through his or her problem with an analyst, effectively finds his or her own cure.

Imagine that you are Lady Macbeth's analyst writing a final report of all the meetings you have had with her. What questions have you asked and what answers were you given? What do you think is the cause of her illness and how might it be cured? Include a transcript from some of your meetings with her, your own analysis of her illness, and your suggested ways of treating it in your final report.

1	way of life	人生之路
2	sere	干枯
3	yellow leaf	黄叶（喻临死前的一段时间）
4	troops	成群结队
5	stead	位置（指代替）
6	mouth-honour, breath	甜言蜜语，阿谀奉承
7	fain	欣然
8	horses	骑兵
9	skirr	快速绕过
10	sick	病（这里指身体生病，区别于精神上的病）
11	thick-coming fancies	老是出现的幻觉
12	minister to	诊治
13	Raze … brain	抹去涂写在脑中的焦虑（此处把大脑比成一张羊皮纸，上面写的东西可以擦去或刮去）
14	oblivious	让人淡忘
15	antidote	解药
16	perilous	险恶
17	staff	长矛
18	dispatch	快点儿
19	cast / The water	验尿
20	pristine	清澈，崭新

I have lived long enough. My way of life[1]
Is fall'n into the sere[2], the yellow leaf[3],
And that which should accompany old age,
As honour, love, obedience, troops[4] of friends, 25
I must not look to have; but in their stead[5],
Curses, not loud but deep, mouth-honour, breath[6]
Which the poor heart would fain[7] deny, and dare not.
Seyton!

Enter SEYTON

SEYTON   What's your gracious pleasure?
MACBETH   What news more? 30
SEYTON   All is confirmed, my lord, which was reported.
MACBETH   I'll fight till from my bones my flesh be hacked.
          Give me my armour.
SEYTON   'Tis not needed yet.
MACBETH   I'll put it on; 35
          Send out more horses[8]; skirr[9] the country round.
          Hang those that talk of fear. Give me mine armour.
          How does your patient, doctor?
DOCTOR   Not so sick[10], my lord,
          As she is troubled with thick-coming fancies[11]
          That keep her from her rest.
MACBETH   Cure her of that. 40
          Canst thou not minister to[12] a mind diseased,
          Pluck from the memory a rooted sorrow,
          Raze out the written troubles of the brain[13],
          And with some sweet oblivious[14] antidote[15]
          Cleanse the stuffed bosom of that perilous[16] stuff 45
          Which weighs upon the heart?
DOCTOR   Therein the patient
          Must minister to himself.
MACBETH   Throw physic to the dogs, I'll none of it.
          Come, put mine armour on; give me my staff[17]. –
          Seyton, send out. – Doctor, the thanes fly from me. – 50
          [*To Attendant*] Come sir, dispatch[18]. – If thou couldst, doctor, cast
          The water[19] of my land, find her disease,
          And purge it to a sound and pristine[20] health,
          I would applaud thee to the very echo

Macbeth leaves, calling for his armour. The Doctor determines to desert. Malcolm orders the army to use branches to camouflage their approach to Dunsinane. He reports many desertions from Macbeth's army.

剧情简介：麦克白离开，命人把他的盔甲拿来。医生决定逃走。马尔肯命令军队用树枝作掩护朝丹悉嫩开进。他通报说麦克白的军队有许多逃兵。

Stagecraft 导演技巧

The coming of Birnam Wood (by yourself)

The approaching forces decide to camouflage themselves by using branches cut from Birnam Wood. How would you stage something this big in a theatre? Write notes to the cast of the play, advising them how this might be done successfully. Suggest the props they should use, as well as sound effects and lighting.

▼ This is how a 2011 production showed Malcolm's army advancing, holding branches from Birnam Wood. Work out how, in your own production, you could stage the approach of the camouflaged army.

1 **rhubarb** 大黄（一种用作泻药的植物）
2 **cynne** = senna（番泻叶，有通便作用）
3 **purgative drug** 泻药
4 **scour** 洗净
5 **bane** 毁灭，灭亡
6 **Profit** 钱（莎士比亚时期的医生常被认为贪财）
7 **chambers** 寝室（邓肯是在寝室被谋杀的）
8 **We doubt it nothing** 我们对此毫不怀疑
9 **hew** 砍
10 **bough** 大树枝
11 **shadow** 遮掩
12 **host** 军队
13 **make … us** 让他们在刺探我方军情时出错
14 **endure** 忍受，经受
15 **setting down before't** 扎营（好围攻）
16 **advantage to be given** 一有机会逃跑
17 **more … revolt** 上至贵族成员下至普通士兵都背叛他
18 **constrainèd things** 受逼迫的士兵

	That should applaud again. – Pull't off, I say! –	55
	What rhubarb[1], cynne[2], or what purgative drug[3]	
	Would scour[4] these English hence? Hear'st thou of them?	
DOCTOR	Ay, my good lord; your royal preparation	
	Makes us hear something.	
MACBETH	Bring it after me. –	
	I will not be afraid of death and bane[5],	60
	Till Birnam Forest come to Dunsinane.	
	[*Exeunt all but Doctor*]	
DOCTOR	Were I from Dunsinane away and clear,	
	Profit[6] again should hardly draw me here. *Exit*	

Act 5 Scene 4
Near Birnam Wood

Drum and colours. Enter MALCOLM, SIWARD, MACDUFF,
Siward's son, MENTEITH, CAITHNESS, ANGUS, *and* SOLDIERS,
marching

MALCOLM	Cousins, I hope the days are near at hand	
	That chambers[7] will be safe.	
MENTEITH	We doubt it nothing[8].	
SIWARD	What wood is this before us?	
MENTEITH	The Wood of Birnam.	
MALCOLM	Let every soldier hew[9] him down a bough[10],	
	And bear't before him; thereby shall we shadow[11]	5
	The numbers of our host[12] and make discovery	
	Err in report of us[13].	
A SOLDIER	It shall be done.	
SIWARD	We learn no other, but the confident tyrant	
	Keeps still in Dunsinane and will endure[14]	
	Our setting down before't[15].	
MALCOLM	'Tis his main hope,	10
	For where there is advantage to be given[16],	
	Both more and less have given him the revolt[17],	
	And none serve with him but constrainèd things[18]	
	Whose hearts are absent too.	

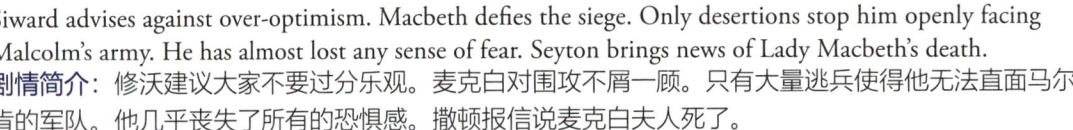

Siward advises against over-optimism. Macbeth defies the siege. Only desertions stop him openly facing Malcolm's army. He has almost lost any sense of fear. Seyton brings news of Lady Macbeth's death.

 剧情简介：修沃建议大家不要过分乐观。麦克白对围攻不屑一顾。只有大量逃兵使得他无法直面马尔肯的军队。他几乎丧失了所有的恐惧感。撒顿报信说麦克白夫人死了。

Stagecraft 导演技巧
Scene contrast, speech contrast

Scene 4 dramatically contrasts with Scene 3. Macbeth's reliance on the Apparition's forecast that he would not be defeated until Birnam Wood came to Dunsinane is followed by Malcolm's order to his soldiers to cut branches from Birnam Wood as camouflage. Now Shakespeare ends Scene 4 with Macduff's calm call for 'Industrious soldiership', then provides an immediate contrast by opening Scene 5 with Macbeth's defiant bravado (虚张声势).

As you read on, make a note of other contrasts that increase the dramatic tension, such as scene length and atmosphere.

1 'I have supped full with horrors' (in pairs)

The sound of women mourning prompts Macbeth to reflect that he has lost almost all sense of fear. Once, an owl's shriek or a horror story would make his blood run cold and his hair stand on end.

a What has caused Macbeth to change? Discuss this in pairs and consider if you think it makes him more or less vulnerable.

b Take turns to speak lines 9–15 in such a way that brings out the differences in tone from Macbeth's first speech in this scene.

Characters 人物分析
'The queen, my lord, is dead' (in pairs)

How did Lady Macbeth die? At the end of the play, Malcolm reports that she committed suicide, but that may not be true (because history is written by the victors). Talk together about how you think she might have met her death, then *either* write her farewell letter *or* write an obituary for a newspaper in which you give an account of her life and her death.

1 Let … event 让我们基于真实的判断决定战事成败
2 owe = own（赢得）
3 Thoughts … arbitrate 推测只是不确定的希望，但战斗决定最终结果
4 war 军队
5 laugh a siege to scorn 让敌人的围攻成为笑柄
6 lie 扎营
7 ague 疟疾
8 forced 得到增援
9 dareful 大胆，无畏
10 beard to beard 面对面
11 fell of hair 发梢；寒毛
12 at a dismal treatise 听到可怕的故事
13 rouse 竖立
14 supped full with horrors 内心充满恐惧
15 Direness 恐惧，可怕之事

MACDUFF   Let our just censures
    Attend the true event[1] and put we on
    Industrious soldiership.
SIWARD   The time approaches
    That will with due decision make us know
    What we shall say we have and what we owe[2];
    Thoughts speculative their unsure hopes relate,
    But certain issue strokes must arbitrate[3].
    Towards which, advance the war[4].

Exeunt, marching

Act 5 Scene 5
Dunsinane Castle

Enter MACBETH, SEYTON, *and Soldiers, with drum and colours*

MACBETH Hang out our banners on the outward walls;
    The cry is still, 'They come.' Our castle's strength
    Will laugh a siege to scorn[5]; here let them lie[6]
    Till famine and the ague[7] eat them up.
    Were they not forced[8] with those that should be ours,
    We might have met them dareful[9], beard to beard[10],
    And beat them backward home.
A cry within of women
           What is that noise?
SEYTON It is the cry of women, my good lord.
MACBETH I have almost forgot the taste of fears;
    The time has been, my senses would have cooled
    To hear a night-shriek and my fell of hair[11]
    Would at a dismal treatise[12] rouse[13] and stir
    As life were in't. I have supped full with horrors[14];
    Direness[15] familiar to my slaughterous thoughts
    Cannot once start me. Wherefore was that cry?
SEYTON The queen, my lord, is dead.

His wife's death sets Macbeth brooding on life's futility. A messenger tells that Birnam Wood is moving towards Dunsinane. Macbeth doubts the Apparition's ambiguous words. He determines to die fighting.

 剧情简介：妻子的死使麦克白忧思生命之徒劳。信使告诉他伯南林正朝丹悉嫩移动。麦克白怀疑起幽灵说过的模棱两可的话。他决心战死。

Characters 人物分析

'Tomorrow, and tomorrow, and tomorrow' (in pairs)

In lines 18–27, Macbeth wearily speaks of time past, present and future, and of how fragile and empty he finds life. Ultimately, he says, it means 'nothing'. This is a profound contemplation about life, and it is worth studying it in depth. Work on one or more of the following:

- Speak the lines in different ways (perhaps sadly or wonderingly).
- Whisper the lines to each other, as though telling a secret.
- Emphasise the bleak fatalism of the words.
- Decide who Macbeth is speaking to (Himself? Seyton? The audience? Or someone else?)
- Devise actions and expressions for each section.
- Talk together about the imagery Macbeth uses. What makes it so powerful?

Themes 主题分析

Fate and free will (in pairs)

The Messenger's announcement that he has seen Birnam Wood raises issues relating to the theme of fate and free will. To what extent do you think Macbeth has control of his fate? Can he alter how he might die and who might kill him?

Script an imaginary dialogue between two students of your own age discussing these issues, with one student arguing that Macbeth is in control and the other arguing that he is not. Remember to use specific examples from the play's events and characters.

1 What does it mean to be brave? (by yourself)

Macbeth is a play preoccupied with what it means to be brave, and each of the main characters has the opportunity to prove their courage in many different ways (even the Messenger, a minor character, has to be brave to tell Macbeth the news about Birnam Wood).

Write two or three paragraphs arguing for the character you think is the bravest of all, using specific references from the play to support your argument.

1. She should have died hereafter （有两种可能的意思：她本应晚点儿死；她本来今后也会死）
2. petty 小，微不足道
3. syllable 说的话
4. recorded 记下来
5. lighted 照亮
6. Out, out, brief candle 灭了，灭了，短短的蜡烛（比喻人生像蜡烛一样短暂且易灭）
7. poor player 蹩脚的演员
8. struts and frets 大摇大摆又焦躁不安
9. report 把……联系起来（即如实禀报）
10. stand my watch 执勤放哨
11. cling 变干瘪，使枯萎
12. sooth 真相
13. I pull in resolution 我撤销决心（pull in表示"勒住马"）
14. equivocation 模棱两可的话
15. the fiend 魔鬼（即第三个幽灵）
16. avouches 断言，声称
17. tarrying 等待
18. 'gin = begin
19. th'estate o'th'world 世间万物
20. undone 完蛋，毁灭
21. wrack 毁灭
22. harness 盔甲

MACBETH   She should have died hereafter[1];
There would have been a time for such a word.
Tomorrow, and tomorrow, and tomorrow
Creeps in this petty[2] pace from day to day
To the last syllable[3] of recorded[4] time;   20
And all our yesterdays have lighted[5] fools
The way to dusty death. Out, out, brief candle[6],
Life's but a walking shadow, a poor player[7]
That struts and frets[8] his hour upon the stage
And then is heard no more. It is a tale   25
Told by an idiot, full of sound and fury
Signifying nothing.

Enter a MESSENGER

Thou com'st to use thy tongue: thy story quickly.
MESSENGER   Gracious my lord,
I should report[9] that which I say I saw,   30
But know not how to do't.
MACBETH   Well, say, sir.
MESSENGER   As I did stand my watch[10] upon the hill
I looked toward Birnam and anon methought
The wood began to move.
MACBETH   Liar and slave!
MESSENGER   Let me endure your wrath if't be not so;   35
Within this three mile may you see it coming.
I say, a moving grove.
MACBETH   If thou speak'st false,
Upon the next tree shall thou hang alive
Till famine cling[11] thee; if thy speech be sooth[12],
I care not if thou dost for me as much.   40
I pull in resolution[13] and begin
To doubt th'equivocation[14] of the fiend[15]
That lies like truth. 'Fear not, till Birnam Wood
Do come to Dunsinane', and now a wood
Comes toward Dunsinane. Arm, arm, and out!   45
If this which he avouches[16] does appear,
There is nor flying hence nor tarrying[17] here.
I 'gin[18] to be aweary of the sun
And wish th'estate o'th'world[19] were now undone[20].
Ring the alarum bell! Blow wind, come wrack[21];   50
At least we'll die with harness[22] on our back.
                              Exeunt

Malcolm instructs his troops to throw aside their camouflage of branches. He issues orders for battle. Macbeth compares himself to a baited bear. He is challenged by Young Siward.

 剧情简介：马尔肯命令军队扔掉用来伪装的树枝。他发出开战的命令。麦克白把自己比作一只被狗围困的熊。他受到小修沃的挑战。

Stagecraft 导演技巧

'harbingers of blood and death' (in threes)

Act 5 Scene 6 is a short, transitional scene of only ten lines. Some filmmakers have used these battle scenes to show the vast scale of the conflict. Theatre directors have to operate with more limitations, including the fact that the actors should be camouflaged with branches. Discuss how you would stage this scene:

- in your school hall or theatre
- in an open-air theatre
- in a big-budget movie.

Now collate your ideas and choose the best (and most workable) of them to write up as advice to a director, outlining how this scene could be staged effectively.

Themes 主题分析

Appearance and reality (in pairs)

In Act 4 Scene 3, Malcolm appears to Macduff to be something he is not; here, he asks his soldiers to discard their branches and 'show like those you are'. The difference between appearance and reality is important in *Macbeth*.

Discuss the key episodes in the play that illustrate the difference between appearance and reality. Talk about why you think Shakespeare and his audience were so fascinated by the interplay between the two. Extend this discussion by talking with other pairs about whether modern society is equally preoccupied with such issues.

1. **leafy screens** 遮挡的树枝
2. **take upon** 承担
3. **trumpets** 军号
4. **clamorous harbingers** 吵闹的先行者（军号吹奏声）
5. *Alarums continued* 持续的战斗声（使观众明白剧情转移到另一个战场，而不是另一个时间）
6. **the castle gate** 丹悉嫩城堡大门
7. **tied** 用锁链锁住
8. **stake** 桩子
9. **course** 攻击（前面麦克白把自己比作被锁住的熊，course 可以具体化为"一轮攻击"）
10. **hotter** 更恶毒

1 Shakespearean sports

Macbeth's reference to being trapped like a baited bear would have created a very powerful image for Shakespeare's audiences. Sports such as bear-baiting and cock-fighting were popular in the area where the Globe was situated. Find out about the sports and other amusements that the audience might have walked past on their way to the theatre. What do these sports tell us about the society of the time, and to what extent have things changed since then? Present your research to others in the class orally, or in the form of posters. These could be displayed to build up a picture of Elizabethan and Jacobean life.

Act 5 Scene 6
Outside Dunsinane Castle

Drum and colours. Enter MALCOLM, SIWARD, MACDUFF, *and their army, with boughs*

MALCOLM Now near enough; your leafy screens[1] throw down
And show like those you are. You, worthy uncle,
Shall with my cousin your right noble son
Lead our first battle. Worthy Macduff and we
Shall take upon's[2] what else remains to do, 5
According to our order.

SIWARD   Fare you well.
Do we but find the tyrant's power tonight,
Let us be beaten if we cannot fight.

MACDUFF Make all our trumpets[3] speak; give them all breath,
Those clamorous harbingers[4] of blood and death. 10

Exeunt

Alarums continued[5]

Act 5 Scene 7
Near the castle gate[6]

Enter MACBETH

MACBETH They have tied[7] me to a stake[8]; I cannot fly,
But bear-like I must fight the course[9]. What's he
That was not born of woman? Such a one
Am I to fear, or none.

Enter YOUNG SIWARD

YOUNG SIWARD What is thy name? 5
MACBETH Thou'lt be afraid to hear it.
YOUNG SIWARD No, though thou call'st thyself a hotter[10] name
Than any is in hell.

Macbeth kills Young Siward and boasts that no man born of woman can kill him. Macduff refuses to fight with mercenaries and seeks only Macbeth. Siward invites Malcolm to enter Macbeth's surrendered castle.

剧情简介：麦克白杀死小修沃并吹嘘凡是女人生的男子都杀不死他。麦克达拒绝与雇佣兵作战，一心想找麦克白对决。修沃邀请马尔肯进入已投降的麦克白的城堡。

Stagecraft 导演技巧

'My name's Macbeth' (in pairs)

This is a very dramatic moment in the scene: Macbeth is clearly aware that his name will strike terror into the hearts of many. Some directors use this as an opportunity to show just how invulnerable Macbeth is to all those soldiers 'born of woman', leading up to the killing of Young Siward. How do you think Macbeth should appear at this point in the play? Does he feel untouchable, or is he deranged (精神失常) and increasingly desperate? Discuss the different ways this might be staged.

1. abhorrèd 可憎
2. haunt （鬼魂）纠缠
3. whose … staves 因受雇于人才抓起棍棒（指雇佣兵）
4. unbattered 未遭损坏
5. undeeded 未使用（未采取行动）
6. There = Where there is most noise
7. clatter 嘈杂，喧嚣
8. one of greatest note 一个最大的人物（麦克白）
9. bruited 高声呐喊
10. gently rendered 不战而降
11. strike beside us 与我们并肩作战（或者"故意不战而走"）

1 'Let me find him, Fortune' (in threes)

On the battlefield, Macduff eagerly searches for Macbeth. Explore Macduff's motives for seeking out the king and discuss how he should act. One person plays 'Revenge', arguing that Macduff should be merciless; another plays 'Forgiveness', arguing that Macbeth should be treated leniently (宽大). The third person is Macduff himself, listening to these arguments. How does he respond in each case? Swap roles to bring out different perspectives.

2 'The tyrant's people on both sides do fight'
(in pairs, then by yourself)

Some of Macbeth's soldiers have deserted and now fight for Malcolm (line 26). In pairs, write some notes for and against defecting from Macbeth's forces. Using these notes, step into role as a soldier and write a private letter to a close friend, explaining why you have chosen to either defect or fight. What are your views of Macbeth? Of Scotland? Of your future happiness and ambition? (Try to refer to the conversation between Malcolm, Macduff and Ross in Act 4 Scene 3, lines 140–79 to develop the personal reasons for your actions.)

MACBETH	My name's Macbeth.
YOUNG SIWARD	The devil himself could not pronounce a title
	More hateful to mine ear.
MACBETH	No, nor more fearful. 10
YOUNG SIWARD	Thou liest, abhorrèd[1] tyrant; with my sword
	I'll prove the lie thou speak'st.

Fight, and young Siward slain

MACBETH	Thou wast born of woman.
	But swords I smile at, weapons laugh to scorn,
	Brandished by man that's of a woman born.

Exit [with young Siward's body]

Alarums. Enter MACDUFF

MACDUFF That way the noise is. Tyrant, show thy face! 15
If thou be'st slain, and with no stroke of mine,
My wife and children's ghosts will haunt[2] me still.
I cannot strike at wretched kerns whose arms
Are hired to bear their staves[3]; either thou, Macbeth,
Or else my sword with an unbattered[4] edge 20
I sheath again undeeded[5]. There[6] thou shouldst be;
By this great clatter[7], one of greatest note[8]
Seems bruited[9]. Let me find him, Fortune,
And more I beg not.   *Exit*

Alarums. Enter MALCOLM *and* SIWARD

SIWARD This way, my lord; the castle's gently rendered[10]. 25
The tyrant's people on both sides do fight;
The noble thanes do bravely in the war.
The day almost itself professes yours,
And little is to do.
MALCOLM   We have met with foes
That strike beside us[11].
SIWARD   Enter, sir, the castle. 30

Exeunt

Alarum

Facing Macduff, Macbeth boasts that no naturally born man can kill him, but Macduff reveals his own Caesarean birth. Dismayed, Macbeth refuses to fight. Macduff threatens he will be exhibited in captivity.

剧情简介：麦克白面对麦克达，吹嘘正常出生的人根本杀不死他，但麦克达说自己是剖宫所生。麦克白感到惊愕，拒绝与他搏斗。麦克达威胁说他将被囚禁起来供人参观。

Characters 人物分析

'play the Roman fool' (in pairs)

With his men deserting him and his castle taken, Macbeth must realise that he has lost the battle. But he rejects the idea of committing suicide ('play the Roman fool') and is determined to fight on, reminding us of the Captain's speech in Act 1 Scene 2, in which he depicts Macbeth as a warrior at heart. Debate which position is the more persuasive: one person argues that Macbeth is foolish, the other that he is admirable. Refer closely to Macbeth's words.

1 Who is the most guilty? (in small groups)

In the previous scene, Macduff admits that he feels guilty for the death of his wife and children (Act 5 Scene 7, line 17). Here, Macbeth admits that he feels guilty for the death of Macduff's family ('my soul is too much charged / With blood of thine already'). But how different are their crimes? In groups, put each character on trial, with a prosecution (控方), defence and judge. You may wish to consider:

- how their crimes are morally different
- why Shakespeare allows us to see this side of their characters
- how our view of both characters changes with these admissions.

2 'Despair thy charm'

Macbeth has been relying on the prophecy that he cannot be killed by 'one of woman born'. Macduff's revelation that he was not born naturally, but by Caesarean section, shatters Macbeth. He realises he has been duped by the Witches and their equivocations. Suggest how Macbeth physically reacts to Macduff's revelation and how he delivers lines 17–22.

Themes 主题分析

Macbeth's guilt (whole class)

The threat of being displayed in a cage in a circus is a humiliation that Macbeth cannot bear to contemplate. What ten crimes of Macbeth's would you write beneath Macduff's proposed sign? As a class, decide on everything he is guilty of, then sequence his crimes in order of importance, with the most serious at number one.

1. play the Roman fool 扮演罗马傻子（古时战败的罗马军人宁可自杀也不愿被俘）
2. lives 活人
3. terms 语言，言语
4. Thou losest labour 你白费力气
5. intrenchant 不怕砍的
6. impress 留下印记
7. crests 头盔
8. Despair 别指望
9. angel 恶鬼
10. Untimely ripped 不合时宜地剖出
11. cowed 吓唬，恐吓
12. my better part of man 我男子汉的勇气
13. juggling 骗人
14. palter … sense 用模棱两可的话骗我们
15. keep … hope 听着是称心之言，却又违背我们的心愿
16. yield thee coward 你认怂吧
17. live … o'th'time 活着供世人观赏
18. underwrit 下边写明

Act 5 Scene 8
Outside Dunsinane Castle

Enter MACBETH

MACBETH   Why should I play the Roman fool[1] and die
On mine own sword? Whiles I see lives[2], the gashes
Do better upon them.

Enter MACDUFF

MACDUFF   Turn, hell-hound, turn.
MACBETH   Of all men else I have avoided thee,
But get thee back, my soul is too much charged   5
With blood of thine already.
MACDUFF   I have no words;
My voice is in my sword, thou bloodier villain
Than terms[3] can give thee out.

Fight. Alarum

MACBETH   Thou losest labour[4].
As easy mayst thou the intrenchant[5] air
With thy keen sword impress[6] as make me bleed.   10
Let fall thy blade on vulnerable crests[7];
I bear a charmèd life which must not yield
To one of woman born.
MACDUFF   Despair[8] thy charm,
And let the angel[9] whom thou still hast served
Tell thee, Macduff was from his mother's womb   15
Untimely ripped[10].
MACBETH   Accursèd be that tongue that tells me so,
For it hath cowed[11] my better part of man[12];
And be these juggling[13] fiends no more believed
That palter with us in a double sense[14],   20
That keep the word of promise to our ear
And break it to our hope[15]. I'll not fight with thee.
MACDUFF   Then yield thee coward[16],
And live to be the show and gaze o'th'time[17].
We'll have thee, as our rarer monsters are,   25
Painted upon a pole and underwrit[18],
'Here may you see the tyrant.'

Macbeth determines to go down fighting, and is killed. Siward reports light casualties. On being told that his son is dead, Siward's concern is to know if Young Siward died bravely.

 剧情简介：麦克白决定去拼死一搏，结果被杀。修沃汇报说伤亡很少。修沃得知儿子战死时，关心的是小修沃死得是否英勇。

Characters 人物分析

'I will not yield' (in pairs)

Lines 27–34 are Macbeth's last lines in the play, and here he chooses life over death. With a partner, discuss how he would give this speech then act out different ways of delivering the lines. Think about the last impression of Macbeth you want to leave with the audience: is his death brave and dignified, or cowardly and abject (下贱)?

1 The death of a dictator

The death of a dictator is always a public (and political) act. Find out how ancient tyrants met their deaths: King Ahab and Queen Jezebel (pictured below), Andronicus I, or, from the modern era, look at how King Faisal II of Iraq, or the Italian leader Benito Mussolini, as well as more contemporary examples. Do their deaths have any similarities with Macbeth's? Share your thoughts with the rest of the class.

1 **kiss the ground** 亲吻地上的土（表示投降的动作）
2 **rabble** 暴民
3 **opposed** 敌对
4 **try the last** 抵抗到底
5 **Lay on** 动手吧
6 **Hold, enough!** 住手，够了！
7 *Retreat, and flourish* （战斗结束时小号齐鸣）
8 **go off** 阵亡
9 **cheaply bought** 以很小的代价赢得
10 **paid a soldier's debt** 偿还了军人的债务（即战死）
11 **He … man** 他刚成人就死了
12 **prowess** 英勇
13 **unshrinking station** 不退缩的姿势
14 **brought off the field** 从战场搬走（加以埋葬）
15 **Had he his hurts before?** 他的伤口在身体正面吗？（问他死时是否面对敌人而不是在逃跑）

MACBETH   I will not yield
           To kiss the ground[1] before young Malcolm's feet
           And to be baited with the rabble's[2] curse.
           Though Birnam Wood be come to Dunsinane   30
           And thou opposed[3] being of no woman born,
           Yet I will try the last[4]. Before my body,
           I throw my warlike shield. Lay on[5], Macduff,
           And damned be him that first cries, 'Hold, enough![6]'
                                   Exeunt[,] fighting. Alarums

           Enter [Macbeth and Macduff,] fighting[,] and Macbeth slain

                           [Exit Macduff, with Macbeth's body]

Act 5 Scene 9
Dunsinane Castle

Retreat, and flourish[7]. Enter with drum and colours, MALCOLM,
           SIWARD, ROSS, *Thanes, and Soldiers*

MALCOLM   I would the friends we miss were safe arrived.
SIWARD   Some must go off[8]. And yet by these I see,
           So great a day as this is cheaply bought[9].
MALCOLM   Macduff is missing and your noble son.
ROSS   Your son, my lord, has paid a soldier's debt[10];   5
           He only lived but till he was a man[11],
           The which no sooner had his prowess[12] confirmed
           In the unshrinking station[13] where he fought,
           But like a man he died.
SIWARD   Then he is dead?
ROSS   Ay, and brought off the field[14]. Your cause of sorrow   10
           Must not be measured by his worth, for then
           It hath no end.
SIWARD   Had he his hurts before?[15]
ROSS   Ay, on the front.

Macduff displays Macbeth's severed head, and hails Malcolm as King of Scotland. Malcolm rewards his nobles for their services, creating them earls. He invites everyone to his coronation at Scone.

   剧情简介：麦克达展示麦克白被割下来的头，接着欢呼马尔肯成为苏格兰王。马尔肯嘉奖为自己效劳的贵族，封他们为伯爵。他邀请所有人参加他在斯贡的加冕仪式。

Themes 主题分析

'I would not wish them to a fairer death' (whole class)

Siward shows such a lack of feeling for his dead son that even Malcolm seems surprised and promises to mourn him as well ('He's worth more sorrow, / And that I'll spend for him'). Do you think Siward is being brave here, or uncaring? As a class, talk about the different representations of bravery in *Macbeth*. Who shows true courage and when, and who is cowardly? The discussion would benefit from forward planning and research: think about the issues involved, and the possible arguments that might be made by other members of the class.

1 knell is knolled 丧钟敲响
2 parted 离世
3 paid his score 还了债（英勇牺牲）
4 Hail 万岁（称颂词；但女巫向麦克白致意时，麦克白在第3幕第1场第61行的独白里也用了该词；因此马尔肯与麦克白有紧密联系）
5 usurper 篡位者
6 compassed with thy kingdom's pearl 被苏格兰的贵族精英环绕
7 reckon with your several loves 计算你们各自表现出的爱戴
8 make us even 让我们扯平（指论功行赏）
9 earls 伯爵（苏格兰新爵位，这里有可能联系到詹姆斯国王，他成为英格兰和爱尔兰王时把子爵和皇亲国戚都封为伯爵）
10 be … time 开启新时代
11 exiled friends abroad 流亡海外的朋友
12 watchful tyranny 让人提心吊胆的暴政
13 ministers 爪牙，走狗
14 by … life 用她暴虐的双手要了自己的命
15 grace of Grace 上天的恩赐
16 measure 适量，适当的程度

1 The restoration of peace? (in pairs)

In most of his tragedies, Shakespeare aims to restore a sense of peace and natural order to society by the end of the play. Here, Malcolm seems to emphasise such restoration by rewarding his allies and asking for the exiled to return. Do you think Malcolm deserves to be king? Knowing what you know about him, and Scotland at the time, do you think he will be a good king? Discuss this in pairs and then take forward your ideas to the next activity.

2 The final curtain (in large groups)

Create a tableau that captures the new hierarchy in Scotland. Where would you place Malcolm, Ross and Macduff (and where would Macbeth's head be placed)? You might want to bring back key players in the future of Scotland, such as Donaldbain and Fleance. If there is more than one group in your class, compare your tableaux and question each group on why it chose its arrangement.

3 Bring on the Witches (in small groups)

Some productions of the play have the Witches present at these final moments of the play. In one, they attended on Malcolm, marking him out as a future victim. In another, they hovered over the dead body of Macbeth – the victim they had enticed to disaster. Work out your own presentation of lines 21–42, and include the Witches to make some comment about Macbeth or the future of Scotland.

SIWARD Why then, God's soldier be he;
Had I as many sons as I have hairs, 15
I would not wish them to a fairer death.
And so his knell is knolled[1].

MALCOLM   He's worth more sorrow,
And that I'll spend for him.

SIWARD   He's worth no more;
They say he parted[2] well and paid his score[3],
And so God be with him. Here comes newer comfort. 20

Enter MACDUFF, *with Macbeth's head*

MACDUFF Hail[4], king, for so thou art. Behold where stands
Th'usurper's[5] cursèd head. The time is free.
I see thee compassed with thy kingdom's pearl[6],
That speak my salutation in their minds;
Whose voices I desire aloud with mine. 25
Hail, King of Scotland.

ALL   Hail, King of Scotland.

Flourish

MALCOLM We shall not spend a large expense of time
Before we reckon with your several loves[7]
And make us even[8] with you. My thanes and kinsmen,
Henceforth be earls[9], the first that ever Scotland 30
In such an honour named. What's more to do
Which would be planted newly with the time[10], –
As calling home our exiled friends abroad[11]
That fled the snares of watchful tyranny[12],
Producing forth the cruel ministers[13] 35
Of this dead butcher and his fiend-like queen,
Who, as 'tis thought, by self and violent hands
Took off her life[14], – this and what needful else
That calls upon us, by the grace of Grace[15]
We will perform in measure[16], time, and place. 40
So, thanks to all at once and to each one,
Whom we invite to see us crowned at Scone.

Flourish

Exeunt

FINIS

 **Macbeth**
麦克白

Looking back at the play 本剧回顾
Activities for groups or individuals

1 The big moments

What are the key scenes in *Macbeth*? In large groups, pick out the pivotal (关键) moments in the play by choosing what you think are the most important lines. Try to condense each act to between twenty and thirty lines; remember, you can cut out lines but you must not alter Shakespeare's language. Now assign parts to each member of the group and think about how you might stage these condensed acts. Ideally, your group will be divided into five smaller groups and each should work on one act. Afterwards, bring them together for a short, focused, blast of *Macbeth* as a whole.

2 Arranging a press conference

Arrange a table with Malcolm, Macduff, Ross, and Siward facing the media after the final battle has taken place. Each member of the 'press pack' should think of questions to ask about what has just happened; questions should be directed at the group and at specific individuals. Write down the answers and then, in groups, put the stories together: choose the medium you want to use to report on this conference (newspaper, radio, television, website blog or something else). You may want to take an editorial line in advance (pro-Malcolm or pro-Macbeth). Now discuss the answers as a class and explore why the various reports were similar and different.

3 Mini-*Macbeth*

Write a summary of *Macbeth* in exactly one hundred words. Then cut that down to exactly seventy-five words (try to stick to complete sentences); then cut that down to exactly fifty words. Continue to do this until you get it down to ten words. Now share these words with the class: you can post these on a designated pinboard, or use sticky notes, or put them on a class website. Discuss the choices made. Select one word that you think captures the most important element in the play.

4 Preparing for your production

How would you move *Macbeth* from being a 'flat text' to a successful performance? Over the course of studying the play, you have come up with many ideas. Now try to bring these together into one consolidated resource for a group of actors who are about to start rehearsing for a production. In addition to your notes to actors and directors, add other essential documents: a letter to potential financial sponsors (why should they invest in it?); posters; advertisements for print and web-based media; a strategy paper for promoting the production via social media; illustrations for the set design, props and costumes.

5 Debate: is Macbeth a tragic hero or, as Malcolm says, 'a butcher'?

In his final speech, Malcolm refers to Macbeth as a 'butcher'. But is he? Copy and complete a table similar to the one below, which outlines the qualities that a tragic hero has, and those that are more closely associated with a butcher.

Butcher	Tragic hero
Ruthless	Having a weakness
Unsympathetic	Sympathetic (feels guilt, shows emotions)

Organise a whole-class debate on this question. Think about the quotations you wish to use to support your points. Make sure you choose a chairperson who will bring in as many different views as possible.

159

MACBETH
麦克白

Perspectives and themes 视角与主题

What is the play about?

Imagine that you can travel back in time to around 1606. You meet William Shakespeare a few minutes after he has finished writing *Macbeth*. You ask him 'What is the play about?' But, like all great artists, Shakespeare doesn't seem interested in explaining his work. He leaves that up to others. He seems to say: 'Here it is. Read it, perform it, make of it what you will.'

There has been no shortage of responses to that invitation! *Macbeth* has been hugely popular ever since it was first performed. The thousands of productions and millions of words written about it show that there is no single 'right way' of thinking about or performing the play. You will probably have noticed this as you looked at the photographs of different productions in this book.

The play is like a kaleidoscope (万花筒). Every time it is performed it reveals different shapes, patterns, meanings, interpretations. For example, you could think about *Macbeth* as:

- a play of political and social realism, which shows how an oppressive hierarchical society produces corrupt individuals
- a tragedy in which a great man falls because of a fatal flaw in his character (Macbeth's ambition causes his death)
- a historical thriller with many elements of a fast-moving, action-packed murder story
- a moral tale advising against regicide (the murder of a king); remember, this would have pleased James I
- a psychological study of a murderer's mind, in which Macbeth constantly reveals his troubled innermost thoughts.

There are also various interpretive standpoints that allow different 'readings' of the play. People have interpreted *Macbeth* according to a number of perspectives. These include:

Feminist perspectives – looking at the way women are represented

Cultural materialist perspectives – looking at the way politics, wealth and power strongly influence every human relationship

New historicist perspectives – focusing on the repressive conditions of Shakespeare's own time

Psychoanalytical perspectives – looking at the unconscious and the irrational, as well as the impact of repressed sexuality and desire

Liberal humanist perspectives – freedom and human progress are the goals of life, and final reconciliation and harmony are possible

- ◆ In pairs, talk about which of the perspectives described above would be most helpful in exploring *Macbeth* further. Then, either individually or together, write the script for a dialogue between two people with different perspectives on the play. Try to show how their conversation develops, and encourage them to agree or disagree with each other about the meaning of *Macbeth*.

Themes

Another way of answering the question 'What is *Macbeth* about?' is to identify the themes of the play. Themes are ideas or concepts of fundamental importance that recur throughout the play, linking together plot, characters and language. Themes echo, reinforce and comment upon each other – and the whole play – in interesting ways. For example, it is hard to write about appearance and reality in the play without referring to the manifestation of evil or the hidden dangers beneath a pleasing exterior. It is equally difficult to write about kingship and masculinity without talking about the themes of loyalty and ambition.

As you can see, themes are not individual categories but a 'tangle' of ideas and concerns that are interrelated in complex ways. In your writing you should aim to explore the way these themes cross over and illuminate each other, rather than simply listing each of the themes.

Perspectives And Themes

You might also like to think about the way the themes work at different levels: the individual level (psychological or personal); the social level (linked to society and nation); and the natural level (the natural or supernatural world). For example, in *Macbeth* you can clearly see how the theme of appearance and reality works across all three of these levels.

The themes of *Macbeth* include the following:

Ambition – the ruthless seeking of power by Macbeth, urged on by his equally ambitious wife. It can be thought of as the tragic flaw that causes his downfall ('I have no spur / To prick the sides of my intent, but only / Vaulting ambition').

Evil – the brooding presence of murderous intention, destroying whatever is good. Macbeth's conscience troubles him, but he commits evil, and finds others to carry out his malign orders (the murders of Duncan, Banquo, Lady Macduff).

Order and disorder – the struggle to maintain or destroy social and natural bonds; the destruction of morality and mutual trust ('Uproar the universal peace, confound / All unity on earth').

Appearance and reality – evil lurks behind fair looks. Deceit and hypocrisy mean that appearances cannot be trusted. The theme occurs throughout. It is introduced in the first scene as the Witches chant 'Fair is foul, and foul is fair'. Later, in Act 1 Scene 5, Lady Macbeth urges Macbeth to 'look like th'innocent flower, / But be the serpent under't'.

Equivocation – telling half-truths with the intention to mislead ('th'equivocation of the fiend / That lies like truth').

Violence and tyranny – warfare, destruction and oppression recur throughout the play. In the first scene, the Witches speak of 'the battle', and in the second, the wounded Captain reports Macbeth's victory in a bloody war. Tempted by the prospect of becoming king, Macbeth embarks on a violent journey that makes him Scotland's tyrant. Malcolm expresses the theme with the words: 'Pour the sweet milk of concord into hell.'

Guilt and conscience – Macbeth knows what he does is wrong, but he does it nonetheless and suffers agonies of conscience as a result ('O, full of scorpions is my mind').

Masculinity – the violent feudal society of hierarchical male power breeds bloody stereotypes of what it is to be a man. 'I dare do all that may become a man', says Macbeth, contemplating murder. But the play offers other visions of manhood: 'But I must also feel it as a man', cries Macduff, weeping at news of his family's murder.

- ◆ Working in small groups, devise a tableau that shows one of the themes of the play. Present your tableau, frozen for one minute, for other groups to guess which theme is being portrayed.

- ◆ Imagine you are asked to explain what *Macbeth* is about by an eight-year-old child, and also by your teacher/lecturer. Write a reply to each of them, using these two pages to help you.

Macbeth
麦克白

The contexts of Macbeth 《麦克白》的创作背景

One way of thinking about *Macbeth* is to set it in the context of its time: the world that Shakespeare knew. His dramatic imagination was influenced by many features of that world. Layers of dramatic possibilities within the script are built on past performances (such as miracle and morality plays), other literary texts (such as Holinshed's *Chronicles*) and contemporary events or topical concerns (such as the accession of James to the throne and the general interest in witchcraft at the time). This layering gives Shakespeare's plays great depth without limiting them to any single or specific social, religious or political meaning.

Writing for a king

In 1603, James, King of Scotland and a member of the Stuart dynasty, succeeded Queen Elizabeth I on the English and Irish thrones. Some critics argue that Shakespeare wrote *Macbeth* partly to flatter the new king (who probably saw a performance in 1606), and that he deliberately included many references to events and issues that would have interested James.

The play has a large focus on kingship, ideas of succession and the health of the nation. *Macbeth* explores the qualities of a good king and the horrors of living in a country ruled by a tyrant. Issues of power and politics are raised through the play's exploration of the sacred power and divine right of kings, the nature of lawful succession, the relationship between England and Scotland, and the dangers of treason and sedition (煽动).

Macbeth refers to the hanging of traitors and to the Gunpowder Plot of 5 November 1605. The king's escape from being blown up was commemorated by a medal showing a snake concealed by flowers. The Plot may be referred to in Act 2 Scene 3, line 50 ('dire combustion'). Sir Everard Digby, one of the conspirators, was a favourite of James (and possibly mirrored by the treacherous Thane of Cawdor). The play's concern with equivocation may also refer to Henry Garnet, who was accused of treason for involvement in the Gunpowder Plot. He was found to have committed perjury (lying on oath), but in self-defence claimed to have the right to equivocate. Equivocation is the use of deliberately misleading half-truths; it was seen as a diabolical use of language that distorted the truth and damned men's souls to hell. Equivocation is a major theme of the play and Macbeth is frequently troubled by it, fearing that the Witches may have lied to him.

▼ The execution of Henry Garnet.

The theme of kingship and ideas of what makes a good king run through the play. In the activities throughout this book, you have had opportunity to consider Macbeth as a political leader. At times it is also possible to compare him to a warrior like Braveheart, especially in Act 1 Scene 2. Further comparisons can be made between Macbeth and historical tyrants, such as Idi Amin.

◆ Draw a table with two columns. In the first column, list all the qualities of a tyrant. In the second column, list Macbeth's qualities. To what extent does he fit the criteria of a bloody tyrant?

The contexts of Macbeth

Witches and witchcraft

Throughout Shakespeare's life, during the reigns of Elizabeth I and James I, many people suspected of being witches were cruelly persecuted, and those who were convicted faced the prospect of being burned to death. Hundreds of pamphlets describing the lurid details of many witchcraft trials were printed. They enjoyed enormous sales: the equivalent of today's popular newspapers, or movies and books about the supernatural.

Witches were credited with diabolical powers. For example, they could predict the future, fly, sail in sieves, bring on night in daytime, cause fogs and tempests, and kill animals. In Act 1, the First Witch describes how she created a storm to destroy the captain of the *Tiger*. The *Tiger* was a real ship that set sail from England in 1604 and undertook a disastrous voyage on its way to Japan. After suffering storms and navigational errors, it finally returned to England around the time Shakespeare was writing this play. Although the voyage of the *Tiger* was a real event, Shakespeare was more interested in the dramatic and imaginative possibilities of attributing this disaster to witchcraft and spells.

It was also thought that witches cursed their enemies with fatal wasting diseases, induced nightmares and sterility, and could take demonic possession of others. People believed that witches allowed the Devil to suck their blood in exchange for a 'familiar': a bird, reptile or beast as an evil servant. Accused witches were examined for the 'Devil's mark': a red mark on the body from which Satan had sucked blood (some of Shakespeare's audience might have interpreted Lady Macbeth's 'damned spot' as evidence of the Devil's mark). Many of those watching *Macbeth* saw in the play the signs of a man and woman seized by demonic possession: disturbed behaviour, lack of fear and indifference to life. Both Macbeth and Lady Macbeth fall into trances (精神恍惚), have strange visions and invite evil spirits to possess their bodies.

King James was as fascinated by witchcraft as any of his subjects. In 1590, a group of witches tried to kill him by raising a storm to sink his ship. Their plot was discovered and they were brought to trial at North Berwick. James personally interrogated Dr Fian, a key witness during the trials. The poor doctor was horribly tortured:

> His nails upon all his fingers were riven and pulled off … his legs were crushed and beaten together as small as might be, and the bones and flesh so bruised that the blood and marrow spouted forth in great abundance.

Fired by his experience of the trial, King James personally investigated other witchcraft cases and, in 1597, he published *Demonologie*, a book on witchcraft. In 1604, an Act of Parliament decreed that anyone found guilty of witchcraft should be executed.

◆ The paragraphs above describe how people in Shakespeare's day understood witchcraft and witches. They also describe how Shakespeare alluded to many of the ideas about evil, the demonic and kingship that preoccupied James I. Re-read this information, then write an opinion article for a local newspaper giving a different perspective on witchcraft and witches. Try to explain why Shakespeare might have included witches in his play about a tyrant-king who murders his way to the throne. Do you think he was influenced by contemporary hysteria about the diabolical powers of witches when he was writing *Macbeth*?

Shakespeare's reading

As he wrote *Macbeth*, Shakespeare had at his side a book published in 1587: *Chronicles of England, Scotland and Ireland* by Raphael Holinshed. Shakespeare had earlier used Holinshed's *Chronicles* extensively as the source for his English History plays. Now, he found in it the Scottish stories that his imagination would turn into the drama of *Macbeth*. But Shakespeare never slavishly followed any source. Holinshed provided details of events, power politics, characters and motivations. Shakespeare selected, altered and added to them to achieve maximum dramatic effect. Here is an extract from Holinshed's *Chronicles*:

> It fortuned as Macbeth and Banquo journied towards Forres, where the King then lay, they went sporting by the way together without other company save only themselves, passing through the woods and fields, when suddenly in the midst of a land, there met them three

Macbeth
麦克白

women in strange and wild apparel, resembling creatures of elder world, whom when they attentively beheld, wondering much at the sight, the first of them spake and said: All hail Macbeth, thane of Glamis (for he had lately entered into that dignity and office by the death of his father Finel [Holinshed 误作 Sinel]*). The second of them said: Hail Macbeth, thane of Cawdor. But the third said: All hail Macbeth that hereafter shall be King of Scotland.*

As well as writing in dramatic form, Shakespeare invented Lady Macbeth's sleepwalking and death, the banquet scene and Banquo's Ghost, and most of the cauldron scene. He also vividly portrayed the changing relationship between Macbeth and Lady Macbeth. He made Lady Macbeth a key character in his story, whereas Holinshed only made a brief comment about her as 'very ambitious, burning in unquenchable desire to bear the name of queen'. Unlike Holinshed, Shakespeare did not make Banquo an accomplice (同谋) to Duncan's murder. Instead, he made the Macbeths solely responsible. This alteration presumably pleased King James because he hated regicides (king-killers) and because he believed he was a descendant of the historical Banquo. See the table below for a summary of the way Shakespeare changed Holinshed's account of *Macbeth*.

Holinshed	Shakespeare
Duncan is an ineffectual king	Duncan is a respected and revered ruler
Macbeth reigns for ten years as a good ruler	Macbeth is a tyrant immediately after he becomes king
Lady Macbeth is described in passing (顺便，捎带)	Lady Macbeth has great prominence in the play
Banquo is an accomplice to Duncan's murder	Banquo is an innocent victim murdered by Macbeth

◆ Step into role as William Shakespeare. Write out what went through your mind as you rewrote Holinshed. Remember, as a playwright you are always asking yourself: 'How can I put this on stage to greatest dramatic effect?'

Mystery plays and morality plays

Shakespeare doesn't limit *Macbeth* to the themes or characteristics of medieval plays, but he does remind his audience of these earlier dramatic traditions. He invites them to make connections and activates their experiences of past traditions to bring greater depth to their understanding of *Macbeth*.

Some critics claim that *Macbeth* shows Shakespeare's recollection of mystery plays, which were dramatised Bible stories immensely popular as entertainment and instruction in the Middle Ages. The mystery play *The Harrowing of Hell* is thought to be the inspiration for the Porter scene in *Macbeth*. In it, Hell is a castle whose gate is guarded by a Porter named Rybald ('ribald' means coarse and vulgar). Christ descends to Hell and hammers on the gate, demanding that Satan release the good souls imprisoned there. In this interpretation of the play, Macduff is the Christ-like figure who knocks at Macbeth's castle door. In Act 5, he enters the castle, kills the devil-tyrant, redeems Scotland and leads its people from darkness into light. Macbeth is singled out as the man who turns his castle and the whole of Scotland into

▼ The Day of Judgement, from the Guild Chapel in Stratford-upon-Avon. As a schoolboy, Shakespeare must have seen this painting often.

a type of hell, and Macduff is identified as Scotland's avenger and rescuer, through this reference to *The Harrowing of Hell*.

Medieval morality plays portrayed the human struggle to choose between vice and virtue. They personified a range of Vices (including the seven deadly sins) and Virtues in stories of temptation and conflict between good and evil. The hero, often given a generic name like Everyman or Mankind, must choose between them. Although the Everyman figure is led astray by the Vice figure, and wallows (沉溺) in sinfulness, he repents and is saved at the end of the play. The point of the plays is that although the hero succumbs to sin, God's mercy is always available to one who repents. In this way, the morality plays made the basic elements of Christianity accessible to those who were unable to read the Latin Bible for themselves. They taught people to watch out for the common vices that might tempt them and to have faith in the mercy of God.

◆ Use the information above to give a context-based alternative interpretation of *Macbeth*. Consider how Shakespeare might have been influenced by medieval religious drama. You might like to reflect on how Macbeth could be seen as an Everyman figure, tempted to evil by different Vices and heading towards either heaven or hell in the course of the play. Also consider whether the link between Macduff and Christ or Macbeth and the devil-tyrant intensifies the conflict between them.

◆ Write a short letter to a younger student telling them about an alternative interpretation of *Macbeth* based on this information. You might like to do more research as you write this letter.

Tragedy

Tragedies were popular in Shakespeare's England. They dramatised the fall from power of kings, princes and military leaders and the way this affected the fortunes of states and nations. Tragedies contained assassination, bloodshed and revenge, and were written to instruct as well as to entertain. Shakespeare was influenced by the Roman playwright Seneca (4 BC–AD 65), whose tragedies included soliloquies, ghosts, witches, magic, violent events, wrongs avenged and moral statements.

Shakespeare was also influenced by the development of tragedy as a dramatic form in England. The most significant aspect of this development was the focus on the protagonist (主人公), who was responsible for his own downfall and often displayed a fatal flaw or essential trait that contributed to his death. Elizabethan and Jacobean tragedy contained sub-plots, spectacle and onstage violence. They also depicted a movement towards isolation and social breakdown – an inevitable sequence of events that led ultimately to the death of the protagonist (and many of the other characters).

◆ Find out more about Elizabethan tragedies and the trajectory (轨迹) of the protagonist towards isolation, chaos and death. How would you plot Macbeth's trajectory? Create a diagram or a graph that charts this trajectory. Beneath it write a description of the characteristics that might contribute to the fatal flaw or essential trait that propels Macbeth towards his downfall. How does this add to your understanding of the play?

Macbeth 麦克白

Characters 人物分析

How are characters created?

The process of creating and developing characters is called 'characterisation'. In *Macbeth*, Shakespeare does this in three major ways:

By their actions – Macbeth murders Duncan; then he has Banquo and Lady Macduff and her family murdered.

By what is said about them – amongst other things, Lady Macbeth is called 'fiend-like'; Macbeth is called 'brave' several times, as well as a 'butcher'.

Through their own language – how they speak with each other and, through **soliloquy**, what they say to themselves when alone.

Each of these is equally important. Soliloquies allow us to gain a deep insight into the innermost thoughts of the speaker, but other characters provide us with different views, and their actions are these words made real. Every character has a distinctive voice, and part of Shakespeare's genius is to explore each aspect while allowing that voice to both change (as events affect the character's mind) and remain unique and recognisable.

The Lady Macbeth we see in Act 5 Scene 1, although recognisably the same character from Act 1 Scene 5, has changed profoundly, and we learn this from her words ('Here's the smell of the blood still; all the perfumes of Arabia will not sweeten this little hand. O, O, O'), her actions (the sleepwalking, the obsessive hand-washing) and what is said about her by the Gentlewoman and the Doctor ('I would not have such a heart in my bosom for the dignity of the whole body').

◆ Which speeches by both characters offer the greatest insight into them? Collect key quotations about these characters and the way they change in the course of the play. Display your choice of quotations on a large piece of paper, with images that symbolise these significant moments.

◆ In small groups, discuss how Macbeth and Lady Macbeth change over the course of the play. Which of their actions most influence how you view them? What comments made by other characters about Macbeth and Lady Macbeth tell us most about them?

Macbeth

Although there are exciting moments in the play, much of the drama takes place in Macbeth's mind. He struggles with good and evil, and believes that his fate is decided by the Witches and other sinister forces. When trying to understand Macbeth, it helps to think about how a performer might approach playing the role: what might the actor feel are the motives that drive Macbeth to act in the way he does?

Below are some views of Macbeth by actors who have played the part and by a director. Read through them, then talk with a partner about which you think is the most striking view.

> *It was Macbeth as a poet, as the creator of a new vision, rather than as a soldier or a king, that I found most intriguing and mysterious. Charting the progress of a man who redefines himself as he analyses his experience became, for me, the single most important and interesting challenge.*
>
> Simon Russell Beale

> *In the last Act he [Macbeth] does, in my view, reach nobility, clarity and strength, a sense of the reality of the consequences of actions.*
>
> Sir Peter Hall

> *[He is] a killing machine with an elegant turn of phrase (措辞; 口才).*
>
> Jonathan Pryce

> *I went through the play marking the times he speaks of fear, particularly in relation to himself. He does so in every scene: it is paramount for him; the man is constantly fearful ... The moment before he does the murder he is afraid – the dagger speech is a fearful speech, the utterance of a terrified man. He does the murder for her, and it destroys them both.*
>
> Derek Jacobi

> *I see Macbeth as ambitious but capable of darkness. The witches saw something in him, they picked the right person. Witches plus Macbeth equals evil. Was evil there before though, I'm not sure you can say. Is anyone evil without input from others?*
>
> Liam Brennan

◆ Rank these quotations in order, with the one that most closely matches your understanding of Macbeth at the top.

◆ In small groups, and then with the rest of your class, discuss which of these comments gives you the greatest insight into the character of Macbeth.

Macbeth appears first in the play as a military hero. King Duncan calls him 'valiant cousin, worthy gentleman', 'noble Macbeth', 'worthiest cousin'. He ends the play as a cruel tyrant, deserted by his soldiers and allies, and finally slain by Macduff. The new king, Malcolm, viewing Macbeth's severed head, dismisses him as 'this dead butcher'.

It is easy to characterise Macbeth as a common murderer, but he is more complex than this – and he changes radically throughout the play. Paradoxically, perhaps, the more he kills, the more aware he becomes of the futility of his actions and even of life itself. Macbeth is revealed as a deeply sensitive man, tortured by his imagination and his conscience. His wife believes him to be a good, and even gentle, man ('too full o'th'milk of human kindness') and he knows that it is wrong to kill Duncan. He struggles to overcome his evil thoughts, but is tempted to criminality by the Witches, by his wife's pressure, and by his own ambition. He murders his way to the throne of Scotland, and then arranges the killing of anyone he suspects to be his enemy.

Macbeth
麦克白

Conflicting thoughts of good and evil constantly torment Macbeth ('O, full of scorpions is my mind, dear wife!'). But as he is drawn ever deeper into cruel and brutal actions, he strives to harden his responses and to lose 'the taste of fears'. Learning of his wife's death, he reflects despairingly on the emptiness of life, saying that it is 'a tale / Told by an idiot, full of sound and fury / Signifying nothing'.

He finally becomes aware that the Witches have misled him ('be these juggling fiends no more believed'). Even in his despair and weariness he determines to die bravely ('Blow wind, come wrack; / At least we'll die with harness on our back'). He slays Young Siward and, coming face to face with Macduff, still fights defiantly to the end although he realises he has met his nemesis (报应) ('Lay on, Macduff, / And damned be him that first cries, "Hold, enough!"'). Whether Macbeth's final words and actions represent heroic endurance or the snarling of a trapped animal is open for each reader or new performance to decide.

Lady Macbeth

For many actors and directors, Lady Macbeth is as difficult to define as her husband: she undergoes profound changes over the course of the play, and can be seen as a fiend or a supportive, ambitious wife.

◆ Just as you did with Macbeth, read the comments below and rank them in order, with the one you feel is closest to the truth as number one. After you have done this, discuss them in groups and then with the rest of your class.

She had no illusions about the evil she was embracing, but the thrill of it drew her back.

Judi Dench

And then she sees the blood ... something happens to her gut. For her, the sight is horrible. It shocks her, the reality of it ... After that we began talking different languages. We who had needed to touch each other all the time grew distant. When he had killed, neither of us wanted to touch each other.

Sinead Cusack

I think first and foremost she's a wife, she's a homemaker, she's a very, very intelligent woman. I think that the audience have to have an affection for this woman to be able to see how far she and her husband fall. I think she's a very strong woman who's the backbone, the crutch of Macbeth. In their marriage she's been the backbone of him.

Allison McKenzie

Lady Macbeth appears first as a supremely confident, dominant figure. She revels in the prospect of Macbeth becoming king, and calls on evil spirits to help her persuade him to kill Duncan. She urges him to use deception to cloak murderous intentions ('look like th'innocent flower, / But be the serpent under't').

When Macbeth's resolve to carry out the murder weakens, she ridicules his masculinity, convincing him to do the deed. She becomes his active accomplice, even returning the bloody daggers to Duncan's bedroom. It is the murder of Duncan that brings the Macbeths most closely together; however, this is also the moment that they begin to move irrevocably apart.

CHARACTERS

From this point, Lady Macbeth's decline seems inevitable. In Act 3, she begins to feel the emptiness of their achievement, seeing only 'doubtful joy'. She appears increasingly isolated and drained of energy as Macbeth moves away from her into his own troubled thoughts. She becomes more of an audience to Macbeth's words, rather than his partner. Although she rallies at the disastrous banquet, she ends that scene displaying none of her earlier dominance over her husband. Shakespeare does not show Lady Macbeth's decline into nervous breakdown and death, giving only one glimpse of that horrifying process: the torment she experiences in her sleepwalking. She dies off stage, an anti-climax (反高潮；高潮突降) of an event that seems to mark out her decline even more sharply.

◆ Study the pictures of Macbeth and Lady Macbeth in this section. Discuss in groups what each of these pictures conveys about the characters. In the same groups, choose one of the following activities:

  a *Hot-seating* One person steps into role of Macbeth. Group members ask him questions about why he did what he did. You can do the same with another person taking the role of Lady Macbeth.

  b *A modern duologue* In pairs, write a duologue between Macbeth and Lady Macbeth reflecting on their actions and trying to explain their behaviour; or if you prefer, improvise this instead of writing a script. Other members of your group watch and give feedback, commenting on how true to the spirit of both characters the interpretations are.

  c *Essay planning* Every member of the group writes one essay question each on:
  • Macbeth
  • Lady Macbeth
  • their relationship.

The group chooses the strongest question and plans an answer collectively. Deliver your essay plans as a presentation to the rest of the class. Keep the presentation succinct, using between six and eight slides (each slide representing a different part of the essay). Each slide should contain only key words: it's up to the group to talk the class through the answer in more detail.

MACBETH
麦克白

The language of *Macbeth* 《麦克白》的语言

Imagery

Imagery is the use of emotionally charged words and phrases that conjure up vivid mental pictures. These words, phrases and images are a kind of verbal painting that stirs the imagination, deepens dramatic impact and gives insight into character.

Macbeth is full of striking visual images. After the disastrous appearance of Banquo's Ghost at the banquet, and knowing that Macduff has turned against him, Macbeth resolves to commit yet more murders: 'I am in blood / Stepped in so far that should I wade no more, / Returning were as tedious as go o'er' (Act 3 Scene 4, lines 136–8). He sees himself wading through a river of blood and is so far in that it does not matter whether he goes on or turns back.

Sometimes an image extends over several lines. For example, in Act 1 Scene 7, lines 25–8, Macbeth soliloquises about whether or not to kill King Duncan, and concludes with an image from horse-riding:

> I have no spur
> To prick the sides of my intent, but only
> Vaulting ambition which o'erleaps itself
> And falls on th'other –

In this image of rider and horse, Macbeth sees himself like a horseman who urges on his mount by digging his spurs into the horse's sides. But he has no such motivation ('spur') to kill Duncan other than 'Vaulting ambition': like a rider vaulting on to his horse, but misjudging his leap and collapsing in failure on the other side.

Examples of how the imagery of the speeches and soliloquies can be illustrated with appropriate pictures can be seen in movies. In Polanski's film of *Macbeth*, for example, a bear-baiting post is used at several points in the play to emphasise the bear-baiting image.

- ◆ In role as a film director, write out your ideas for how the imagery in certain passages might be visualised in a film production. Prepare a screenplay or script to illustrate your ideas.

Recurring imagery

Macbeth is rich in imagery and certain images recur through the play, contributing to its distinctive atmosphere.

Blood

Images of blood carry great emotional force in *Macbeth*. The play begins and ends with bloody battles, and much blood is shed throughout, from that of 'blood-boltered Banquo' to Lady Macduff and her children. Macbeth is obsessed with blood and imagines himself wading through a river of blood, while Lady Macbeth, sleepwalking, smells blood and tries to rub away the spot of blood on her hands.

Darkness

Much of the action takes place at night, and the frequent images of darkness create a pervasive sense of evil. The Witches' presence and their spells and incantations heighten this, as does Lady Macbeth's invocation of evil spirits and darkness in Act 1.

Theatre

Shakespeare's fascination with his own profession provided him with a recurring theme: the world as a stage. On this stage, humans make brief, insignificant appearances to play their parts. Macbeth uses imagery relating to acting and theatre when he hears of the death of his wife in Act 5 Scene 5:

> Life's but a walking shadow, a poor player
> That struts and frets his hour upon the stage
> And then is heard no more.

Falconry and bear-baiting

Falconry (the art of training and hunting with a falcon) was also used as a key image by Shakespeare. Macbeth calls on 'seeling night' to come and 'Scarf up the tender eye of pitiful day', referring to the practice of sewing up hawks' eyes during the training process. Macduff describes the death of his wife and children in 'one fell swoop', referring to the way a falcon descends on its prey.

The bear-baiting that Shakespeare saw near the Globe Theatre also inspired an image for Macbeth as he is

The language of Macbeth

surrounded by his enemies and facing death at the end of the play:

> They have tied me to a stake; I cannot fly,
> But bear-like I must fight the course.

Disease
The Witches' 'fog and filthy air' in the first scene begins the imagery of sickness. This continues in references to the poison that goes in their cauldron and the 'infected' air they ride on. Disease and sickness affects both Scotland, 'the sickly weal', and the Macbeths – Lady Macbeth has a 'mind diseased' and Macbeth describes his mind as 'full of scorpions'.

Nature
Frequent images of animals, birds and insects are often ominous, and there are recurring images of ferocious creatures. Shakespeare shows how evil overruns Scotland by using images of nature disturbed.

◆ **Choose one example of recurring imagery in the play and collect as many pictures from magazines or the Internet as you can that represent this. Find quotations from the play that link to the images you have chosen, then think of an appropriate way to display them, such as in a collage.**

Metaphor, simile and personification
Shakespeare's imagery uses metaphor, simile and personification. All are comparisons.

A **simile** (明喻) compares one thing to another using 'like' or 'as'. Macbeth challenges Banquo's Ghost to approach 'like the rugged Russian bear'; the First Witch threatens the sailor she will 'drain him dry as hay'.

A **metaphor** is also a comparison, suggesting that two dissimilar things are actually the same. Donaldbain says 'There's daggers in men's smiles'.

Personification is a special kind of imagery that turns all kinds of things into persons, giving them human feelings or attributes. The bleeding Captain speaks of Macbeth as 'Valour's minion' (bravery's favourite) and of 'Fortune' smiling on the rebel Macdonald. In Act 4, Scotland is described as weeping, diseased and suffering under the evil rule of Macbeth.

▼ Imagery of blood recurs throughout the play. After murdering Duncan, Macbeth wonders 'Will all great Neptune's ocean wash this blood / Clean from my hand?'. Later, Lady Macbeth asks 'will these hands ne'er be clean?'.

Macbeth
麦克白

Verse and prose

Shakespeare's audiences expected tragedies to be written in verse, because verse was thought to be appropriate to great men, affairs of state, and moments of emotional or dramatic intensity.

Macbeth is written mainly in **blank verse**, which is unrhymed lines that have carefully placed stressed and unstressed syllables. Each line has five feet (groups of syllables) called iambs, each of which has an unstressed (×) and stressed (/) syllable that sounds like a heartbeat (da DUM, da DUM, da DUM, da DUM, da DUM):

> × / × / × / × / × /
> So foul and fair a day I have not seen.

The Witches almost always speak in four-beat rhythm (tetrameter), a style appropriate to spells, incantations and the supernatural. The rhythm is the opposite of the heartbeat rhythm described above (DUM-da, DUM-da, DUM-da, DUM-da):

> / / / /
> Fair is foul, and foul is fair

Shakespeare uses a varied rhythmic pattern throughout the play. He sometimes wrote lines of more or fewer than ten syllables, sometimes changed the pattern of stresses in a line, and sometimes used rhyming couplets for effect. He ensured that the rhythm of the verse was appropriate to the meaning and mood of the speech: reflective, fearful, apprehensive, anguished or confused.

These rhythmic patterns are what distinguish verse from prose, not whether they rhyme. Prose is different from blank verse: it is everyday language with no specific rhythm, metric scheme or rhyme. Shakespeare uses prose to break up the verse in his plays, to signify characters' madness or low status, or to draw attention to changes in plot or character. It is easy to tell the difference: verse passages begin with a capital letter and the lines do not reach the other side of the page, whereas prose passages have lines that reach both sides of the pages and only use capital letters at the beginning of sentences.

Shakespeare also used **caesura** ([诗行中的] 切分处；停顿处) and **enjambement** (跨行) to add to the rhythm of his blank verse. A caesura is where the phrasing of the line is broken to create a pause or a break in the dialogue or action. With enjambement, the end of one sentence carries over into the next line of poetry, giving the impression that the phrases are spilling over and building up from one line to the next.

◆ The human heartbeat is the rhythm of iambic pentameter (抑扬五音步). Put your hand on your heart to hear the basic rhythm of weak and strong stresses.

◆ Choose a verse speech. Explore ways of speaking it to emphasise the metre (four or five beats). For example, you could clap hands, tap the desk or walk five paces to accompany each line. Then write eight or more lines of your own in the same style.

Antithesis (对偶) and repetition

Antithesis is the opposition of ideas, words or phrases against each other. It expresses the conflict that is at the heart of the play. In 'When the battle's lost, and won' and 'Fair is foul, and foul is fair' the conflict is shown in 'lost' against 'won', 'fair' against 'foul'. Antithesis is especially powerful in *Macbeth*, where good is set against evil and where deception and false appearances are major themes.

Shakespeare used **repetition** to give his language great dramatic force. Repeated words, phrases, rhythms and sounds add to the emotional intensity of a scene. This repetition can occur on many levels:

Repetition of words Sometimes the same word is repeated in a short space of time in order to increase pace and tension. The following exchange between the Witches illustrates this:

> Show!
> Show!
> Show!
> Show his eyes and grieve his heart

At other times a word is repeated throughout a passage so that the idea can be developed or extended:

> Still it cried, 'Sleep no more' to all the house;
> 'Glamis hath murdered sleep', and therefore Cawdor
> Shall sleep no more: Macbeth shall sleep no more.

The language of Macbeth

Repetition of sounds Alliteration is the repetition of consonants (at the beginning of words): 'Fair is foul, and foul is fair' and 'Double, double toil and trouble'.

Assonance is the repetition of vowel sounds (in the middle of words):

> *Thrice to thine, and thrice to mine,*
> *And thrice again, to make up nine.*

These repetitions are opportunities for actors to intensify emotional impact. Rhyming couplets, which often end long speeches in blank verse or signal the end of a scene, also show this repetition of sound:

> *Hear it not Duncan, for it is a **knell***
> *That summons thee to heaven or to **hell**.*

Repetition of patterns Anaphora (首语叠用) is the repetition of the same word at the beginning of successive sentences:

> ***Though** bladed corn be lodged and trees blown down,*
> ***Though** castles topple on their warders' heads*

Epistrophe (尾词重复) is the repetition of a word or phrase at the end of a series of sentences or clauses:

> *When you durst do it, then **you were a man**.*
> *And to be more than what **you were**, you would*
> *Be so much more the **man**.*

Polyptoton (一词多形法) is repetition of words derived from the same root word, but with different endings or forms:

> *But yet I'll make **assurance** double **sure***
> *And take a bond of fate*

◆ Turn randomly to any two or three pages of *Macbeth* and identify all the ways in which Shakespeare uses repetition on those pages. Try out different ways of speaking the lines to discover how emphasising or playing down the repetition can contribute to dramatic effect.

Soliloquies and asides

A **soliloquy** is a monologue, a kind of internal debate spoken by a character who is alone (or assumes they are alone) on stage. It gives the audience direct access to the character's mind, revealing their inner thoughts and motives. Macbeth often 'thinks aloud', expressing doubt, fear, guilt and confusion. His soliloquy in Act 5 Scene 5 conveys his overwhelming despair, and in Act 1 Scene 5, Lady Macbeth's soliloquy is an impassioned appeal for demonic spirits to possess her.

An **aside** is a brief comment or address to the audience that shows the character's unspoken thoughts, unheard by other characters on stage. The audience is taken into this character's confidence or can see deeper into their motivations and experiences. Asides can also be used for characters to comment on the action as it unfolds.

◆ Identify some of the play's soliloquies and asides. Choose one and write notes on how you would speak it on stage to maximise dramatic effect.

◆ Copy and complete the table below as a summary of the information in this section.

Quotation	Language use	Its effect and meaning
'Fair is foul, and foul is fair'	Antithesis	The tension and confusion in this antithesis adds to the evil atmosphere and the sense of foreboding in the whole scene.

MACBETH 麦克白

Macbeth in performance 《麦克白》的演出

Performance on Shakespeare's stage

Many people believe that because of the references to the Gunpowder Plot of 1605, *Macbeth* was first written and performed in 1606 as a tribute to King James I (who was also King James VI of Scotland). The first record of a production was written by Simon Forman, who described a performance he saw at the Globe Theatre on Bankside in 1611. Many of Shakespeare's plays were performed at the Globe, one of the many specially designed outdoor playhouses built at the end of the sixteenth century. They were modelled on the public amphitheatres (竞技场 [剧场通常是半圆形，两个剧场并在一起就成为一个圆形剧场，用于举行角斗或斗兽]) like the bear-baiting rings that existed in the seedier locations outside the city walls (and the city's jurisdiction).

During Shakespeare's lifetime, plays in outdoor amphitheatres like the Globe were performed in broad daylight during the summer months. So, at 2.00 p.m. people would assemble with food and drink to watch a play with no lighting and no rule of silence for the audience. There were high levels of background noise and interaction during performances, and audience members were free to walk in and out of the theatre.

In the Globe, the audience was positioned on three sides of the stage: the 'groundlings' (站票观众) stood in the pit ([圆形剧场中的] 无座观众池) around the stage, while those who paid more were seated in three levels around the pit. Actors would see around three thousand faces staring up or down at them. The positioning of the audience made it difficult for everyone to hear all that was going on. Inevitably the actors would have their backs to sections of the audience at times. The best place for an actor to stand, especially for a soliloquy or an aside, was at the front of the stage, so that he could directly address almost all of the audience. However, it would be tedious if all the action occurred there!

Shakespeare's use of repetition helped to overcome this problem. Sometimes the same idea is stated or developed in three ways, to allow an actor to address each section of the audience. These repetitions were never simply word-for-word, but were used to create rhythm, accumulate details and build on an idea through different metaphors and imagery. If you spot significant repetition, it may be a clue that Shakespeare intended the character to move around the stage to engage the audience.

▼ This map from 1647 shows the Globe Theatre (the circular building, centre left), built for the second time in 1614 after the first one burnt down. It was mistaken by the artist Wenceslaus Hollar for a bear-baiting pit that was nearby.

Macbeth in performance

◆ Look at some of Macbeth's and Lady Macbeth's soliloquies and identify where repetition might allow an actor to use the stage space in different ways. Imagine you are on the Globe stage and read out the lines while addressing different parts of your (imaginary) audience. Experiment with other ways of enacting repetition of words or ideas in the soliloquy for dramatic effect.

Shakespeare included many other clues for his actors in his play scripts. These clues are known as 'embedded stage directions' because of the coded instructions they gave to the actors about who to talk to, when to move or gesture and when to exit. Clues about setting, weather, clothing, other characters' appearances and onstage action were also placed in the scripts. In Act 4, when Macbeth sees the Apparitions, eight kings and the Ghost of Banquo, his dramatic exclamations can also be seen as embedded stage directions so that the actor knows how to respond: 'A fourth? Start, eyes!' His words a few lines later could also prompt the actor playing Banquo's Ghost (or prompt the imagination of the audience if no Ghost is present): 'the blood-boltered Banquo smiles upon me, / And points at them for his.'

Embedded stage directions were invaluable for early modern actors, who had little time to rehearse and not much opportunity to study the whole play before a performance. When a play was written, a scribe would make a copy. This was then cut up and each actor was given a scroll with his speeches stitched together along with basic cues and stage directions. The actors would memorise their lines, taking particular care that they knew their cues so they would understand when to enter and speak. A summary of the play, known as a 'backstage plot', was hung up backstage, so actors would know the main story and the context for their entrances and exits. Players who knew only their parts and a plot summary relied heavily on their cues and embedded stage directions to piece together information about what was going on, who they were addressing and who was going to respond.

The pressured system of rehearsal and performance was confusing for inexperienced actors, especially young ones, who were sometimes apprenticed to older actors while they were new to the workings of the stage. The apprentices, also known as boy actors, were usually aged between six or seven and thirteen or fourteen, and learned the art of acting from more established actors. Female roles were played by boy actors because women were not allowed to act on stage.

◆ Some of the activities throughout this book have asked you to look out for embedded stage directions. Look at these, or find some more, then discuss with a partner what a modern director might say to actors at these points. Are all of them necessary on a modern stage? Would you consider cutting some lines if they are not necessary? How should the actors perform the lines?

▼ An illustration from 1595 showing the Swan Theatre on Bankside in London. Wealthier people paid to sit in the levels that surrounded the stage on three sides.

Macbeth
麦克白

Stage sets were limited in terms of scenery and lighting, so Shakespeare included detailed and often poetic descriptions of the time and place in various scenes. Audiences needed to use their imaginations to compensate for the bare stage! However, actors wore lavish costumes and a range of visual and sound effects were used to add spectacle to a performance. For example, animal organs may have been used on stage – including pigs' bladders filled with animal blood – during murder scenes. Cannonballs were rolled along tracks backstage to simulate thunder. Storm scenes such as the opening of *The Tempest*, or the scenes on the heath in *King Lear* and *Macbeth*, were probably accompanied by such sound effects. Bells, trumpets and drums were also used, as were a range of songs, background instrumental music and dance music.

A trapdoor on stage was also used in performances, allowing for such effects as a cauldron ascending with the Apparitions in *Macbeth*. The space above the stage, the upper structure known as the 'heavens', was decorated on the underside with stars and zodiac signs, and used for characters to descend and ascend during a performance.

Performance after Shakespeare

Since Shakespeare's time, *Macbeth* has always been popular. But like all of Shakespeare's plays, it has been rewritten, revised and adapted through the centuries, reflecting the tastes and the social and political circumstances of different times. Indeed, the playwright Thomas Middleton changed some of the Witches' scenes and further revised the play as early as 1610. It has been altered many times since then.

We might revere Shakespeare today, but writers, actors and audiences from earlier periods felt that his plays needed to be salvaged and rewritten. They 'improved' the perceived flaws in the plays and adapted them to suit the tastes of the day. Sir William Davenant (who claimed to be Shakespeare's illegitimate son) presented a radically changed version of *Macbeth* from that first published in the 1623 First Folio edition of all Shakespeare's plays. A record of this production in 1672 reads:

The Tragedy of Macbeth, altered by Sir William Davenant; being dressed in all its finery, as new clothes, new scenes, machines, as flyings for the witches; with all the singing and dancing … being all excellently performed being in the nature of an opera.

This version was published soon after the Civil War and, in new scenes, it asked the audience to consider the role of the monarchy. But the changes were so extensive that it could be argued that the play was no longer Shakespeare's at all, but rather something entirely new. Davenant cut the Porter and the Doctors, had Seyton change sides at the end, and altered the language so as not to offend his audience of gentry. Scenes were added: Lady Macbeth and Lady Macduff talked together; Macduff's role was greatly enlarged at the expense of Malcolm's; and the Witches turned up to support Macduff against Macbeth.

Davenant's version of the play remained the standard theatre script until the eighteenth century, when the actor David Garrick sought to stage a production of *Macbeth* 'as written by Shakespeare'. However, even Garrick could not resist the temptation of writing a long farewell speech for Macbeth, full of sorrow and self-condemnation. Some critics believe that Garrick's production, staged in 1744, marked a new phase in the play's performance history, a process of returning to the integrity and purity of the 1623 Folio script.

Successive actors and directors continued in this, and looked for new ways to explore Shakespeare's language, as well as to make each production relevant to the values of their society and culture. It seems that every society projects its own values on *Macbeth*. Even Davenant's now-derided version can be seen as a response to the growing interest in opera (it involved much music and dancing) and the political situation of the time.

From early in the twentieth century, the spectacular operatic effects were removed. Staging became simpler, partly in an attempt to return to the plainer values of Shakespeare's own stage. The creative tension between the script and the staging continued to mine rich new

Macbeth in performance

ways of imagining the play, and modern productions have radically reinterpreted and re-presented *Macbeth* in order to explore and stress different aspects of the play.

The Witches, in particular, have proved to be a source of inspiration for directors and actors. They have been presented as creations of Macbeth's mind and as puppet masters controlling each of the characters on stage. They have been shown as children, as a family unit of husband, wife and child, and as ugly old women. Other productions have portrayed them as sexually alluring young women, disruptive young men who merge with other characters, and even refuse collectors. They can be entertainers, dancers, roller-blading teenagers – anything that the director thinks articulates an aspect of the play that will further develop or frame key themes.

There is perhaps less freedom to experiment with the leading characters of Macbeth and Lady Macbeth, but again, both these parts have drawn radically different interpretations from some of the greatest actors of their age. Both characters challenge those playing the roles to decide whether to make them fully 'human', or to demonise them. Henry Irving's 1888 production was characterised by its dark, sombre atmosphere, and Irving played Macbeth as a liar and a murderer. In contrast, in this production Lady Macbeth was performed by the renowned Ellen Terry. She played the character as an 'enchanting being', free of malice, a doting wife who simply loved her husband (see the picture bottom right p. 169).

▼ **David Garrick in the title role during his 1744 performance of *Macbeth*. Lady Macbeth was played by Mrs Pritchard.**

Macbeth
麦克白

Gradually, our understanding of the complexities of human behaviour developed, both through modern clinical medicine and, perhaps even more importantly, through the pioneering work done in the late nineteenth and early twentieth centuries by psychoanalysts such as Breuer, Freud (who wrote a brief study of Lady Macbeth) and Jung. As this understanding grew, artists became increasingly interested in the conscious and subconscious urges of individuals, and *Macbeth* lent itself very easily to interpretations that accentuated the inner lives of the main characters.

The relationship between Macbeth and his wife is fundamental to the play. Macbeth has wide-ranging relationships with almost all the other characters, but Lady Macbeth relates only to her husband. Actors have to decide how to play the relationship between these two characters as they grow estranged from each other.

A crucial aspect is how much they are in love, and some productions have presented their initial relationship as passionate and sensual. One famous remark about the production that starred Laurence Olivier and Vivien Leigh as the Macbeths was to remind audiences 'that Macbeth and his Lady were lovers before they were criminals'. Retaining both the light and darkness of each character – the love and criminality, so that one does not extinguish the other – is a challenge that will undoubtedly continue to interest actors and audiences in the future.

Other changes in society, including the rise of left-wing political parties and an increasingly radical feminism, saw productions focusing on areas of the script that emphasised certain political positions. For example, the feminist critic Janet Adelman claimed that Macbeth acts in the way he does because he is insecure about his own masculinity. Other feminist critics believe that the families represented in the play are essentially patriarchal, with children and wives largely absent or inconsequential. The only family we see that has a young (male) child is Macduff's, but his family is abandoned by the patriarch of the house, and then brutally murdered by the patriarch of Scotland.

Macbeth in performance

Macbeth resonates with all societies, regardless of culture and time. An all-black adaptation of the play, *Umabatha*, has toured the world. It transformed *Macbeth* into a play about Zulu identity in early nineteenth-century South Africa. Chanting, drumming, and rhythmically beating shields, the huge cast created a tribal *Macbeth* of immense ritual power. The Zulu warriors grieved, rejoiced, welcomed and fought throughout their own unique re-staging of Shakespeare's tragedy.

The play has also been a rich source of inspiration for artists to reinterpret it in different forms. It has been made into opera, ballet, novels, movies, television programmes, songs, graphic texts, political cartoons and adverts. Now, in the age of the Internet, it has taken on a new life, as bloggers, amateur filmmakers and musicians adapt the text, perform it, and render it in new forms, spreading it to fresh and increasingly diverse audiences. *Macbeth*'s popularity can be explained in a number of ways: it has a relatively straightforward story, strong characters, powerful themes with universal appeal, and an economy of action that makes the plot unfold rapidly. And perhaps the key theme, ambition, resonates with everyone.

Whose *Macbeth* is it?

We tend to treat the script of *Macbeth* as something untouchable. As you will have seen in the various activities throughout this book, interpreting an episode in a particular way means focusing on certain aspects that we believe exist in the words. It is rare to see productions (other than those in translation) that change Shakespeare's language. But, as mentioned earlier, this has not always been the case.

◆ As a class, discuss how much freedom directors and actors should have in adapting *Macbeth*. Should every word remain untouched? Or is it permissible to cut scenes if they are not felt to be necessary (or if they are probably not by Shakespeare), such as the scene featuring Hecate? Is it right to make the play overtly political? Is it possible to keep the interpretation of the play separate from the society in which it is performed? Who judges such adaptations a success – the director, the cast, critics or the audience?

Macbeth
麦克白

Macbeth on stage and on film

Macbeth is best experienced live, but if you are unable to see a production, or take part in one, there are many different film versions available for you to watch. Take time to find different versions of the text, but remember to view each one actively rather than passively. If you are analysing a movie adaptation of the play, think about:

- camerawork (angles, movement, shot type [镜头类型])
- sound (dialogue, sound effects, music)
- lighting (back light, key light)
- editing (simple cuts, montages, fade-out shots, dissolve cuts).

For each of these, consider what their effect is on the viewer, and how they add to (and sometimes detract from) the original script.

Write a review

Now try reviewing different versions of *Macbeth*. You could compare and contrast two movie versions, or two play productions. It might help to read film and theatre critics' reviews of past productions to get a sense of what they focus on and their depth of analysis. There are many very different interpretations of this play, so remain open-minded about each.

As you watch the productions, ask yourself what each is saying about its time and its culture. Above all, retain your own distinctive voice as you assess the qualities of the performances you watch.

Posters

Promotional posters provide a snapshot of a production. Their layout, typography (版面设计) and use of images convey the qualities of the movie or play as well as the period and culture in which it was devised.

◆ Look at the posters on these pages, then discuss in groups of three what key elements in *Macbeth* you think each production might highlight.

◆ Stay in your groups and design your own poster to promote a production of *Macbeth* that conveys the main values of a particular community. This community could be a school, an area of a town, a financial district or a whole society. Think carefully about the images and text you would include and why are they relevant to *Macbeth*.

MACBETH IN PERFORMANCE

Macbeth 麦克白

Writing about Shakespeare 笔论莎士比亚

The play as text

Shakespeare's plays have always been studied as literary works — as words on a page that need clarification, appreciation and discussion. When you write about the plays, you will be asked to compose short pieces and also longer, more reflective pieces like controlled assessments, examination scripts and coursework — often in the form of essays on themes and/or imagery, character studies, analyses of the structure of the play and on stagecraft. Imagery, stagecraft and character are dealt with elsewhere in this edition. Here, we concentrate on themes and structure. You might find it helpful to look at the 'Write about it' boxes on the left-hand pages throughout the play.

Themes

It is often tempting to say that the theme of a play is a single idea, like 'death' in *Hamlet*, or 'the supernatural' in *Macbeth*, or 'love' in *Romeo and Juliet*. The problem with such a simple approach is that you will miss the complexity of the plays. In *Romeo and Juliet*, for example, the play is about the relationship between love, family loyalty and constraint; it is also about the relationship of youth to age and experience; and the relationship between Romeo and Juliet is also played out against a background of enmity between two families. Between each of these ideas or concepts there are tensions. The tensions are the main focus of attention for Shakespeare and the audience; this is also how the best drama operates — by the presentation of and resolution of tension.

Look back at the Themes boxes throughout the play to see if any of the activities there have given rise to information that you could use as a starting point for further writing about the themes of the specific play you are studying.

Structure

Most Shakespeare plays are in five acts, divided into scenes. These acts were not in the original scripts, but have been included in later editions to make the action more manageable, clearer and more like 'classical' structures. One way to get a sense of the structure of the whole play is to take a printed version (not this one!) and cut it up into scenes and acts, then display each scene and act, in sequence, on a wall, like this:

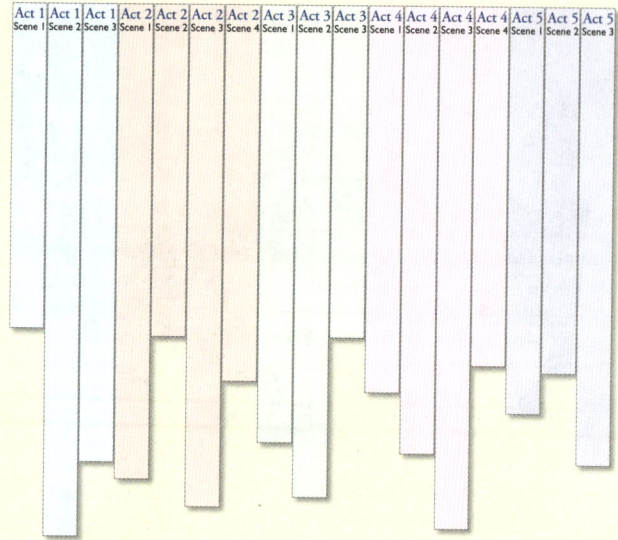

As you set out the whole play, you will be able to see the 'shape' of each act, the relative length of the scenes, and how the acts relate to each other (such as whether one act is shorter, and why that might be). You can annotate the text with comments, observations and questions. You can use a highlighter pen to mark the recurrence of certain words, images or metaphors to see at a glance where and how frequently they appear. You can also follow a particular character's progress through the play.

Such an overview of the play gives you critical perspective: you will be able to see how the parts fit together, to stand back from the play and assess its shape, and to focus on particular parts within the context of the whole. Your writing will reflect a greater awareness of the overall context as a result.

The play as script

There are different, but related, categories when we think of the play as a script for performance. These include *stagecraft* (discussed elsewhere in this edition and throughout the left-hand pages), *lighting*, *focus* (who are we looking at? Where is the attention of the audience?), *music and sound*, *props and costumes*, *casting*, *make-up*, *pace and rhythm*, and other *spatial relationships* (e.g. how actors move around the stage in relation to each other). If you are writing about stagecraft or performance, use the notes you have made as a result of the Stagecraft activities throughout this edition of the play, as well as any information you can find about the plays in performance.

What are the key points of dispute?

Shakespeare is brilliant at capturing a number of key points of dispute in each of his plays. These are the dramatic moments where he concentrates the focus of the audience on difficult (sometimes universal) problems that the characters are facing or embodying.

First, identify these key points in the play you are studying. You can do this as a class by brainstorming what you consider to be the key points in small groups, then debating the long-list as a whole class, and then coming up with a short-list of what the class thinks are the most significant. (This is a good opportunity for speaking and listening work.) They are likely to be places in the play where the action or reflection is at its most intense, and which capture the complexity of themes, character, structure and performance.

Second, drill down at one of the points of contention and tension. In other words, investigate the complexity of the problem that Shakespeare has presented. What is at stake? Why is it important? Is it a problem that can be resolved, or is it an insoluble one?

Key skills in writing about Shakespeare

Here are some suggestions to help you organise your notes and develop advanced writing skills when working on Shakespeare:

- Compose the title of your writing carefully to maximise your opportunities to be creative and critical about the play. Explore the key words in your title carefully. Decide which aspect of the play – or which combination of aspects – you are focusing on.
- Create a mind map of your ideas, making connections between them.
- If appropriate, arrange your ideas into a hierarchy that shows how some themes or features of the play are 'higher' than others and can incorporate other ideas.
- Sequence your ideas so that you have a plan for writing an essay, review, story – whichever genre you are using. You might like to think about whether to put your strongest points first, in the middle, or later.
- Collect key quotations (it might help to compile this list with a partner), which you can use as evidence to support your argument.
- Compose your first draft, embedding quotations in your text as you go along.
- Revise your draft in the light of your own critical reflections and/or those of others.

The following pages focus on writing about *Macbeth* in particular.

MACBETH
麦克白

Writing about *Macbeth* 笔论《麦克白》

Any kind of writing about *Macbeth* will be informed by your responses to the play. Your understanding of how characters, plot, themes, language and stagecraft are all interrelated will contribute to your unique perspective. This section will help you locate key points of entry into the play so that your writing will be engaging and original. The best way to capture your reader's attention is to take them with you on a journey of discovering a new pathway into *Macbeth*.

But first, how do you find your unique perspective? You may want to start with a character – say, Lady Macbeth. From here, allow yourself to make free connections with the rest of the play. If you think about the development of her character throughout the play, and her relationship with Macbeth, you might reach the conclusion that in some ways she is similar to the Witches. Like them, Lady Macbeth is linked to evil, and she calls on familiar spirits to possess her. This may lead you to a consideration of how Shakespeare's representation of witches was influenced by historical events and people. You may also find yourself thinking about the way the play links evil and gender, and questions ideas of masculinity and femininity.

Lady Macbeth also tempts and torments Macbeth. This may lead you to consider the language she uses: is it similar to the Witches' language at any point in the play? Or does it create a menacing and tense atmosphere in a different way? You might want to compare the language Lady Macbeth uses at the beginning of the play with her broken, strained language at the end of the play.

You will need to refer to the poetic, linguistic and dramatic features of the language, and in order to do so, you will want to focus closely on some key speeches. These key speeches may draw your attention to one of two themes that open up more of your ideas about Lady Macbeth. For example, the theme of appearance and reality is a fruitful one for exploring her language and the way she displays a deception and manipulation similar to that of the Witches.

As you can see, your unique perspective of *Macbeth* will begin to develop as you think about what you are interested in, and allow yourself to make connections between the dramatic, contextual, linguistic and thematic features of the play. As you formulate your ideas into a coherent piece of writing, by using mind maps and essay plans, remember to refer back to the characters and events in the play, and to quote from the play to develop and extend your ideas further.

- ◆ Generate five of your own essay titles for writing about *Macbeth*. Try to compose your 'dream' questions that will give you plenty of scope to pull together all your ideas about the play and allow you to investigate new and interesting areas. These could be a mixture of creative and analytical: be as open-minded as possible. For example, you could start with 'Ambition, fate or bloodlust: what motivates the Macbeths to act in the way they do?'

- ◆ Once you have your five titles, work with a partner or in a small group to build up ten titles that are varied and clear, and that inspire you to actually write an essay in response.

Creative writing

At different times during your study of *Macbeth*, and during assessments and examinations, you will be writing about the play and your personal responses to it. Creative responses, such as those encouraged in the activities on the left-hand pages of this book, can allow you to be as imaginative as you want. This is your chance to develop your own voice and to be adventurous, as well as being sensitive to the words and images in the play. *Macbeth* is a rich, multi-layered text that benefits from many different approaches, both in performance and in writing. Don't be afraid of larger questions or implications that cannot be reduced to simple resolutions. The complex issues that have no easy answers are often the most interesting to write about.

Writing about Macbeth

Macbeth (the director's cut)

◆ Imagine that you are directing a movie version of *Macbeth*. As Shakespeare's shortest play, the producers want it to have additional scenes. In pairs, look at each act and think about where an extra scene could be used to develop key themes. Would you add a scene that explains what happened to the Macbeths' child? Or would you include Lady Macbeth's death scene? Now choose one and write it yourself in Shakespeare's language (using iambic pentameter if you can).

◆ As part of the promotional material, the characters are going to be interviewed so that they can explain their actions and give their views on the others. In pairs, write twenty questions that you would like to ask them. Then, in small groups, conduct the interviews and film them, if you can, so that the rest of the class can view them.

Essay

Some responses, such as essays, have a set structure and specific requirements. Writing an essay gives you a chance to explore your own interpretations, to use evidence that appeals to you, and to write with creativity and flair (才华, 天赋). It allows you to explore *Macbeth* from different points of view. You can approach the play from a number of critical perspectives or in relation to different themes. You will also need to explore the play in the social, literary, political and cultural contexts of its production (Shakespeare's day) and reception (today or at any point since Shakespeare's time).

An essay can be seen as an exploration of the play in which you chart a path to illuminate ideas that are significant to you. It is also an argument that uses evidence and structural requirements to persuade your readers that you have an important perspective on the play. You must integrate evidence from the script into your own writing by using embedded quotations – and by explaining the significance of each quotation and reference to the play. Some people like to remember the acronym PEA to help them here. P is the POINT you are making. E is the EVIDENCE you are taking from the script, whether it is a direct quotation, a summary of what is happening, or a reference to character, plot and themes. A is the ANALYSIS you give for using this evidence, which will reflect back on the point you are making and contain your personal response and original ideas.

◆ Put the following essay questions in order of difficulty (with number one being the most challenging) and discuss with others why you put them in that order. Choose a few to construct a detailed essay plan that reflects the advice given in these two pages.

1 Look at Act 1 Scene 3 of *Macbeth* and explore the ways in which Macbeth and Banquo are presented in this scene and elsewhere in the play.
2 'Macbeth is a plaything of the Witches: he has no free will and is therefore innocent of his crimes.' Discuss.
3 'The play is an analysis of male values; ultimately it sees masculinity as a destructive force.' To what extent do you agree with this statement?
4 Why is Act 2 Scene 1 so dramatically effective?
5 '*Macbeth* is an ancient text that has no relevance or parallels with my society.' How far do you agree with this assertion?
6 How does Macbeth change during the play?
7 Who is most responsible for Macbeth's fate?
8 Look at Act 3 Scene 4 of *Macbeth* and comment on how Macbeth and Lady Macbeth are presented in this scene and elsewhere in the play.

MACBETH
麦克白

William Shakespeare 莎翁年表
1564–1616

1564	Born Stratford-upon-Avon, eldest son of John and Mary Shakespeare.
1582	Marries Anne Hathaway of Shottery, near Stratford.
1583	Daughter Susanna born.
1585	Twins, son and daughter Hamnet and Judith, born.
1592	First mention of Shakespeare in London. Robert Greene, another playwright, described Shakespeare as 'an upstart crow beautified with our feathers'. Greene seems to have been jealous of Shakespeare. He mocked Shakespeare's name, calling him 'the only Shake-scene in a country' (presumably because Shakespeare was writing successful plays).
1595	Becomes a shareholder in The Lord Chamberlain's Men, an acting company that became extremely popular.
1596	Son, Hamnet, dies aged eleven. Father, John, granted arms (acknowledged as a gentleman).
1597	Buys New Place, the grandest house in Stratford.
1598	Acts in Ben Jonson's *Every Man in His Humour*.
1599	Globe Theatre opens on Bankside. Performances in the open air.
1601	Father, John, dies.
1603	James I grants Shakespeare's company a royal patent: The Lord Chamberlain's Men become The King's Men and play about twelve performances each year at court.
1607	Daughter Susanna marries Dr John Hall.
1608	Mother, Mary, dies.
1609	The King's Men begin performing indoors at Blackfriars Theatre.
1610	Probably returns from London to live in Stratford.
1616	Daughter Judith marries Thomas Quiney. Dies. Buried in Holy Trinity Church, Stratford-upon-Avon.

The plays and poems

(no one knows exactly when he wrote each play)

1589–95	*The Two Gentlemen of Verona*, *The Taming of the Shrew*, *First*, *Second* and *Third Parts* of *King Henry VI*, *Titus Andronicus*, *King Richard III*, *The Comedy of Errors*, *Love's Labour's Lost*, *A Midsummer Night's Dream*, *Romeo and Juliet*, *King Richard II* (and the long poems *Venus and Adonis* and *The Rape of Lucrece*).
1596–99	*King John*, *The Merchant of Venice*, *First* and *Second Parts* of *King Henry IV*, *The Merry Wives of Windsor*, *Much Ado About Nothing*, *King Henry V*, *Julius Caesar* (and probably the Sonnets).
1600–05	*As You Like It*, *Hamlet*, *Twelfth Night*, *Troilus and Cressida*, *Measure for Measure*, *Othello*, *All's Well That Ends Well*, *Timon of Athens*, *King Lear*.
1606–11	**Macbeth**, *Antony and Cleopatra*, *Pericles*, *Coriolanus*, *The Winter's Tale*, *Cymbeline*, *The Tempest*.
1613	*King Henry VIII*, *The Two Noble Kinsmen* (both probably with John Fletcher).
1623	Shakespeare's plays published as a collection (now called the First Folio).

Acknowledgements 鸣谢

Cambridge University Press would like to acknowledge the contributions made to this work by Rex Gibson.

Picture Credits

p. iii: Battersea Arts Centre 2000, © Donald Cooper/Photostage; p. v: The Independent Players and New Vision Theatre 2011, © Charlie Neuman/ZUMA Press/Corbis; p. vi top: *Shogun Macbeth*, Pan Asian Repertory Theatre 2008, © Corky Lee; p. vi bottom: Out of Joint/Arcola Theatre 2004, © Donald Cooper/Photostage; p. vii top: Albery Theatre 2002, © Donald Cooper/Photostage; p. vii bottom: Albery Theatre 2002, © Donald Cooper/Photostage; p. viii top: West Yorkshire Playhouse 2007, © Donald Cooper/Photostage; p. viii bottom: Ludlow Festival 2001, © Donald Cooper/Photostage; p. ix top: *The Kingdom of Desire*, The Contemporary Legend Theatre 1990, © Donald Cooper/Photostage; p. ix bottom: English Shakespeare Company/Peacock Theatre 1992, © Donald Cooper/Photostage; p. x left: RSC/Royal Shakespeare Theatre 1996, © Donald Cooper/Photostage; p. x right: RSC/Royal Shakespeare Theatre 2004, © Donald Cooper/Photostage; p. xi left: RSC/Barbican Theatre 1983, © Donald Cooper/Photostage; p. xi right: Out of Joint/Arcola Theatre 2004, © Donald Cooper/Photostage; p. xii top: Open Air Theatre 2007, © Donald Cooper/Photostage; p. xii bottom: Ludlow Festival 2001, © Donald Cooper/Photostage; p. 6: RSC/Royal Shakespeare Theatre 1996, © Donald Cooper/Photostage; p. 8 top left: Three witches of Belvoir woodcut 1600s, © Topfoto; p. 8 top right: © Gordon Anthony/Hulton Collection/Getty Images; p. 8 bottom left: Woodcut book illustration c. 1500, © Bettmann/Corbis; p. 8 bottom right: Battersea Arts Centre 2000, © Donald Cooper/Photostage; p. 10: Open Air Theatre 2007, © Elliott Franks/ArenaPAL; p. 14: RSC/Swan Theatre 2007, © Donald Cooper/Photostage; p. 20: 'The Family of Henry VIII: An Allegory of the Tudor Succession' by Lucas de Heere c. 1572, © Getty Images; p. 22: Albery Theatre 2002, © Donald Cooper/Photostage; p. 28: Shakespeare's Globe 2001, © Donald Cooper/Photostage; p. 30: Center for New Theater at CalArts/Almeida Theatre 2005; © Donald Cooper/Photostage; p. 37 top: Schiller Theatre Company/Mermaid Theatre 1992, © Donald Cooper/Photostage; p. 37 bottom left: Minerva Theatre/Chichester Festival Theatre 2007 © Donald Cooper/Photostage; p. 37 bottom right: Ludlow Festival 2001, © Donald Cooper/Photostage; p. 44: RSC/Swan Theatre 2007, © Donald Cooper/Photostage; p. 50: RSC/Royal Shakespeare Theatre 1996, © Donald Cooper/Photostage; p. 54: Minerva Theatre/Chichester Festival Theatre 2007, © Donald Cooper/Photostage; p. 63 top left: Out of Joint/Arcola Theatre 2004, © Donald Cooper/Photostage; p. 63 top right: Gielgud Theatre 2007, © AlamyCelebrity/Alamy; p. 63 bottom left: Ludlow Festival 2001, © Donald Cooper/Photostage; p. 63 bottom right: *Shogun Macbeth*, Pan Asian Repertory Theatre 2008, © Corky Lee; p. 64: RSC/Barbican Theatre 1989, © Donald Cooper/Photostage; p. 70: Ludlow Festival 2001, © Donald Cooper/Photostage; p. 74: Cheek by Jowl/Barbican Theatre 2010, © Robbie Jack/Corbis; p. 82: RSC/Royal Shakespeare Theatre 2004, © Stewart Hemley/RSC; p. 86: The Royal Opera/Covent Garden 2002, © Donald Cooper/Photostage; p. 94: RSC/Royal Shakespeare Theatre 2004, © Donald Cooper/Photostage; p. 96: Cheek by Jowl/Barbican Theatre 2010, © Robbie Jack/Corbis; p. 97 top left: Bell Shakespeare/Melbourne Arts Centre 2012, © Silas Brown; p. 97 top right: TR Warszawa/Edinburgh Festival 2012, © Robbie Jack/Corbis; p. 97 bottom: *Umabatha: The Zulu Macbeth*/Shakespeare's Globe Theatre 1997, © Donald Cooper/Photostage; p. 104: Opera North 2008, © Donald Cooper/Photostage; p. 108 left: West Yorkshire Playhouse 2007, © Donald Cooper/Photostage; p. 108 right: RSC/Royal Shakespeare Theatre 2011, © Donald Cooper/Photostage; p. 110: RSC/Barbican Theatre 1993, © Donald Cooper/Photostage; p. 116: *The Kingdom of Desire*, The Contemporary Legend Theatre 1990, © Donald Cooper/Photostage; p. 120: Out of Joint/Arcola Theatre 2004, © Geraint Lewis; p. 122: RSC 1999, © Geraint Lewis; p. 126: RSC/Royal Shakespeare Theatre 1996, © Donald Cooper/Photostage; p. 131 top: Out of Joint/Arcola Theatre 2004, © Geraint Lewis; p. 131 middle: RSC/Barbican Theatre 1983; © Donald Cooper/Photostage; p. 131 bottom: RSC/Royal Shakespeare Theatre 2004,

Macbeth
麦克白

© Geraint Lewis; p. 134: 'Lady Macbeth Sleepwalking' by Henry Fuseli 1783, © Roger-Viollet/Topfoto; p. 136: Cheek by Jowl/Barbican Theatre 2010, © Geraint Lewis; p. 142: The Royal Opera/Covent Garden 2011, © Donald Cooper/Photostage; p. 150: RSC/Barbican Theatre 1993, © Donald Cooper/Photostage; p. 154: 'The Death of Jezebel' by Gustave Doré, © Ann Ronan Picture Library/HIP/TopFoto; p. 159 top left: Battersea Arts Centre 2000, © Donald Cooper/Photostage; p. 159 top right: The Royal Opera/Covent Garden 2002, © Donald Cooper/Photostage; p. 159 bottom: Salzburg Festival 2011, © Barbara Gindl/epa/Corbis; p. 161: Shakespeare's Globe 2010, © Donald Cooper/Photostage; p. 162: 'Henry Garnet Executed', © Mary Evans Picture Library/Alamy; p. 164: 'The Day of Judgement' illustration from the Guild Chapel, Stratford, by permission of the Shakespeare Birthplace Trust; p. 166 top: Cheek by Jowl/Barbican Theatre 2010, © Geraint Lewis; p. 166 bottom: RSC/Barbican Theatre 1993, © Donald Cooper/Photostage; p. 167: RSC/Royal Shakespeare Theatre 2004; © Donald Cooper/Photostage; p. 168: RSC/Swan Theatre 2007, © Geraint Lewis; p. 169 top: The Metropolitan Opera 2012, © Marty Sohl Photography; p. 169 bottom: 'Miss Ellen Terry as Lady Macbeth' by John Singer Sargent, © The Print Collector/Corbis; p. 171: Birmingham Repertory Theatre 1995, © Donald Cooper/Photostage; p. 174: 'The Long View of London from Bankside' by Wenceslaus Hollar; p. 175: Swan Theatre, Bankside, London c. 1595, Heritage Images/Corbis; p. 177: 'David Garrick and Mrs Pritchard in *Macbeth*' by Johann Zoffany 1768, © Topfoto; p. 178: Ninagawa Theatre Company/Lyttelton Theatre/National Theatre 1987, © Donald Cooper/Photostage; p. 179: *Umabatha: The Zulu Macbeth*, Shakespeare's Globe Theatre 2001, © Adrian Dennis/epa/Corbis; p. 180: WPA Federal Theatre Negro Unit poster c. 1936, © Corbis; p. 181 top: Japanese film poster for *Throne of Blood* 1957, © TOHO/The Kobal Collection; p. 181 bottom: Film poster 2006, © AF Archive/Alamy.

Produced for Cambridge University Press by White-Thomson Publishing
+44 (0)843 208 7460
www.wtpub.co.uk

Managing editor: Sonya Newland
Designer: Clare Nicholas
Concept design: Jackie Hill